Charlotte Nash was born in England and grew up riding horses in the Redland Shire of Brisbane. After completing degrees in mechanical engineering and medicine, she fell into eclectic jobs, among which she counts the best as building rockets, traversing the Pilbara mines and scrambling over shiploaders in Newcastle. These days, she is a writer of both technical material and fiction, and teaches creative writing at the University of Queensland. Charlotte took part in the QWC/Hachette Australia Manuscript Development Program in 2010. *Ryders Ridge* is her first novel. Charlotte's next novel, *Iron Junction*, is set in the Pilbara region of Australia.

Also by Charlotte Nash

Iron Junction

RYDERS RIDGE

CHARLOTTE NASH

hachette
AUSTRALIA

First published in Australia and New Zealand in 2013
by Hachette Australia
(an imprint of Hachette Australia Pty Limited)
Level 17, 207 Kent Street, Sydney NSW 2000
www.hachette.com.au

This edition published in 2014

10 9 8 7 6 5 4 3

National Library of Australia
Cataloguing-in-Publication data

Nash, Charlotte.

Ryders Ridge / Charlotte Nash.

978 0 7336 3262 4 (pbk.)

Romance fiction.

A823.4

Cover design by Xou Creative
Cover photographs courtesy of Age Fotostock and Thinkstock
Text design by Bookhouse, Sydney
Typeset in Sabon LT Pro
Printed and bound in Australia by Griffin Press, Adelaide, an Accredited ISO AS/NZS 14001:2009 Environmental Management System printer

The paper this book is printed on is certified against the Forest Stewardship Council® Standards. Griffin Press holds FSC chain of custody certification SGS-COC-005088. FSC promotes environmentally responsible, socially beneficial and economically viable management of the world's forests.

Ryders Ridge has been written with the encouragement of Queensland Writers Centre (QWC).

Charlotte Nash participated in the 2010 QWC/Hachette Australia Manuscript Development Program, which received funding from the Queensland Government through Arts Queensland.

For Dad . . .
I wish you could have seen this

Chapter 1

Dr Daniella Bell knew that for many people, hospitals were scary places. But that had never been true for her. At least, not until recently.

The plain health-service clock showed twelve after midnight. She stood in the intimate familiarity of an emergency bay, the starched white bedsheets forming an island within the multicoloured wall-mounted equipment bins. She could just as easily have been in a hospital in Brisbane and not several thousand kilometres away in the small town of Ryders Ridge, north-west Queensland.

Daniella's hands clenched the chart as a sickening panic rose inside her. That wasn't familiar. She didn't panic, never lost control. She was Dr Bell of the Zen calm.

Or rather, she had been. It was the patient who'd triggered this response. Sarah, a little girl with asthma, now resting under a gurgling nebuliser mask. In fact, everything was already done. Daniella's supervisor, Dr Martin Harris, the one doctor of this formerly one-doctor town, had responded to the emergency call. He had administered the steroids and bronchodilators. Sarah's breathing had become less laboured. Oxygen sats were excellent. The danger was past.

But Daniella couldn't relax.

As she watched Dr Harris work, she poked at her memory. She had no good reason to panic about asthma; she'd seen dozens of cases in Brisbane. But that had been *before*. She tested herself, checking off the elements of asthma management on her fingers, relieved by how easily they came to her. But she was still a long way from her usual self, calm and non-emotional. It frightened her: she wanted to be sure of herself. She wanted to forget.

It wasn't that she was hiding out in this far-from-nearly-everywhere town . . . well, maybe she was. But she preferred to think of it as a sabbatical. Ryders Ridge was as different from Brisbane as she could imagine. And here she worked one on one with an experienced doctor. A perfect place to restore her confidence.

Sarah's parents, Mac and Susan Westerland, were both concerned, but they were familiar with both their daughter's condition and Dr Harris; they had been unobtrusive and comforting. Dr Harris pushed his glasses up his nose and stepped away, leaving the family alone. Daniella followed him out of the room.

'Everything all right?' asked Dr Harris, adjusting his cuffs. He'd asked this question many times since she'd started four days ago, his tone always one of fatherly interest, his white brows raised, glasses slipping down his nose. But Daniella was never sure if he was just keeping an eye on her, or if he saw through her.

'Fine,' she said brightly as they walked down the hall.

'You'll have been on call in Brisbane, I know,' he continued. 'But it's a different beast here. You won't get calls every night, but there're more nights on. As I've said before, I'm very glad to have you here. Until you're comfortable, though, I'll just call you in on the interesting cases.'

Dr Harris stepped towards the sink. Daniella watched as he washed his hands: rinse first, two pumps of pink soap, lather, rinse again. Then a squirt of alcohol gel to finish. The man was meticulous; dressed in a crisp white shirt and navy trousers, even though he'd probably got out of bed to attend the call.

'Sarah comes in quite frequently,' he said over his shoulder. 'I've asked Mac and Susan to bring her to the clinic tomorrow so we can review the management plan. She's a good case, so let's discuss it then.'

He was a real old-school doctor. He exuded confidence and care. One of the nurses had told Daniella that Dr Harris held regular dinner parties at his house and expected the staff to come. She wasn't quite sure what to think of that yet; such familiarity was unheard of in Brisbane.

'I'll stay until the nebs are finished, but you can go now,' he said. 'See you in the clinic at eight.'

When he'd gone back down the hall, Daniella slid Sarah's plump file into the inpatient rack. Everything in Brisbane had been going electronic, but there seemed no sign the trend had spread this far north. She hovered a moment in the hall; it felt wrong to just leave. In Brisbane, there was always something more to do: discharge papers, bloods, rounds. But this wasn't really a proper hospital as far as she was concerned; it only had two beds. It was a glorified emergency room, with a basic X-ray machine and well-stocked shelves, but nothing sophisticated. For anything serious – surgery, intensive care – it was a stop-over point to call for an evac.

She glanced at her watch. The GP clinic next door opened in seven hours; she worked there each day, with Dr Harris in the next room, then they alternated nights on call for the hospital. Or at least they would, when Dr Harris was happy she could do it on her own.

Daniella pushed open the double doors, then walked across the verandah and down onto the concrete path. As she left the lights behind, the sky became a mass of star-punctured indigo, a vaulted roof high overhead. About her, the air swirled silently, her own footsteps the only sound.

She strode around the hospital's bore-fed lake towards the town of Ryders Ridge. She was only ten minutes' walk from her house; the town itself perhaps the same distance. Eight hundred people lived there, and about as many again in the surrounding district, which spanned hundreds of kilometres. A few hours' drive away was the mining town of Mount Isa, which had the nearest serious medical facility. Anything else seemed an incredible distance: several hours by Royal Flying Doctor Service. All that space was occupied with pastoral farms and the occasional mine. It was strange to think there were people out there, tiny presences in the mass of land.

And all potentially her patients.

Daniella sighed, remembering the panic she'd felt when Sarah had come in. When she'd decided to take up the job here Daniella had told her colleagues she wanted to go bush . . . but really, she hadn't been able to face Brisbane anymore. She ran her thumb across the mobile phone in her pocket. She had left her father behind, too. He would still be up, no doubt; a surgeon himself in a busy hospital. But she couldn't call. They'd argued about her taking the job; he believed she was throwing herself away up here.

Once she'd skirted a dark paddock and trekked past sleeping houses, her own place appeared, white and ghostlike in the glow of the moon. A little fibro cube, generously provided by the health service. At first she'd thought of it as quaint, but after four days she'd abandoned delusions in favour of truth: it was merely functional, and she spent little time there anyway. She climbed the two steps and walked inside, discarding her shoes on the lino by the door. A stale smell of smoke clung to the curtains and the living-room carpet, no doubt from a previous occupant flouting the no-smoking rule.

She collapsed on the couch without bothering to undress. The bed was too firm and too far from the television, so the couch was where she'd been sleeping. The blanket was still twisted, as she'd left it when Dr Harris called. She shook it and laid it out again.

She lay awake a long time, thinking of her family: her father so far away in Brisbane, and further down south, her brother in the army. She tossed, trying to get comfortable on the old couch. It was better she was alone here, she thought. She wanted to trust herself again, to make this dark terror inside her leave and never return.

She burrowed her face into the couch, then recoiled; the fabric reeked of musty, stale smoke. She twisted back over, willing sleep to come.

Daniella woke after precisely five hours of sleep, a wicked crick in her neck. Yawning, she peeled off yesterday's clothes, pulled on clean trousers and a knit top, and opened the pantry. A daddy-long-legs scuttled into the very empty corner. A single packet of ancient cup-a-soup sat on the middle shelf, the last of the food that had been left there by the previous inhabitant. She'd found a few meals in the freezer, too. Daniella glanced at her watch. No, boiling the kettle would take too long. She'd eat a couple of biscuits from the clinic kitchen, and after work make herself find the supermarket.

She brushed her teeth with her head tilted sideways, trying to undo the crick. Her blonde streaks were growing out, leaving a light brown stripe down her part, as though her internal unrest was starting to show through. Six months ago, she would never have let it get this bad. After she found the supermarket, she'd have to find the hairdresser.

Once she'd spat out the toothpaste, she scrutinised her face: dark circles under her grey eyes, sallow skin. She was only twenty-seven – why did she look so tired? She pulled a face at the fluoro light over the mirror and wondered how long the country air and sun would take to defeat her indoorsy city complexion.

Time to find out.

From the top of the pantry she pulled down a battered brown felt hat. Left by the previous occupant, it was the first thing she'd seen when she arrived. There'd been a note too: *You'll need this.*

She struck out into the morning, down the straight street lined with neat houses, past the little church at the end of the row. A group of loose-limbed boys rode by on bikes, shouting to each other, weaving over the asphalt, helmets dangling from their handlebars. Daniella grimaced, hoping they wouldn't end up at the hospital later.

She reached the shimmering lake by the hospital and clinic in no time at all. She was glad of the hat. Even early in the morning, the light was harsh and raw. The sky was an enormous blue, a silent, tangible presence, and she felt as though she could confess all her fears up to it. In fact, if she had been sure no one else was listening, she might have done just that.

She arrived at the clinic at half past seven. The two nurses were already there. Jackie, a young woman with dark curls, was shuffling files behind the desk. The other nurse, a quiet but savagely efficient woman, was fiddling with the coffee machine.

'Hi, Jackie,' Daniella called.

'Hi, doc – I mean Daniella,' Jackie returned, smiling as she looked up from the files.

'Hi . . .' Daniella racked her brains, trying to remember the other nurse's name. They'd only been on one shift together, but Daniella was dismayed. She could remember a long list of causes for a cough, but not a nurse's name? Fortunately, the woman's back was turned.

'Roselyn,' mouthed Jackie with a grin as she tucked an escaping curl back behind her ear.

'. . . Roselyn,' finished Daniella, shooting Jackie a grateful look.

'Nice hat,' said Jackie.

Daniella whipped it off and put it on top of the filing cabinet just as Dr Harris came in. As usual, he was dressed in beautifully ironed trousers and shirt, with braces and a bow tie.

'Good morning, Daniella. How did you sleep?'

The pleasantries continued as they all sat down for the morning briefing at the laminex table in the clinic kitchen, which functioned as both lunch and meeting room. Daniella could hardly believe the sum total of the staff to cover sixteen hundred people: two doctors, two nurses and some community volunteer ambos for the four-wheel-drive ambulance – it hardly seemed enough. Dr Harris had been here ten years, he'd told her proudly, much of that time as the only doctor. From the awe the nurses she'd met so far held him in, and her own research, Daniella knew that staying so long was almost unheard of in such an isolated place.

Dr Harris scrutinised the appointments, sorting the charts into two piles, one for him, one for Daniella. 'Now, Mr McLeod . . . I'd better see him today . . . and Mrs Blake . . .'

By the time the meeting ended, the waiting room was nearly full, and Dr Harris's pile was twice the height of Daniella's.

This wouldn't keep her busy. She took a breath and leaned forward. 'Dr Harris, do you want me to take the on-call tonight?'

The nurses glanced at each other. Dr Harris looked at Daniella over his glasses.

'I just mean, since you were called out last night,' she clarified, hoping her cheeks weren't as red as they felt.

Dr Harris shook his head. 'I appreciate the offer, but let's stick to the roster for now.'

As Jackie and Roselyn left to check the rooms, Daniella picked up her pile, feeling chastened.

Dr Harris smiled at her kindly. 'Keen to get into it? I know it must seem like I'm being overly cautious, and I admire your enthusiasm. It's good. But I know you've only worked in the city before: things are a bit different out here. I want you to be prepared and comfortable, let yourself get settled in. I'll always call you if there're any good things to see, like last night. All right?' He smiled again.

Daniella nodded, swallowing hard. In the city, the policy was often the opposite: throw the young ones in at the deep end, let them sink or swim. She'd done her time being terrified of being on call – a year of internship, two as a house officer. She'd loved the job, and managed to get past the fear. So after that, feeling lost inside a big hospital had been a shock, a large part of why she'd come to Ryders. She didn't want similar terrors sneaking up on her here.

She placed the files on the front desk and picked up the first one. Mandy Rawlinson. Daniella looked around the waiting room. A greying couple sat by the door. A young woman in jeans and a windcheater was next to them, leafing through an old *Woman's Day*. Then a woman with watchful eyes and a toddler on her lap, and a young man in a flannelette shirt with a grease-smeared face and some papers in his work-scarred hands. Daniella could seldom tell just by looking why patients had come. It was one of the reasons she loved her job: what people told her once they were behind closed doors implied a trust that she cherished.

Jackie caught her eye, nodding towards the little girl in the woman's lap. Daniella took a deep breath, summoning her courage. 'Mandy?' she asked.

Mandy and her mother rose at once. Daniella looked for any signs of illness. Despondency. Dull eyes. Listlessness. But the girl skipped happily down the hall and climbed up on the treatment couch.

'Daniella Bell,' she introduced herself, sticking out her hand to Mandy's mother.

'I know, you're the new doc,' said the woman. 'I'm Kirsty.'

'And you're Mandy,' said Daniella, turning to the little girl, who nodded, looking at her mother for approval. 'How old are you, Mandy?'

'Four,' said the girl.

'When's your birthday?'

Another glance at Mum. 'Tomorrow.'

'Fantastic! Are you having a party?'

The girl nodded.

'So, what can I do for you today?' Daniella addressed the question to Mandy but included Kirsty in her glance. This was the trick with children – treating them as individuals without leaving out the parents.

Kirsty gave her daughter a quick encouraging nod and Mandy solemnly pulled up her sleeve.

'Oh, you're here for your immunisations? Wonderful.'

So this was the kind of thing Dr Harris was putting on her pile. She was glad it wasn't something more serious, but couldn't help feeling a little frustrated at the same time.

'Well, Mandy, there're three needles. We might get Nurse Jackie and do them all at once. Then, we'll get you some special bandaids and you can get on with planning your party.'

Daniella grabbed a handful of colourful Mr Men bandaids and let Mandy pick the ones she wanted. 'So, do you live in town?' she asked Kirsty once she'd called Jackie in.

'No, on Benders Station.'

'Where's that?'

'North-east, about three hours' drive.'

'Three hours?' Daniella paused in laying out the needles in the little tray. 'Wow, you must have been up early.'

Kirsty laughed. 'No – about the usual time.'

'And what do you grow at Benders?'

'Cows!' answered Mandy.

Daniella and Jackie laughed and Mandy swung her legs happily.

'Sounds great,' said Daniella. 'Okay, Mandy. Here we go then.'

Jackie was an expert with two needles in one hand. A moment later, the swabs and injections were all done, and the special bandaids applied. Jackie dispensed a bright pink lollipop, and Kirsty administered cuddles until Mandy's bottom lip stopped quivering.

'You're the bravest girl I've ever seen,' said Daniella in genuine amazement.

'She's just like her dad,' said Kirsty, kissing her daughter.

Jackie gave them a quick smile and turned away.

Kirsty paused as they were leaving the treatment room. 'Say, if you want to see the place, you're welcome anytime. Come for dinner. We'd love to have you.'

Daniella smiled and said she'd try. As the pair left the clinic, she shook her head. 'Incredible. Never seen a four-year-old like that.'

Jackie nodded and handed her the next file.

Daniella glanced at it, then looked around the waiting room. 'Shaun?'

Shaun Groves was a sheep farmer needing a script refill for his blood pressure meds. As she took his vitals, he told her at length about his sheep and then his wife, whom he seemed to hold in equally high esteem.

'You should come to dinner,' he finished.

'That's very generous of you,' said Daniella, writing out the script refill, amused at the second invitation in one day. 'I'll try to do that if I'm ever off duty.'

''Course, 'course,' said Shaun. ''Magine you've got a lot on, getting settled in and all.'

And so the day passed. Shaun was followed by two more children for shots, then two pairs of grey nomads from the caravan park, both with gastric complaints. In between appointments she ate biscuits to appease her grumbling belly, avoiding the awful coffee that Roselyn drank like a camel. Later, Dr Harris called her in to help (or, as she soon realised, watch) him cut a skin cancer from a patient called Garry, a jackeroo. Daniella had done many such minor surgeries in Brisbane, but she watched patiently. At least Garry didn't invite her to dinner.

In the mid-afternoon, Sarah, the little girl with asthma from the previous night, came in for a check-up. Dr Harris watched as Daniella listened to Sarah's chest and chatted to her mother about her asthma action plan.

By the end of the day, Daniella was exhausted. It hadn't been flat out, but she'd had to concentrate on each unfamiliar thing, from the new patients to where they stored prescription pads.

She stepped outside the air-conditioned rooms. It was early July, but the heat hit her immediately. Leaning against the wall, she soaked up the sun like a lizard. It was clinical inside, clean and bright and cool, but out here a thin film of dust covered everything, glittering with minerals. The big blue sky was a tent sheet flung high above.

The sliding door opened beside her. 'Going home?' asked Jackie, pulling her bag over her shoulder.

'Yes,' said Daniella, then remembered the cup-a-soup. 'I mean, no, I need to find the supermarket. Can you tell me where it is? I was given a lightning-fast tour on Monday and I can't remember.'

'God, you've been eating soup and biscuits for five days, haven't you!' said Jackie, shaking her head. 'You docs are all the same. Come on, I'll give you a lift. I'm picking up my boy from Mum's – it's right next door.'

Daniella gratefully followed Jackie to her crew cab ute. As she opened the passenger door, she had to shield her eyes against the glass-reflected sun. She was missing something.

'Just a sec,' she said, running back to the clinic.

Dr Harris was collecting his bag from behind the desk as Daniella retrieved the battered hat from the filing cabinet. He smiled at her.

'That old dust bag,' he said. 'You don't know how many heads have been in that thing. Probably every single locum who's lived in the health-service house, at least.' He tapped his chin, remembering. 'I think the first registrar I had here brought it with him and left it behind. Someone should have retired it years ago.' He stepped forward and ushered Daniella and her hat ahead of him. 'But I guess it'll do a while yet. Oh, and before I forget: I'm making a roast on Sunday night, having a few people round. You must come. Jacqueline, too.'

Chapter 2

Fifty k's away, on the back verandah of Ryders homestead, Mark Walker shook the dust from his own hat, muster dirt clinging to every surface. The honey-coloured stone of the house was the same shade as the natural timber floors, and were lovely at any time of the day. But at sunset they were spectacular. Mark had seen a fair bit of Australia, and particularly of Queensland, but nothing he'd seen out there made him feel the way these stones did. They were home, part of his soul.

He paused to look down the property from the wide verandah. The Mitchell grass country ran all the way to the horizon, across ditches and fossil-rich rises, punctuated only by scrappy trees, fences and cattle. Nearer the house, the machinery sheds and stables were etched with the last orange light against the fading sky.

The rich grass was what made Ryders one of the premier grazing stations in the state; or at least it had been. Ten years of drought had worn away at prosperity, and although the rains had finally returned a few years ago, cash flow had been slower to follow. Mark looked at the blackened fence post his father had mounted near the yards – a reminder of a grass fire that had destroyed fences and sheds at the end of the drought, just before the rains had come. All those fences had had to be replaced on barely any sales. Then had come the live export ban.

Mark pressed his knuckles into the railing. Those had been dark times. But they'd always come through, one way or another. Six generations of Walkers had loved this land, even as helicopters and quad bikes replaced stock horses, and they'd taken on loans and outside interests – the dust was in their veins. And here they were, rebuilding again.

Right now, the somewhat diminished herd was being mustered in the top paddock; Mark had been out there to check on the work, satisfied they would finally bring a sale this year. He squinted at the pink-sky horizon, which made the soil blush and the grass turn grey, his chest swelling with pride. This was his family's place. And it always would be.

It was just a pity they weren't all there to share it.

Mark brushed a hand through his hair and felt it stand up on its own, thick with sweat and dust. He removed his boots at the door and, in his grubby socks, silently paced down the long hall to the living room with its big stone fireplace. He was about to walk past when he noticed his father standing at the bureau, gazing at the rows of photo frames touched in orange and pink light from the west-facing window.

'Hi, Dad,' he said.

William Walker glanced around. In many ways, he was the same as he'd always been: a big, burly man of the land who was equally at home outside in the dust and in an elegant house. But Mark's mother's death had changed him. Almost overnight, he had more grey hair. Then he'd had a health scare for the first time ever: chest pains for which he'd been given medication. But he wouldn't talk about it. Now, dressed in clean trousers and linen shirt, hair combed, hands scrubbed, no one else would have known.

But Mark sometimes saw through the veneer.

He knew which photo his father was looking at: the one of the whole family, taken twenty years ago, when Mark was eight or so. The shot had been taken in front of the Ryders homestead. His father and mother had their arms around each other, their affection belying the volatile nature of their relationship. Mark's elder brother, William junior, rode a low fence rail; at ten he had a wide, cheeky grin, his eyes screwed up against the sun. Mark sat cross-legged on the ground, while his sister, Catrina, who was then just walking, proudly held his hand.

'We don't look much like that anymore,' his father said, turning away to squint out the window. Mark knew it. Will was working in the Isa mines now. Catrina was finishing uni in Brisbane, her last semester of agricultural science after four months' travelling in Europe. Since his wife's death and his own health scare, William had had to retire from the rural firefighters. But Mark had never caught his father being sentimental before.

Swiftly, William dismissed the subject. 'How's the muster?' he asked.

'Going well, all the herd moving. A few hands short as usual, and we probably haven't got enough work for the ring-ins after it's over.'

His father compressed his lips. 'They'll go to the mines, I guess.'

Mark let that slide. 'Who knows? If we need to replace anyone, I'll start looking tomorrow. And we should start planning for cash flow after the sales. See whether the Roma station can take up any slack.'

His father nodded. 'Well, scrub up,' he said. 'Kath's going to serve in an hour and Stephanie Morgan is joining us.'

Mark stilled. 'Is everything all right?'

'As far as I know. Steph's spending a few days here organising some local events, so she said she'd drop by. She'll be overnighting in the cottage before she goes back to town.'

Mark relaxed fractionally. 'Maria here too?'

'Not yet. Though Steph said she's coming out over the weekend.'

'I'll go wash up,' said Mark. He tried to sound unconcerned but the qualm remained. He and his father both disliked outside interests, but after the drought and the live export ban they hadn't really had a choice when the Morgans offered to invest substantially in the station. And he hadn't seen Stephanie in a while; they'd seldom seen each other since she'd moved to Townsville a few years ago. That had been just before the Morgans' investment, and after he'd ended his and Stephanie's brief involvement.

In the bathroom, he pulled off his filthy work shirt, took down the buckskins and inspected a cut on his ribs, courtesy of some barbed wire. He took a long soapy shower until his conscience grated at him for wasting water and he shut it off.

Back in his room and dressed in a clean shirt and jeans, Mark sat on his bed, facing the big window. He was almost too tired for company, but outside, in the rapidly failing light, he could see the sheds: the stable roof needed repairs, among a dozen other things. He loved this place, had loved growing up here; he'd shaped the land under his hands, and it had shaped him back. He wanted Ryders Station to be here in ten years, in twenty. And that meant finding a way to make it work. He'd better show up for dinner.

He glanced over his shoulder at the phone on the hall table, an antique piece of his mother's, with a matching carved chair alongside. He would have liked to call someone to talk things through, but his best mate Dave was out on the muster, flying the chopper and supporting the men on the ground, his father didn't want to acknowledge that times had changed, and Catrina was just back from a long trip.

No, he'd have to face this one alone. So he sat, mulling on the station, as the pink glow slipped away and night came.

~

On dark, Mark came out for dinner. From the hallway, he heard Stephanie and Kath, the housekeeper, talking in the kitchen. Mark tried to squash any lingering anxiety as he walked in.

'Smells amazing,' he told Kath, appreciating the rich, caramelised scent of roast beef and perfectly crispy potatoes as she opened the oven. 'Hi, Steph,' he added.

Stephanie paused in slicing tomatoes to smile at him. 'Hi, Mark.' She looked suntanned and sleek in her jeans and checked shirt, with pearls at her ears and painted nails. She was obviously doing well in Townsville, and Mark was relieved to find no uncomfortable undercurrents lingering from their brief relationship.

She put down her knife and passed him a beer. 'Can I borrow you for a sec?' she asked.

'Sure.' Mark stepped outside, his nerves increasing once more.

Kath called after them, 'I'll be serving in five, Mark.'

Out on the terrace, Stephanie leaned against the railing, a small frown pulling between her eyebrows. 'Sorry to call you out here like this, but is your dad all right? I haven't had a chance to really talk to him yet.'

Mark rubbed a hand through his hair, pulling a half-truth neatly to the surface. 'I think so. I mean, it's been hard, but he's doing okay. Why?'

'I wanted to talk to you about the fundraiser over dinner, and I thought he might find it upsetting because it's for the firefighters.'

Mark shrugged and leaned on the railing beside her. 'He knows about it already. He's not going to be upset, or at least he won't show it. He's just frustrated he can't help more, especially after we had the fire here.' He glanced at Stephanie, who nodded matter-of-factly.

'Okay, well. It's going to be a movie night at the oval in town. There'll be heavy gear to move from the hall into the park, and then it'll all need to be packed up again afterwards. I'm going to do the ticket sales and the bar, and I imagine we'll need a few hands. Can I count on you? Dave too?'

'When is it?'

'A few weeks yet,' she said.

Mark looked upwards, calculating the next few weeks' work. 'I'll do my best, but you know what things are like here.'

'I know, absolutely, thanks.' Her hand settled on his arm.

She smiled and quickly released him, but Mark felt a wave of discomfort and took a step away. 'How's Townsville?' he asked.

They made small-talk for a minute: her mother was well, the firm making progress. Then Stephanie asked, 'How's the muster going?'

Mark's discomfort returned, for a different reason this time. The stock were recovering. But with the Morgans' money invested in the property, it wasn't like talking to a friend. The Morgans had moved away from town; focused on building their legal firm in Townsville. Stephanie was now the face of their business with Ryders. Things had changed a lot since he and Stephanie had been at school together. 'Really well,' he said carefully. 'All the head look good. Might even get you a return this year.'

Stephanie gave him a quick smile. 'Good to hear. And I might even find some other ways to help with that.'

Before Mark could ask her what she meant, Kath called, 'Dinner!'

~

The four of them ate around the big scrubbed table. The conversation flowed easily, but Mark soon began to push the potato around his plate as the bone-aching tiredness took over.

He felt Kath's hand on his shoulder. 'You're going to fall asleep in that gravy in a minute,' she whispered.

Mark forced his eyes open. His father was in the middle of explaining to Stephanie the breeding strategy he and Mark had planned for rebuilding the herd, and Stephanie was listening attentively. Mark was trying to catch up when she turned to him and said, 'What do you think, Mark?'

'It's sound,' he said. 'And we're getting further input from the market and the breeders' association.'

She nodded slowly. 'Yes, but will it cover your expenses into the next few years?'

Mark swallowed, trying to decide how to answer. He believed it wouldn't, but his father disagreed.

'Don't worry about that at all,' said his father, patting Stephanie's arm.

She flashed him a practised smile. 'I'm not worried at all, William. I'm only concerned that the station keeps going. I want to help you with that. There are some other ways to ensure cash flow.'

Trying to deflect his father, Mark said quickly, 'Yes, of course.'

It didn't work. 'I'm not letting those mining bastards come and poke around on this land,' said William. Then he paused. 'Sorry about the language, Steph.'

'That's quite all right. Naturally, while the land is yours you want to make sure it's treated with respect, and your privacy protected. But don't forget there's overseas interest, too.'

Mark heard this with a winding panic. 'Overseas interest? Are you serious? You're talking about a foreign investor?'

Stephanie laughed lightly. 'I'm only talking around it, Mark. Of course the control is yours, absolutely. And I'm not in favour of anything intrusive. God, no. I love this place. We made this investment three years ago and like you we want the best outcome. But there're opportunities out there. Mum just wanted to make sure you're aware of them. You know, have all the information in front of you. I promised her I'd mention it.'

'Where's all this coming from?' asked William sharply.

For the first time, Stephanie looked uncomfortable. She glanced at Mark as though seeking his assistance. 'We've been approached by an overseas party who are interested in buying the station. And we know there's at least one other group who want to explore for minerals here. Just tests, that's all. Nothing serious. It's early days, but you'll be aware they don't need the owner's permission to do preliminary exploration. I'm so sorry, but I wanted to let you know. I meant what I said: the control is yours. But there it is.'

She made an apologetic face at Mark. For a moment, he wondered if she did mean it, but he couldn't blame her; her family had money in the station and she was just doing her job. But if they lost the Morgans' support . . . He was considering how to reply when the phone rang. Excusing himself, he went down the hall to answer it, leaving his father to ask questions. The gnawing dread stayed with him as he picked up the phone.

'Oh, Mark, good,' came the voice on the other end.

Hearing his brother's voice Mark slumped down in the chair. 'Will, how's it travelling?'

'Working for the man, little bro. Dad okay?'

Mark glanced down the hall to make sure their father was out of earshot. 'Yeah. He's taking the pills, I think. Not talking about it, though.'

'Yeah, well, that's his way. He's tough. Always has been.'

Mark reflected that this slightly reverential view of their father was something Will could only express when he was in another town, or, preferably, another state. They both knew that their father considered Will a disappointment; going off to the mines rather than staying on the beloved property was the worst thing a son of William Walker's could have done. But Mark had seen how unhappy Will had been; how he and their father had struck sparks off each other. Will could never have stayed.

'So, how's the Isa?' he asked.

'Busy. Big shut coming up. Wanted to know if you're interested.' Pragmatic Will, straight to the point.

'You're asking me if I want to come work in the mines?'

'Not for good – this would be two months, max. Good money, good work, good times. Bit of space, that's all. You know, if you need it.'

Mark grunted. Leaving Ryders was a foreign concept. Yes, he'd travelled when he was younger, but the last time he'd come back he'd known it was for good. This was his place for life. 'Look, thanks, mate. But no.'

Will laughed. 'Hey, I didn't really expect you to say yes. But it's not for a while yet. Offer's open. Do you know if anyone else is looking for work? I wouldn't mind having a few hands you'd trust.'

Mark didn't have to think long. 'Dave's good on the tools. He's here for the muster, but he said pilot work's been slow and he's doing more mechanical stuff. He might be interested.'

'Sure, sure. Let me know,' Will said, and rang off.

Some time later – probably only a few minutes – Mark became aware that he'd been dozing in the hall chair. The familiar whine of a dirt bike coming in from the back paddock had roused him. He hauled himself up and went to the back door to find Dave, thick with grey dust, kicking out the stand and peeling himself off the bike. Dave rolled his thick shoulders, his blue eyes the only clean part of him.

'Everything all right?' asked Mark in surprise. Dave must have ridden at least an hour from where he guessed the herd was now.

Dave shook a cloud of earth from his shirt front; dark hair curled from under his cap, damp with sweat. 'One of the quads is down with a busted brake cable. I've got a spare here and we need it, so here I am.'

'Jesus,' said Mark. 'Why didn't you drive the ute back?'

Dave grinned. ''Cause it was bogged and had a flat too. I left Simmo working out how to extract it.'

'I'll go back with you, then,' said Mark. 'Give you a hand.'

'Nah, we're right,' said Dave. 'Besides, you boss types just get in the way, and I've gotta be out of here in two days.' He winked and chucked his filthy cap in Mark's direction, which Mark managed to dodge. 'Give us a hug, then,' he went on, dedicated to the task of transferring dirt onto someone else.

Mark laughed. 'Get off. All right – but let Kath feed you before you head back.'

Dave retrieved the hat and plastered it back on his head as he and Mark walked around the side of the house to the kitchen door.

'Will just called from Isa,' Mark said. 'You interested in some shutdown work? They've got one coming up.'

'How soon?'

'Few weeks yet.'

Dave clicked his tongue thoughtfully. 'Yeah, maybe. I'll be out that way in a week or so anyway. I'll give him a call.'

They reached the kitchen door and Kath greeted Dave with hands on hips. 'Look at you! More dust than man. If you're coming in, at least take off your boots.'

'Can't do it,' said Dave. 'Socks'll walk away on their own if I do.'

Kath laughed. 'Wait there, then,' she said. A minute later, she returned with a plate groaning with beef and potatoes.

Stephanie followed behind. 'Hi, Dave. Didn't know you were here,' she said, standing close to Mark.

Dave, who was leaning against the wall, had his mouth full. He raised his fork in acknowledgement but said nothing. Mark felt tension creep into the air; he knew they'd never got along particularly well.

'Uh-huh,' said Stephanie. 'How's it all going?'

Dave kept chewing. 'Busted quad,' supplied Mark, easing her away. 'Dave came back for spares.'

'Ah. Well, are you going to be around for a few weeks?' she asked Dave, who only shrugged. She pressed on. 'We could do with a hand at the fundraiser, and you should come to the ball in a few weeks. It'll be fun.'

Kath interjected. 'Let the man eat, love!' she scolded Stephanie. 'Plenty of time for that later. But the lot of you need a night out. Why don't you go into the tav tomorrow after the muster's in? Nice cold beer?'

'Just like old times,' said Stephanie, smiling at Mark.

Mark didn't share the nostalgia, but he hadn't been into town in a while, and Dave and Stephanie would both be heading back there anyway. 'Sounds good. Be able to check it's still there.' He gave Kath a wink.

'Ah ha. It's still there, don't you worry. There's a new extension on the butcher's, lots of posters up for the rugby comp next week – oh, and there's a new doc at the clinic.' Kath was always up with gossip.

'Where's he come from?' asked Stephanie.

'She.'

Mark raised his eyebrows. 'Dr Harris isn't leaving, is he? Dad's supposed to go in for a check-up, and you know how he is with doctors – it's hard enough to convince him to see Dr Harris, let alone someone new.'

'Is he sick?' asked Stephanie, that little frown of concern returning.

Instantly, Mark regretted mentioning anything. He didn't want the Morgans worrying that his father might have a health problem. Anyway, it had been six months since the scare and his father seemed fine.

Having cleared his plate, Dave excused himself and strode towards the machinery shed. 'Can you help me look for that spare?' he called back. Mark left Kath stacking pots; Stephanie watched them go from the doorway.

As soon as they were inside the main shed, its metal shelves crammed with boxes, Dave asked, 'What's up with the Morgans? Everything sweet?'

Mark rubbed his face. 'Yeah, why?'

Dave glanced towards the house, then began rummaging in the parts boxes. 'No reason. Just, well, things are a bit down everywhere at the moment and I heard one of the big stations in the Territory was trying for a foreign sale. People reckon overseas buyers are offering big bucks. Plus I don't trust the Morgans. Always looking out for themselves.'

'They're just checking in. Seeing how things are,' said Mark. But his sense of unease grew stronger. He'd better talk to his father about the books and check everything really was fine.

'Found it.' Dave pulled out a box from the second shelf.

Dave didn't hang around, but Mark's anxiety did. The world was changing, and he knew that sooner or later the station would have to as well. He paced into the station office, his mind racing. Stephanie's references to mining rights and foreign investors couldn't be a coincidence. It would look attractive compared to being patient as the station recovered. Thank God the Morgans' stake wasn't enough for them to make decisions alone. He should make sure it didn't come to that; it was time to think of different ways forward. Other stations were doing it, finding new ways to generate income, even bringing in tourists.

His eyes fell on the office phone. Again, Mark thought about calling Cat, who loved to talk through new ideas, but she was probably in the grip of jet lag. So Mark walked back to the house through the darkening night and collapsed against his pillow, exhaustion pulling him to sleep.

Chapter 3

After the comparative calm of the week, the Saturday morning clinic was bedlam. As well as more patients than usual in only a half-day clinic, new issues had arisen that Daniella hadn't anticipated.

One of the patients in her pile insisted on seeing Dr Harris instead of her. In itself, that was fine. She could understand. The man, who went by the name of Rusty, was a tough-looking type with a weather-beaten face and a work-broken body, grey chest hairs sprouting from his blue singlet, wiry arms folded. Probably Dr Harris had worked hard to gain his trust and it wouldn't be easily given to someone else. But it meant the appointments were backing up. And one of the guys waiting was getting agitated.

'How much longer?' Daniella could hear him ask. She was contemplating another lunch of dry biscuits, an early one today because of Rusty's refusal to see her. She glanced through the mirrored bars of the window between the kitchen and reception. The guy was leaning on the counter, hunched over on himself as though in pain.

A moment later, Jackie joined her in the kitchen.

'Problem?' asked Daniella.

'New patient,' said Jackie. 'Says he's got a headache. Made the appointment earlier this morning and got a cancellation.'

'He a local?' asked Daniella, wondering about Dr Harris's reaction if she swiped his patient.

'No, haven't seen him before and he gave a Mount Isa address.'

'Okay, I'll take him.' Daniella grabbed the empty manila folder and read out the name. 'Peter?'

The man was tall and thin, and dressed in a T-shirt and blue King Gees like the mine guys wore. Daniella had seen them a lot in Mount Isa but not around here. As he walked towards the exam room she noticed that he looked nervous and didn't meet her eyes. Then again, maybe he'd come about something sensitive and was embarrassed.

'What can I do for you today?' she asked after he had sat down.

'Got a bad headache, doc. Need something for it.' He was sweaty around the hairline.

'What sort of headache?'

'Real bad.' He gripped a hand to his head, grimacing.

'Have you ever had this type of headache before?'

'Not this bad. Can you give me something for it?'

'Okay, Peter,' she said calmly. 'Where is the headache?'

'Kinda all over,' he said, shifting in his seat.

'Can you rate the pain out of ten, if zero is no pain, ten is the worst you could imagine?'

'Ten, definitely a ten.'

Daniella frowned, and wondered if it could be a bleeding cerebral aneurysm. She had to rule it out. 'How long have you had the pain?' she asked.

'About an hour.'

'Okay, hop up on the couch and let's have a look at you,' she said, grabbing a flashlight.

'Can't you just give me something for it?'

Daniella paused; her instincts were telling her that something was wrong. She'd heard another doctor describe it as a twinge in the bullshit-o-meter. Trying to sound firm and relaxed, she simply said, 'A quick look.'

He reluctantly got up on the exam couch where she quickly ran through a neurological assessment. She didn't find any signs – no weakness or dysfunction in his face – but then, with an aneurysm, she might not. The clinic didn't have a CT scanner, or even a pathology lab; it only had an X-ray, a centrifuge and some basic assays. She could do a lumbar puncture – to take a sample of fluid from around his spine to help with diagnosis – but they'd just lose valuable time that they could spend getting him somewhere with more facilities.

'Okay, Peter, how quickly did this pain come on?'

'Real fast,' he said.

'Anything make it worse? Or better?'

'It's just bad,' he said.

Daniella chewed her lip. 'Peter, there's a chance you might have something serious. I'm worried about a bleed in your head, and I'd like to ask Dr Harris to step in.'

That seemed to make him all the more agitated. 'Look, doc, I get migraines. My doctor usually just gives me the Endone.'

Daniella stopped. Endone was an opiate drug. 'Endone? For migraines?'

'Yeah.'

'But you said you hadn't had this pain before.'

'Not this bad.' The guy licked his lips.

Suddenly, Daniella suspected what was going on here. She tested the theory. 'I'm worried you might have an aneurysm, which is very serious,' she said. 'I need the more experienced doctor to take a look at you, because if that is what you have, we'll need to get you flown out to a larger hospital.'

'I don't have an aneurysm, I just need some Endone.' Scowling, he got down from the couch and crossed his arms.

'I can't prescribe that for a migraine,' she said, moving past him slowly and carefully. 'But I can take a quick history of your migraines and find something appropriate.'

'Look, lady, just gimme the Endone!' he said, his voice rising.

Daniella opened the door. 'Thank you. Please wait outside so I can consult Dr Harris.'

The guy's eyes went back and forth between her and the corridor beyond. 'Fuck you, bitch!' he yelled, and ran out.

Daniella heard the clinic door close with such force that it bounced on the slider. She put a hand out to the wall. Three. Deep. Breaths.

Jackie burst into the room. 'Daniella, you okay?'

Daniella could hear patients in the waiting room exclaiming and talking at once. Then, she heard gravel spraying as a car fishtailed out of the car park. Dr Harris was asking everyone to remain calm. He appeared in her room a moment later.

Daniella shut the door, proud to note that her hand was only shaking a little. That would probably get worse as the adrenaline kicked in.

'Are you hurt?' asked Dr Harris.

'No, he didn't touch me. I'm fine.'

'What happened?'

'He was looking for Endone. Reported acute onset headache with ten-out-of-ten pain, nothing on the neuro. When I mentioned I was going to consult you, he said it was a migraine and Endone the regular script. I asked him to wait outside, but he took off.'

Dr Harris's mouth compressed in a censorious line, his eyes making a rapid assessment of her face. Daniella tried to maintain her calm expression. 'Right,' he declared, as if he'd come to a conclusion, and walked out.

Daniella raised her eyebrows at Jackie, who said, 'He's probably calling the pain clinic in the Isa to find out why the guy ended up here. I've never seen him before, but we've had other people come down from there and try it on with us.'

'Really?'

'Yeah. They know there's only one doc, and no security. They think it'll be easier to get bolshy.'

'Wow.' Daniella swallowed. She'd never felt so close to danger before.

'You really okay?'

Daniella thought she was, but if someone asked again, she might not be. She cleared her throat. 'Would you get me the next file, please?'

Jackie duly did so. The next patient had a throat infection; nothing to be done but reassure him that he'd recover soon. When she emerged to walk the patient out, Daniella saw that Rusty, blue singlet and all, had disappeared and Dr Harris's door was closed. She pushed on with the patient list as the raw northern sun burned its way across the perfect sky. Inside the clinic, its movement was evidenced only by the shifting arc of the venetian-blind shadows. Each time she returned to the room with a new chart and patient, the column of lit dust motes had moved a little, as if the whole world was turning without her. She'd been in this savagely beautiful place for nearly a week and she'd seen nothing of it but the inside of the hospital and clinic. She may as well have still been in Brisbane.

By the time she returned the final patient file to the front desk the sun was halfway down again; it seemed 'morning clinic' was a misnomer. Was this what it was going to be like, living in one of the hottest places in the state but never seeing the sun? It seemed an awful waste.

A hand tapped her shoulder. 'Daniella?'

'Sorry, what?' She'd been staring out the window, slumped in the chair, and she sat up quickly.

Dr Harris sat on the edge of her desk and filled her in on his call to the Mount Isa pain clinic. He'd been asked to put things in writing. 'Usual run-around,' he said, shaking his head. 'You did well today,' he continued. 'I'm wondering if you could do me a favour – only if you feel all right?'

Daniella straightened further. 'Sure.'

'Mrs Turner lives in town and doesn't have much mobility. She has a diabetic ulcer at the moment and can't get to the clinic easily. Could you call in? I usually go, but I think she'd enjoy a fresh face.'

'Of course,' she said, eager to keep going.

Dr Harris left and Daniella took a few moments to collect herself and then dust off the mobile kit that had sat under her desk for a week.

When she came out, Jackie was pulling her dark curls out of their band, a thick file tucked under her arm. She turned to Daniella and smiled. 'I hear you're doing the Turner call. Shall I come with you and show you where it is? Moral support, too?'

'That would be great,' said Daniella, taking the file, which was stuffed with a multicoloured array of paper and labelled *Turner, Valerie*.

'Jamie's with Mum. How about a drink afterwards?' suggested Jackie.

'Where do we go?' asked Daniella, wondering if it would be better to go straight home.

Jackie grinned. 'The tav of course! It's the only place in town. Come on, I'll buy and everything.'

'What about Dr Harris? Should we invite him?'

'He's gone shopping for the meat for dinner tomorrow. He said to be there at six. I imagine he'll be thick in marinades all evening.' Jackie rolled her eyes. 'So it's just us.'

Daniella rubbed her face, considering. Her professionalism hadn't allowed her to admit that the incident with Peter *was* a big deal. Sure, she'd had close calls before – in the A&E, and with a few psychiatric patients – but she'd been in a large hospital where there were lots of other people around, and security. Today, the boundary between herself and real danger had been paper thin. She suddenly wanted to find a crowd, and she could really use a drink.

'Okay, great,' she said.

They walked out into the dusty afternoon, with the heat surrounding Daniella like a lustful caress against her skin. She climbed into Jackie's ute and rested the file and her kit on her knees. It only took a few minutes to drive into town and pull up outside a pale brick house. Across a well-tended lawn, the house was ringed with paperbark trees and the eaves groaned under hanging baskets. The whole place was as green as St Patrick's Day.

'Mrs Turner isn't shy about using the bore,' said Jackie as they got out.

A long pause followed their knock. Finally, a voice hollered from inside that it was open.

Jackie led Daniella down a hallway into an L-shaped lounge room crowded with squat brown couches and a solid dining table, which was covered in photo frames and pushed against the wall. In the corner, more framed photos balanced on a TV set, which displayed a muted fishing program. A few of these photos showed a young man in a graduation gown and mortar-board.

Valerie Turner herself occupied the corner of a three-seater, her bandaged leg up on a stool. She wore a floral-print dress and a squashed expression, her grey hair tamed with a savage part. Heavy glasses, currently dangling on a chain around her neck, had left a red mark across the bridge of her nose.

The remainder of the couch was devoted to an apathetic elderly kelpie.

'Thought you'd come, did you?' the old woman said to Jackie. Valerie didn't look as if she could move too far; a walking stick was propped against the couch. But the place seemed in good condition. Clean, despite the worn grey carpet and old furniture.

'Hello, Valerie. This is Dr Bell,' said Jackie smoothly. 'She's going to check your dressing.'

'Is she?' asked Valerie, peering shortsightedly at Daniella.

'Call me Daniella, please. It's nice to meet you, Valerie.'

'Mrs Turner,' corrected Valerie. 'Dr Harris finally given up on me, then? How do I know you're even a real doctor?'

Daniella took a slow breath as she put her kit down on a side table. So, this wasn't going to be easy. She tried for humour. 'Well, I've got the kit.' Valerie gave her a glare, and Daniella quickly changed tack. 'I just need to take a look at your ulcer and make sure there's no infection or other problems. I'll go as slow or as fast as you want.'

Valerie grunted, which Daniella took to be all the permission she'd get. She put on some gloves and gently eased off the dressing. Diabetes could impair circulation and feeling in the legs – the very reason for the ulcer to begin with – and she didn't want to do any more damage. The ulcer was right over the protruding bone – the malleolus – on the inside of Valerie's ankle. The dressing had left the ulcer looking slightly swollen with fluid, but it was otherwise a fairly shallow wound, only involving a few layers of skin. Daniella soaked a cotton bud with sterile saline and carefully cleaned around the edges.

'It looks all right,' she told Valerie. 'There's no sign of infection.'

'Not going away yet though.'

Daniella caught the desperation beneath Valerie's peevish tone. It must be horrible to have something like this: a wound that seemed not to heal. 'Not yet,' she said soothingly. 'But let's get it re-dressed.'

When the ulcer was covered again, Daniella tried to go through the history with Valerie: how long had she had the ulcer, what medications was she taking, and any other symptoms. But the old woman had other ideas. 'Didn't you bother to read that thing?' she asked, pointing at her file.

Daniella persisted a little longer, trying to establish how mobile Valerie was and whether she was getting any exercise. Valerie stared fixedly at the muted fishing program, and refused to answer or cooperate. Finally Daniella gave up.

Her back ached as she packed up the kit. She could tell Jackie was keen to go, but this hadn't gone well. She didn't want to leave feeling that she'd failed to make any connection with Valerie. She cast around for something to save the situation.

'Is that your son?' she tried, nodding towards a photo on top of the television. Surely family would be a good starting point.

'What business is that of yours?' snapped Valerie.

Two minutes later, Jackie and Daniella were back out on the kerb.

'Charmer, isn't she?' said Jackie.

Daniella didn't want to talk about it. Something about Valerie tugged at her. She had wanted to get away but she also felt dissatisfied. She wanted to go back in and try again. With an effort, she pushed her thoughts away from work. 'Jackie, tell me something.'

'Mmhm?'

'Where's a good place to go to, you know, see the country around here? I have a day off tomorrow and I want to see something besides the house and the clinic.'

Jackie removed the keys. 'Been cooped up all week, huh?'

'Yeah.'

'Well, come with me and Jamie to the dam tomorrow.'

'That's your boy? How old is he?'

Jackie opened her door. 'Nearly three,' she said, then gave Daniella a grin. 'Now, to the tav.'

'Okay,' said Jackie. 'The first rule is, don't show any fear. They can smell it.'

Standing inside the door, Daniella looked around. The 'tav' looked like most of the country pubs she'd seen before, the decor straddling both the wood-and-felt quaintness of yesteryear and the chrome and glass of modern shop fitting. This one had the obligatory neon, denser around the pokie room – a glorified name for a corner with two machines. Daniella realised she had her hands stuffed in her pockets, her shoulders hunched, as she always did when she felt unsure of herself. She stood up straighter. 'Okay, check rule one,' she murmured.

Faces turned in their direction. Yep, thought Daniella, you're not in Brisbane anymore. Two out of every three people wore a wide-brimmed hat, from the well-worn and ugly to gracefully curving, bone-coloured ones that reminded her of rodeos. She couldn't help doing a quick scan for any scruffy men wearing T-shirts and King Gee pants, and was relieved to see there was no one fitting that description.

They approached the bar and Jackie ordered two beers. 'You must be the new doc,' said the woman behind the bar, smiling as she gave Daniella the once-over. The woman had a mop of tight curls, a splash of broken capillaries across her nose, and a warm smile. 'How're you finding it?'

'Great,' said Daniella. 'Busy, but great.' It seemed the required response, but she felt the lack of enthusiasm in her voice.

The woman stuck out a chubby hand, wet from the beer glasses. 'Donna,' she said kindly. Daniella shook awkwardly over the bar, surprised at the warmth in Donna's palm. 'Well, great to have you, doc. Kitchen's open in a half hour and the band starts at seven.'

Daniella and Jackie carried their pints over to a table near the bar, away from where most of the men were congregating. In the far corner, a young man in a faded black T-shirt was fiddling with some speakers.

'Do you know the band?' asked Daniella.

Jackie rolled her eyes. 'Probably the Shania Twain tribute band again. I heard they were coming back.'

'They any good?'

'Oh, I suppose. But, you know, it's Shania Twain. They think 'cause we're in the outback that's the only stuff we like.'

'What do you like?'

Jackie grinned. 'Well, mostly the Wiggles these days. But I've heard you get them in Brisbane too.'

'Been to Brisbane recently?' asked Daniella.

Jackie's eyes dipped. 'Not for a while.'

There was a pause. Daniella sensed a touchy subject, so she left it alone. It was too soon to start delving into personal matters with co-workers. She wondered if she should ask Jackie about her son when Jackie got in first. 'Right, so you should know who to avoid in town.'

Daniella laughed. 'Jackie, I'm a doctor. I can't avoid people!'

'You know what I mean – not professionally, just when you're at the supermarket or community events, right?'

'Are there a lot of those?'

'Supermarkets or community events? I'm kidding. Two supermarkets – that one I dropped you at yesterday is the best one. But events, yeah. Most weekends there's something on in the district. In a couple of weeks there's a B&S outside Julia Creek. And let's see . . . rugby match on the oval next weekend. Ugh. That's going to be a great day on duty.'

Daniella raised her eyebrows.

'Bunch of guys who don't usually play rugby fanging down the field knocking into each other? All we gotta do is sit back and wait for the concussions,' Jackie explained. 'You'll see, the X-ray will get its annual workout.'

'Interesting,' said Daniella. 'Is Dr Harris trained to X-ray here? We didn't have to do any this week and I forgot to ask.'

'He's never been able to get enough time off to go and do the training. It's me,' said Jackie, her eyes shining. 'Master of the electrons.'

'Oh really?'

Jackie gave her a mock glare. 'Yes, the lowly nurse. Just kidding. Out here, you have to be ready to do everything. I did the training with a radiographer in Townsville. Got a licence from Queensland Health and everything.' She took a long pull on the beer and changed tack. 'Oh, and there's some movie thing coming up too, at the oval. They put the big screen up on the goalposts.'

'What're they playing?'

Jackie snorted. 'Probably *Jurassic Park*. You know, because of the fossils.'

'Fossils?' asked Daniella, raising her eyebrows.

'Oh yeah. Marine dinosaurs and heaps of other stuff. We get fossil hunters around here all the time. Sometimes from universities, but the caravanners try their luck, too. It's been going on for at least a hundred years. The biggest finds were in the twenties, though; quite a while ago now.'

Jackie went on in some detail about the region's ancient inland sea geography and how the fossils had ended up here.

Daniella found herself remembering snatches of her early science studies at uni, before medicine had occupied all her brain cells.

'How do you know all this?' she asked finally.

Jackie gave a mock groan. 'Jamie's mad about dinosaurs, so my reading's been compulsory. There's a big Kronosaurus display in Richmond, not too far away. I don't want to tell you how many times we've been there.' She laughed.

As more people arrived, Donna turned up the mix tape volume to compensate. 'The Gambler' came to an end for a second time. Looking around, Daniella saw couples in matching flannelettes, workmates, grown families out for dinner. The band stage now had instrument stands, a drum kit and microphones. Kasey Chambers began blaring from the bar speakers, and a screen showed the latest Keno draw.

'Sorry, I got distracted,' said Jackie suddenly. 'I'm meant to be telling you survival stuff.'

'Like show no fear?' Daniella laughed, feeling the beery glow. She was enjoying watching the tav customers. Working in hospitals, it was easy to get the impression that the whole world was unwell. But here were normal people, most of them in the prime of their lives, talking, joking, having a great time. Daniella had seldom gone out in Brisbane, and when she had it had not been particularly enjoyable. The tav was refreshing, without big-city pretensions. Non-threatening, despite her initial reservations.

Then, abruptly, she remembered Peter.

Jackie poked her in the arm. 'You okay?'

Daniella dragged herself out of the bad memory. 'Yes. Sorry.'

Jackie raised a finger. 'Right, first, any man who asks you on a date to the dam, you say no. Got it?'

'Okay,' said Daniella, smiling. Somehow she couldn't see a situation arising where anyone would ask her out.

'And ditto to anyone who asks you to join an organising committee. I'm not saying they don't do good things; they do. All that stuff I mentioned is for the Flying Doctors or the Red Cross or the firefighters. And they bought our centrifuge at the clinic. But those committees will suck the life out of you. You don't want to be part of it. Trust me. Morgans' territory.'

'Morgans?'

'Old family from the area. They used to have a station out here, but they were in lots of other ventures – exports and business; legal stuff I think. Lots of money. They mostly live in Townsville now and come in to organise things. They've got some kind of law firm there. Mrs Morgan's a lawyer, sold the station years ago, but they like to pretend they still live here – all appearances – so they come back regularly to keep the roots strong. I went to school with Steph. When you meet them you'll see what I mean.'

'Any other old families I should know about?'

'Well, there's the Walkers. Ryders Station is theirs, about forty minutes out of town. Big cattle station. The family's been here forever.'

'They named their station after the town?'

Jackie swallowed and coughed, as if the beer had gone down the wrong way. 'No, no. Town's named for the station. It's been here longer than anything else. William Walker runs it. His wife died earlier this year. Really sad.'

'Oh?' Daniella asked idly, carefully stacking beer coasters into a card house. When the base was finished, she looked up. There was a queue at the bar now; she could see a lot of the RM Williams catalogue lining up. As two men moved aside after being served, one of them caught Daniella's eye. Unlike many of the guys, he looked good in his jeans. Tall, perfect-length leg, shirt tucked into a wide belt, broad back.

Above this was a tousle of sandy hair and, as he turned to take his beer, a pleasing profile.

Daniella felt herself go still. 'Who's that?'

Jackie followed her gaze. There was a distinct pause. 'Speak of the devil. That's Mark Walker.'

'Really?'

'Yeah. Nice guy, actually. William's son.'

At that moment, Mark Walker turned and his eyes fell directly on Daniella. His gaze stopped momentarily, then shifted to her coaster card house. He smiled. Daniella felt embarrassed to be caught in such a childish activity, but simultaneously intrigued. He had a very open face, interested, intelligent. Her hand jerked involuntarily and the coaster house tumbled.

Jackie helped her pick them up off the floor. 'Quite a looker, too, isn't he?' she whispered.

Daniella made no comment, hastily pushing the coasters into a pile. When she looked again, Mark was talking to the man beside him, who had dark hair and was a few inches shorter. They both glanced in her direction. A woman had joined them, wearing jeans and a checked shirt; she leaned in to hear whatever was being said, then laughed, her hand touching her throat.

'Who are they?' Daniella asked Jackie.

'Double devil,' muttered Jackie.

'What?'

'That's Steph Morgan. I mentioned her before. Avoid the committees, remember?'

'And the other guy?'

Jackie spoke quickly. 'Dave Cooper, Mark's mate. Went to school with all of them.'

'What's Dave do?' Daniella asked.

Jackie grimaced. 'You might never see him again – he

travels round a lot. He's a pilot, mechanic, general fixer, among other things.'

'Mmm,' said Daniella, filing details. As Jackie chatted on, she could sense Mark looking her way and she surreptitiously smoothed her hair and checked her shirt buttons were done up. Then, to focus on something else, she rebuilt the coasters.

The next thing, a shadow fell across her card house. 'Hi,' said a deep male voice.

Daniella looked up. Mark Walker was standing right beside their table. Up close, he was even more impressive, exuding a confidence and authority beyond his years. She fished around for the right word and settled on *gravitas*.

'Hi, Mark,' said Jackie. 'Haven't seen you around lately.'

'Yeah, I haven't been to town for a while,' he admitted. 'Lots going on, as always. How's Jamie?'

'Fine – a handful, and getting bigger. How's your dad?'

'Doing all right.' Even though he was talking to Jackie, Daniella couldn't help noticing that his eyes kept sliding in her direction. She sat there, self-conscious about having not been introduced, but at the same time feeling the warmth of his attention.

Jackie noticed too. 'This is Daniella Bell,' she said. 'Daniella, Mark Walker.'

'Nice to meet you,' said Daniella.

'Likewise.' Mark smiled back at her, and Daniella felt her shyness melt away. In spite of his intimidating appearance, his manner was natural and unassuming.

'Daniella's the new doc,' supplied Jackie.

'Oh really?' Mark slipped into a seat at their table. 'I heard about you from Kath.'

Then, before Daniella could ask who Kath was, a hand shot into her line of sight. 'Steph Morgan,' said the woman in the checked shirt.

Daniella shook the other woman's hand, uncomfortably aware of how cold and damp her hand must be from the beer glass. 'Hi,' she said.

'So what are we talking about?' enquired Steph, putting her hand on Mark's shoulder as if keen to claim him. Daniella wiped her hand on her trouser leg under the table. Steph's tone had injected an uncomfortable scrutiny into the conversation.

Jackie waved dismissively. 'Nothing, really. Just catching up with Mark.'

But Mark shifted his shoulders so that Steph removed her hand and continued easily, 'Do you want to join us?' he asked, gesturing towards the bar. 'We brought the muster in today so a few beers are in order.'

Daniella glanced over. Mark's mate Dave had his back to them as he chatted to a group of men in blue overalls. Mark seemed an island of calm, but Steph hovered, her eyes full of questions, clearly itching to dominate the conversation. After the long day, a dull ache started up in Daniella's head at the thought of a quiet beer turning into twenty questions.

She was relieved when Jackie said, 'No, thanks. We're just having a quick one.'

'No worries,' said Mark. He stood up reluctantly and moved back to the bar. Steph lingered, casting an appraising glance at Daniella and Jackie before she followed.

Daniella looked at Jackie. 'It's okay – we can join them if you really want to,' she said, even though it wasn't. Steph didn't seem like easy company.

Jackie downed the end of her beer and shook her head quickly. 'Nah, it's all right. Look, you finished? Why don't we take a walk?'

A moment later, they were walking along the tav's verandah, then out into the street beneath the darkening sky.

'So, you've survived your first social encounter,' joked Jackie. 'Don't worry, being the new thing will fade. Listen, do you still want to come to the dam tomorrow? Less people there.'

Daniella laughed. 'I thought you said not to accept invitations to the dam?'

'Ha ha! You passed the test. But that only applies to men, and Jamie doesn't count. Come on, I'll give you a lift back.'

Daniella looked up at the sky. 'Actually, I think I'd like to walk. What time tomorrow?'

'Pick you up at ten. You need a sleep-in.'

Soon, Jackie's ute had bumped its way down the road and Daniella was alone. The street was full of cars; mostly utes and dusty four-wheel-drives. The land was really flat; that must be why the sky seemed so big. Jackie had told her that the whole area was once a huge sea, which explained both the flatness and the fossils. Now, it was as if the sea had been upended to become the great bowl-shaped sky overhead.

The air had cooled during the evening and the walk to her place wasn't far. As the happy rumble of the tav receded, Daniella found herself thinking of Mark Walker. He seemed to have left an indelible imprint on her retinas. She tried to reason with herself; now was not the time to be noticing attractive men. She'd come to this town for one reason only – to get her confidence back – and she didn't need any emotional entanglements, anything that might impede her recovery.

But her thoughts returned to him anyway, like a scratched record that kept skipping the needle back to the same place. When she got home, she shut Ryders Ridge out for the night and settled onto the couch, her mind still with Mark as she fell asleep.

Chapter 4

Daniella crammed her battered hat down over her ears as Jackie's ute rolled up the next morning. The sun was shining in all its savage brilliance, puffy white clouds hanging on to the far horizon, and she was already sweating. Again, she checked that she had her phone in her pocket.

'Hi!' called Jackie across the seat and through the open passenger window.

'Morning,' said Daniella, yanking the door open. 'Hey, is there any reception out at the dam?'

'Off and on, and only if you've got Telstra.'

'Okay.' Daniella bit her lip. Dr Harris was again on call, but if something came in . . .

'Don't worry, Dr Harris will be cooking all day. If he gets a call, it'll be a welcome distraction. And I thought you wanted to see some of the country?'

Daniella got in. She twisted around to smile at the little boy strapped into his car seat. He had dark curls and dark eyes, just like his mother, and three plastic dinosaurs in his lap.

'Jamie, this is Daniella, the new doctor,' said Jackie.

'Hi, Jamie,' said Daniella.

'Jamie, are you going to say hi to Daniella?'

'Hi, Nella,' said the little boy with a flash of dimples.

Daniella grinned at him. 'Wow, are they dinosaurs?'

The boy gathered the plastic figurines tightly into his chest, a smile of pure glee plumping his cheeks.

'Do you think we can look for dinosaur bones at the dam?' Daniella suggested.

He nodded fervently, clearly too excited to speak.

'He's beautiful, Jackie. He looks so much like you,' said Daniella.

Jackie kept her eyes on the road. 'Yes, he certainly does.' Daniella caught an edge in Jackie's voice, but then she seemed to shake it off. 'Hey, do you like sci-fi?'

'You mean like *Star Trek*?' asked Daniella.

'Well, I suppose if you want to be vintage. But there's heaps of other good stuff. You seen *Firefly*? No? Oh dear. I'll educate you.'

They drove on for five minutes before the road became dirt, then ten more until the corrugations started up and they all rattled around in the cab. Jamie found this hilarious and giggled uncontrollably as his teeth chattered.

'Ugh, road's overdue for a grade,' complained Jackie.

After five more minutes they crested a gentle rise, and a sparkling expanse of water opened up before them, a sheet of diamond lights, kissing the eucalypts from shore to shore. The glare was incredible, and Daniella pulled out her sunglasses. She knew the dam wasn't natural, just like the hospital's lake; both had the feel of being crafted by human hands. Still, it was pretty. Beyond it she could see glimpses of the country diving off towards the shimmering grey horizon. Evidently other people liked it too. Four vehicles dotted the shoreline, three of them campervans, the occupants under pop-out side shades pouring tea from thermoses. They all waved as Jackie drew up nearby.

She produced a blanket from the crew cab and the two women stretched out in the shade of a gum tree, watching Jamie tearing along the shore with his dinosaurs. After a comfortable silence, Jackie asked, 'So, you got a man back in Brisbane?'

'No, haven't had much luck with them.'

'Too busy?'

'I had a boyfriend for a while. He was an A&E registrar. We didn't see an awful lot of each other.' In fact, this had been true of the two boyfriends before the registrar, too. She was attracted to driven, professional types, men with intelligence who knew what they wanted. But inevitably she'd found herself taking second place to the same ambitions that had drawn her in, and the relationships had drifted apart.

'That's not why you're here, is it?' asked Jackie.

Daniella swallowed. 'No. That's been over for a while. I came here to get more experience, and I wanted to live in a smaller place. Brisbane was too big. And Dad had just taken a job at the hospital where I was working. Kinda felt like time to do something different.'

'Ah, daddy issues,' said Jackie, nodding. 'He want you to settle down and have kids?'

Daniella let her eyes wander over to the edge of the dam to where Jamie had flopped down on his stomach, happily making tracks in the mud with the toy dinosaurs. 'Just the opposite, actually. He's a surgeon. He wants me to do the same. But I don't want that life,' she said, confidently. And she didn't, did she?

'What does your mum think?'

Daniella didn't miss a beat. 'She died a long time ago.'

'Oh, I'm sorry,' said Jackie.

'It's all right. I was really young, and I hardly remember her. When I was growing up it was always just Dad and me and my brother Aiden – we were all really close. Then Aiden enlisted and it was just the two of us. I think Dad thinks of me as an extension of himself – that's why the whole surgeon thing.'

Jackie looked thoughtful. 'Wow, that's so different from the attitude around here. You should've heard the way people talked after I had Jamie. It was like I should've been chained to a sink or something. Everyone expected I'd just settle down and be a mum and that'd be it. But that's not for me. I want to do more.'

'Like what?'

'You know, study. See the world. I want to travel again. Go back to live in Brisbane for a while. Don't get me wrong, I love the town, and Mum's here. But I want to know what's over the hill. When I was studying down in Brisbane, that was the best time of my life.'

Daniella smiled at the passion in Jackie's voice. 'I didn't realise you'd studied in Brisbane. Is that where you did nursing?'

'Yeah. I didn't quite finish, though. Had to do some tricky external juggling to become registered. But that wasn't what I wanted to do.'

'So what do you want to do?'

'Radiography,' said Jackie. 'Remember I told you I trained for a rural licence in Townsville? That was when Jamie was really small – it nearly killed me, but it was so interesting. The licence I have is pretty restrictive and the equipment isn't anything flash: I'm supposed to consult a radiologist for anything other than X-raying a leg or an arm, but you can't always get on to them when you need them, so I've started looking at proper courses. Apparently there's one at QUT. Have you heard of it?'

Daniella thought. 'Yes – I don't know much about it but I can ask some friends down there if they could find out more, if you like?'

'That'd be great. But quietly, okay? I don't want anyone in town gossiping about me going away. It's been hard enough the last few years, and I still need to save some more money before Jamie and I can go. I could work some shifts down there, but I'd need a bunch to start out with for bond and rent. And there'll be textbooks, too, and childcare. Meanwhile things seem to keep coming up that need paying for.'

'How long have you been saving?' Daniella asked. She was impressed by Jackie's determination.

Jackie's gaze drifted over to Jamie, who looked up and gave them a mischievous smile. Both women grinned back stupidly and waved. 'A while,' murmured Jackie.

'What about Jamie's dad? Could he help?'

Jackie shook her head. 'He's just someone I went out with in Brisbane – he's not involved in our lives.'

At that point, Jamie got up and came tearing back across the sand. He flung himself at Jackie, who caught him in a rough hug, kissing him until he squealed. 'What's this, you mad ruckus!' she jabbered, tickling him. Daniella watched them, smiling. In spite of Jackie's difficult situation, the deep loving bond between them was obvious.

Finally, the little boy stopped wriggling and dropped the plastic dinosaurs. 'Bones now?' he asked.

Daniella jumped up. 'You bet. In fact . . . I think I see one!' And she went tearing off across the sandy shore with Jamie and Jackie laughing as they tried to keep up.

~

Daniella was still picking the sand out from under her fingernails as she thought about what to wear for dinner at Dr Harris's. She and Jamie had dug at dozens of spots for bones. They hadn't found any, but Jamie didn't seem to mind. He'd been snoozing in the car when Jackie dropped Daniella back at the house. Jackie was exhausted and told Daniella she'd call Dr Harris and apologise that she wouldn't make it to dinner.

Knowing she was going into another six-day week, Daniella would also rather have spent the evening crashed out in front of the TV or reading a book. But it sounded as though Dr Harris was going to a lot of effort; she really should put in an appearance.

She decided on the same pair of jeans she'd worn that day; all her trousers seemed too work-like, and she didn't own a dress. Her shirts still lay in a rumpled pile after the work week. Bugger, she'd forgotten to do any washing. She brought the least crumpled one up to her nose. Ugh. All right, she wasn't wearing one of those. Which left the T-shirts. In the end, she went for a plain white one. It was creased from being folded up in her suitcase, but it would have to do.

She pushed the laundry pile aside with her foot as she slipped the T-shirt onto a hanger. She'd hang it up in the bathroom and hope some of the creases would come out during her shower.

If only the same thing would work on her face. Daniella didn't know what was wrong with her. She generally ate pretty well. Well, all right, she had in Brisbane – she just hadn't yet managed to get a routine in place here. She exercised when she could. Did a job she loved. Even so, she looked . . . tired.

Just after six thirty she knocked on Dr Harris's door. He lived not far from her, in a nice double-brick, two-storey home with shrouding gardens. The front door was on the second level, up a long flight of steps.

Dr Harris opened the door, his grey hair yellowed by the porch light. 'Come in, come in, my dear,' he said, ushering her past a plush lounge room, neat but crammed with furniture. Crocheted throws over the backs of chairs, frilly lamp covers and deep red walls announced a decorator in love with 1976, but it looked cosy all the same. After the lounge, the house opened out into a well-appointed, reasonably modern kitchen facing a huge deck. The mouth-watering smell of lamb and rosemary filled the room. Standing by the kitchen bench were two tall blonde women, wine glasses in hand. Daniella recognised Steph Morgan from the tav.

Dr Harris made the introductions. 'Daniella, this is Maria Morgan and her daughter, Stephanie. Maria and Stephanie, Dr Daniella Bell.'

Both women turned towards her and Daniella had the random thought that they were a matched pair. Both wore impeccable white jeans and tailored blue shirts beneath tanned faces, sun-bleached hair and tiny stud earrings. In Maria's case, the tanning was a little more leathery, the studs diamonds rather than pearls.

Daniella was hugged and kissed, with many exclamations of 'how wonderful'. Uncomfortable with such physical familiarity, Daniella took a step back, but the Morgans seemed not to notice. Then the two women spent ten minutes praising the smell of Dr Harris's cooking and asking about the recipe. He modestly claimed that it was nothing to do with him, simply that Ryders-district meat was the best in the world. With further pressing he revealed that his secret was wrapping the meat in foil and adding milk. By this time, the famous roast had been removed from its resting plate and more gushing ensued.

Daniella had the impression that this conversation had happened before. She watched the Morgans, mesmerised by their ceaseless chatter and perfect teeth. She was definitely outside the conversation. That was fine, really. Once the food had been carried to the deck and they'd all sat down, the women's focus moved to her.

'So, Daniella, you're from Brisbane?' Maria began.

Daniella straightened. ‘Yes. I was at the PM, the Princess Mary Hospital, on the north side, and before that, the PA. The Princess Alexandra, that is. On the south—’

‘And how long are you staying?’

Daniella paused, taken aback by her directness. ‘Well, I’m planning to apply for a training program.’ That part was true at least. ‘I could train as a rural specialist GP, so this is the perfect area—’

‘What was the name of that other registrar you had, Dr Harris?’ Maria cut in. ‘That lovely young doctor from Sydney?’

‘Stuart Masterson,’ supplied Dr Harris, cutting at his lamb with great concentration.

‘Ah, yes,’ said Maria to Daniella. ‘Talented. Very attractive. He went on to specialise, didn’t he, Martin?’

‘Anaesthetics,’ said Dr Harris.

‘Well, everyone was a little bit in love with him, I think.’

Daniella had nothing to add to this, so she swallowed the unsaid end of her sentence and followed it with food.

As Maria plied Dr Harris for details of registrars past, Steph plucked at Daniella’s sleeve. ‘Dani, we’re organising a movie night soon to support the fire service,’ she said. ‘The community does a lot of things like that. You should consider joining the committee.’

No one had called her Dani since primary school, and Jackie’s warning about committees rang bells. ‘Thank you, but since the clinic is six days I think I’d better stick to that for now. How long have—’

But Steph had turned away. ‘Dr Harris, you didn’t invite the Walkers tonight?’

‘I did. Mark apologised and said they had some business to attend to.’

'Oh well, we'll find out about that later,' said Maria, waving her hand. 'The muster came in yesterday.'

As the conversation continued, Daniella found herself always at its edge. Dr Harris tried to bring her in, but inevitably the Morgans spoke over the top of her, or talked about relatives or locals she didn't know. She tried to follow the details, thinking it could be useful to understand the relationships between people who were potential patients. But after a few minutes she was hopelessly lost, so she sat quietly and sipped steadily at her wine.

When Dr Harris and Maria took the dishes into the kitchen, she found herself alone on the deck with Stephanie. The silence was uncomfortable, and Daniella looked out into the gum trees that shielded the back of the block, searching for something to say.

'So, Dr Harris does this pretty often, I hear,' she tried.

'Yes. He likes to cook. His wife died not long after he moved to town, and he's been on his own ever since.' Steph lowered her voice. 'He's pretty keen to retire now though. Did he tell you that?'

Daniella frowned slightly. 'No, I—'

'Oh well. I guess he's looking for someone to take over the practice. You know, be here for the long haul.'

Daniella didn't know what to say; her position here was temporary, but the thought that Dr Harris hadn't mentioned his plans was unsettling somehow. But something about Steph made her wonder whether to believe it.

'So anyway, think about the committee,' Steph burbled on, brightly. 'I know you'll be busy, but it's for good causes and we always need more people for ideas and posters and all that. Everyone who can usually helps out.'

'Well, I guess so,' said Daniella, feeling herself giving in.

'Oh, and you should come to the rugby next week and the ball the week after. Tickets are ninety dollars – it all goes to the Red Cross. Can I put you down for one?'

Daniella felt bulldozed by sheer force of personality and looked for a way out. She got up from the table. 'I'll be on duty,' she said quickly. 'Excuse me a minute.'

She escaped into the house and asked directions to the bathroom. Once there, she sat down on the cool seat and pressed her hands to her burning cheeks. She missed Jackie, who she was sure would have handled Steph with a witty reply. Interacting with the relentless Morgans was making her bones ache. She counted the towels, neatly stacked beside three bottles of hospital-grade soap, then splashed some water on her face.

When she finally stepped out into the hall again, she noticed a framed photo on a small table facing a window. It showed a young man and woman together, arm in arm, both in flares, with some kind of arch behind them. The photo was so faded and splotched that it was hard to make out their faces, but even so it exuded joy. She wondered if the young man was Dr Harris, so very different, so long ago.

When she got back to the kitchen, she was surprised to find that both the Morgans had departed.

'They never stay long when they're on their own,' said Dr Harris apologetically. 'But it's a very good idea to get to know them. They're important in the area. Do a lot of fundraising. Makes the medical work much easier, believe me.'

'Are they always so . . .' Daniella reached for a word that wasn't *overbearing*.

'Self-absorbed?' He chuckled. 'They love to talk but you get used to it. Their hearts are in the right place. And city hospitals won't teach you how to survive out here. I don't just mean the medical stuff – you have to work with the community, understand them. It takes a while.'

Daniella eased onto a stool. 'Yes, I imagine.'

'So, your father's a surgeon, I think you said?'

Daniella shifted. 'Yes, he is.'

'What's his specialty?'

'Trauma,' she said.

Dr Harris smiled knowingly. 'Ah, so a bit of an ego, then?'

She let herself smile back. She found it hard to see her father from an outsider's perspective. 'I guess people might say that. He's very sure of himself, and he has set ideas about my career.'

'My dear, all fathers do,' said Dr Harris. 'Especially if they're doctors too.'

'He transferred to the Princess Mary just before I decided to come up here. They have a specialist trauma centre. It was probably a good thing that I left, really.' Daniella thought about saying more, but she couldn't see a safe out if she got started. Instead she said, 'I think I'll head home. Thank you for the lovely meal. The meat was delicious.'

'You're very welcome, my dear. We'll do it again soon. As I said, the best meat in Australia comes from this town, and after that whole export drama, the farms really need the support. Take some home with you.'

And so Daniella walked home under the big sky with her thoughts caught between the Morgans and her father, an alfoil pack warm in her fingers.

Chapter 5

Tuesday afternoon on Ryders Station found Mark and Dave both sweating in the machinery shed and struggling to get the day on track again.

'Pass me that,' said Dave, on his back underneath a quad bike, his eyes fixed on something deep in the engine bay.

'What?' asked Mark, pausing in his bridle repair to reach for the tools.

'*That*,' insisted Dave, jabbing a grubby finger in the general direction of the toolbox. 'I'm going to jam the whole bloody lot up here. Goddamn.' He grunted, trying to get his finger onto something just out of reach.

'You fixing that thing or just playing with it?' joked Mark.

'I could try to explain, but I know you'd only understand if this was a cow's rear end. Torque wrench.'

Mark passed it over. 'Smartarse.'

'Takes one to, you know,' Dave managed while working the torque wrench. 'Okay. Try that.'

Mark put down the bridle and reached for the key. Mechanical failures had a way of accelerating time, and today was already disappearing. He had to get to a fence repair, and then look at the plan for next year's baseline. When that was done, he was determined to give some thinking time to Ryders' future, if something else didn't come up that needed his attention.

'Anytime today would be good,' called Dave.

'Sorry. Hands clear.' Mark turned the ignition and the quad bike roared to life.

Dave slid out, wiping his hands down the once-blue coveralls. 'How big's this fence break?' he asked as he packed away the tools.

Mark started loading gear into the quad-bike tray. 'Not too big. We'll get it done today. You off back to town later?'

'Yeah. Fridge at the supermarket's playing up – Tony wants me to take a look tomorrow morning before he puts in for a service call. Not much else on for the week though.'

Mark nodded. 'We'll have to do a complete check in the next few months, right down the long fence. Need you in the chopper for that.'

'Right,' said Dave. 'Unless you'd prefer a long trek on the horses?'

Mark laughed. One summer, when they were eleven, William had sent them on a long ride out to check fences, their first real taste of freedom and responsibility. 'If only I could spare the time. But no boys' adventures this year – just have to make do with rugby.'

Mark was actually looking forward to the annual community game on Sunday. Even though much of his work on the station was physical, it always had a practical purpose; the simplicity of a bunch of men knocking each other around just to chase a ball down a field was appealing.

'So, how many of those Julia Creek wankers are we going to put in the hospital this year?' asked Dave, cleaning his hands on an old rag.

Mark grinned. 'At least Dr Harris's got help.' He regretted the statement instantly.

Sure enough, Dave socked him on the arm. 'Don't think I didn't notice you staring the other night.'

Mark didn't rise. But since their encounter at the tav, he'd been thinking rather a lot about the new doc. He remembered the way she'd looked around, as if absorbing every detail, and the interest in her face when she'd looked at him. It was true that young, attractive women didn't often move to town, but Mark had met plenty of them before, particularly on his travels, and this was the first time he'd felt such a strong interest. Ever since, whenever he got a break in his work, he found himself wondering when and where their paths might cross again.

Abruptly, he realised he'd come to a complete halt halfway to the quad with a roll of wire. He quickly loaded the roll and went back for the tools.

Dave went on, 'Yeah, well, Steph Morgan isn't so impressed.'

'No?'

He hefted a pole driver into the tray. 'She caught me when I was leaving town this morning. I tried not to listen, of course, but she said something about the new doc refusing to join a committee. They were both at Dr Harris's on Sunday night.'

Mark smiled to himself. 'Resisting the Morgans. She must have a backbone.'

Dave gave him a look. 'Or Steph could just be stirring. I noticed that, too; she's still keen on you.'

Mark remembered the brief, uncomfortable conversation they'd had at the tav where, after quite a few beers and getting tired of shrugging her off, he'd said he just wanted to be friends, and she'd laughed and acted as if he was imagining things. Mark made a face. 'Not interested, and I think I was pretty clear about that.'

Dave climbed onto the bike, and fired it up, shouting over the engine, 'Yeah, well, let's see how long the new doc lasts.'

Mark started his own quad and they rolled out of the workshop, cruising past the shed where the nose of the chopper

– a Robinson R22 – peeked from under its dustcover. As they passed the chopper, leased from a Northern Territory aviation company with the Morgans' money, Mark found himself returning to an idea that had been in his mind since Steph turned up on Friday. He knew the station's future was on a thin edge, but he believed with enough time they would return to success. They'd been hit hard, but they were still here. He was proud of the station's beauty, and it was even more spectacular from the air. Maybe the chopper could help them through the next few years, earning income from tours. They could keep building the herd while people paid to experience the life out here – if it didn't just generate more work than it brought in. Maybe they'd need to change the lease, get an R44 with the extra seats. As he and Dave bumped down the ridge and started to ride along the fence line he mulled over the issues. He wanted to be sure it was a good idea before he mentioned it to anyone. But the Morgans talking sale options made him feel like he didn't have much time.

So why was he thinking about the new doctor?

On Wednesday morning, Dr Harris finally told Daniella to take the night on call by herself. She wasn't sure what had changed since last week, but she stopped thinking about it when at around eight that evening she was called in to the hospital. Nineteen-year-old Robert, evidently fresh from training for the upcoming rugby match, had rolled up with a broken finger. He'd driven himself to the hospital directly from the field, the broken hand stuck out the window, changing gears and steering one-handed. Daniella examined the finger and decided it was a clean break, no X-ray required, so Jackie could stay in bed. She then used local anaesthetic to numb the finger (noting Robert's white-as-a-sheet reaction to the needle), straightened and braced the finger, gave him the rest-ice-elevation spiel, and made him a follow-up appointment for Monday.

When Dr Harris heard about her handling of the case the next day he looked impressed, and so Thursday morning found Daniella alone in the clinic while Dr Harris went to Mount Isa for a local health board meeting. He had originally scheduled the clinic to be closed that day, so appointments were sparse, but the autonomy felt very good.

The first appointment slot was empty and no one was in the waiting room yet. Jackie was at the desk, ready to take calls or walk-ins as they happened. Daniella went out to join her.

'How's Jamie?' she asked, sorting through the slim patient-file stack.

'Wonderful. Terrible. Everything together.'

'He's with your mum today?'

'Yeah, and he's staying there tonight for some more Grandma time. You want to come over for dinner? I can show you *Firefly* like I've been threatening. I swear, I don't know how you've lived the last decade without seeing it.'

'Well, the wards were my spaceship,' said Daniella. But she felt the lovely glow of being sought out. Since arriving in Ryders Ridge she'd felt as if she was floating somewhere between the dry earth and the big sky. Jackie's friendship made her feel as though some part of her had touched down. 'Sure,' she said. 'Dr Harris will be back at five to take tonight's on-call, so I'm all good.'

At that moment, they both spotted a plume of dust coming up the hospital drive. 'Uh-oh, I smell a bleeder,' chuckled Jackie.

A minute later, as the dust cloud was tinkling down on the verandah roof, Robert (complete with braced finger) hauled a younger boy in through the clinic doors. Both were dressed in grotty Auscam fatigues, and the younger guy was grey behind patchy teenage stubble. His left hand was wrapped in a dirty

T-shirt and there was blood all down his front. Given their physical similarity, Daniella picked them for brothers.

'Doc!' said Robert. 'Joe got his hand bit.'

'This way,' Daniella said calmly while her mind moved quickly. She led them through the back door of the clinic, along the connecting walkway and into the hospital's suture room; better to have everything to hand. She installed Joe on the bed. Robert hovered on the other side, his arms crossed, the broken finger sticking out.

Daniella turned to Jackie, who had followed them. 'Could you get me the antivenin chart and also check the X-ray is prepped? We might need it.'

Jackie stepped out and Daniella turned to Joe. 'Okay, what happened? What bit you?' She was trying to remember back to med school, which was the last time she'd seen a snake bite.

'A goddamn pig,' declared Joe.

'I'm sorry?' replied Daniella.

'Pig,' said Robert. 'He got too close an' the boar weren't dead. Not a bite so much. Got tusked. Got him good.'

'Wait – I'm sorry, what were you doing?'

'Pig shootin',' said Joe and Robert in unison, as if it wasn't obvious.

Daniella turned to stare at Robert. 'You went pig shooting with a broken finger?'

He shrugged. 'I'm a leftie. Trigger finger's the other one.' He illustrated this with an imaginary rifle. 'Anyways, I can't play the game on the weekend, so we thought we'd go for a week's shootin'.'

Daniella took a deep breath and decided to let it pass. She put a thick hospital towel on Joe's lap, then pulled on a pair of gloves. 'Well, let's take a look,' she said.

Joe didn't move, just sat staring at her, his Adam's apple

bobbing up and down. He looked petrified, and absurdly young; Daniella picked him for maybe fourteen.

'Joe,' she said gently. 'I have to look. I won't touch, all right? Just put your hand down on the towel and let me unwrap it. You can tell me to stop anytime.'

Slowly, Joe complied. There was one bad moment when Robert encouraged him with a slap on the shoulder and Joe told him solidly to *fuck orf*, but soon the hand was down and the wound exposed.

'Hmm . . . he got you good, didn't he?' said Daniella.

Joe's middle finger was ripped lengthwise from just within the crease where it joined his hand to just above the last joint. It was smeared with sand, grass and mud, but the bleeding was a slow ooze, and the finger itself wasn't deformed.

'Is it bad?' Joe asked tremulously. He was staring at the wall, avoiding looking at his hand.

'It's a bit dirty, so we're going to have to clean it,' said Daniella. 'And you'll need stitches. I'd like to check a couple of things first: can you move your fingers? Just do it slowly if you can.'

After some complaining that it hurt, Joe managed to do this. Good sign.

'Okay, now I'm going to touch your fingers very lightly. Close your eyes and tell me when you feel the touch.'

By this, Daniella established that his sensation was intact, as was a very low pain threshold. She was satisfied he didn't have any neurological damage.

'Joe, are you left-handed too?' she asked.

'No, right,' he said.

Daniella relaxed a little more. If she'd been in Brisbane, she would probably have requested a consult with a hand surgeon. Hands were serious business; significant injuries could impair someone's whole life. Some of her father's colleagues regularly took toes from people's feet to replace amputated thumbs: hand function was that important. But a non-dominant hand was slightly less of a concern.

She put a fresh gauze pad over the wound. 'Press gently,' she said. 'We're going to do an X-ray to make sure nothing's broken, then we'll start cleaning it up. Are you allergic to anything? Good. You're going to need some serious antibiotics for the next ten days, and I'll need to see you in a few days to make sure it doesn't go septic.'

'But we're going roo shootin' tomorrow,' Joe objected.

This argument continued through the X-ray (which Jackie produced with perfect contrast and showed no broken bones) and then Joe's awful fear of needles. The aversion clearly ran in the family.

'It's just like I had,' said Robert, sticking his now-filthy finger brace in Joe's face. 'Stop being a sissy and get the shot.'

'Fine for you. You didn't have half yer finger comin' off!'

Eventually, after more tears than little Mandy had shed over her vaccinations, Daniella got the anaesthetic shot into each side of Joe's knuckle, carefully turning the needle to inject a little between the fingers to cover the small return branches of the nerves. She didn't dare mention yet that he'd need to have a tetanus booster too. After laying out two sterile pre-packed wash trays, she scrubbed up, put on gloves and carefully cleaned the wound. All the shiny tendons were intact, she was pleased to see. The pig must have just got a grip on the skin and twisted, tearing rather than biting through.

It took ten stitches to close, and she put in two mattress sutures near the knuckles for better support. Dressing, bandage, sling, tetanus shot, done.

Joe grinned at her, looking slightly sheepish. 'Thanks, doc,' he said.

Daniella pursed her lips. 'I don't want you boys going bush tomorrow. If that hand gets infected, you could be in serious trouble.'

'It's okay, doc, I'll take the pills,' said Joe casually. Now the ordeal was over, his bravado had returned.

'Monday,' she said firmly. 'I want to see you both here on Monday. No excuses.'

Once she'd extracted a promise that they'd return, Daniella emerged to find the waiting room was now full. Jackie handed her the next file.

After the pig bite, the rest of the day went past in a blur. All the other appointments were fairly mundane: some workers' comp forms, a sore knee, two sore backs, three colds, one mole biopsy. When she and Jackie closed the doors at five, Daniella stretched her aching back. But it was a satisfying ache, this one. She'd handled her first solo clinic, she was going to a friend's for dinner and her boss was beginning to trust her. She smiled as she walked back down the hall, sticking her head into the consulting rooms to see if anything needed straightening, or wall bins refilling. Everything looked in order.

Jackie came in the back door from the hospital side. 'All done,' she said. 'You want a lift?'

'No, I think I'll walk home and take a shower,' Daniella said. She wanted to savour this feeling a little longer. 'Be at your place in an hour?'

'Sure.'

'You want me to bring anything?'

'No.' Jackie laughed. 'I've got frozen pizza and beer. All you've got is cup-a-soup.'

Daniella laughed too. 'True.'

When Jackie had left, Daniella took one last walk through the clinic, making sure the drug cabinets were secure, the computer off, the alarm ready. She was just going out the front door when her mobile rang. She looked at the caller ID with a sinking feeling.

'Hi, Dad,' she said, stepping back inside the clinic.

'Dr Bell,' came her father's voice down the line. This greeting used to be a joke between them, something that had started when she'd graduated from medical school. But now Daniella heard only a signal from an earlier time, when they'd been on better terms than they were now. 'How's work in the great red yonder?' he teased.

Daniella grimaced. 'Fine,' she said, sinking into a waiting-room chair. 'How's the Princess Mary working out?'

'Great place to be,' he said. 'Still feels new and well equipped. Good staff. Looking forward to the opportunities. Seeing any surgical cases up there?'

'Did one today,' she said.

'Ah. Tell me about it?'

Daniella quickly regretted mentioning it. Her father was a perfectionist who liked to analyse everything. Even when she'd first started medical school, he'd enjoyed analysing cases in detail, discussing what had gone well, what could be improved on, what she should be thinking. In person, sitting across from him at their dining table, able to read his expressions, that had been fine. But he was a different man on the phone: straight to business, no warmth. Now he asked her difficult questions, and she skirted round the details. She didn't want her day picked apart from afar.

'Hmm,' he said finally. 'I'm concerned you're going to waste up there. Don't let them convince you to stay longer. You need to get back into the tertiary hospitals.'

'I'm fine,' she said tightly.

'At least come down to the surgeons' college conference.'

'I'm not sure I can – the roster's pretty full.'

'Well, be sure to make some time for studying. It's easy to let the anatomy slip. You'll want to be applying to the college soon and it's very competitive – you don't want the other registrars to get ahead of you.'

She felt the urge to argue but didn't really know why. She knew that he was proud of her, but he didn't know the real reason she'd come north. She'd let him believe it was for rural experience, which he grudgingly admitted one had to do at some stage these days. She didn't really intend to stay in the long run, but he was so belligerent about the city being the place for her. She wanted to go back when she was ready, not because he said so. The silence drew out too long.

'Something wrong?' he asked at last.

'I'm a bit tired, that's all. Just closed a solo clinic, Dad.' She affected a yawn, imagining a big void within her needing air. But when she breathed out, the empty space remained.

She waited for him to say *That's my girl* or *Get some rest* or *You'll do fine.* Instead he said, 'Good for you. Keep building up your endurance – it'll be good practice for next year. Talk to you soon.'

He rang off before she did. Daniella let the phone fall into her lap and looked around. She was sitting in her own waiting room, seeing it for the first time from a patient's perspective. Ten padded chairs, a coffee table piled with magazines and a kids' toy tub in the corner. The reception desk with its perspex information holders, the call bell and the posters on the walls about skin cancer and osteoporosis . . .

The consultation rooms were dark. There was no one here but her.

Physician, heal thyself.

She laughed until her ragged breaths turned into sobs. Then, she told herself to get a grip. Set the alarm, locked up and went outside.

The sky was the blushing pink of day's end, the town twinkling across the lake. As the breeze brought the first of the night air against her cheek, Daniella counted the few stars just appearing in the perfect sky. Something about it was different tonight: more majestic, fathomless. The town invited her steps, and as she walked, the star cradle briefly lifted her heart above the grief she had carried inside ever since the night three months ago that had changed everything.

By the time she reached the house, she felt temporarily absolved. It wouldn't last, but it was enough for tonight.

Chapter 6

Sunday dawned clear-skied and bright: a perfect day for footy. Or, as Mark kept hearing, for kicking the shit out of the Julia Creek guys – all for a good cause, of course.

After a chaotic start spent getting things in order so they could take the rest of the day off, Mark and his father drove down from the station mid-morning. When they arrived, the oval was already ringed with utes and four-wheel-drives, with a few town cars thrown into the mix. Scenting action, some of the tourist campers gradually crept in and formed a posse beyond the eastern dead-ball line. Beside the campers were two ambulances brought in from Mount Isa in anticipation of trouble. Two refs chatted on the sideline amid a motley collection of balls, and some of the team members were warming up.

As soon as he was out of the cab, Mark spied Steph advancing. 'Mark, you'll never guess!' she called, as if the night at the tav had never happened.

Mark warily grabbed his bag from the Rover's back seat. 'What's up?'

'Robert broke his finger during the week and then took off shooting.'

Mark laughed. 'Right, of course.' They were always short.

She smiled back, seemingly hopeful. 'Listen, can I grab you for a few minutes after the game?'

Mark nodded noncommittally. After the tav, he thought it should have been pretty clear that he wasn't interested, but Steph could be determined. On the other hand, maybe she wanted to talk about the station, which gave him no choice.

He shrugged this off as he reached the Ryders team, all dressed in similar footy shorts with mismatched blue shirts. Handshakes and back-slaps went all round. He'd known the guys for years, and had been to school with many of them, including Dave. No one would mistake them for professionals, but they played well together and made a professional art of ribbing the Julia Creek boys. Mark sized up the rivals across the field in between pulling off his work shirt and extracting his three-year-old team jersey from his bag. It was still loose about the waist but tighter across his shoulders. Must have been all the fence repairs.

'So, we going to talk tactics?' asked one of the blokes, who'd been sucking on a Gatorade. 'Or, we just going to smash 'em like last year?'

Cheers and whistles. 'We better bust out the pineapples!'

Mark grinned, enjoying himself. They spread out in a circle and began to pass a ball around. Mark looked over to the sideline where the crowd were setting up with blankets, chairs and umbrellas. His father was chatting to Tony, who owned the larger supermarket, and Donna, who owned the tav. Mark knew his father hadn't been very social since his mother's death, so he was glad to see it. Mark made one more search of the crowd, looking for Dr Harris and hoping Daniella might be there too. But he couldn't see either of them; most likely they were on duty.

They lined up. Julia Creek had the kick-off, and Mark was way down the field as full-back. He waited with his arm up against the sun. The kick came; the ball floated, an easy mark against the crisp blue sky. He caught it solidly against his chest and tucked it under his arm, tearing down the field to meet the opposition's line. Three red shirts came at him, one going for his legs, the other two high on his chest. He stepped around the legs guy, and shoved his shoulder forward into the others. Their bodies met with the bone-jarring impact of heavy muscle propelled in opposite directions. Mark made another three metres before they wrestled him into the dust. The ground was hard, and their combined weight crushed him like a vice. Then it lifted. He was on his feet again, the ball rolled under his foot and was taken by someone else. Mark tasted dirt and a little blood; sweat trickled off his forehead and his breath stretched his shirt. He hurt, but he was energised. First tackle done. Getting hit was good sometimes. The second tackle finished up field, and he ran to join the line.

They played for a half without significant incident. The Creek's five-eighth rolled his ankle on a hard divot and went limping off to ice and a cold beer. Another two players clashed heads, opening up face cuts that bled impressively. The Creek guy got his taped and came back on. The Ryders' player went off to the hospital to get stitched.

Half-time came and went, Ryders only two points ahead. Mark stayed on the field during the break. He was enjoying the brutality of the game, and that they could get out on the field and act like thugs while raising money for services the area desperately needed. His father would be pleased about that. Hell, he was pleased. Steph arrived with oranges, which the team received gratefully. Mark left her to enjoy their attention while he paced around, waiting for play to restart.

In the second half, desperation crept into Julia Creek's play. Ryders had won the last two years, and the boys in red knew it, as did their sizable cheer squad, who'd all driven several hours to be there. The tackles got heavier, tactics a little dirtier. When a few forward passes and shepherds went unpunished, Ryders started to grumble about where the ref was from; some goodwill was lost. So, when a turnover came and they were back on offence, Ryders wanted ground, they wanted points.

Mark had the ball and was about to run into a solid tackle when he spied Dave tearing up the inside. He flicked the pass and Dave caught it solidly; only then did Mark see the four Creek players already closing in on him. Shit, he'd just given his best mate a hospital pass. Dave hit them hard and went down, still fighting. One of the Creek guys lost it, grabbed Dave's legs and upended him. Dave's head hit the dry field, his body went limp, the ball came loose. Someone picked it up and ran with it, but Mark was running straight to Dave; he'd seen the nasty angle of Dave's neck as he'd hit the ground.

Since the impact, Dave hadn't moved. People were rushing over, the ref trying to hold them back. One of the first to arrive was William, running across the ground as though he was twenty years younger.

Mark knelt down with his hand on his mate's shoulder. 'Dave!' he yelled. 'Dave, buddy, you got hit.'

'Mmmph,' mumbled Dave, slowly coming round and trying to turn his head.

'No, no, buddy, keep your head still.'

'All right, let's make some room.' The ref muscled in, clearing a path for the ambos and the stretcher. Mark was pushed back with the others. As the ambos carted Dave off the field, Mark glanced up and saw his father. William Walker had broken out in a sweaty film, his chest heaving, a tight grimace on his face. Mark's heart tripped and he moved quickly towards him. 'Dad, you all right?'

William waved a hand. 'Fine.'

By the time Mark reached him, William did indeed seem

fine. He wiped his forehead on the back of his arm. 'Let's go see about Dave.'

~

Mark and his father drove behind Dave's ambulance on the five-minute trip to the hospital. By the time the ambos were unloading him at the Ryders A&E, Dave was fully awake again, making jokes and complaining about the neck collar they'd slapped on him.

Roselyn ushered the stretcher inside and into one of two bays, then set the wheel brakes with practised moves. Swiftly, another woman appeared, dressed in a blue shirt, her fair hair drawn back to her nape and a stethoscope slung around her shoulders. With a pleasant surge of interest, Mark instantly recognised Daniella Bell from the tav.

'I'm Dr Bell. What have we got?' she asked Roselyn, her face serious.

William got in first. 'Could we see Dr Harris, please?'

Mark saw her absorb this with a tiny twitch of apprehension, before she calmly replied, 'Dr Harris is treating another patient at the moment, so let's get started here. What happened?'

Mark spoke quietly to head off his father. 'Dave got spear-tackled. Came down on his head pretty hard.'

Daniella turned to Mark, her grey gaze steady. 'Was he knocked out?'

'Yes.'

'For how long?'

'A minute,' chipped in his father.

'No, it wasn't that long,' Mark disagreed. 'Five seconds, maybe.'

At this, Daniella turned all her attention on Dave. 'Okay, can you tell me your full name?'

'David. Cooper,' said Dave. 'Dave is fine though, doc.'

'Dave, we're going to do a few quick tests, all right? Can you wiggle your toes for me?'

Dave's grubby football socks moved up and down. 'I've done this before,' he said, sounding amused.

She gave him a little smile back. 'Now, follow my finger . . . Good. Okay, I'm going to ask you some questions but I don't want you to move your head, so just say yes or no, all right? Have you got any pain, anywhere at all?'

'No.'

'Tingling, pins and needles, or numbness?'

'No.'

Daniella ran through a few more questions. Mark watched her as she worked. She was sure of what she was doing. Her hands were always moving, checking, gentle but capable. He saw confidence and skill, and passion for her work. Dave answered her, Roselyn followed her direction. She'd clearly already earned the nurse's trust, and Mark found her knowledge and assurance mesmerising.

Daniella straightened up. 'Here's the deal. I can't find anything wrong, but I want to make sure your neck's okay. So we're going to take an X-ray. If that's all clear, we can think about taking the collar off. If not, or if I'm not sure, you might be getting on a flight out, all right?'

'Damn it,' said Dave.

'What?' she asked warily.

'Just played sixty minutes to make money for the community, not to spend some of it.'

Daniella's mouth pulled into a sympathetic smile, which Mark rather liked. 'Those are the risks, I guess,' she said. 'Maybe you could buy a ticket to the movie night to make up for it? I heard that's on soon.'

Mark chuckled.

'Excuse me, but when will Dr Harris be available?' asked William.

'*Dad*,' said Mark, embarrassed.

'I'm sorry,' Daniella didn't blink, 'but as I said before, Dr Harris is occupied. He'll be reviewing the films once they're done. Since we don't have a lot of room, I'd appreciate it if you could step out into the waiting room while I organise the X-ray.' She waited calmly, avoiding Mark's eyes, not even appealing to him as someone she'd met before.

Mark steered his father out. 'What's got into you?' he asked. His father was certainly difficult in medical situations – refusing check-ups or suggested procedures – despite respecting Dr Harris. Even when he'd had that bad chest pain six months ago, he hadn't wanted to go to the hospital.

William sat heavily in the chair, arms crossed. Mark was reminded of when his mother had been sick, and they'd spent frustrating hours waiting in oncology; his father had always sat in that same pose.

'I'm fine,' William said. 'I just want Dr Harris to see David.'

Mark watched him carefully. His father was a bit pale, and Mark remembered that moment at the oval. 'Dad, are you feeling okay?'

William dismissed his question with an impatient wave of his hand. Mark knew how stubborn his father was, but they were inside the hospital now. He glanced around, hoping Roselyn or Jackie might be nearby and he could ask if his father really looked all right. The nurses' desk was empty, so he paced back down the hall, also feeling he ought to apologise to Daniella for his father's behaviour. The bay where Dave had been was now vacant. He encountered Daniella as she came out of the X-ray room.

She dragged her eyes up from the chart in her hands.

'Mr Walker. Is there a problem?' Some strands of her hair were coming loose, and a little frown folded between her eyebrows.

Abruptly, Mark realised what he'd done. Not only had his father been rude but now he'd gone and wandered into the only-if-you-were-invited parts of the hospital while she was busy, and interrupted her. What had got into him? Mortified, he only managed to say, 'Mark.'

Daniella filled the gap. 'All right. I'm sorry, Mark, but if you could please wait, I'll let you know when Dave's back.'

Way to make a good impression. Mark cursed himself as he went back to the waiting room where he found Roselyn standing over his father, who was waving a hand at her. 'Roselyn, my dear, I'm fine,' he was saying.

'What's going on?' Mark asked, noting Steph and Maria Morgan now hovering nearby.

'So, I just took two squirts under the tongue, that's all. That's what I'm *meant* to do with this stuff.' William waggled a small pump-pack spray that had been prescribed for his angina. Mark hadn't been sure his father was even using it.

'Do you have any pain now?' Roselyn persisted, watching him narrowly.

'No, my dear, I'm fine,' William repeated, and stood to indicate the subject was closed. 'I haven't seen you in a while, Roselyn. You're looking very well. How's your dear mother?'

Mark looked at him closely: his father didn't seem to be in pain right now. Roselyn kept him chatting for a few minutes, then excused herself and disappeared down the hall. His father relaxed, back in his chair. Mark understood better than anyone the pride of the man, and that he wouldn't want to show any weakness in front of the Morgans, but he wondered how serious the problem would have to be before his father admitted it.

Steph eased in beside him and whispered, 'Mark, shouldn't he see Dr Harris?'

'I can't *make* him do anything,' Mark said. 'He looks fine.' He hoped appearances weren't deceiving.

'He's your *father*.'

Mark summoned all his strength not to bite back. He was just as worried, but he knew it would be impossible to force William Walker to do something against his will. The next moment, the door opened at the end of the hallway and Dr Harris emerged, drying his hands on a bunch of paper towels.

'William Walker, my dear fellow!' he said. 'How lovely you took me up on that offer of a social call.'

'Doctor,' William acknowledged with a nod.

'I'm just about to take a break. Why don't you join me?' said Dr Harris, not missing a beat. 'Come through, come through. How's that grand property of yours?'

Mark knew Dr Harris was being shrewd, and seizing the opportunity – probably on Roselyn's advice – knowing that William wouldn't refuse out of respect. The two of them disappeared down the hall, and Mark exhaled in relief. Tactfully he suggested Steph and Maria return to the field; he would let them know how Dave was. Steph particularly wanted to stay, but in the end conceded she would need to supervise the fundraising.

When they had gone, he glanced down the hall and saw Daniella standing in one of the doorways; he could have sworn she was watching him. He met her eyes, unable to help the smile that came to his lips. For a moment she smiled too, then glanced away as if embarrassed to have been caught out.

'Dave's back now if you want to see him,' she said, and was gone.

~

Jackie waited for the film to develop. In a quirk of the hospital layout, she could see straight into Dave's room from the X-ray room. She clucked her tongue at the film, impatient to see if she'd got the exposure and angle right. This was important. To avoid watching the pot, she eased towards Dave's door. He looked bored, tapping his thumbs together, his head and neck immobilised by the hard collar. Jackie chewed her lip, watching his arm muscles moving under his tattoo, and hoping any damage was minor.

'Any pain?' she asked finally, then quickly added, 'No, don't move,' as he instinctively turned towards her voice.

'Sorry,' he said, eyes fixed back on the ceiling. He sounded uneasy. He cleared his throat. 'And no, feels all right.' A pause. 'How does the X-ray look?'

Jackie tapped her foot, watching him for any signs of discomfort, her chest a tangle of emotions. 'Not sure yet. Still waiting.'

'You sound worried.' His mouth pulled upwards, not quite a smile.

Jackie didn't want to entertain bad scenarios. She saw Daniella coming down the hall and checked her watch. 'Should be ready now,' she said instead.

She zipped back to retrieve the film, then went out to where Daniella was washing her hands, looking tense and distracted.

'You okay?' asked Jackie. 'What else is in?'

Daniella laid it out. 'Two eyebrow stitch-ups – one of them had a whole roll of tape around his head that I had to pull off first. A spectator with chest pain, and just now, a six-year-old with a rock stuck in a grazed knee.'

'Let me guess, imitating a slide try?'

Daniella tapped her nose. 'You got it.'

Jackie handed her Dave's film and hovered. 'Sorry, I don't think it's my best effort,' she said softly.

Daniella slapped it up on the light box, and Jackie watched her follow the lines of the vertebrae with her finger. Daniella made a satisfied noise. 'No, it's a nice one. Good work. And this looks okay.'

'What's next?' asked Jackie, her heart pounding with relief.

'A palpation. If there's no pain, we can swap the stiff collar for a soft one. But I want to keep him in overnight. He was pretty concussed. Wouldn't want to miss a slow bleed.'

'Okay,' said Jackie.

'Hey – you all right?' asked Daniella. 'The film is fine, really. It's good work.'

'Yeah.' Jackie gave her a heartfelt smile. 'That's great. No need to call for an evac.'

As Daniella headed for Dave's room with the good news, Jackie called after her, 'Oh, sorry, I forgot too. Dr Harris asked earlier if you could call in on Mrs Turner on your way home.'

Daniella raised her eyebrows. 'You forgot, huh?'

Jackie tried to look sheepish. 'Can't give you all the good news at once.'

Chapter 7

Daniella found Valerie Turner in the same spot on the couch as last week. The ancient kelpie tracked Daniella's entry with one eye, apparently unable to muster any further muscle activity. The muted TV showed a cooking show this time.

'Hello, Mrs Turner,' said Daniella, trying for a friendly tone.

'Hmm. I thought they'd send you back,' said Valerie. 'I don't see that nurse Jackie braving another round though.'

'She had to pick up her son,' said Daniella, unpacking her kit. She wanted to get this over with as quickly as possible and have this long day at an end.

Valerie grunted. 'She would. Bad business that.'

Daniella looked up. 'What is?'

Valerie briefly met her eye. 'Nothing,' she said, and went back to staring at the TV.

Daniella knelt on the floor and eased off the dressing, wondering if Valerie had moved at all since she last visited. Lack of exercise wouldn't be helping her condition, but Daniella suspected she'd get her head bitten off if she mentioned it now. She tried to think of a way to casually bring it up later.

The couch creaked and Valerie's floral-print dress slid up

two inches. 'Doesn't look much better than last week,' she commented, peering over Daniella's shoulder.

Daniella shifted to let her look, and sighed. 'Yes, it's not too different. But no worse.'

'Not better *is* worse,' grumbled Valerie, collapsing against the couch again.

Daniella sat back on her heels and chewed her lip. 'Mrs Turner, how much does this affect you? Does it stop you from getting around?'

'I get around just fine, missy.'

'Do you have anyone who could help out?' Daniella asked gently, nodding towards the photo frames, aware that this line of enquiry hadn't gone well last time.

'No,' declared Valerie. She seemed to be about to say something else, so Daniella waited, resisting the impulse to prompt her or fill the silence. Eventually, Valerie sniffed. 'I suppose they'll have to take the leg, if it doesn't heal.'

Daniella frowned. 'Well, that's really the last resort, Mrs Turner. I think we're a long way off that yet.' She thought harder. 'Hyperbaric therapy can be very good for these kinds of ulcers.'

'Hyper-what?'

'Hyperbaric. It's a treatment where you breathe pressurised air and it helps with healing.'

'Sounds like quackery,' said Valerie. The kelpie punctuated this with a sigh that sounded equally unimpressed.

Daniella pressed on. 'No, really. They do it in Brisbane. And I think there's a facility in Townsville too. I can find out.'

Valerie pressed her lips together, but the scowl that had seemed permanently mounted between her eyebrows like a car-hood ornament had gone.

Daniella reapplied the dressing and packed up her kit. 'I'll come back on Monday and see how it is then,' she said.

She was moving to the door when Valerie said, 'He works in Townsville.'

Daniella turned back. 'Who does?'

Valerie nodded towards the frames on the television. 'My son. His name is Bruce.'

~

Later that evening, Daniella walked home from Jackie's, full of pizza. She went the slightly longer way, down the street on the town's edge, leaving behind the glowing yellow house lights that obscured the stars. After a few minutes she reached a gentle rise. Below, the hospital and its lake nestled together, and beyond, the dark land rushed to the horizon. She knew people were out there, human outposts on remote properties, but nothing indicated their existence. Daniella hugged herself, feeling lonely for them. They were all under the same sky, yet so far away.

But Daniella knew you could be just as lonely among other people. She remembered her first experience of that vividly: in primary school she'd been intelligent and shy, no match for the boisterous games that made friends. Then, already feeling awkward and out of place, she'd had to wear a patch to correct a lazy eye. The other children had shunned her; even when the patch was removed, she'd never really been let back in. Once uncool was always uncool. She'd become good at passing time alone, but it had still been awful. She thought of Valerie Turner, alone in her house. It was easy to be bitter when no one wanted to see you. Maybe that was why she was so prickly.

At the top of the hill, just off the road, was a little wooden bench. Daniella sat down on the cool wood, not wanting to go home yet. Her back touched something cold; she turned and saw a little bronze plaque. Using her phone as a torch, she read: *For Margaret, who loved this place. Gone too soon.*

Daniella sighed. She wondered who Margaret had been, and what she'd come here to think about; how many others had done the same. The vantage point was perfect: the hospital lake a dark patch to her right, the sky balancing the endless deep blue earth. She slouched down to rest her head on the back of the bench and looked up. In Brisbane the stars had been murky, but here the heavens had depth, layer upon layer. She picked out the Southern Cross, low over the hospital where Roselyn was on night duty; and then, high above, the dull red eye of Scorpio. She wondered if Valerie was still sitting on her couch, and whether she ever saw the stars.

Daniella's phone buzzed in her pocket, scaring her stupid. She swore softly and sat up, her eyes drawn to the hospital. It must be Dr Harris calling her in; at least she wasn't far away.

'Hello, Dr Harris?' she said, not stopping to check the number on her phone.

'Dr Bell?'

It wasn't Dr Harris. The voice was familiar, though, deep and engaging, but she couldn't quite place it. 'Yes?' she said uncertainly.

'This is Mark Walker. We met last week, and earlier today at the hospital.'

Her heart gave a bound, even while she wondered why he was calling. 'Dr Harris is on call tonight,' she said apologetically. 'I'm not sure why they gave you this number.'

'No, I wanted to talk to you, so I asked a friend. I hope you don't mind.'

'Is your father all right?' she asked automatically. 'Dr Harris mentioned he has angina and Roselyn told me he was having some chest pain after the rugby.'

'Yes, he's fine. But that's sort of why I'm calling. I wanted to apologise for what he said at the hospital today. He's difficult around doctors, I guess maybe because he's never had any health problems until this last year. But still, it was rude, and I'm sorry about that.'

Daniella laughed, taken aback. She hadn't enjoyed fielding William Walker's mistrust, but she certainly hadn't expected an apology. It was part of the job, dealing with wary patients. Disarmed, she said, 'It happens. People are stressed in those situations. Don't worry about it.' She took a breath, then couldn't think of what to say.

'I'm sorry, is this a bad time?' he asked.

'No, not really,' she said, surprising herself. Normally she would have been happy to keep the conversation short. Solitude was more comfortable. 'I was just walking home, and I'm sitting on the bench looking at the hospital across the lake. It's rather nice here.'

'Really?' He paused, as if choosing his words carefully. 'That's a special place. How are the stars?'

'Oh, amazing, much better than in Brisbane.'

'That's where you're from?'

'Yes.'

'Nice city,' he said.

She laughed, genuinely amused. 'That's the first time anyone's ever said that to me. Usually it's put-downs, you know? Big country town, parochial . . . Sydney's so much better . . . blah, blah.'

'Well, the RNA show is a big deal,' he said with mock seriousness.

She laughed again. 'Oh, right. Cows. I get it. We call it the Ekka. I just used to go for the Dagwood dogs and bumper cars, to be honest.' She cut herself off, aware she was hunched around the phone, cradling it as though talking to an old friend.

'Hey, you want to know something?' he said into the brief, awkward silence.

'What?' she asked, curiously.

'Look straight ahead, then right about ten degrees or so.'

'Ten degrees?'

'Look for a tiny hill on the horizon.'

Daniella sat up straight, then turned her head slightly until she saw a little bump in the distance. 'Okay, what am I looking at?'

'Me,' he said.

'You?'

'You're looking roughly at Ryders Station homestead. It's about forty minutes out of town.'

'That's where you are?'

'Yes. Well, down the ridge a little. I came out to look at the stars too.'

Daniella tried to picture him. 'What does the town look like from there?'

'Pretty much nothing,' he said. 'Just a faint glow way out on the plain.'

Daniella was nodding now. 'Yeah . . . I was just thinking about that before,' she said. 'You know, how big the land is, how many people are out there – I was wondering if they're lonely, what they're doing right now. And weird, there you are.'

She stopped, embarrassed to realise that she'd just been voicing her private thoughts to a stranger. She rubbed her arms. A chill was creeping in. She was about to make an excuse to ring off, but she hesitated, and Mark spoke first.

'I won't keep you, but can I call you tomorrow?' he asked in a rush.

'About Dave? Probably better to call the hospital, then you can get whoever's on.'

'Okay, yeah. Dave,' he said sounding disappointed. 'Well, goodnight.'

Rather than going straight home, Daniella sat for a while looking at her phone and then the horizon. After he'd hung up it had occurred to her that he might have meant something else. Like, that he wanted to *call her*. That he might be interested in her. The idea was both appealing and a complication. But she was getting ahead of herself. She really had no idea what he was thinking. By the time she'd finally made it home, switched on the insipid fluoro lights and turned on the shower her thoughts had muddled. But she fell asleep thinking of when she might next see Mark Walker.

Chapter 8

After the Sunday spent on-call for the rugby Daniella slept well for a change, and the next morning she went to the hospital long before the clinic start. The hospital was at capacity with two inpatients, so she wanted to make sure everything was in order before Dr Harris arrived at seven to do rounds. She might even have time for bad biscuits before the first clinic appointment.

She tiptoed past the night-duty nurse's room only to find Roselyn already up and folding sheets. Daniella hoped she had slept enough; Roselyn was rostered on in the clinic today as well. Even if it had been a bad night, Daniella knew she wouldn't hear about it; Roselyn kept complaints to herself and took obvious pride in her silent efficiency. Daniella admired the support. They exchanged a quick greeting before Daniella went to check on the patients. The first, Dr Harris's chest-pain patient, was still sleeping soundly. But she was surprised to find Dave awake.

'I was hoping I wouldn't disturb you,' she said, coming in and looking over the observations chart Roselyn had filled out until midnight in her neat, careful hand.

'No way. Usually I'd be at work by now,' Dave said. He tried to prop himself up in the bed and winced.

'Any pain?' Daniella asked quickly. He looked awful, actually. But then, so did every patient after a night in hospital.

'No, but I feel ratshit. Didn't sleep well.'

'Sorry about that,' she said, still tracking through the numbers. 'Being woken up so someone can shine a light in your eyes and take your blood pressure probably didn't help.'

'Nope. But you gotta do it, I know that.'

Daniella glanced up. Dave had stuck an arm up behind his head and was looking out the window. She saw the edges of a tattoo under his upper arm. He was nice looking with blue eyes and dark hair that tended to curl, and seemed friendly enough. But she felt as though he was keeping her at a distance. He probably just wants to get out of here, she thought. That was fine with her.

'Well, thanks for being an easy patient,' she said, flipping through the chart. 'But . . . you had a bit of a BP spike last night. Did Roselyn tell you?'

'Yeah,' he said with a sigh. 'Is that bad?'

Daniella put down the chart. 'Not necessarily. Could be caused by a lot of things. How do you feel?'

'Woke up with a headache,' he admitted.

'Still there?' she asked.

'Yeah, but not as bad as when I woke up.'

'Okay.' Daniella spent a few minutes examining him. She found the painful spot on his skull where he'd met the playing field yesterday. Everything else was normal, except that his pupils were slightly unequal. She frowned and repeated the light test twice.

'What?' he asked.

'Your pupils aren't quite the same,' she said.

'Are you saying I've got wonky eyes, doc?'

Daniella glanced at him to see if he was joking. He raised his eyebrows, half serious. 'Not at all,' she said.

'It's okay, Roselyn already told me.'

'She did?'

'Yeah, she said they've been like that for a while. See, I got kicked in the head a few years back and she noticed my pupils back then too.'

'What kicked you?' Daniella asked.

'A bull.'

She laughed. 'I'm sorry, that's not funny. But seriously?'

He smiled this time, looking up at her as if he were proud of the experience. 'That's okay, it was a bit funny. I was helping with a breeding program, and I was doing things he only wanted a cow to do for him, if you know what I mean. Poor bastard. He didn't get me too bad. Probably knocked some sense in. Went down the coast to do my pilot's licence soon after that.'

'I see . . . Sorry about this, but I'd like you to stay a little longer, maybe just until the afternoon. I think we should check you out once more before you go.'

He shrugged, looking towards the door. 'Can I get up?'

'Yeah, you can shower and everything. But take it easy – no sudden movements. Move slowly in case you get dizzy. Any pain, buzz straight away. Got it? Do you need some clothes?' she asked. He was wearing a hospital gown.

'Nah, I got my after-match stuff here.'

'All right. Well, I'll check back in around lunchtime.'

She was almost out the door when he said, 'Doc?'

'Yeah?' She stuck her head back in.

'Thanks.'

'No problem. Do you think you can survive the morning occupying yourself?'

He reached over to the side table and wagged a dog-eared paperback in her direction. 'It's okay. Roselyn gave me Matthew Reilly.'

The morning passed smoothly. Dr Harris was happy with her discharge plan for Dave. They organised the charts for Roselyn, who rechecked them anyway, and the early appointments soon rolled in. Around eleven, Daniella had an empty slot and Dr Harris called her in to his consult. A wiry man was seated on the edge of the exam couch.

'Hugh, this is our new doctor, Daniella Bell,' said Dr Harris.

The man stuck out his hand. He was wearing stubbies above two long, grey-haired legs, which then disappeared into explorer socks and beaten Steel Blue boots. His obviously once-fair skin was now a riot of pink splotches and sun spots, and Daniella noticed that parts of his ears were missing.

She shook his rough, scarred hand. 'Nice to meet you, Hugh.'

Dr Harris continued, 'Hugh has a concern with his chest. Take a look.'

Hugh pulled aside his shirt collar. 'Right here, doc,' he said, pointing at the skin below his collarbone.

Daniella looked. Amid the patchy skin was a colourless lump, maybe a centimetre across. She gently stretched the skin around it. The lump was pearly looking, and a tangle of blood vessels was visible within.

'Probably a BCC – basal cell carcinoma,' she said. 'Pretty classic, really.'

'Yep,' said Hugh. 'I've had lots of 'em.' He pointed at his ears, then pulled at the skin of his neck, highlighting faint white scars. Daniella wondered why Dr Harris had asked her to look at such an obvious skin cancer diagnosis; basal cell carcinomas were the most common skin cancer, especially among people who'd spent their life in the sun.

'How would you remove it?' asked Dr Harris.

Daniella straightened. 'Standard elliptical excision, lidocaine with adrenaline. Maybe a number four suture,' she said.

Dr Harris twitched his lips. 'I think it's too large for that,' he said. 'Take another look at where it's sitting, at how thin the skin is there.'

Daniella did. The skin on Hugh's upper chest was thin with age; the bulk of muscle had wasted, making his ribs visible. 'A flap could give a better result,' she said.

Dr Harris looked pleased. 'Yes. We're going to do a spiral flap – I think that will give Hugh the best possible result.'

Daniella was initially surprised. Doing a flap would take longer, and for someone who already had so many scars, what did the aesthetic result matter? She stopped herself, ashamed. Dr Harris was enthusiastically gathering the materials, telling Hugh about where he'd first learned to do this technique, why he was choosing it. It didn't matter how many other scars Hugh had. This wasn't a big, city clinic where the doctors might not see this man again; here it was personal. Dr Harris would give him the best result because it was the right thing to do.

And as they started on the procedure, marking out the cut lines, injecting the anaesthetic, Daniella felt a surge of excitement. This wasn't just a straightforward, everyday excision; there was an art to it. She had never seen this technique done before. Dr Harris drew the spiral ends of the flap together with a fine suture. It looked like a galaxy, something from the deep dark sky. She saw how the wound would come together, how much better the result would be than a standard cut.

Dr Harris let her finish it. He scrubbed out, saying he would go and clear Dave for discharge. When he was gone, Daniella chatted with Hugh. He told her he was a stationhand on one of the nearby properties but that he often moved around for work. His stories were full of animals and the land; of difficult steers and loyal stock horses. For the first time, Daniella glimpsed understanding: why Dr Harris had stayed for so many years. It was a tribal feeling beyond just a job. In this place, patients were part of your life, and theirs became a part of yours.

Hugh left with a wave. Daniella knew he would be back in a week to have the stitches out and she liked the fact that she was sure to see him again.

She went out to the desk for the next patient. 'Walk-in,' said Roselyn. 'Cora Matthews. Her daughter, Astrid, stuck something in her ear. I took a look, but I can't see it. I've put her in your room already. '

'How old?'

'Five.'

Daniella's heart rate ratcheted up and the familiar nausea settled deep in her gut. She talked to herself as she walked to her room, telling herself not to be silly, it was only something stuck down an ear.

Even so, it wasn't until minutes later, when she was peering into Astrid's ear with the auriscope, that she began to feel in control again. A little bribery had been required to get to this point, but as much as she tried, she couldn't spot the offending object.

'What sort of sequin was it?' she asked Cora again, sitting back.

'A pink one. It came off one of the jackets we made for the play last year. She just loves it and wears it all the time.'

'I bet. Okay, once more, Astrid, hold nice and still for me.' Daniella took another look. She could see the eardrum clearly; ironic really. Usually when she examined a child's ear she was looking for otitis media – a middle ear infection – and Daniella had often had trouble seeing the eardrum in those cases. Now, though, she had a beautiful view of a very healthy tympanic membrane, but no pink sequin.

Then again, maybe that was the problem. With kids you normally had to pull gently down on the ear to get a good view, which was what she'd been doing. With adults the change in the ear canal anatomy meant you pulled up. Daniella gently shifted direction; the eardrum slipped out of view and she saw instead the bright red-orange of the ear canal lit by the auriscope. And there, deep down, right on the side, was a shadow . . . yes, it was pink. A dark pink edge.

'Ah ha!' she exclaimed.

'You see it?' asked Cora.

'Yes.' A rush of satisfaction and relief swept through Daniella. 'And I think we can get it. We'll just have to do a little flush. Really easy.'

She'd need an ear syringe, so she stuck her head out of the consulting room, looking for Roselyn. Dr Harris's door was closed and the reception station was empty. She was pretty sure she'd seen some ear syringes among the hospital supplies. 'I've just got to duck down to the hospital to grab my special squirter,' she explained. 'Sit tight, Astrid, and if you like, you can listen to your heart with that stethoscope there.'

Daniella stepped out the clinic's back door and across the short covered walkway to the hospital's side door. After the cool air-conditioning, the mid-afternoon heat rolled across her in a great wave. Inside, she strode towards the treatment room, her soft shoes silent on the lino.

She opened the first equipment drawer before she stopped, her senses prickling. She glanced over her shoulder towards the pharmacy store attached to the treatment room. The light was on inside. Then something fell to the floor. It was a medication box; she heard the pills rattle in their plastic cards.

Daniella stepped towards the doorway, then pulled up sharply. A man was inside, facing the narcotics cabinet, a screwdriver in his hand. She recognised him instantly: Peter, in blue King Gees, and the same T-shirt he'd had on a week ago.

Peter glanced around and saw her. He stumbled backwards. 'Fuck!' he declared as he collected the phlebotomy trolley. It fell with a crash, spilling its plastic-wrapped innards everywhere.

Daniella was frozen with surprise, and Peter recovered faster than she did. 'Back off!' he growled, brandishing the screwdriver.

Daniella took one step back, but irrationally, she didn't want to clear a path for him. He was stealing from their drug stores, taking medication the hospital needed. It made her angry.

'I said, back the fuck off!' he hissed. 'Where's the key?'

Finally she found her voice. 'Just stay calm.' She put up her hands.

'The key, bitch!'

'I'm not going to get that for you,' she said. A cold sweat broke out under her hair. He was at the doorway now, coming forward, the screwdriver weaving. Her adrenaline kicked in. She wanted to yell *Security!* but there wasn't any. She wanted to run, but she didn't want to take her eyes off him either.

Then Peter's gaze flicked sideways. Something collected him hard and shoved him into the wall. The screwdriver hit the lino. Daniella grabbed it, and backed away until she hit the scrub sink under the window. From there, she had a perfect view of sandy-haired Mark Walker, his fists full of Peter's T-shirt.

Mark shoved him against the wall again, making his head rock. 'All right, who are you, you fucker?' he demanded.

'Fuck. You!' Peter tried a headbutt, connecting awkwardly. Mark's head went back sharply.

'You little prick,' he growled, getting right into the guy's face. Blood dripped on the floor. Daniella winced; this was going to get ugly.

The shelves bounced as Mark forced Peter back against the wall again.

'Arright . . . Pete,' the guy coughed out with a bunch of spit.

'Pete what?'

'Stein.'

'Where are you from, Pete Stein? Sure as hell ain't Ryders Ridge.'

'Isa,' Peter ground back.

'You know this guy, doc?' Mark asked over his shoulder.

'He came in last week,' Daniella managed. 'Wants the drug cabinet, I think.'

At that, Mark hauled Peter off the wall and frog-marched him towards the treatment room door. Daniella followed them into the hospital hallway. Two doors up, Dave appeared, dressed, rugby bag over his shoulder. When he saw Peter and Mark he dropped the bag.

'You right, Mark?'

'I got this,' Mark shot back.

Once they'd all reached the reception area, Daniella's legs started to shake. She leaned against the triage desk, watching as the glass sliding door opened and Mark dragged Peter outside. Dave moved around her and put himself in the doorway.

'Go back to fucking Isa. Don't let me see your face here again,' she could hear Mark say as he deposited Peter in the dirt. He and Dave stood there watching until Peter had scrambled into a beat-up Camry and taken off down the road.

Only then did Mark return inside. He came straight towards Daniella. 'Are you all right?' he asked.

As he stood before her, he seemed enormous, his broad chest expanding with each breath. He was bleeding above one eye, not much, but a drop had started to run around his brow.

'You're hurt,' she said. 'No, don't touch it.' She reached for the triage tissue box, grabbed a handful and pressed them to the cut. His fingers replaced hers in a brush of warm skin: a tiny shock of contact. Daniella took a shaky breath; his eyes found hers, searching, concerned. They were deep green, she noticed, almost brown.

'Your hand's shaking,' he said gently. 'Do you want to sit down for a moment?'

Daniella shook her head. She wasn't going to admit how upset she was. She'd never had a patient threaten her like this, but this was her clinic. The situation was over. She wasn't going to lose it now. 'Come through and let me clean that up,' she said.

He followed her back to the treatment room and sat down on the bed without being asked. She squirted a saline bottle into a tray and grabbed a gauze square. She turned towards Mark. The first time she tried to clean the cut with the saline, her hand shook so much she had to stop.

'Give me a minute,' she said, dropping her head, feeling like a fool.

'Take your time,' he said, his voice full of comfort.

After a moment, she pulled the tissues away from his eyebrow and threw them in the bin. The cut was no longer bleeding; it was just a little break. She wiped the blood ooze away, her hands now steady. 'What were you doing here anyway?' she asked.

'Picking up Dave. I heard the crash.'

'Ah.'

He kept his eyes lowered as she closed the cut with tape. She was grateful for his silence but she wanted to talk to him, which felt dangerous. She finished without saying more.

Mark stood up. 'I have to give Dave a lift to his place, but I'm going to call Rich. Don't worry, that guy isn't coming back.'

'Rich?'

'The copper.' He went to leave the room, then stopped in the doorway. 'Can I call you tonight?' he asked. He waited, his face kind, open and hopeful.

Daniella took in the long line of him, boots to sandy hair, aware that this experience connected them, and that it couldn't be taken back. She had no confusion this time; she knew he was interested in her, and that she was attracted to his ease and confidence. She was torn, knowing she was still vulnerable – not just from today but from the last few months – and yet wanted more. *He looks good in those jeans*, said a small, irrational voice in her head. But she didn't have to get involved with him. It was just a phone call.

'Okay,' she said.

Dr Harris was appalled when he heard about the incident. He fumed for the afternoon, and kept asking Daniella if she was all right. Roselyn uncharacteristically swore under her breath and rushed off to check the lock on the hospital door before calling Rich herself. Appointments were delayed. Daniella returned to her consult room as soon as she could, apologising profusely to Cora. Once the ear syringe was finally located and put to use, Astrid went away happy with her sequin rattling around in a yellow-lidded sample pot. Finishing late, Daniella was about to leave when a highway patrol car rolled up and Richard, the cop who covered the district, came in and introduced himself. He'd been several hours away at another call and apologised for having taken so long. Mark and Roselyn had clearly filled him in by phone, but there was paperwork to do, and Daniella had to make a statement. When that was done, Richard insisted on giving her a lift.

Daniella had to convince him to drop her at Valerie Turner's place for the promised visit, and not to hang around until that was done to make sure she got home safely. After all this, Daniella felt galvanised against whatever atrocities Valerie's tongue could muster: surely things couldn't get any worse.

'What's the matter with you?' Valerie demanded as Daniella walked in. For once the kelpie was absent, though Daniella could hear scratching coming from the back of the house, so she assumed the dog was outside.

She set her face in a neutral expression. 'Bad day,' she said, hoping that would suffice.

Valerie narrowed her eyes. 'I suppose someone died, then.'

Daniella almost laughed; the glass was definitely half-empty for Valerie, and its contents were probably poisoned too. But she thought better of it. 'No, nothing like that. I found someone trying to steal drugs from the hospital. He had a go at threatening me with a screwdriver.'

'Bloody lowlifes,' declared Valerie. But interest sparkled in her eyes. She flicked off the television. 'I suppose he was from Isa?'

'That's what he said.'

Valerie muttered to herself while Daniella unpacked her kit. She didn't expect the old woman to inquire after her welfare, and it was actually a relief not to be asked every few minutes if she was okay. Valerie instead quizzed her on the particulars of the incident; she clearly had an investigative bent, and Daniella began to think she would give Richard the copper good competition.

'I thought my Bruce would go after criminals,' Valerie said finally.

'Oh?' said Daniella, pouring saline into the sterile tray.

'But he went into corporate. He's a lawyer,' the old woman clarified. 'I suppose he makes a lot of money.'

'Sounds like he's successful, then,' Daniella said carefully; it was hard to tell whether Valerie and her son were on good terms or not.

'Of course he's good at his job,' Valerie said sharply. Daniella glanced up, wondering if she'd said something wrong. But Valerie's face simply wore the fierce, proud look of a parent.

'Of course,' said Daniella softly.

'He pays for my lawns to be mowed and the cleaning, you know,' said Valerie. 'I still do the gardening when I can. I don't want strange people in here – they're always moving things – but I suppose it makes Bruce feel better.'

Daniella focused back on the ulcer. 'He sounds like a good son. Do you see him much?'

The spite seemed to have gone out of Valerie. 'Not much. He's very busy. Hard to get on the phone. Always working.'

'Does he write?' Daniella asked idly, inspecting the edges of the wound. She could see granulation there now. Excellent. Healing had started. Then she looked up again to find Valerie blinking, her eyes suspiciously red. 'Are you all right? Did I hurt you?' she asked.

'He writes,' Valerie said tightly. 'I don't.'

Daniella took a moment to process this. 'Mrs Turner . . . can you write?'

'Of course I *can*,' Valerie said, offended. 'But my eyes . . . I can't see to do it well enough. And I won't send something he can't read. I don't want him coming back here trying to fix that too.'

This made sense, and it explained the thick glasses, and perhaps Valerie's comments about cleaners moving things. Diabetes advanced enough to give her ulcers would likely affect her eyesight, too. Gently, Daniella asked how her eyesight was being managed. For once, Valerie answered the questions. Beyond managing the problem, Daniella knew she couldn't do much about the damage already done; she explained how exercise would help, but Valerie only scowled – clearly, she'd heard it all before. The woman didn't even show any pleasure when Daniella told her the ulcer was looking better.

Daniella packed up feeling heavy and helpless. She didn't want to internalise Valerie's problem, but it was nearly impossible not to. Although she thought it was probably a waste of time, as she was walking away she said, 'If you'd like to write to your son, I could help. Think about it and let me know.'

Valerie didn't look up, and Daniella quietly closed the door behind her.

Chapter 9

Valerie's was only a few minutes away from her house, so Daniella had missed her usual, meandering big-sky walk, and went straight to the shower when she arrived home. It was her turn to be on call tonight; Dr Harris had tried to convince her to swap but she had refused. She knew she was rattled, but like hell was she going to stand down because of it. She'd just got him to let her go on call; she wasn't backing out now, and she knew she had to push through these jitters. Dr Harris had only agreed on the condition she let him know if there were any calls.

Daniella got the water cranking, scrubbing away the day. Between her conversations with Dr Harris, Richard and Valerie, she had gone over the incident several times. Richard had taken the screwdriver, making a joke about its being a Phillips head, and what kind of self-respecting crook used one of those? Now, after so many retellings, instead of a rolling video reel of the incident, she had established an impartial list of events. The only part of the events she hadn't managed to detach from was the part that involved Mark Walker.

She heard her phone ringing over the falling water.

'Shit.' She fumbled to turn off the taps and grab a towel. She'd left her phone on the kitchen bench. Big wet puddles grew on the lino as she padded out. The front blinds were open. 'Shit.'

She answered the call as she twisted the closer, keeping the towel up with her elbows. Wired and expecting an emergency call, she dropped the handset and caught it with her forearm.

'Daniella?' came a voice from the faraway tinny handset speaker. A male voice. This time she recognised it instantly.

All right, this was not an emergency. And yet her heart was still thudding in her chest.

'Sorry, hello,' she said, putting the phone onto the kitchen bench and punching loudspeaker while still tugging on the towel.

'Bad time?' Mark Walker's rough baritone wasn't at all marred by the phone's tiny speaker.

'No,' she said quickly, then admitted, 'I was in the shower. I'm dripping water everywhere.'

She bit her lip, cursing herself; would Mark now be imagining her stark naked in her kitchen? Would he think she was flirting with him? She braced for the crass joke, but Mark offered none.

'I'll call you back,' he said.

Daniella found herself amused. 'No, it's all right. I'm on call. I left the phone out in the kitchen. It's not the first time I've done this.'

She heard him laugh. 'All right. How do you like your place? I dropped a doc off there once, a long time ago.'

Daniella tightened the towel back around her. 'Ah, it's . . . functional. I don't spend much time here.'

'Always at work?'

'Yeah.'

'Me too, except work's at home.'

She suddenly felt curious about his life on the station. 'What's it like out there?' she asked.

Down the phone line she heard footsteps, maybe boots on a wooden floor. He was walking as he talked. 'Quiet, right now,' he said. 'I've got the house to myself. It's a bit lonely, but I can always sense what's outside the door.'

'Which is?'

'The sheds and the herd. Miles and miles of Mitchell grass country.'

'Sounds restful,' Daniella said, holding the phone with her shoulder as she padded into the living room and rummaged in her case, still unpacked at the end of the couch. Her track pants and shirt were in there somewhere.

He laughed. 'I wish. There's always lots to do. But even when it's tough, it's worth every minute.'

She could hear the passion in his voice. She could picture him in her head, looking off into the distance, his handsome profile as she'd first noticed it in the tav. She shifted the phone to her other shoulder as she pulled on her clothes. 'Sounds amazing,' she said softly.

'Did Rich come down?' he asked, changing the subject.

'Yes. Did a binderful of paperwork.'

She meant it to be funny, but Mark didn't laugh. 'Good. I gave him the plates. He's taking it back to Mount Isa so they can follow through.'

Finally dressed, the fleece inside the trackies softly caressing her skin, Daniella felt comfortable enough to be honest with him. 'Mark?'

'Yes?'

'I don't really want to talk about it.'

'All right.' He was quiet for a moment. 'Well, I should let you get to bed. Or do you not sleep when you're on call?'

'No, I sleep and wait for the calls.'

'Okay.'

They both paused. But now the silence had a new warmth to it. Daniella didn't want to hang up, and she suspected he didn't want to either. She still wasn't sure it was a good idea, but she wanted to keep talking, exploring the connection they'd made earlier. Their conversation made the long night ahead seem less lonely.

'Well, goodni—' she began, reluctantly.

'Wait, Daniella,' he said. 'Can I take you out?'

'Take me out?' she asked blankly.

'Yes. Tomorrow night.'

Suddenly, she realised what he was asking and her stomach turned over. 'I'm not sure,' she said.

'Are you on call?'

'No . . .'

'You don't want to?'

She bit her lip. It wasn't that. The idea of spending time with him was definitely appealing – he was a nice guy, easy to talk to, not to mention those gorgeous green eyes. Just . . . it was a complication she didn't need, and she wasn't sure it was a good idea.

Mark took her silence for affirmation. 'All right, well, sleep—'

'Okay,' she said quickly. 'Okay.'

He laughed, relieved, a lovely sound. 'What time do you finish?'

'Usually five, but it often runs over.'

'So I'll pick you up at six?'

'What if it runs over?'

'I'll wait. See you then.'

Daniella waited for him to end the call. Then she just stood there in her trackies, wondering what impulse had driven her to accept the invitation.

She flopped down on the couch, determined to get some rest. During her internship and then two years as a resident, she had become very good at sleeping early on her on-call nights, banking rest before the phone inevitably rang. But now all that training deserted her and her brain wouldn't switch off. She imagined all the ways the date with Mark could go awry. One of the scenarios was that it went well and he wanted to do it again. God, what was wrong with her? Had she become so comfortable being alone that the idea of a second date was frightening?

Sleep seemed impossible and needing a distraction, she flicked on the TV. Only one channel had decent reception, and *Offspring* was starting. Daniella snorted. She'd never really liked the show; too quirky for her taste. But today, she got it. One half-crazy doc watching another. She settled in.

As it turned out, there wasn't a single emergency call all night. After eventually drifting off, she woke once, suddenly at 2 am, convinced she heard a phone ringing, but when she checked, the screen was blank, no missed calls. Bathed in the mobile's blue-screen glow, she sat back down on the couch. It was funny, she hadn't imagined a ringing phone since the first months of her internship. In her strange half-asleep logic, she saw herself regressing. Soon, she knew, she would forget how to deal with real patients and become as she had been in med school: all book learning, no substance. Before long, all of that would be forgotten too and she'd be back at her all-girls high school, a bookish teenager again, mooning over boys – mostly her brother's friends – who would never look her way. Ugh. That was years ago, but in the depth of night, it seemed real and now. She found sleep again some time before dawn.

Five minutes before her alarm Daniella woke, face squashed against the musty couch. Fortunately, the night-time thoughts soon evaporated.

It was a busy day in the clinic. Jackie was on, but they could only grab snatches of conversation between patients.

'Oh my God!' was Jackie's opening line. 'Roselyn told me all about it! You're okay, right?'

Daniella had a mouthful of biscuits, slightly stale milk-coffee ones from the bottom of the barrel. She chewed furiously, nodding. 'Fine,' she got out. Fortunately Jackie didn't ask about Mark's involvement. Roselyn had obviously left out some details.

Patients kept coming, but everything went smoothly, and remarkably the clinic closed at exactly five o'clock.

'I'll call you,' said Jackie apologetically as she rushed out to pick up Jamie.

So it was that Daniella arrived at her house, even after dawdling on the big-sky walk, with nearly a full hour before Mark was due to collect her. She paced around, not sure what to do first.

Where would he be taking her? The options were reasonably limited. She knew there were a couple of cafes in town, but they didn't open in the evenings. Probably they would go to the tav. What to wear? Black might be preferable – then she could melt into a corner. She searched through her case and held up a wrinkled T-shirt. She'd slept in it a few times already. Okay, next. Underneath a folded coat she was yet to wear, she found a black knit top, crushed like tissue paper. She shook it out. Another one to be subjected to the steamy bathroom treatment.

After her shower she tugged on jeans. The top stuck to her skin, its scoop neck only just covering the lacy edge of her only non-work bra. She inspected herself in the mirror. Still pink from the shower, her hair damp. The dark circles were still beneath her eyes, but they looked fainter. She didn't have a hairdryer, so she brushed her hair and swept it up into a clip. That would have to do.

Then as she stepped into the living room, she suddenly saw it through an outsider's eyes. It looked like a squat. The old couch with her blanket and pillow strewn across it, her case at the end vomiting clothes. She would never tolerate such a mess at work, but her living space had a free pass. It was simply a place where she touched down briefly between more important things, and chaos tended to reign.

She dumped the blanket and pillow in the bedroom, the dust making her sneeze. Then she hauled the case in there too. Now the living room was neat, but utterly spartan. It didn't even look lived in. Hearing an engine outside she peeked through the blinds. A four-wheel-drive had pulled up. She panicked, unable to face the thought of Mark seeing inside. Grabbing her bag, she went out to meet him.

Mark Walker was actually nervous. He'd dated a few girls over the years, but not many since he'd returned from travelling. He knew everyone in Ryders anyway, and younger people tended to leave town, not move to it. Steph was the last Ryders girl he'd dated, and she'd left, too. Besides, people noticed what he did, who he saw, and he didn't want that kind of scrutiny now, for himself or Daniella.

Daniella Bell. She'd been in his thoughts for the past week, and he was looking forward to this evening. He wanted it to be special . . . and private. So, he had the perfect plan.

He felt a flutter of excitement as he stepped down from the Rover. Daniella was locking up her front door, her back towards him; her blue jeans and black shirt were outlined against the pale house paint. She turned, waved to him and dumped the keys in her bag. He stopped to watch as she jogged down the path, just like he'd been watching her when she'd been working on Dave. He liked the way she moved with such captive energy, every action precise and fluid.

~

'Hi,' she said. He saw indecision flash across her face, sensed her uncertainty as to the appropriate greeting. Should they hug? Shake hands? He answered it by opening the passenger door for her. 'Thanks,' she said, blushing.

Mark walked around to the driver's side, knowing that he was grinning like an idiot. He got in and turned over the engine.

As they started down the road, Daniella glanced at him. 'You look good,' she said. He'd gone to a lot of effort, she could tell. Well-pressed bone-coloured jeans, his blue shirt tucked in and belted. Polished boots. He smelled amazing. *And* he'd opened the door for her. Who did that anymore? She smoothed her own top, checking for residual wrinkles.

'Thanks.' He smiled, but kept his eyes on the road.

'So, where are we going?'

'Not too far. Somewhere quiet. Didn't feel like braving the locals,' he admitted.

'Glad you said it,' she said gratefully. Maybe he knew an out-of-the-way restaurant or cafe she hadn't seen yet.

This thought persisted right up until they hit the dirt track at the end of the main street. Then Daniella knew exactly where he was taking her.

'Wait a minute, are we going to the dam?' she asked.

'You've been there already?' He sounded a little deflated.

'Yeah, but . . .' She laughed, shaking her head. 'Jackie told me never to go to the dam with anyone.'

He laughed. 'She did, did she?'

'Yeah. She was pretty clear about it.'

'That's good advice . . . if you're sixteen! I think I even told Cat that once.'

'Cat?'

'My sister. She lives in Brisbane – for uni. She's twenty-one now, and I'd say she definitely survived a few dodgy boyfriends thanks to that advice.'

The awkwardness was broken. They'd just acknowledged to each other that they were on a date; they were adults, they could laugh about it.

'Let me guess . . . it's the local make-out spot?' joked Daniella.

'Yep, well, part of it is. That's not where we're going, though.'

Daniella felt a twinge of disappointment that she quickly suppressed. 'All right. Where are we going?'

That smile again. 'The best part. You'll see.'

For the rest of the drive they talked easily – about her day at the clinic, about the bad condition of the road, the different animals they could see diving off at the edges of the headlights. Eventually they reached the hill at the dam's head. Mark drove straight down and along the shore where Jamie had played with his dinosaurs. Then he hooked the Rover off into a path between the trees, down a steep slope, and around a grove of eucalypts. Daniella watched him handling the vehicle easily; she had the sense he'd done this many times before. He came to a stop facing the water, the car shielded from the main parking area by the grove. To their right, the scrub was already blue with dusk, stretching to the horizon where the last licks of sun coloured the sky.

With the engine off, the silence was vast. There weren't even any crickets. Just stillness, a moment so perfect, so fragile, it should have evaporated. Daniella sat motionless, trying not to mar it with squeaks from the seat. Mark slowly released the wheel and rested his hands on his thighs.

Finally he said, 'Yeah, that's why I come here.'

They got out and wandered a little. Mark explained where they were – north of town – and pointed out the species of trees in the grove. They fell into step together along the little private patch of shore.

'You must be hungry,' he said.

'I am, actually,' said Daniella, though she could have happily kept walking just to feel the cool quiet air against her cheeks.

'Come on.' He took her hand, and turned back to the Rover. Daniella's stomach tightened pleasantly as she felt the pressure of his skin against hers, and then a sadness crept over her; she didn't want to go back to town yet. She had just found this place: a perfect escape, where she wasn't herself at all. She was a dreamlike creature here, treading softly, whole and complete.

But Mark released her hand only to open the Rover's back door and wrestle out an esky.

Daniella laughed. 'How did you do that?'

'Do what?' he asked, moving around the car and throwing a blanket over the bonnet.

'Know exactly what I was thinking.'

'What were you thinking?'

'That I didn't want to go back to town yet,' she said softly.

Leaning against the Rover, he stopped and gave her a very country look, head tipped down as if embarrassed, smiling at her sidelong. Completely charming. 'Give you a lift up?' he asked.

He lifted her as though she was nothing, and precious besides.

~

On the bonnet, the engine warmth kept any night chill at bay. They ate sandwiches, sitting together, as the moon and stars rose. Daniella inspected her sandwich.

'What's on this? It's the best thing I've ever eaten,' she said.

'Ryders beef,' said Mark. 'But I can't claim credit. Kath made them – she's the housekeeper at the station.'

'You have a housekeeper?' She was surprised. She thought housekeepers were found in big-city mansions.

'Yep. Kath's been with us a long time. She started out as a stationhand, came with her husband. He was one of the stockmen. He died on a property in the Territory, a long time ago now, and Kath stayed on with us and started looking after the house. It worked out well. Dad probably couldn't do without her now.'

Daniella took a breath, remembering that Jackie had told her his mum had died this year. 'How's he doing?' she asked gently.

Mark blew out his breath. 'Honestly? Not that great. He's had a bad year and he's really worn down. Not physically, really. I mean, he's had some heart problems but that seems to be under control. But he gave up the rural firefighters. He's frustrated about the station and how the future will be. I get it, I really do.'

Daniella saw the fierceness in him now; the place was in his blood. 'Does the station take a lot of people to run?'

'Most of the time it's me and Dad, Kath and a couple of hands. More when the mustering's on. When the herd was bigger, before the drought, we had even more. And it's tricky now with the mining boom – it can be difficult to get tradesmen. Dave's a mechanic as well as a pilot, so that's a help – when he's around. We're not too badly off for stockmen, but anything specialist, we're just doing it ourselves.'

He rubbed his hands, unconsciously. Daniella admired the strong fingers; he looked capable of anything. 'You saying if I need a plumber, I should call you?'

He chuckled. 'Yeah, probably be faster than trying anyone else around here.' He continued, 'When I was young, we had a schoolteacher too. That was when we were on a different station down near Roma for a while. It wasn't so close to town. But we always came back to Ryders.'

'Any brothers and sisters besides Cat?'

'One older brother, Will. He's in the mines at Isa now. Catrina's at uni in Brisbane as I said, doing ag science. She went to school there, too, as a boarder.'

'Really? Where?'

'Girls Grammar. You know it?'

'Of course, up on the Terrace. I used to go to debates there.'

'Where did you go to school?'

Daniella had meant to say as little as possible about her background. She was more comfortable asking the questions, like when she was taking a history in the clinic. But he drew out the details, and she found herself telling him how lonely and friendless primary school had been, the better time she'd had at high school, where her academic bent had been encouraged, then university.

'I think sometimes I started med because of those mean kids in primary school,' she reflected. 'Because no one would play with me I studied harder, and I asked Dad heaps of questions, which kept me going. Then I'd force Aiden to be my patient. Once, I bandaged him all over and he couldn't move. Dad had to help me unwrap him. The cat was luckier, though; she could run faster than Aiden.' Mark laughed.

He listened attentively, as if her stories were the most important things in the world. Soon the sandwiches were all eaten, the stars out in full. They lay back on the bonnet, shoulder to shoulder, looking up. The quiet was comfortable. Daniella felt completely relaxed. Any thoughts that she shouldn't get involved with this man while she was trying to sort herself out were fading.

'What made you go to that bench the other night?' he asked suddenly.

Daniella pushed herself up on her elbow. 'I was walking that way. I . . . wanted to look at the land and sky. Like this. It was a pretty spot.'

He made a sound in his throat. 'It is.'

She looked at his face. He was leaving something unsaid. His dark green eyes were black in the moonlight, his face unreadable.

'Would you like to see it?' he asked.

'What?'

'The station.'

She nodded slowly, feeling herself smile. A delicious tension crept between them as they stared at each other. Then, Mark leaned forward as if to kiss her.

In a moment of uncertainty, Daniella glanced down at her watch. 'Oh my God, it's eleven!' she exclaimed. 'I have to go. I have an early start tomorrow.'

He began to apologise for keeping her, but she assured him it was fine, scrambling to climb down from the bonnet before he could help her. He still managed to get to her door first and open it.

She paused before she got in. 'Thank you, this was really lovely,' she said, feeling awful and regretting breaking the moment. The drive back went too quickly.

But when Mark pulled up outside her house, he caught her hand. 'Listen, Daniella. There's a ball on this Saturday, outside Julia Creek. Will you come?'

'What sort of ball?'

'A B&S.'

'Aren't those . . . kind of rowdy?' Even back in Brisbane she'd heard stories about the rural singles balls – drunken escapades and injuries that would put city events to shame.

'Yeah,' he said, releasing her hand. 'Lots of people treat them as a drunken rite of passage but they can be fun. I wasn't sure about going, but Dave wanted me to drive there with him. I'd love you to be there, too.'

Daniella felt torn between the warm glow his words had sparked in her, and duty. 'I'm not sure. Dr Harris usually takes Saturday night, but still, I'm not sure if I should go out of town . . .' Say no, she thought. 'I'll have to check.'

Mark nodded, stepping back. 'I'll call you.'

Daniella thought, after all that, she would be awake for ages, going over everything she had said, everything that had happened. But sleep came swiftly, and she dreamed of stars and a soft breeze on her lips.

Chapter 10

'You did *what*?' demanded Jackie.

Daniella took a gulp of tea and nearly burned her tongue. Wincing at both the burn and her friend's tone, she turned on the cold tap to cool her tea. 'I know, I know . . . you said not to go to the dam with anyone, but I didn't know that's where we were going, I swear. And he was perfectly civilised.'

Dr Harris was on a call to a supplier in the hospital meeting room, but it would be done soon. The clinic hadn't started yet; they would open the doors in ten minutes. Daniella hoped that would be enough time for Jackie to get over her shock.

'Of course he was perfectly civilised,' said Jackie. 'This is *Mark Walker*. Holy shit. Who else have you told?'

Daniella dunked her biscuit meditatively. 'No one. Just you.'

'Did anyone see you?'

'What? I don't think so. Why, what would that matter?'

Jackie looked around and lowered her voice. 'Look, he's the catch of the whole district. Just watch yourself, that's all. People talk. And the Morgans will take an interest. Steph's been circling Mark for years.'

Daniella shrugged. What the hell did she care about the Morgans?

Jackie was frowning, but then she seemed to catch herself

and smiled apologetically. 'Hey, I'm just shocked, I guess. He never asks anyone out. You must have made a big impression. How was it?'

Daniella blushed. She'd mentioned the date to Jackie because it felt wrong not to, but she didn't really want to discuss the details. 'Nice. But I think he just did it to make up for his father being rude last weekend.'

'He said that?'

'No, just a feeling I got.' She wasn't going to talk about the other feelings Mark had given her.

Jackie looked sceptical, clearly scenting deception. 'Somehow I doubt it. You don't see it, do you?'

'What?' Daniella responded impatiently. This was ridiculous. She'd been on one date with Mark. They'd eaten some dinner, talked, and looked at the stars. He hadn't even kissed her. What was the big deal?

Jackie put her head on one side. 'It makes sense now. I saw him looking at you. You know, in that way.'

Daniella rolled her eyes. 'What way?'

'*That* way.' Jackie grinned, then met Daniella's unamused expression. 'I'm just surprised, that's all. Not that someone would notice you – it's just that I haven't seen much of Mark since his mum died.'

'Mmmm,' said Daniella, trying to dampen the intrigue. She wasn't actually sure how she felt about Mark Walker. As much as she tried not to think about him, her mind kept coming back to the subject. He was different from the men she'd met before; considerate and attentive. This very fact made it seem wrong, unnatural – what had she done to deserve such attention? She tried repeatedly to shut her thoughts down; she'd even tried to think about him clinically: their relationship was like a new case, she reasoned, in the early days of diagnosis. She needed to run more tests, get more data. Only then would she know the prognosis. But her attempts to be detached never worked for long. Soon, she'd find herself thinking again about how he'd looked at her as they lay on the Rover's bonnet, or wondering what it would be like to kiss him. Lord, she had to get herself together.

She glanced out the window. A car was just pulling into the lot. First patient, no doubt.

'Do you like him?' Jackie asked in a concerned whisper.

'Why are we whispering?' said Daniella.

Jackie screwed up her face. 'Because it's more fun to be conspiratorial,' she said, leaning on the kitchen wall. 'Well?'

'I'm not sure,' said Daniella. 'There's a lot going on.' Like the patients she hoped were about to descend on the clinic and save her from this conversation.

'Did he ask you out again?'

Daniella hesitated before saying, 'Yeah. To the B&S this weekend.'

'Oh God,' said Jackie. 'Tell me you said no.'

'I didn't say anything. I might have to be on call. Mark's going to ring me about it.'

Jackie shook her head again. 'Daniella, have you ever been to a B&S?'

'No.'

'They're mindless piss-ups.'

Daniella went out into the reception area and picked up the file stack again, pretending to go through it so she could get some breathing space. 'Mark said the exact same thing,' she called back. 'He also said Dave was driving there with him.'

Silence.

'Jackie?' Daniella went back into the kitchen where Jackie was sitting on the table with her arms crossed, staring into space. Then she refocused on Daniella. 'You're going to go,' she said. 'I can tell.'

To her surprise, Daniella realised she wanted to go, as long as it was okay with Dr Harris and the roster. Despite the stories about the B&S balls, she felt safe with Mark, especially remembering how he had handled himself with Peter Stein, how fearless and strong he'd been in her defence. And besides, it would make a good test. 'Why don't you come?' she asked impetuously. 'If Dave's going too, there'll be four of us – safety in numbers. I'm sure Mark wouldn't mind.'

Jackie chewed her lip. A knock came at the clinic door, and the phone rang.

'Opening time,' said Jackie, standing up quickly. 'I'm not sure if I've got anything to wear,' she called back as she went to open the door.

'Can't be worse off than me.' Daniella frowned as she wondered how she was going to find a dress before the weekend. It was bliss to have patients to attend to, to take her mind off it. She picked up the first file: Sarah, the little girl with asthma, back for a check-up.

But as the door opened, in came not Sarah but Robert and Joe, pig-shooting brothers extraordinaire. Instantly, she remembered: Joe hadn't come back on Monday as she'd insisted; with all the drama with Pete, she hadn't registered the no-show.

She met them before they could sit down. 'Joe, Robert. What's happening?'

Joe's mouth tugged to the side. 'Doesn't feel too good, doc.'

Daniella looked down at the filthy bandage. 'Through here,' she said. She didn't bother with the consulting rooms, taking them straight to the hospital room where she'd first stitched up his hand. They met Dr Harris coming the other way.

'Starting early?' he said good-naturedly.

'Hi, doc,' chorused the brothers.

'You right with this?' Dr Harris asked Daniella.

'Actually, I'd appreciate you looking in. You remember I told you about this bite, from last week when you were in Mount Isa?'

'Oh yes,' said Dr Harris, pushing up his glasses with interest and following them to the treatment room.

Daniella peeled the bandage off the wound and chucked it in the biohazard bin. It hit the side and she heard the dirt trickle down the plastic liner.

'Did you change the dressing?' she asked.

Joe was unapologetic. 'Nah, seemed cleaner just to leave it.'

'Christ,' she muttered. 'Tell me you took the antibiotics?'

'Sure, doc, I said I would.'

Joe complained as she eased the dressing off the wound. His finger was swollen into a pink, slug-like thing. The skin around the sutures was inflamed and angry; some of the suture knots had pulled so tight they had disappeared into the flesh. She couldn't see any obvious pus, though, just some skin flaking away from the edges of the tear. She was glad to have Dr Harris by her side. If she'd been in Brisbane, there would have been a registrar to call, a pathology lab to send swabs to. Here, pathology took at least twenty-four hours.

She was aware that Dr Harris was waiting for her to speak first. She asked Joe some basic questions: how long had it been like this? Was he getting any fevers or chills? She took his temperature and blood pressure: no fever, at least for now.

'Let's take some blood,' she said. 'We'll have to wait for the results, but I'd like to establish a baseline in case this gets worse.'

'And the wound?' prompted Dr Harris.

Daniella chewed her lip. If the wound started to fester, it might have to be left open, to granulate and heal. This was the most extreme response, and the scar would be disfiguring, or worse. She felt momentarily out of her depth.

'What would you advise?' she asked Dr Harris, hoping she didn't sound too breathless. 'I don't want to open the wound, and it looks as though it's mostly knitted anyway.'

He nodded. 'I would release every second suture to relieve the pressure, plus any where the knots have pulled under the skin. We'll keep a track of his temperature and send off some swabs. And I'm sorry, young Joe, but you'll be staying with us tonight.'

'Aw, man, what?'

Relieved to have a plan of action, Daniella backed up Dr Harris. 'Sorry, Joe, if you go shooting with an open wound, this is what happens.'

Joe swore, then apologised for swearing. Daniella had to coax him to have the blood test needle, which he swore about some more, this time without apology. Robert thought the whole thing was hilarious, until he discovered that, all going well, he'd have to come back to pick Joe up the next day. By the time it was all sorted out, Daniella was sure it must be the afternoon, but it was only nine thirty: a full day remained ahead.

Normally, Daniella would have been fully absorbed in her work, but something in her head had shifted. At unexpected times, even in the middle of consults, she found herself thinking about Mark and looking forward to his call. It was surprising to have more to her life than her work.

For the first time, she accepted a lift home from Dr Harris, not feeling up to conversing with the sky and letting all her apprehensions reign. Despite her uncertainties, when Mark Walker called, she wanted to tell him she was going to the ball.

As she got out of Dr Harris's car, he said, 'Oh, Daniella, I nearly forgot. Valerie Turner called. She said to bring some paper when you see her on Saturday. Does that make sense to you?'

Daniella managed a half-smile through her surprise. 'Yes, it does.'

'You two are getting along all right, then?' asked Dr Harris, looking at her closely.

'Seems like it,' said Daniella.

'One more.'

'Steady on, what's the rush?' called Dave. He hefted a roofing sheet from the quad's trailer and sent it up. Mark already had his hand out. They'd been working on the front paddock feed-shed roof for an hour, and the job was nearly done. A pile of rusted metal was ready for scrap and Simmo, one of the younger stationhands, was moving it into the trailer.

This did nothing to lessen Mark's impatience; he wanted everything in order so he could relax at the ball tomorrow. 'Lots to do,' he said, crab-walking to slip the new sheet in place. As it found the right spot, he caught the view from the roof down the ridge and all the way to the horizon. He paused and straightened up, remembering his idea. 'Hey, Dave. What do you think about chopper tours over the station? Get you more flying work. Lots of people pass through town who might be interested.'

Dave tipped his head to follow Mark's gaze. 'Sure. I guess. Only got one passenger seat in it though. You need more Tek screws?'

'No, I'm good.'

Mark went back to lining up the corrugated sheet to overlap with the next one, then hefted the cordless drill and screwed the Tek straight down into the batten. After the first screw was in, the rest followed in rapid-fire fashion. A few minutes later he was done.

'Here – catch,' he said, dropping the drill and the screw box down to Dave. Then he climbed down the ladder and started helping load the scrap. 'Hey, Simmo, where's your other glove?' he asked a second later. The boy had a roping glove on his right hand, but the left was bare.

'Um, lost it somewhere,' said Simmo, turning red under his freckles.

Mark looked at all the sharp rusty edges, and then at the boy. Simmo's arms and legs were still lean like a colt's. He was keen to learn and his youth and enthusiasm made Mark feel fiercely protective. The station needed more like him.

'Here,' he said, chucking his own left glove to Simmo. 'You can tie it all down, too.'

'What's up with you?' asked Dave. 'Never seen you in this much of a rush.'

'Lots to do,' repeated Mark. 'Need to go check that windmill up the back mile. Plan the brand program, stocktake the feed, work out the cut for the next sale. Want it done before dark today. Simmo's learning too, aren't you?'

Simmo gave him the thumbs-up in the baggy gloves.

'You planning on being out the whole weekend or something?' asked Dave.

'I am,' said Mark. 'Or at least half of it. As are you.'

'Yeah, Mark, look. We really can skip this ball thing. You know that. I bought the tickets because Steph got me at a weak moment during the rugby. I'm happy to pay the money, but we don't have to show up.'

Mark ignored him and threw the last pieces of roofing into the quad trailer. He was trying very hard to be nonchalant.

Dave gave him a sly look. 'Ah. Now I understand. Let me guess. Daniella Bell?'

'Yes,' said Mark shortly, stowing the drill and roofing screws in the trailer's front end. He went to check Simmo's work with the tie-down. 'Simmo, come here a sec.' He brought the lad back to look at the lopsided load and limp ropes. 'That's not going to hold it. Here.' He went through the truckie's hitch again until Simmo had it right. Mark finally stepped away, satisfied, letting the boy finish on his own.

'So, Dr Bell? Since the other night?' asked Dave incredulously.

Mark gave him a hard stare. 'Yes.'

'When you asked me to get her number, you said it was so you could apologise!'

'It was.'

Dave pointed a finger at Mark. 'B&S, mate. Bachelors and spinsters, remember? You can't invite someone to a singles ball.'

'You can too. You did once, as I recall.'

Dave was silent for a moment, then said, 'That was years ago. And it wasn't exactly a good night.'

'Thanks for your support.'

'She's only been in town five minutes.'

Mark knew and he didn't care. He wanted to see Daniella again.

Dave went on, 'I don't want to be a third wheel, so just go without me, all right?'

'You won't be. She rang to ask if it was all right if Jackie comes too. So don't go piking on me now. You can make it up to Jackie for getting pissed and passing out before ten o'clock all those years ago.'

Dave dropped his head. 'Bloody hell,' he said. He turned away and climbed onto his quad bike. 'I was hoping to get out of finding a tux.' Then he gunned it back towards the homestead.

Simmo threw the last of the gear into the tray. 'Are you really going to the B&S, Mark?'

'Yes, afraid so.'

Simmo nodded, dejected. 'My brother's going too. Wish I was.'

Mark well understood the frustration of being seventeen and having an elder brother who got to do everything first. 'Next year, Simmo. Be here before you know it. Now, let's get to that windmill.'

Simmo jumped in the trailer. 'Right-o.'

Chapter 11

'Oh my,' said Daniella.

Jackie glanced across the cab. 'Doesn't look so unpopulated now, does it?'

Daniella could only nod in stunned agreement. They'd been passing signs to the B&S for the last half hour, but now, creeping in the snail-slow convoy of utes and trucks they could see the venue spread out under the darkening sky.

'Usually these are the saleyards,' said Jackie. All Daniella could see was miles of canvas tents rimmed with parked vehicles and a crowd of young people, the black and white of tuxes interspersed with colourful dresses. She had always avoided balls in Brisbane – even ones for special events like her graduation – because she found such crowds so intimidating. She was much more suited to one on one. Although, of late, she'd started to wonder about that too. Earlier in the afternoon she'd spent half an hour at Valerie Turner's, dutifully taking dictation of a letter to the son in Townsville. Valerie had been particularly prickly today, making Daniella spell out the longer words so she could check they were correct. After all that, she'd insisted on keeping the letter rather than letting Daniella post it. Daniella had left feeling exhausted, and unsure whether the letter would even be sent. Crawling into a dark cave had never seemed so appealing.

'I can't go in there,' she whispered.

They were driving alongside an improvised fence now, the type used around construction sites. Ahead of them, Mark and Dave's ute made a right turn and followed the marshals directing them to the parking around the rim. On the phone yesterday, Mark had suggested they all drive down together, but later Jackie had pointed out that two cars would give them much more room if they ended up sleeping here overnight, as so many people would do (though Daniella knew Jackie herself wasn't keen on the idea). Besides, as it was a singles ball they would need to make a show of only meeting up once they had actually arrived. Daniella had heard the disappointment in Mark's voice; he'd obviously wanted to spend the almost three-hour drive with her.

An uneasy silence had punctuated the first half hour of the trip and Daniella wondered whether Jackie was cross at being dragged along. When Daniella had finally asked if everything was all right, Jackie had responded brightly that it was fine, and proceeded to change the topic completely. Daniella didn't believe a word of it, but she hoped once they arrived, Jackie would have a good time.

Both utes pulled up in the last row of parking in the section, angled so the trays faced the tents. Daniella climbed out gingerly. She'd borrowed a little black dress from Jackie: a figure-hugging number with a plunging neckline and cut even lower at the back. She felt almost naked in it, and it was so tight she had to manoeuvre her legs sideways to get out of the ute. When Daniella tried it on, Jackie had wistfully recalled that the dress had fitted her just fine before Jamie came along. Daniella would rather have gone in a set of scrubs from the hospital, but after she and Jackie had been worked over by the Ryders hairdresser – a home business hiding in a side street – at least her hair was soft and silky, and back to its natural light brown. Jackie was beautiful in a deep blue wrap dress of soft jersey, her dark curls pinned up.

Daniella stood with one hand clutching the ute tray, trying to work out how to approach the main area. Music pounded from the white and yellow canvas tents, almost drowned out by the clamour of voices. All around them, people were excitedly hugging and shaking hands, some obviously old friends who hadn't seen each other in ages. Daniella watched one girl skilfully hug a tux-clad boy in a hat while carrying four open beer stubbies and a lit cigarette. The air was a potent mix of dust and perfumes.

'How does it work?' Daniella asked.

'Work?'

'Where do we go?'

Jackie laughed. 'Anywhere you want. That tent ahead probably has a DJ – there'll be a couple of them around. And live bands in some of the other tents.'

Mark and Dave approached, both looking tall and positively regal in their tuxes and cowboy hats. In Brisbane, the combination would have seemed out of place, even ridiculous, but here, it was the done thing. Jackie had obviously seen it before, and glanced towards the tents.

'Ladies,' said Mark, tipping his hat. 'Fancy seeing you here.'

Daniella laughed as he offered her his arm. She slipped her fingers onto his forearm and felt the strong warm muscle beneath her hand. She leaned into him. Being with him here felt as familiar and easy as it had by the dam.

'You look amazing,' he whispered.

'Let's get a drink,' said Jackie from behind them.

They walked towards the tents, and Dave soon peeled off to greet a group of men. From all sides, people hailed Mark. He shook a lot of hands, and introduced Daniella to most of the people, but she found herself shrinking back. She could hardly hear the names over the music, and the crowd jostled around her. She was nearly trampled by a group in bedsheet togas doing some kind of line dance. Mark kept her arm firmly against his body, but he was turned away, talking to a guy in a sheet. Finally they reached the drinks queue, and Jackie was beside her again.

'This is insane,' Daniella shouted.

'I know!' Jackie laughed.

The queue moved fast (kegs of beers and goon wine seemed a wise choice for the no-glass event) and Daniella soon had a drink in her hand. She released Mark's arm to keep a better hold on the plastic cup and a moment later he was lost in the crowd.

'I'm going to go find a band,' said Jackie as Daniella craned her neck, trying to catch sight of Mark. 'You want to come?'

Daniella didn't. Her ears were ringing. She wanted clean air and quiet. Coming here had been a massive mistake. She didn't want to abandon Jackie, though. Mercifully, Dave reappeared and stepped in.

'I'll go,' he said, neatly dodging sideways as an already-drunk line dancer careened past. 'Mark won't be long,' he added to Daniella.

'Fine,' said Jackie tersely, then waved to Daniella. 'Find you in a bit.'

Alone again, Daniella rubbed her arm, an old tic from years ago when she had often been by herself in social gatherings. Balancing the drink, she edged towards a tent pole, which made a small island in the crowd. She leaned her back into it, feeling adrift in the throng.

Then a strong arm came around her shoulders, and Mark's voice was in her ear. 'There you are,' he said. 'I was afraid I'd lost you. Let's get out of here.'

Daniella could have cried with relief.

Soon, they had left the noisy tent far behind. They sat on the tray of his ute where Daniella put her plastic cup of wine aside. Mark had drunk about half his beer, but now it too was forgotten. From the car park the B&S was a dull roar, and away from the tents she could see the sky again.

'This is much better,' Mark said. 'Every time I forget what a shambles it is. Great fun when we were younger, but I'm twenty-eight and feeling like I'm getting a bit old for it.'

'Do you think everyone noticed you haven't been in a while?' asked Daniella.

'Well, everyone knows everything about everyone out here. Gets tiring, sometimes. When I travelled, I actually liked some of the bigger places that felt more anonymous. But then they didn't have the quiet, and the same stars, and I started to miss home. That's mostly why I came back.'

'Yeah, I understand. I don't want to go back to Brisbane,' Daniella said in a rush. 'I mean, I didn't want to work there anymore. Too big.' Uh-oh. She hadn't meant to get into this.

Mark gave her an appraising look. 'That makes you pretty unusual.'

'What do you mean?'

'Most docs who come to this town are here for a few months, no more. Dr Harris is a pretty amazing exception. Some people feel a bit jaded by the high turnover. They want to build a relationship with someone.' He looked at her and smiled.

Daniella swallowed. 'I can understand that.' She breathed out. 'Where did you travel?' she asked, moving closer to him.

He put an arm around her, a warm shock against her night-cooled skin. She shivered and huddled into his shoulder. 'Lots of places,' he said. His words hummed through her. 'All across the Top End. The Pilbara, for a while. Perth. Adelaide.

Tassie. Melbourne, Wagga, Sydney. Brisbane, of course. Rocky, Emerald, Cairns. I was gone about two years.'

They compared notes on the few places they'd both been. For the first time all evening, she began to think she wouldn't mind sleeping in the back of the ute – if she was with him. He was solid and steady, and sure of himself. She liked that right now. And even tucked against him, she felt in control of herself. It felt safe.

'So you didn't find anywhere you'd rather be?' she asked eventually.

He spoke after a brief pause. 'No. This is home. But I had to go away to make sure. I love this place, but there's a big amazing world out there and I needed to see it. The Walkers, especially Dad, tend to stay put, but Mum told me all the Camerons – that's her side of the family – are travellers. She always said Will and Cat and me ended up with some of that in us. Cat took last semester off and went overseas, but she'll come back here when she's finished uni, I think. Dad's going to be waiting a long time for my brother to come home, though.'

Daniella heard how carefully he said 'Mum'. He was tapping his hat against his knee now, looking down at the ute tray, a little pensive crease between his brows. She turned her head, feeling the muscular curve of his shoulder under her cheek. 'Can I ask what happened to her?'

'Cancer,' he said quietly. 'Got picked up late and took her pretty quickly.'

'You must miss her,' she said.

Mark's nods slowed. 'Every day. When she died, some of the life went out of the station – and out of Dad, too. Sometimes I forget she's gone, but that's getting better. Dad's still finding it hard though. He wants things to be the way they were.'

'Mmm,' Daniella said softly. 'My dad was the same, I think.'

Mark turned his head; she felt his lips brush her forehead. A pleasant warmth radiated from the spot. 'Your mum, too?' he asked.

Daniella took a moment to think through the words. 'Yeah, but it was such a long time ago. I don't really remember her. I just remember her smile, and Dad's when she said something funny. He didn't smile like that for years afterwards.'

Mark nodded against her forehead. Daniella let the silence settle as they sat close together, linked in these words and their touch. Her thoughts then turned to her own family, her father and brother.

'You said your brother was in mining?' she went on eventually.

Mark shifted. 'Yeah, he's a leading hand at MIM now. Doing his engineering degree at night, too. He coordinates the shutdowns for the plant equipment maintenance – he rings now and then to try to get me to do some work for him. I think that's his way of staying in touch. He left around the time I came back from travelling, and Cat left for uni not long after. Broke Dad's heart, I think. He wanted Will to stay in the business, running the stations like him. Then Mum got sick. Cat always comes home for holidays but Will's never done that. I don't think he's coming back.'

'How long's it been?' asked Daniella. Without realising what she was doing, her hand had crept up to play with the buttons on Mark's shirt.

'Four years, and I miss him like hell.'

Daniella let her fingers drift across the crisp white shirt, then slipped her hand between the buttons and brushed smooth warm flesh. Mark caught his breath and Daniella realised with a shock what she'd done. She couldn't understand it – she wasn't usually this forward.

'Sorry,' she said, embarrassed. 'My hand must be cold.'

He caught her before she could pull away, closing his warm fingers around hers. His other hand was making small circles on her shoulder, tiny meditative movements that matched the careful tone of his voice as he spoke. 'I'm really glad you came to town,' he said.

Daniella looked up. He was smiling at her, his eyes intense. 'Really glad,' he whispered.

Gently, he kissed her. Daniella felt the glow of being in his arms as she returned the pressure, exploring his mouth. It was too lovely – his hair soft under her fingers, his arms protecting her, the warm feel of his skin.

He broke away briefly, but didn't let go, stroking her jaw with his thumb. Daniella experienced a wave of certainty: she could do this. She could mend herself and see where this might lead.

Across the field, a crowd of revellers fell through the side of a canvas tent, scattering plastic cups and cowboy hats. Mark chuckled softly, brushing his lips against hers. The partygoers soon untangled themselves and staggered back inside, but Mark showed no signs of interest in anything but Daniella. Instead, he lifted her further back in the tray so they could rest against the cab.

'That's better,' he said, kissing her again.

The B&S grew more rowdy as the stars turned overhead, but Daniella hardly noticed. Cuddled into Mark's side, she was content to be kissed, and enjoy the warmth of him against her. Only when a particularly loud cheer erupted from a nearby tent did she glance around.

'I hope that's not bound for the emergency department,' she said.

Mark grinned at her. 'What's it like, working in a big hospital?' he asked.

She hesitated, tried to be objective. 'There's always lots going on. You're usually in one area at a time though. And it's easy to get a bit . . . lost in it.' Careful, she told herself.

'Lost?'

Daniella played with her skirt, avoiding Mark's eyes. She really didn't want to talk about Brisbane, even in the security of his embrace. 'Like I said before, it's just a big place.'

'And you mentioned your dad works there?'

More difficult territory. Daniella nodded, still looking down. 'He's a trauma surgeon.'

She felt a gentle pressure under her chin. With one finger, Mark turned her face towards his. 'Hey. Things not so good there?' His face was full of concern.

She shook her head. No, they weren't. But she didn't want to talk about it. She was about to say she'd prefer he kissed her again when she spotted Dave trotting down the hill from the party tents. With a wave of guilt, she realised she'd abandoned Jackie.

Dave had lost his hat somewhere, his jacket and bow tie were both undone and he had a big blue stain on his white shirt. Through the material, Daniella could see that the tattoo on his arm extended across his chest.

'What happened to you?' she asked, appraising the damage as he approached.

'Someone's got the dye out,' Dave said quickly.

'Dye?'

'Food dye,' supplied Mark. 'They ban it, but people still bring it and throw it on each other.'

'Jackie needs some help,' said Dave.

Daniella was up in a second. 'Is she all right?'

'Few too many,' said Dave apologetically. 'But she won't let anyone touch her. I can't leave her there – you know what happens at these things.'

Mark took off his jacket and slung it in the ute tray. 'Let's go,' he said grimly.

They found Jackie propped in a plastic seat at the edge of a band tent, an empty beer cup in her hand. Standing guard over her was Stephanie Morgan, who was wearing a tight white dress that had also taken a big hit of blue dye.

'Few too many,' said Steph brightly when she saw them, but Daniella noticed Stephanie's mouth tighten as she took in Mark with his arm around her.

Jackie's mascara had run. 'Hi,' she said vaguely, peering at the cup as though hoping it might refill itself.

Daniella's doctor brain kicked in, scanning for injuries, assessing mental state. She concluded pretty quickly that Jackie was simply toasted. 'Thought you were going to go easy,' she said, moving to help Jackie up.

Mark got in first, easily hoisting her out of the chair. 'Okay, easy there, Jack,' he said. 'Dave, get over here. Thanks, Steph,' he added.

'No problem. I'll leave you to it,' she said, melting away into the crowd.

Between the two of them, Mark and Dave got Jackie in a fireman's lift and carried her out to the car park. The movement clearly wasn't helpful; sending the boys away, Daniella spent a long time holding Jackie's hair as she threw up against a gum tree. Finally, Jackie stopped being sick. 'I'm sorry,' she muttered, over and over.

'It's fine, really,' said Daniella. But she was worried. Jackie was normally so sensible, and she'd been so critical of the B&S being a piss-up. 'What happened?'

Jackie just smiled, a wide, unhappy smile, and wouldn't say anything more. Perhaps she just hadn't been out in a long time. Daniella managed to steer her back to the ute and got her into the passenger seat. Then she went to Mark and Dave, who were sitting on the back of Mark's ute.

'What really happened?' she asked Dave.

He rubbed his forehead, looking tired. 'Beats me. It was loud in there with the band. We were trying to talk over it. Then Steph turned up and butted in, and a few people I knew came over to say hello. I went to get another round and when I came back Jack was pissed off about something. Then she started on the Bundy shots. Someone emptied the blue dye over Steph and me and things went pretty much down the crapper from there.'

Daniella chewed on this. Attuned from taking medical histories, she suspected Dave was leaving something out. She'd have to try to find out the real story from Jackie later. 'Look, I think I should drive her back,' she said. 'Tomorrow she'll probably have a wicked hangover and the drive then will be murder.'

Mark nodded. 'We'll drive ahead of you. We've got a bullbar and you need to watch out for roos.'

As Dave turned away, Mark pulled Daniella into a quick hug. 'I had a really good time,' he whispered. 'I'll call you tomorrow.'

~

Only a few hours after arriving home, Mark headed up the stockmen's meeting in the stable office, feeling the impact of the late night. His father was supposed to take the meeting, but instead he'd waved Mark on and sat down next to Steph, who was looking sleek and unaffected by the night before. Now Mark faced the room. Leaning against the back wall was Darryl, the regular vet, his burly arms crossed, ready to get on with the job.

'So, let's get this started,' said Mark. 'Darryl will go through each pen, then as we get the okay, the teams move those pens onto the loader. We cut out any without the okay, same as usual. Any questions?'

There weren't; the stockmen knew the drill. Mark sent Simmo to help with cutting the weaners into branding groups. Then, pen by pen, Mark went through all the mustered stock with Darryl.

'Spectacular as always, Mark,' pronounced the vet. 'Larger herd next year too, I'll bet.'

Mark watched the glossy hides on the animals with a mixture of pride and exhaustion. He was glad it had all gone well, especially in front of Steph Morgan.

Darryl asked, 'How's Simmo working out?' Simmo was his nephew.

'Good. Works hard. Very teachable,' said Mark, as they stopped and leaned against a railing. Both men turned to watch Simmo straddling a pen chute, opening a gate for the weaners.

'That's great. He thinks a lot of you, Mark, and he really wants to stay here.'

Mark nodded, not letting on how much this meant to him.

But Darryl, blunt as ever, clearly had other things on his mind. 'Your dad's maybe not doing as well as he pretends, though,' he observed.

Mark turned and saw his father and Steph standing close together in intense discussion as they watched all the goings-on: the herd stamping around the yards, the dust rising and floating across the homestead, the trucks at the loaders. Physically, William looked fine. But anyone who knew him well could see the difference. The spark was missing. In previous years William Walker had been the animated station head, across everything.

'Yeah,' said Mark slowly.

'Well, it's only been six months,' said Darryl. 'Can take a while to get the head back in. See it all the time. How you doing with it?'

'Okay,' Mark said. 'We all miss her.' In truth, he'd been so busy with the station that he hadn't had a chance to start processing the full impact of his mother's death. But then, getting the station right again was part of that. She'd always backed him with the things he'd wanted to achieve. And somehow, knowing she would have encourged his efforts made it easier.

Darryl slapped him on the shoulder. 'Yeah, that's right. But you're doing great here. Lovely country. Always enjoy coming here.'

Mark straightened. 'Thanks, Darryl.'

'Any time. Give my best to Cat. And, hey, just remember: us vets have the strong stuff. If you're going to have a meltdown, talk to me first.' Darryl gave him a wink.

Mark shook his head at the departing back, uncertain whether the man was serious or not. Knowing Darryl, he probably was.

~

That evening, when Mark came into the homestead, filthy after checking the holding yards and the cattle loader, he ached to call Daniella and he wanted to be clean first. Revived by a hot shower, he pulled on fresh jeans and a shirt and went barefoot from his room into the hallway. He found his father sitting in the hall chair, in the green jacket he wore to every Sunday evening meal.

'Did you have a good time last night?' William asked.

'Yeah, not bad,' said Mark, surprised at his father's interest. 'Went well today.'

'Yeah. Darryl was very pleased.' Mark saw his opportunity. 'Look, Dad. I think there're some other ways we could generate income here, while the herd's recovering. To take the pressure off.'

William's mouth turned grim. 'I've already made myself clear, Mark. I'm not having those mining bastards here. I know Steph is only doing her job, but I'm not going to see this place being picked over by vultures. End of story.'

Mark bunched his fists in frustration. 'That's not what I'm talking about. What about looking at some of the methods we're using here, or even bringing in tourists? We could leverage off the Roma station—'

'Mark,' his father cut in. 'I've had enough of deflecting this kind of talk from the Morgans. It's been a good day. I want a nice dinner without any of this nonsense. I heard you're taking out that new doctor.'

Mark took a moment to navigate the abrupt change in topic; then he figured Kath had probably heard gossip from someone in town. 'Yes.'

His father grunted. 'You need to think about what you're doing, Mark. You want someone who knows the country, who's lived on the land and wants to be here. Look at Steph.'

Mark raised his eyebrows, astonished. Had Stephanie put him up to this? 'Steph's fine, Dad. But not like that. We went out a few times years ago and that was it. And she lives in Townsville.'

William shook his head. 'My point is they have roots here. Look at how much she does for the town. How's it going to work with someone who goes away, chasing their career? Don't let me see that happen again.'

Mark could only think how strange this was. His father had never shown the slightest interest in who he'd dated before his travels. But it was more than that. These complaints were too specific, too personal. He thought of his father when he'd been younger; his mother had travelled a lot. 'Are you saying that's what happened to you?' he asked.

William stood, and put his hands on Mark's shoulders. 'It ruined everything, what she did with her work and those trips,' he said. 'Courses. Conferences. Studies. She never really wanted to settle here.'

Mark's frown deepened. 'Hold on, that's not true—'

'Just think about it. I mean it.'

Stephanie appeared at the far end of the hall. 'Dinner's ready,' she called.

His father strode away, leaving Mark baffled. He stood there thinking for a long time. His parents' relationship was something that had always been there in the background. He'd known it was volatile, but he'd never thought about why. And he really hoped Steph hadn't heard any of that conversation.

Finally, he swallowed this new information and headed for dinner. He'd have to call Daniella later.

Chapter 12

After the weekend shemozzle, Daniella was glad to get back to the clinic on Monday. Dr Harris had had a quiet night on Saturday – he'd only been called in once, for Sarah, who again needed the nebuliser and steroids – so Daniella didn't feel as guilty as she might have. And Mark had rung her last night and they'd talked for nearly an hour. Yes, she didn't feel guilty at all.

Dr Harris spent a long consult in the morning with Mac and Susan Westerland, reviewing the plan for Sarah's asthma, which was becoming increasingly difficult to manage. Daniella took appointments as usual, which today was mainly grey nomads on holidays with various complaints: sun spots, script refills, piles.

As they met up between appointments over the biscuit barrel in the kitchen, Dr Harris pursed his lips. 'The health system really needs to examine the true cost of all these southerners spending their retirement in Queensland,' he complained.

Daniella rummaged in the biscuit tin. 'How so?'

Dr Harris dunked his tea bag with fervour. 'Well, health is funded on a state-by-state basis, based on population. The biggest cost comes from older people, always will, but there are far more retired southerners up here than Queenslanders going south. And for the smaller regional centres, like Cairns or Isa, and even here, we get the extra cost of caring for all those travellers, but no increased funding.'

He went on for a few more minutes until Daniella's eyes began to slide sideways towards the next appointment file. Dr Harris shook himself. 'Sorry. But these things are important round here. And you'll find that more and more as you practise here. We've got to stand up for ourselves, otherwise we get nothing. No support, and no respect.'

'Gotcha,' she said, nodding. In Brisbane, discussions of the resourcing of regional centres had always felt like an academic exercise; out here, the issues were starkly apparent.

'Say, Daniella? Are you busy next weekend?' he asked.

Daniella's hand stopped on its way to the file. 'Just the usual Saturday clinic.'

'You should throw a dinner party on Sunday. You can use my kitchen, invite a few people.'

'Like you do?' she asked nervously.

'Well, you know, do your own thing. But basically, yes. Best way to get to know people away from the clinic.'

'I'm not sure that's a good idea . . .'

'Nonsense,' said Dr Harris. 'It's a great idea. If you take Thursday night on call, I'll cover Saturday. Give you plenty of time to prepare.'

Daniella, however, still thought it was a bad idea as she trolled the supermarket that evening. It wasn't that she was a bad cook (though she didn't cook much), it was simply the weight of expectation. Everyone knew Dr Harris, he was famous for his roasts. How could she follow that? Besides, she wasn't Dr Harris. She didn't flourish in group situations. And she didn't want to create the idea it was something she'd be doing regularly.

She strolled down the few aisles, thinking about what she could cook, but procrastinating by picking out other things.

New toothbrush. Weet-Bix. Milk. Corn chips to eat when she watched *Offspring* later. Crap, what about dinner tonight? She was tired of tinned soup, and she'd had every one of the supermarket's range of pre-packed microwave meals a million times. She stopped in front of the vegie section, frozen like a roo in headlights. When was the last time she'd bought a leafy green? She picked up a lettuce, then quickly put it back. Who was she kidding?

'Hi, Dani.'

Daniella jumped. Stephanie Morgan had come up beside her. Balancing a basket on her hip, she raised an eyebrow at the discarded lettuce. Daniella felt caught out and found herself confessing, 'I'm not much into salads.'

'Then I'll pounce,' said Stephanie lightly, picking up the reject. 'Good to see you at the B&S on Saturday,' she continued, now sorting through the tomatoes. 'They're always fun. Did you have a good time?'

'Yes, thanks,' said Daniella. 'Thanks for looking out for Jackie, by the way.'

'Hey, no problem. I haven't seen much of Jackie lately. No doubt she's been busy with Jamie, and I've been in Townsville a lot. Not my favourite place, though, I have to say. It's always so nice to come back here and see real people – all the friends we went to school with, you know, all the new partners and kids. Funny who people end up with, isn't it? Dave was there, too. Seen a lot of him recently – doesn't he usually travel more?'

'Er, I'm not really sure. I don't know him so well,' Daniella said, following Stephanie's lead and braving the tomatoes while trying to keep up with her rapid conversation.

'Probably best,' said Stephanie.

Daniella looked up, not sure what she meant. 'Sorry?'

But Stephanie just handed her a dusky orange tomato. 'Here. Probably the best you'll get right now. Meat's always good, but sometimes fresh produce is limited. What I wouldn't give to be in a Townsville grocer right now.' She made a face. 'I was surprised to see Mark at the ball. Made it a big weekend for him. He looked like he was about to fall over last night, he was so tired.'

Daniella felt a strange and unpleasant sensation. 'Last night?'

Stephanie had started rummaging through the carrots. 'Mm-hmm. At dinner. The muster came in two weeks ago, so everyone's flat out. Mark's really committed to the station, just like his dad. Sometimes I think it's all he cares about. But he's great to work with. They've got some really good opportunities out there. Can't wait to see them happen.'

Daniella sneaked a glance at Stephanie's face. She looked perfectly innocent, focusing on selecting carrots. 'Oh?' she responded.

Stephanie smiled. 'Yes. We work pretty closely. And who wouldn't want to, with him?' She gave Daniella a little wink, then sighed. 'Then again, he'd give anyone up for the station. Probably not the best move to go after him, you know. You'll only get hurt.' Steph turned back to the veg.

Daniella knew she was being warned off. Doubt sprouted in her heart. How well did she know Mark, really? Was he really serious at all, or had she let herself be led on? She remembered the first time she'd seen him at the tav, and how Stephanie had behaved around him. She had the awful feeling she had everything all wrong. Maybe that was a good thing, she tried to tell herself. She should stick to her original resolve, keep it simple, avoid attachments. But the thought sent her mind into full revolt. Hadn't they spent the whole evening at the ball talking and kissing in his ute? Oh no, she realised with dismay, she was already involved.

All she wanted right then was to get out of the supermarket. She quickly stuffed a zucchini into her basket and turned away. 'Excuse me.'

'Can I help you find anything?' Stephanie asked, following behind. 'Sometimes things are in funny places in here, you know, little items ending up in completely the wrong aisle, all mixed up where they don't belong. Happens all the time, especially with new things.'

Daniella gritted her teeth. 'I'm sorry, did you want something from me?' she asked.

'Just making sure you don't get lost on the way out,' said Stephanie crisply.

Daniella let Stephanie follow her as far as the checkout, where a bored-looking teenager was slumped on her stool, picking at her nail polish. Her name tag read, *Hi! I'm Becky.*

Suddenly Daniella saw a way out. 'You know,' she said, facing Stephanie and not bothering to lower her voice. 'I don't really know off the top of my head what those symptoms could be, but why don't you make an appointment tomorrow and we can discuss it further.' She stood stiffly, her heart hammering in her throat.

Stephanie eyed the teenager, who had perked up and was now hanging on every word. 'Becky, remember you're helping me with posters tomorrow,' Stephanie said sharply, and retreated back down an aisle.

Daniella breathed out. But her temporary victory over Stephanie didn't do anything for the empty feeling in her stomach. Had she been wrong about Mark?

After she'd walked home, she switched her phone to silent and unpacked her groceries. Shit. One zucchini, the corn chips, toothbrush, milk and cereal. Nothing she could actually eat for dinner. She peered in the freezer. There was one meal left from her first shopping trip. She scraped the frost off its cardboard face. Apricot chicken. Ugh. She'd been avoiding it for a week; tonight would have to be the night. With a sigh, she stuffed it in the microwave. While it cooked, she put the zucchini in the middle of the kitchen bench and stared at it meditatively. She wanted to call Jackie, but that might require disclosing more than she wanted to right now.

She absolutely didn't want to talk to Mark. She couldn't bear to have her new and tender expectations of joy taken away. It made her feel like a teenager again; liking a boy and thinking he liked you back, and then finding out you were wrong.

She flicked on the TV. No, tonight would be bad dinner, and corn chips and someone else's drama. At least that couldn't disappoint her; she knew what she was getting.

Mark called that night, and again on Tuesday, but Daniella let the calls go through to voicemail and didn't listen to the messages. She knew she was being immature, avoiding the problem, but it seemed easier to focus all her attention on work. In a few days, she'd have some perspective back, she was sure; she would deal with it then.

The Wednesday clinic began the same as any other. Then, at around eleven, as Daniella was getting her first tea fix of the day, Jackie stuck her head around the kitchen door. 'Walk-in to fill your gap,' she said, and handed over a slim file.

Daniella tipped the rest of her tea down the sink. In the waiting room, she was surprised to see the checkout girl from the supermarket.

'Rebecca?' she read off the file.

The girl came forward without making eye contact. Daniella led the way to the consulting room and closed the door. The girl sat down in the patient chair with her arms folded around her bag, chewing her lower lip.

'What can I do for you, Rebecca?'

'Becky,' said the girl.

'Okay,' said Daniella. She waited. The girl sat up and leaned forward, but didn't seem to find any words. Daniella pushed the file away and put down her pen. 'It's all right, take your time.' Looking at the girl's troubled face, she had a pretty good idea what this was about.

She was right. 'I think I'm pregnant,' said Becky. As soon as she'd uttered it, she looked terrified. Daniella understood: the awful secret had been spoken to someone else. Right now, Becky probably felt the most vulnerable she had ever been in her life.

Daniella kept her face impassive. 'All right, when was your last period?'

The girl's eyes rolled up, thinking. 'Six weeks ago, I think. But they're not, you know . . .'

'Regular?'

'Yeah.'

'Okay – that can be perfectly normal at your age. First things first: we should do a quick test and make sure. Then we'll talk about where we go from there, all right?'

A look of pure terror crossed Becky's face again. 'What sort of test?'

'Urine dipstick. It'll just take a couple of minutes.' Daniella spoke matter-of-factly, trying to look reassuring. She stood up. 'Come back through the clinic and we can go into the hospital rooms. I'll get you a sample pot there, completely private.'

It took a little coaxing, but Daniella got Becky into the hospital and then sent her to the bathroom to provide the sample. She waited three minutes for the test to develop, then did another one just to be sure.

'Becky, you're not pregnant,' she said finally.

Becky gaped. 'I'm not? But what if that test's, you know, defective?'

'These are pretty accurate. We'd have to do a blood test to be absolutely sure, but based on this, you're not pregnant.'

'Oh my God,' said Becky, putting her hands over her mouth. 'I was so sure, you know, and I know you can't wait too long if . . .'

'You did the right thing coming in so soon. But come back to the clinic and let's talk a little more.'

Back in the consulting room, Daniella took the full history and encouraged Becky to ask her own questions. Becky was only fifteen, so irregular periods weren't unusual. She had a boyfriend. They'd had sex a few times; he hadn't used anything, and she'd been too embarrassed to ask him. Daniella explained about STIs, at which Becky's brow furrowed with concern; Daniella made a mental note to come back to suggesting she be tested.

But most of all, she didn't want to see Becky back here in two months' time with her fear realised. After a moment's silence, she said, 'Becky, I think it's really important for any woman to be in control of her own body. There're a few options for avoiding this situation again, and I'd like to go through them so you can think about what you'd like to do.'

'Okay,' said Becky, seeming more responsive.

'Right. Well, the only guaranteed way to avoid pregnancy is to not have sex. With any form of contraceptive there's still a risk, but if you take care to use them properly the risk will be minimised. First of all, there're condoms, which can protect you from both pregnancy and the STIs I mentioned before. I can give you some here, and you can buy them from the supermarket.'

Becky flushed red. 'I work there,' she said.

Daniella nodded in understanding. From what Becky had told her, she wasn't confident they would be used anyway. 'There are also a few other options. The most common is the pill. Do you know about that?' she asked.

Becky squirmed. 'Sure, yeah. But do my parents have to know?'

Daniella took a breath. Becky was clearly frightened of being found out. But from her point of view, the rules were clear. 'They don't have to. Everything that happens between us is confidential. I think it's a very good idea for you to talk to your parents about this if you can, but I know that can be difficult. As long as you understand the things I'm telling you, I can write you a script. Shall we go through that now?'

She spent some time explaining when to start the pill, how to take it and side effects to look out for, and how long before it would be effective. 'I can get you started with a sample pack,' she said. 'And give you a script for when that runs out. How does that sound?'

'Good,' said Becky, looking relieved for the first time.

Daniella made a follow-up appointment for a few months' time to check how she was going, and impressed on Becky that she must come back sooner if her period didn't start in the next week.

'Come and see me anytime, about anything at all,' she said as she stood to open the door.

'Thanks,' said Becky. 'By the way, that was amazing the other day, with Steph Morgan. Did she really have something wrong with her?'

Daniella groaned inside, embarrassed to be reminded of how unprofessional she'd been. 'Thanks,' she said weakly. 'And no, she didn't – I just wanted her to leave me alone for a moment.'

Becky sighed. 'Know what you mean.'

As Becky walked away, Daniella felt a rush of satisfaction. She knew this appointment might just have changed the girl's life trajectory.

~

It was dark when Daniella got home. She'd gone to the other supermarket to pick up food for dinner, avoiding the usual shop in case it made Becky uncomfortable to see her again so soon.

As she was on call that night, she plugged her phone in to charge and turned on the oven. Frozen pizza tonight, but she'd bought an actual salad to eat with it. Feeling almost pleased with herself, she opened her front door and sat on the top step. The night sky was quiet; calm and clear. There were hardly ever clouds here at night. She felt an urge to take a walk. The oven was craptacular and would take at least twenty minutes to heat up, so she unplugged her phone, put it in her pocket and pulled the door closed behind her.

Wondering if there would be any calls tonight, she walked towards the corner of the main street, where Margaret's bench looked down on the expansive plain with the lake and hospital off to the side.

Sure enough, her phone rang as soon as she sat down. It seemed very loud in the still night and she answered it without checking the caller ID.

'Daniella?'

It was Mark. Daniella felt her throat close up. She didn't know what to say to him. She knew she'd been avoiding him, and prepared herself for him to be angry or hurt.

'Hi, Mark,' she got out.

'I missed you the last two nights. Everything all right?' He sounded neither angry nor hurt.

'I'm fine.' She didn't know how to ask him about their relationship without seeming jealous; she didn't yet understand what they were to each other, whether she even had the right to be.

'I can hear everything's not okay,' he said, sounding worried. 'What happened? Something at work?'

'Is there . . . anything going on between you and Stephanie Morgan?' she blurted. Her throat stung.

'No. Where did you get that idea?'

She couldn't think of a way to explain what had happened at the supermarket. 'Are you sure?' she croaked. She looked out towards the horizon, to that little bump she knew was Ryders Station.

He laughed. 'How would I be unsure about something like that?'

'Sorry, that's not what I meant . . . dammit.'

His voice was serious as he continued, 'I would never lie to you. And I sure as hell wouldn't be seeing two girls at once. Jesus.' He sounded scandalised, then sighed. 'Look, we went out a few times before she moved to Townsville, years ago. It never came to anything and I was happy to leave it there. Do I need to have a talk with Steph – did she say something?'

'Oh no, please don't. I might have already stuck my foot in it. Besides, aren't you too busy? Someone said you didn't have time for anything but the station.'

'Someone?'

'Yes. Not saying who.'

Mark laughed shortly. 'Not going to give in, huh? I can admire that.' Then he cleared his throat. 'Okay, here's how it is. The Morgans have a stake in the station. Three years ago we needed cash just to keep the place going and the banks wouldn't lend us any. We'd had a long drought, and then a big fire came through. We had to rebuild fences and a shed, and feed the cattle while the grass recovered. The Morgans offered to step in, and we didn't have any other options. My connection with Steph – it's business. That's all there is to it.'

Daniella was struck by the matter-of-fact way he relayed

these huge things. Drought. Fire. All part of his life. 'Oh,' she said, unsure what else to say.

'Daniella, I really like you. I *make* time for you. I want to see you again.'

She took a breath, remembering his kisses. 'I'd like that, too,' she said. She was amazed how quickly he'd reassured her. She wished he was there right now so she could lean into his warmth, his strength, and tell him some of the reasons she was uncertain about being involved with him. She quickly changed the subject. 'Hey, you know where I am right now?'

'Where?'

'Sitting on the bench on the main road, looking at Ryders.'

He sighed again. 'I'd love to show you the station. Are you rostered on this weekend?'

Daniella groaned, remembering the approaching dinner. 'Actually, I'm not. But Dr Harris wants me to give a dinner party – he's taken over the weekend roster so I'll have time to prepare.' He had even insisted on taking over her usual Saturday afternoon house call to Valerie Turner. To her own surprise, Daniella was almost sad about that. She wanted to find out what had happened with the letter. 'But I'll probably only need Sunday to prepare,' she went on.

'So, Saturday? Pick you up at eight?'

Daniella looked at her watch, a reflex whenever time was mentioned. 'Sure . . . uh-oh.'

'What?' he asked.

'I left the oven on at home – I completely forgot.'

He laughed. 'Good start.'

Daniella had to laugh too as she ran back to the house, where she found not a disaster but the oven at the perfect temperature. She hoped it was a sign of good things to come.

Chapter 13

On Saturday morning, Mark turned up promptly at eight. This time, the battered Rover was nowhere in sight; instead he pulled up in a very dusty white Commodore SS ute. Daniella eyed it off as she locked the house door. With its streamlined body, low-profile tyres, huge bullbar studded with spotlights, and CAT in orange on the rear mudflaps, it looked reckless and uncontrollable. Aiden had been into cars like this before he'd joined the army, and she'd always worried about him driving them.

Mark stepped out to greet her, and Daniella pursed her lips to stop herself from smiling crazily. Wow. Talk about performance body. His blue jeans were like a second skin, and the sleeves of his checked shirt were rolled up, showing thick biceps. His sandy hair was ruffled as if he'd just run his hand through it; she'd noticed he did that when he seemed nervous or was thinking.

'Nice car,' she said carefully.

He made no effort to suppress his own smile as he opened the passenger door for her. Daniella had to admit, the seats were spectacular – deep and enveloping. She dropped her bag and the old battered felt hat to the floor and leaned back.

'My brother's,' explained Mark, as he climbed back in the driver's side. He twisted the key and the engine growled to life.

'Doesn't look like something from a cattle station,' she said, running her eyes over the stitching on the gearstick, extra dials and custom dash-mounted units.

He gave her a sidelong glance. 'No. Very impractical. The cattle grids – oh man. But Dad took the Rover and the stockmen took the other two cars, so I was stuck with it. All the other vehicles on the station are just bush-bashers – unregistered.'

'Is that a radar scanner?'

'Yeah.' He pointed at the different dials: 'Separate oil gauge, fuel-line flow meter, emergency frequency scanner. Wouldn't surprise me if Will had a satellite phone in here too.' He pulled slowly away from the shoulder and threw a U-turn to head to the highway.

'I thought your brother was away in Isa?'

'He is. Do you know what circle work is?'

Daniella shook her head.

'You want me to show you?' He gave her a wicked grin.

Daniella felt a surge of dangerous excitement, but she quickly tamped it down. 'Um, maybe you can just tell me?'

Mark grinned. 'Probably for the best. My brother was the one who was really into it. He taught me, but I was never as good. It's basically burning out, round and round, turning the loop tighter and tighter. Will's really good. He used to do demos at the ute musters and B&S balls. This car was his favourite.'

'Did he get a new one?'

'Sorta. He got a Pathfinder. That's a four-wheel-drive. In Isa, all the mine boys make good money and spend it on cars like this. There's not a lot to do on weekends, so they take 'em racing out on the highway. Been some bad smashes. Will got out of that stuff all of a sudden. I think he realised what a risk it was, and it's easier to avoid temptation if he doesn't have this thing in his driveway.'

Daniella nodded. 'Good move.'

They hit the highway and the ute growled its way to a hundred, where it sat comfortably for the next fifteen minutes. Then Mark took an unmarked turn north onto a narrow sealed road. After two minutes it turned into a dirt road, not unlike the one to the dam but in better repair. Mark explained that they had to keep it well graded for the cattle roadtrains that regularly visited the station.

They drove for a while in silence, and then Mark slowed as they came up a hill.

Daniella leaned forward in her seat. Just over the ridge, in the shelter of the hill, was a sprawling honey-coloured stone homestead. It had large dark windows behind deep verandahs and a pale roof that was the same colour as the clouds dotting the sky. It faced the wide plain that seemed tacked to the distant horizon, and was flanked on each side by sheds and outbuildings. Some were new, made of Colorbond; others were older and worn with weathered wooden walls and corrugated-iron roofs. A short distance away was a cluster of fenced yards; Daniella could see that the road continued around the ridge, behind the sheds to the edge of the yards, where it joined a fence line. In a fenced paddock, three horses tugged at the grass. To Daniella, the land was a perfect curve holding the house and its familiars, and echoing the sky above; two concavities joined only at the horizon.

'Oh, it's lovely,' she said.

Mark pulled up in an otherwise empty carport. Opening the doors, they emerged into the silence. Daniella heard a crow call, but then nothing at all. She was aware of her feet on the earth, of the land and sky surrounding her. Mark put an arm around her shoulders.

'It's so quiet . . . where is everyone?' she asked.

'Well, the stockmen are driving one of the herds down from the middle paddock. They won't arrive until tomorrow morning at the earliest. We've got cutting out and tagging to do this week. Dad's gone to the saleyards. Kath's probably down in her cottage.'

'Ah,' said Daniella. She cleared her throat. 'Where does it end?' She pointed towards the long fields below them.

Mark scratched his head. 'You can't actually see the edge of it from here.'

Daniella looked at him, astounded. She couldn't believe that everything she could see belonged to the station. 'Wait – I thought you could see the town?'

Mark gently turned her towards the west. 'Not quite from here – you have to go up the ridge a little. But, technically . . . the town's on our land.'

'Really?'

He nodded, his green eyes sparkling. She saw how much he loved the place. He was proud of it. Daniella found it overwhelming, and not just its sheer size. The blue sky made her throat pulse, and she wanted to draw the air into her, to smell the dusky grey-green grass and the red ochre dirt. The weight of so much space slowed her mind.

She sighed deeply. 'This is amazing, Mark.'

He took her hand, warm palm to palm. 'Come and see the house?'

The homestead was as beautiful inside as it was out. Mark took her through the kitchen, the dining room, the offices, and finally to the lounge with its vast open fireplace and framed photos. Daniella admired the rooms, tastefully decorated with antiques that set off the warm wooden floors and exquisite rugs. Many of the pieces had an exotic flavour to them, carved with elephants or jaguars. She stopped to look at a beautiful teak-wood chest with snarling faces carved into its lid and sides.

'I think I told you Mum liked to travel,' Mark explained. 'She brought things back. Kath complains they take a lot of time to clean.'

Daniella turned to look at him. He was leaning against the big mantelpiece, comfortable and at home. Daniella sensed the memories all around her; Mark was a result of all this. He had a heritage: he knew where he came from and where he belonged. It made her feel strangely adrift. Her family was scattered. Her career anchored her, but that felt new and tenuous compared to the heritage of this place. She and Mark shared one similarity – they had both followed their father's profession. But in almost every other respect, his world was both foreign and alluring. She breathed out.

She pointed to a closed door in the far corner of the room. 'Where does that go?'

'Which one?' he asked. Without taking his eyes off her, he stepped forward and pulled her towards him.

'That one.' She pointed again.

'It's a hallway,' he teased.

'Hallway to where?'

He tightened his arms around her. She could feel the tension in his body, his focus on her complete. Her heart pounded. His green eyes caressed her face as he raised one hand and carefully tucked her hair back behind her ear.

'Bedrooms,' he whispered.

A smile flickered across his face, and Daniella felt again the abandon she had felt in his car. Unable to stop herself, she slipped her arms around his neck. 'Oh yes?' she responded.

His face grew very serious, and he kissed her, tentatively, his soft lips moving over hers. Daniella felt her body go faint with desire. She kissed him back, gently caressing his mouth.

Familiarity came fast; there were no awkward first moments such as she could remember with other boyfriends, when teeth clashed and embarrassed laughter ensued. Mark was all beautiful rhythm, his movements perfectly attuned to hers. Soon, their kisses were deep and hungry, his tongue moving in her mouth and exciting her as nothing had ever done before. She pressed herself into him, feeling her own softness against his solid muscle; if his arms hadn't been holding her up, she thought she might have melted into the floor.

But at a certain point, it could not go on like this. Such passion demanded they must either begin to undress, or stop entirely. In a pause, Daniella looked into Mark's eyes and saw he knew it too. He was waiting for her to make the choice. She stopped. If it had been starlight and not daylight, she considered it could have gone either way. But the sun was high, the house unfamiliar.

'You are so lovely,' he whispered, resting his forehead against hers. Daniella couldn't speak.

They made lunch in the big farmhouse kitchen, joking and kissing each other between getting the bread and mayonnaise and sliced roast beef. They took the sandwiches outside and sat on the verandah, watching the horses turn lazily around the paddock. Daniella commented again on how beautiful and peaceful it was compared to the city.

'I know,' said Mark. 'It always struck me, coming back. Actually, I've been wondering if we could make more use of that.'

'How do you mean?'

'After the drought and the fire, the herd was really depleted. We're building it up again now, but the thing is, there's always going to be ups and downs. I'd like to set up more sources of income, ways to iron out the peaks and troughs a bit. I've been thinking that maybe people would pay to visit the place. That'd help when something else goes wrong unexpectedly. We're far away from anything here, and we have to be self-reliant, plan ahead.'

Daniella nodded. 'Yeah, I didn't realise until I came here how different it is. In the clinic we have to think of ways to do things you don't need to think about in the city. Dr Harris said he used to deliver babies when he first came here. But the service wouldn't support him for the insurance, so now the women have to go to Mount Isa or somewhere miles away like that.'

Daniella stopped. She sounded like Dr Harris himself.

But Mark was nodding. 'Yeah, that's it. But we know that's how it is, so the key is to be smart about it. Plus,' he paused and gave a cheeky smile, 'this place is incredible and I want to make sure it's still here to show off in the future.'

Daniella laughed. 'Well, you should see the number of grey nomads we get coming through the clinic, in search of the "real Australia". Maybe they don't have to continue on to Isa – it's right here.'

Mark's eyebrows drew together thoughtfully. 'Yes, that's something I've been thinking about. We could maybe do tours in a chopper – we use it for work anyway. But I'd also like to find ways for us to survive as a farm, not just a destination. I've heard of a few things people are doing, diversifying their business; technology stuff.'

They bounced ideas back and forth for a while, Daniella remembering tourism ads she'd read in the paper from Brisbane, and Mark telling her some of the things he'd begun to discuss with Cat. As they talked, he put his arms around her again, and she enjoyed the excitement of having his body next to hers.

Finally, when they reached a natural lull, Daniella's gaze returned to the horses. 'I used to go riding, years ago.'

'Yeah?' he prompted her.

'Mum was into showing – Dad kept the photos of her. As soon as I was old enough, I went to the same riding school she'd gone to. But when I got to high school I had to give it up – too busy studying. I learned English-style,' she added apologetically. 'I saw the rodeos when they came in, but I've never ridden stock, or western.'

Mark stretched out his long legs. 'It's not that different.'

He got up, and took her on a long walk down to the paddocks and the yards. Daniella ran her hands over the tubular railings around the yards and laughed as they ran up the cattle loader ramp. They wandered along the line of sheds and Mark showed her the chopper they used for mustering and fence checking. To Daniella, it looked like a big plexiglass bubble set on two skids with a two-bladed rotor. It was much smaller than the emergency evacuation choppers she'd seen in Brisbane. Then again, she reminded herself, this wasn't used for transporting patients.

By the time they returned to the homestead, late in the afternoon, she could feel the dirt between her fingers and wanted to wash her hands. Mark showed her to the main bathroom so she could clean up.

She peered in surprise at her dusty face in the mirror. For the first time in a long while, she didn't look tired. Even once she'd cleaned her face, her eyes were bright, the blue end of grey, like the evening sky. She smiled at herself.

After knocking, Mark came in behind her and kissed her on the neck. 'Have I told you how gorgeous you are?' he murmured.

Daniella leaned back into him, feeling playful. 'No . . .'

He nodded earnestly against her skin. 'Since that night at the tav – I turned around and there you were. Then I saw you in the hospital, watched you work. Such skilled hands.' He caught her right hand and kissed the fingers. 'Want to go for a drive?'

'Where to?' She watched him in the mirror, his large body wrapped around her, protective and powerful. She didn't want the moment to end.

'Down the ridge a little. Show you the view.'

It was only a short drive. As the sun went down they sat in the ute's tray on an old but clean foam mattress. Behind them, the eucalypts whispered softly on the spine of the ridge, but overhead was nothing but stars.

'This is the most relaxed I've ever felt,' Daniella marvelled. The clinic seemed so far away. Even what had happened in Brisbane before she'd come here felt removed, hidden behind a veil. She pushed at the barrier, and it held. She found she could choose not to relive the guilt of that night.

As the chill crept in, Mark pulled a bag out of the ute's cab. He unpacked a padded swag for them to lean against, and spread out a blanket that smelled wonderfully of horses. Then he pulled her into his side. It felt so perfect.

'How long has this place been in your family?' she asked.

He told her the story. In the 1850s, his many times great-grandfather had first settled the station, his sons seeing a prosperous enterprise and growing town over the next fifty years. Then disaster had struck – a major drought whittled all the resources and forced the Walkers off the land, returning to England. Mark's grandfather had been born in the 1920s and had lost both his parents during the Second World War. When it was over, he'd come to Australia as a young man with nothing, dreaming of the property in his father's stories. He'd married, learned all he could about grazing and worked his hands to stumps to make good. He and his wife had been frugal, both taught by the austerity of the Depression and war. When the opportunity came, they realised their dream, reclaiming Ryders for the Walkers. Their children, including Mark's father, had been born on the station.

'Dad was always going to stay here. But after he met Mum they moved around for a while. She was a teacher and did a lot of relieving.' There was a pause. 'Daniella, that night I first called you, when you were sitting on the bench up by the main road . . .'

'Yes?'

'Did you look at the plaque on the bench?'

'Yes. I think it said, *For Margaret, who loved this place—*' She saw the look on his face. 'Oh . . . Margaret was your mother?'

Mark took a slow breath. 'That's where she used to sit, looking at the station. She said in her will that she wanted a plaque put there, to record how much she loved the place.' He took Daniella's face in his hands. 'I don't believe in fate. But, Christ, I wondered that night. When I went outside to look at the stars I was thinking about her, wondering what to do about the station, what she would have told me. And then I started thinking about you. I wanted to apologise for Dad, but that was only an excuse. I wanted to know more about you. I don't usually get reception down on the ridge, but that night I did. I called you and then you told me where you were, right in her spot. I haven't stopped thinking about you since then.'

Daniella was breathless; she had never had a man speak to her so openly, without embarrassment, and without alcohol. But when he looked at her, when he kissed her and she felt his passion, she had no choice but to believe him. Her heart thundered. 'Mark, I've never felt like this before. I don't know what to say,' she admitted.

'Then don't say anything.'

They kissed again, only this time there was no lightness, no hesitation. He was fierce in his gentleness, worshipping her with his lips and tongue. Daniella unbuttoned his shirt, marvelling at the flat planes of his pec muscles, the tight washboard stomach. Trying to slow down her raging desire, she found herself feeling for his heartbeat, naming the muscles under her fingers.

'What are you doing?' he asked.

Daniella bit her lip, embarrassed. Then she confessed that she was practising anatomy.

He burst out laughing. 'All right, Dr Bell, let me test you . . . What's this one?' He ran his fingertips across her lips, and then proceeded to ask all the Latin names for the things he wanted to touch. Some of them she couldn't remember; or, at least, she couldn't find the breath to voice them as his lips moved down her neck to her naked chest.

'What about this?' he asked, his tongue finding the sensitive tip of her breast.

'Areola,' she gasped.

He kissed his way back up to her mouth so they could move their naked skin together again. Daniella felt his belt buckle against her belly.

'Test me some more,' she whispered.

'But you've already named everything,' he teased, gently biting the base of her neck, sending shudders up her spine.

'Not everywhere.' She pushed him onto his side and reached for his belt, undid it and slowly pulled it from the loops of his jeans. He watched her from hooded eyelids. Then he tucked an index finger into her jeans and pulled her towards him.

'Ah, doctor,' he said thickly, as he eased the denim down over her hips. 'I see you need further testing.'

'You're next,' she warned. And he laughed and pulled her into his arms.

~

Morning brought a sprinkle of dew. Mark woke in the back of the ute with Daniella in his arms, both of them still naked under the blanket and swag. He put an arm up behind his head. It was probably already seven, but he wasn't moving yet. Ultimately, he knew they would both get hungry, or someone would need him, but for now he wanted this to be all there was in the world.

Daniella was the most amazing woman he had ever met. She was gorgeous, curious, intelligent and driven; she excited him like no other woman ever had. He wanted to do things with her – and not just physically like last night; he wanted more. He wanted to build things with her. Help her with her work. He wanted her to love the station, maybe even as he did. He wanted her to feel that she had a home here . . .

Except . . . dammit. He knew these were only his dreams for them both. What were her plans for her life? How would she feel about being drawn into the demands of this place? He looked down at her. Her light brown hair had flared out over her bare shoulder. Her skin glowed like the sunset on the dam on a red-sky night. She was beautiful and talented and from somewhere else.

He made a soft groan in his throat, then leaned down and kissed her gently. Her eyelids fluttered as she woke. He watched as she blinked, registering where she was. Then memories of the night before must have flooded back, and her cheeks flushed.

'Good morning,' he whispered.

'Morning,' she said with a sleepy smile, snuggling shyly against him. 'What time is it?'

'Hmm . . . I think it's about seven.'

'And it's Sunday, isn't it?' she asked, with a tone that said she hoped it wasn't.

'I'm afraid so. Why?' He stroked her hair.

'I'm giving the dinner party tonight. I have to do all the shopping and cooking. And first, I actually need to think of something to cook!'

'Can I help?' Mark offered, looking for an excuse to spend more time with her.

'Umm . . . maybe. Can you come? I might need someone to say it's edible.'

'I'd love to,' he said. 'Come back to the house and raid the cookbooks.'

Mark drove them back to the homestead, and gave Daniella the run of the bathroom while he raided Kath's bookshelf. Or, at least, that's what he'd intended to do. In reality, he spent a fair bit of time in the shower with her, before he left her to wash her hair and went to find what he promised was a fantastic lasagne recipe.

When Daniella emerged ten minutes later, dressed but still wet-haired, she found Mark in the kitchen, thumbing through Country Women's Association recipes. Then she heard a car pulling up outside and a minute later, William Walker came through the door, a rolled-up catalogue under one arm. On his home turf, he looked even more imposing than he had at the hospital. When he saw her, surprise flickered in his eyes, and Daniella felt like disappearing into the pantry.

'Good trip?' Mark asked his father, as if there was nothing unusual about Daniella being in the house.

'It was all right,' said William, looking expectantly from Daniella to Mark.

'Dad, you remember Daniella Bell? She looked after Dave after the rugby. I've been showing her round the station,' said Mark, putting an arm around her shoulders.

'I remember,' said William, extending a hand to Daniella. 'William Walker.' They shook stiffly. Daniella was sure he was looking at her damp hair.

'Daniella's from Brisbane,' Mark went on, filling the silence.

'I see,' said William. 'Where did you work down there?'

'The PA, and the Princess Mary,' she said automatically.

William nodded, some kind of recognition registering in his eyes, but no warmth. 'And where will you be moving to next?' he asked.

'Um,' she stumbled, taken aback. 'I have no plans to go anywhere.'

At this, William Walker took the catalogue from under his arm and refolded it. 'Well,' he said, glancing at Mark. 'Take care.' He strode off down the hallway.

Daniella felt Mark stiffen beside her, then he kissed her lips. 'Sorry about that,' he said. When she looked at him questioningly, he went on, 'Don't worry about it. Let's go.'

Chapter 14

By six thirty, Daniella finally began to relax. Dr Harris's kitchen was certainly far better appointed than the one in her health-service house, and the lasagne – Mark's recipe – had come together well. The béchamel sauce hadn't gone lumpy; the mince mixture was stuffed with basil she'd discovered at the bottom of the supermarket's fresh vegie fridge (Becky had helped with that one); and she'd bought enough pasta sheets to fill the dish Dr Harris had produced. Now, the cheese was happily bubbling in the oven, and it smelled amazing.

As the small group chatted at the kitchen bench, Daniella put together the side salad. Dr Harris had invited Mac and Susan Westerland, who were staying in town for a few days to be close to the hospital while they tried out Sarah's new treatment. In the living room, Sarah and Jamie were happily playing with Dr Harris's extensive toy collection – brought down from the clinic reception – and Jackie and the Westerlands knew each other very well now from their many visits to the clinic.

The doorbell rang and Daniella downed tools to answer it. 'Don't touch that,' she called ineffectually to Dr Harris, who had swooped and taken over the salad faster than a vulture on a highway carcass. She didn't really care, because she knew who had rung the bell.

She opened the door to find Mark, her tall handsome Mark, looking perfect in bone-coloured trousers, RM Williams boots and a blue shirt, smelling clean and fresh and familiar.

'Hi,' she said softly, feeling the blush in her cheeks.

'Hi.' He kissed her as though he hadn't seen her for a week. Conscious of the guests at the other end of the hall, she tried to pull away, but he only kissed her harder.

'Here,' he said, finally releasing her and handing over a bottle of wine.

'You weren't supposed to bring anything!'

'It's not entirely altruistic. I don't like red, and I wanted to get rid of it. Dr Harris loves it and besides, it's rude to come empty-handed.'

Mark and his manners. She laughed. 'Come on in.' She led him along to the kitchen.

'Mark, my dear boy. It's been too long,' said Dr Harris.

Mark and the Westerlands were obviously old friends, and he was soon talking with Mac about cattle exports. Jackie and Susan were swapping notes on their children. Daniella looked around and rubbed her arms; Dr Harris had gone to take a call and everything was ready to go.

Mark glanced towards her. 'Daniella?' He beckoned her over to the dining table. 'I was just telling Mac you'd been to see the station.'

'That's great,' said Mac. 'Ryders is fantastic country. Ours is better, of course, but the Walkers' place is closer to town.' He gave a cheeky grin and the men exchanged a few good-natured digs about whose property was superior. Mark drew her into the conversation; Mac wanted to know what she'd thought of the set-up at Ryders, if she had any ideas how the health service could better serve them all out on the stations, and what she thought of telemedicine. All the while, Mark had his arm around her, making their connection clear to everyone.

When Daniella had to go back to the kitchen to check the oven, she felt light and airy. She was fitting in, managing a social situation (albeit a small one) without disaster, and Mark was hers.

Jackie and Susan both followed her into the kitchen and out of general earshot.

'I've never seen him like this,' said Jackie, clearly amazed.

'You look so good together, if you don't mind me saying so,' said Susan. 'Anyway, I'm so glad you're staying in Ryders Ridge.'

Daniella didn't mind, except for the part about her staying, which tugged uncomfortably, but nothing could dent her happiness right now. She was even starting to think – quite irrationally, she reminded herself – about whether this could be home after all.

The lasagne came out of the oven on cue at seven, a magnificent, golden-brown-crusted thing. Everyone gathered round to issue the obligatory praise. Daniella duly redirected the compliments to Dr Harris's oven, which had perfect air circulation.

They were about to sit down when the doorbell rang again. Dr Harris looked at Daniella. 'Were you expecting anyone else?' She shook her head. 'Could be a clinic call then. Excuse me. Please start.'

He went off down the hall. Daniella carried the lasagne dish to the table on the deck where Mark was pouring wine into Dr Harris's glass, which he managed to do while pressing a kiss to her cheek. She had her back to the hall, and Mark's arm was still around her waist when he looked around and went still. Daniella felt a qualm and turned.

Coming down the hall after Dr Harris was Dave, and behind him, Stephanie and Maria Morgan.

Initially, Daniella felt oddly calm, almost as though she was under water. Then the questions began. What was happening? Was she at the wrong dinner? Dr Harris gave her an apologetic shrug, then squeezed her shoulder. 'I'm sure we have enough,' he whispered.

Daniella saw Dave's eyes track sideways to the lounge where Sarah and Jamie were now sprawled on the couch, then flick to Jackie. She saw Stephanie's gaze fall on Mark's arm around her.

Stephanie inserted herself at the table on Mark's other side. 'Dani, thanks so much for having us, and sorry we're late.'

Daniella bit her tongue. A small frown settled between Mark's brows. Dave hovered as if unsure where to sit.

'Dave, there's a space next to Jackie,' said Stephanie. 'I want to chat to Mark about the Isa rodeo.'

So Dave sat, but the conversation no longer flowed easily, even with Dr Harris chatting smoothly as he collected more settings. Daniella escaped to the kitchen to help him with the plates and cutlery. She had a sinking feeling. The mood was definitely black between Dave and Jackie. What the hell had happened at the B&S?

She felt a warm hand on her back. 'Let me help with those,' said Mark, taking the plates. 'Are you all right?'

'Freaking out – this wasn't in the plan,' she admitted, then dropped her voice. 'Did Dave and Jackie have a fight about something? They look like they hate each other.'

'No idea. But look, don't worry about it. Everything'll be fine.' He took the plates, leaving her alone with Dr Harris.

'Did you invite them?' Daniella whispered desperately to him.

'No, my dear. It's possible they mistook the date. I invited them next week. Then again,' he said more quietly, 'deliberate misunderstandings have occurred.'

The night went rapidly off track, at least as far as Daniella was concerned. Nothing was overtly wrong, but silences came too often, wafting from both Maria and Stephanie. Mark did his best to open up the conversation, but Stephanie seemed determined to keep him in a verbal headlock, monopolising his attention. Daniella was constantly up and down, offering to refill glasses and clearing empty plates to make room at the table, which wasn't big enough to easily accommodate so many guests. Mac and Susan tried to engage Dave and Jackie, but they both seemed unusually quiet, more intent on ignoring each other. Daniella felt Maria watching her more than once.

'This is excellent,' said Mark, in praise of the lasagne. Mac agreed.

'It is. I'm just surprised you don't like the local beef,' said Stephanie.

Daniella blushed. 'It is local. I made sure I asked.'

'Oh. Well, it's a bit hard to tell with mince.'

Mark shot Stephanie a frown, but she was already chatting about something else and was oblivious. Daniella had no idea how to handle Stephanie's animosity; she couldn't very well repeat her supermarket performance in front of Dr Harris. She just wanted the night to end. In the meantime, she once again escaped to the kitchen to take some deep breaths.

As she was returning to the deck, she heard Stephanie ask, 'Jackie, how old is Jamie now?'

'He'll be three in a few weeks,' said Jackie stiffly.

'Wow, he's getting big!' Stephanie went on. 'I haven't seen him in such a long time. Can he come out to the table for a while?'

Jackie took a long drink of water. Even though she didn't understand what was going on here, Daniella could sense how upset Jackie was. She sat down at the table again. 'He's sleeping, Steph,' she said quickly, earning a grateful glance from Jackie.

'Oh, well then.' Stephanie looked briefly put out, but then she beamed at Daniella. 'You were telling us last time you're from Brisbane, isn't that right, Dani?'

'That's right,' said Daniella.

'And you're from a medical family, aren't you?' asked Maria.

'My father's a surgeon,' Daniella said flatly. 'Now, would anyone like—'

Stephanie interrupted, 'Quite a famous surgeon by all accounts.' She then proceeded to lay out a fair few of Peter Bell's career achievements, which unnerved Daniella no end. She must have googled him.

The night seemed interminable but to Daniella's surprise, it was only eight thirty when Mac and Susan made their apologies, carrying away a sleeping Sarah. Jackie escaped to the lounge to check on Jamie, then left shortly after. Stephanie was reluctant to leave without Mark, until he told her pointedly he'd see them outside.

Once the Morgans had gone down to their car, he turned to her. But Dave got in first. 'I'm so sorry, Daniella. I was told we'd been invited. The food was really good.'

She waved a hand weakly. 'It's fine,' she said.

Mark's mood was thunderous; Daniella could feel the anger coursing through him as he hugged her.

Dave went to walk out. 'No, stay,' Mark said. 'You'd better walk me down.'

'Why?' Dave asked.

''Cause otherwise there's a chance I'll knock them both out.' Mark kissed Daniella swiftly. 'I'll call you. I'm going to sort this out.'

And then he was gone, leaving Daniella with the crusty baking dish. She looked at the rim of burnt cheese. The whole evening felt like that; once so filled with promise, now hollowed out.

Dr Harris had already started on the cleaning up. He saw her face. 'Don't let it worry you, my dear. I think you did very well.'

Daniella couldn't help but feel that didn't really matter. Her earlier happiness now felt like an illusion. And she started to wonder what more might be in store.

'Oh, Daniella,' said Dr Harris, as if he could hear her thoughts. 'I saw Valerie Turner yesterday. That ulcer is looking much better. She asked for you to call in tomorrow. Take it as your last appointment for the day. I'm glad she likes you.'

'I'm not sure she does,' said Daniella, but too quietly for Dr Harris to hear.

Jackie swapped the Monday shift with Roselyn, but in the afternoon she rang to ask Daniella over that evening. Relieved to hear from her, Daniella said she'd come after her appointment with Valerie Turner.

At five o'clock she duly found Valerie on the same couch, in the same position. This time, though, the television was off, and she had a kitchen tray and several pieces of paper in her lap. The kelpie was sprawled on the floor and gave Daniella a baleful look as she walked in. The room smelled of industrial cleaner.

'Shoes off,' said Valerie. 'Carpet's just been done.'

Daniella slipped off her flats and padded in with her kit.

'Don't need that today,' said Valerie, and she pushed a handwritten page at her. 'You'll have to read that,' she said. 'And mind you remember your doctor–patient privilege.'

'Bruce wrote back?' asked Daniella, taking up the paper, noting the neat handwriting.

'Read, read,' said Valerie.

'*Dear Mum*,' Daniella read obediently. '*Thanks for your letter. I took it with me on a trip to Cairns and I'm writing back as I sit in the airport waiting to go home.*'

Valerie snorted. 'As if I wanted to know that.' Then, when Daniella paused, 'Well, keep going then.'

Daniella read the rest of the letter, which mostly described the business trip Bruce had been on, without mentioning any of the business itself. He said he'd taken a hike behind the Tablelands, and he described the landscape there, which he said reminded him of the country around Ryders Ridge, and then the way it suddenly changed from plains to rainforest west of Atherton.

'*I hope you'll write again soon, and I hope you'll reconsider my offer to come and see us here for Christmas. Much love, Bruce*,' finished Daniella.

'Hmph,' said Valerie, but Daniella could see how much the letter meant to her. Bruce's descriptions of the landscape had reminded Daniella of the station Mark had shown her on Saturday, and she had a sudden longing to see him.

'What are you thinking about?' asked Valerie, as if noting her distraction.

'About Ryders Station,' said Daniella before she could stop herself.

Valerie was onto her in a flash. 'Ryders Station? So you *are* seeing that Walker boy. The cleaner was talking about that, and I usually have a hard time getting anything out of her.'

Daniella turned red. 'We've been out a few times.'

Valerie actually cackled, then looked serious again. 'Bet William Walker's pleased about that.'

Daniella raised her eyebrows. 'Not entirely. I've only met him twice, but I don't think he likes me.'

'Of course not.'

Daniella waited for a moment, but Valerie offered nothing more.

'I had to give a dinner party last night at Dr Harris's,' Daniella continued, taking the blank sheets from Valerie's tray without being asked. 'It didn't turn out overly well.'

'Did you poison them? Imagine you're not much of a cook,' declared Valerie, but with less malice than normal.

Daniella bristled. 'The food was fine. But the Morgans invited themselves and so it turned into a squeeze.'

After this, Valerie demanded a blow-by-blow account of the evening, and of her encounter with William Walker at Ryders. Then Daniella was mortified as Valerie made her transcribe a great deal of it into the letter to Bruce. Valerie dismissed all her protests, and once again insisted on keeping the letter.

At least by the time Daniella finally managed to get away, explaining that she was expected at Jackie's, Valerie seemed to be in what passed for good spirits. She even hauled herself up on her stick and shuffled with Daniella to the door.

'Friends with that nurse, then, are you?' she asked before Daniella could escape.

'Yes,' said Daniella warily, wondering what criticisms Valerie would make of Jackie.

'Good,' said Valerie unexpectedly. 'Hard to be doing what she's doing, raising that little boy all alone, and everyone talking behind her back about who the fella was. Think it's their business, but it isn't. I know something about that.'

Daniella nodded, surprised and feeling a kernel of liking for the old woman. Encouraged, she asked a question that had been nagging at her. 'Mrs Turner, why wouldn't William Walker like me? You seemed like you had an idea.'

Valerie gave her a shrewd look. 'Because he won't like any woman he thinks will make his son choose between her and that station. Had that enough with his wife.'

And so Daniella went out into the night with that knowledge turning in her mind. She felt partly reassured; perhaps William's dislike wasn't personal. And, she told herself, it was a long way from coming to Mark making such a choice.

Daniella arrived at Jackie's just as she was putting a sleepy Jamie to bed. Jackie looked tired herself, and upset.

'I'll just wait out here,' Daniella said.

'No, no, come and listen,' said Jackie, her voice high with unspilled tears. Wondering what was going on, Daniella went and sat in the corner chair in Jamie's room.

Jackie read Jamie's favourite Thomas the Tank Engine story until the little boy was asleep, his dark curls framing his face. Jackie sighed and stroked his hair. Then she put the book aside. She didn't look at Daniella.

'Let me tell you another story,' she said in a low voice, as if she were still talking to Jamie. 'Once upon a time there was a girl in a small town who liked a boy she knew at school. The girl went away because she wanted to study. The boy didn't want her to leave, but she was determined. Then, one day, the boy showed up in Brisbane. The girl was really excited, because she'd just finished her exams. She really liked the boy – his name was Dave – and she thought she could have everything. She wasn't careful enough.'

'Oh God, Jackie.' Daniella saw it now. So that was why they were always distant with each other. Jackie got up. She put a finger to her lips and they went out into the hall.

Daniella put her arms around her friend. 'Why didn't you tell me?'

Jackie sniffed and Daniella grabbed a handful of tissues from the box on top of the TV. She sat Jackie down on the sofa.

'Because – because . . .' sobbed Jackie. 'Stupid reasons. Dave . . . he was wilder back then, and he was living down the coast finishing his pilot training. After I found out about Jamie, I told Dave and he wanted us to be together. But I wasn't sure – I didn't want it to just be about obligation, and then I heard about things he was doing behind my back, playing around. We had a big fight and I told him I never wanted to see him again. I was so upset, and Mum was here so I came home. Dave came back too, but I didn't want to see him. He travels all over with the flying and his other work he does, and I don't think anything's changed – he's still out all the time. I didn't want to be hurt like that; I couldn't do it. Jamie looks so much like me no one has guessed. Even Mum gave up asking about who the father was.'

Daniella was appalled at Jackie's heartbreak.

Jackie blew her nose. 'In a moment of rage I even shredded Jamie's birth certificate,' she admitted. 'So no one could find out. I guess I'll have to replace it before he needs it for something.' She laughed a little, then her eyes welled up again. 'I didn't have any money back then. And I resented Dave for the whole situation, too – I knew it was unfair, but I couldn't help it. The more he argued he wanted to help financially, the more I pushed him away. Eventually, he left me alone.'

'What happened at the ball last week?'

'We actually had about five minutes of civil conversation. You see, when he was hurt at the rugby I was really worried about him. I hardly ever see him, but he always gets my heart in knots. I didn't even give him a hard time when he called me afterwards, asking for your number – I didn't realise it was for Mark. But then, at the B&S, Steph started hovering around and butting in, trying to talk to Dave about Ryders. I was pissed off and wanted him to just tell her to bugger off, but he didn't. And that old anger came back, you know . . .

like when I was pregnant and I really wanted things to work out between us, but then I'd hear about him seeing other girls.' She shook her head, remembering. 'Look, I love Jamie to bits, but given a do-over? It'd be so different.'

Daniella held Jackie as she cried.

'You can't tell anyone about this, right?' Jackie said finally. 'You're the first person I thought I could tell.'

Daniella rolled her eyes. 'Do you even have to say that? I'll take it to the grave.' She put her hand on her heart and stuck out her tongue, playing dead.

Jackie laughed. But Daniella was troubled by the story. It seemed utterly wrong that Jackie should be bearing all of this alone. She thought for a moment.

'Jackie . . . I'd like to help you more with your training. I know I promised to ask my friends, but I remembered someone else I know who works in the scholarships area. Maybe there's some assistance you could apply for. If you really want to go, I think you should. Jamie's a bit older now. You'll make it work. You're amazing, what you've done till now.'

Jackie took a big breath. 'Sure, can't hurt.'

'What are you going to do in the meantime?'

Jackie sighed. 'Mainline my sci-fi, eat comfort food. Also, I hear you can buy voodoo dolls on the web now. Maybe they have ones that looks like Steph.'

~

Daniella had an uneasy night. What a wretched situation. She was still thinking about Jackie, Dave and Jamie when she arrived at the clinic the next morning. Dr Harris greeted her grimly.

'Daniella, let's have a chat,' he said.

Uh-oh. That didn't sound good. They went into Dr Harris's room and he shut the door. Daniella sat down, wondering what was going on.

'Did you see Rebecca White last week?' Dr Harris asked, referring to Becky.

'Yes.'

'And you wrote her a pill script, and gave her a starter pack?'

'Yes – what's this about?'

Dr Harris sighed. 'I just wanted to make sure that part wasn't made up. Here it is: her parents have made a complaint about you.'

Daniella felt a needle plunge into her heart. It was a word that made any doctor cold with horror. 'What kind of complaint?' she asked thickly.

'That you're encouraging promiscuity, overstepping boundaries, prescribing to a child.'

Daniella threw up her hands. 'It was entirely appropriate. The guidelines are pretty clear for someone her age: if she can understand the implications of what she's doing, she doesn't need parental consent. I encouraged her to talk to her parents, if she could. That's straight out of the GP college advice.'

Dr Harris waved his hand. 'I know, I know. It's ridiculous. She's a competent minor, I have no problem backing you on that. This will blow over, but it's a tough thing to handle when you've just got here. So this opportunity may be good timing . . .'

A second needle. Daniella felt as though she couldn't breathe. 'What do you mean? What opportunity?'

'Before you took up this position, I'd organised an old student of mine to come in from Isa to relieve. I was going to tell him not to bother, but he was keen to see the town again. So, I've arranged for you to swap with him for the next week at least. I want you to go and work those Isa shifts. It'll be a change of environment – bigger hospital, more specialties. Good for you.'

'You want me to hide?' asked Daniella incredulously. This felt like betrayal, and so wrong. She wanted to fight this complaint, not run away. Also, the mention of a bigger hospital hit her panic button.

'No, absolutely not,' Dr Harris said firmly. 'But this is a good opportunity for you to experience a different side of work out here, and it will take the pressure off. Besides, the rodeo's on in Isa this weekend, and it's a great event. You should see it.'

Daniella straightened. 'I won't go,' she said stubbornly.

'My dear, I like you very much, but I'm not asking. Do this for me.'

No matter what she said, he wouldn't relent. Eventually she gave up, feeling she was in danger of breaking down. She felt so ashamed. Even though she knew she had done nothing wrong, somehow being sent away made it feel like she had.

'When?' she croaked finally.

'Let's rip the bandaid off quickly,' said Dr Harris. 'There's a coach out at five today.'

Daniella barely took this in. In her daze, all she could think was that at least it wouldn't take her long to pack.

Chapter 15

Daniella had a lot of time to think on the three-hour coach ride up to Mount Isa and more after she'd installed her case in the temporary room they'd given her for the week ahead. Not that thinking was a good thing. Ever since the night she'd spent with Mark on the station, unpleasant things had been surfacing. The dinner party. Dave and Jackie. The complaint. She wasn't superstitious – she normally considered such ideas to be silly – but now, in her turmoil, she couldn't help but feel there was some connection.

She wanted to call Mark, but she forced herself not to. He'd have his hands full with the station, she knew, and in any case she didn't know what to say to him. She missed him desperately, which only made her feel even more out of control. She told herself that it was better to cool off for a few days at least. Maybe then she could be more detached, look at everything more rationally – like she used to.

Her accommodation was in the hospital's student quarters, two 'pods' of dorm-style rooms that each clustered around a central kitchen and lounge, and was just five minutes' walk from the hospital. As she lay in the unfamiliar bed (but a bed, no less) she could hear some of the students in the next pod crashing around the kitchen. On her side, only one other room seemed in use: another doctor or maybe a nurse, currently absent and with a sign on their door indicating night shift.

Daniella left for her first shift at noon the next day, trekking down to the hospital. In the distance she could see the mine flanking the town, which you could see from everywhere in Isa. Somehow, even though it was only a few hours from Ryders and up on a plateau, the sky wasn't the same here. Earlier that morning, she'd hiked up to the eastern end of the street where the road ran out at a little hilly bluff. She'd crunched across the mineral-rich soil – grey and silver sand mingling in the deep red dust – climbing until she reached the top. There, a little lookout bench had mocked her; it faced not endless plains but houses and mine stacks. Nothing like Margaret's bench. Disappointed and heart-sore, she'd climbed down and gone back to her room.

The hospital's white edifice appeared. Mount Isa had a population easily ten times that of Ryders and a hospital to match. It wasn't Brisbane by any stretch, but it was big enough to put the fear back into her. She was rostered into the A&E, just as she had been that night in Brisbane. What if it happened again?

She smothered the feeling as best she could and stuffed her bag in a locker. Then she greeted the nurses on triage and went to find her supervisor. They'd spoken by phone when she'd arrived last night, and he now gave her a speedy, well-practised induction.

'It's pretty standard. Patient list on the computer screen. Phleb cart there. Resus bays here, but I'll just start you on the lower end today, no pressure. Give me a yell if you need anything.'

Her first patient was Stan, a regular in the department. 'I'm here to have my blood taken,' he said.

Daniella saw from his chart that he had haemochromatosis, a disorder where people accumulate excess iron in their bodies, which could be deposited in the liver and kidneys, or anywhere in the body, eventually causing organ failure. Taking blood regularly removed a big hit of the iron and helped to prevent this.

'So you have blood taken how often?' she asked.

'Around about three months.' He showed her his arm, complete with track marks as good as any junkie's.

Daniella checked the details on the computer record, then came back with a blood donation bag and needle the nurse had given her. 'Wow, sixteen gauge,' she said, as she uncapped the thick needle.

Stan nodded. 'Yep. Got me over my fear of needles, that's for sure.'

Daniella found the vein and chatted with Stan while the blood drained into the bag.

'You going to the rodeo this weekend, doc?'

'Oh, maybe. I just got here, though,' she said.

'You should definitely go,' he encouraged.

After Stan, there were a couple of cuts needing sutures, and then an older man called Rick who came in very stiffly. He showed her his problem – his feet and lower legs were angry red and swollen.

'It's from my boots,' he said. 'I got this lovely new pair of biking boots for the ride up here, and after the first day, this is what happened.'

'Have you taken anything for it?' she asked.

'They gave me antibiotics.'

Daniella checked the records. He'd been prescribed antibiotics five days ago. She peered at the inflamed skin. It was starting to peel on the top and was hot to the touch. It was certainly cellulitis, but antibiotics were for an infection. And she wasn't sure there was one.

'Any improvement since you started taking the tablets?'

Rick shook his head. Daniella looked at the inflamed skin again. The swelling ended in a neat line, right at the knee.

Suspicion dawned. 'You're not still wearing the boots, right, Rick?'

He looked at her sheepishly.

'I'm almost sure this is an allergic reaction,' she said. 'Probably to something in the leather. You can't wear those boots. You need to throw them out. And I think you need some steroid treatment and antihistamines.'

'But they're works of art!' he complained.

'Then you can hang them on the wall,' she said firmly.

She cleared the change of treatment with her supervisor. 'Christ,' he muttered to her outside the curtain. 'Thanks for picking that up. Looks like a junior might have got him first time on a busy night shift. Dermatologist's going to be here tomorrow to review him. Best we correct things before then.'

He walked away, leaving Daniella unnerved; her heart was pounding. A junior on a busy night shift . . .

Her own shift ended at midnight, and she walked back to her room. The sky was full of stars, but she refused to look at them because she knew they would remind her of Mark. She wanted to be with him again, but she had to get a hold of herself first.

When she got back to her small, bare pod room, she plugged in her phone, but left it off.

The next day she started at eight, and the shift passed in much the same way. Daniella began her work mechanically, trying to ignore the fear that lurked just below the surface. Every time she went to the triage computer for the next patient, she held her breath in case it was a sick child.

But everything went smoothly, and her supervisor was usually close by. As the day went on, her worries began to recede. Her supervisor seemed to like her, and told her a couple of times that she was doing a good job. He didn't have the unflappable confidence of Dr Harris, but she felt supported. Although the reason she'd been sent there still stung, she began to think that maybe she could do this again; she could cope in a bigger place.

The clock crept into a quiet afternoon, though the nurses told her it wouldn't last, what with the weekend coming up and the rodeo starting the next day. But Daniella was able to leave on time when her shift ended, after half an hour of re-stocking and chatting.

She went the long way home, which took her on a loop down the main road and past the video store. The traffic was heavy with trucks and horse floats, all heading to the rodeo grounds. Daniella didn't go that far; all those men in RM Williams clothes would only remind her of Mark, and the fact that she hadn't yet spoken to him. The shame of being sent away was now compounded by hiding. She made a quick stop at the supermarket and returned to her pod to heat up a microwave dinner.

Her phone lay on the desk where she'd left it, now fully charged. Unable to delay any longer, she flicked it on. Five missed calls. She didn't need to scroll through the numbers. She wondered what to say.

Almost straight away, the phone rang. In her dark little room, the screen was like an interrogator's light. All right, it was time to face him. She trotted out of the room, letting the phone ring until she was in the doorway where she could see the sky.

'Hey.' Mark's tone was all warmth.

'Hey,' she managed, sitting down on the doorstep. The sound of his familiar, deep voice undid her, and she felt her tenuous self-control melt away.

'Are you at the A&E?' he asked.

'No,' she said softly.

'Out walking?'

'No, I'm just sitting here.'

'You're at the bench?'

Daniella took a deep breath, her eyes suddenly brimming. 'Why?'

''Cause you're not at home. I was hoping we could have dinner.'

'You're at the house?'

'Yes.'

The tears spilled over. 'Mark, I'm in Mount Isa.'

There was a moment of silence. She could almost hear him putting things together. 'What happened?' he asked.

The words tumbled out. The complaint, Dr Harris sending her away. She told him almost everything, except the details about who had made the complaint and Becky's name in case, by some miracle, the story wasn't already widely known. He listened to it all.

'None of that is true,' he said gently. 'None of it. You were doing just fine. If Dr Harris thinks it will all blow over, then it will. I hate hearing you so upset,' he continued. 'I'm going to drive up there tomorrow.'

'I don't – I mean . . . you don't have to do that,' she said. She didn't feel she deserved his kindness and support, especially when this was a work issue. And if she saw him, would she just be pathetic and emotional? She didn't want to lean on him like that. Besides, the idea that he would drive for hours just to see her made her stomach tighten.

'Like hell,' he argued. 'Babe, you know how much I . . . Look, I want to see you. I miss you.'

Steadily, he talked her down. When they hung up half an hour later, she had pulled herself together again and agreed he would visit. But she sat on the step a long time, looking at that bare patch of sky between the roofline and a tree, and wondered what the hell she'd been thinking when she decided to move to a small town. She had no head for the politics or hosting dinner parties. She had only intended it as a temporary measure; perhaps it had been long enough. Maybe she would be better off in Isa. Maybe she could even go back to Brisbane if she applied for something like dermatology. Something safe like that.

Daniella was rostered on again the next morning, and arrived to find the department in full flight. She spent the day constantly in motion between her cases. Three patients with chest pain, all grey nomads overexcited at the rodeo or overstressed trying to park their giant caravans in the choked city. A lady who had fallen on the footpath and broken her wrist. Another woman turned up with an early diabetic ulcer, and Daniella thought momentarily of Valerie – would anyone be helping her with her letters to Bruce? The afternoon threatened to be even busier, as the rodeo kicked off at midday.

Daniella was in the minor procedures room extracting a broken needle from a woman's foot when one of the nurses stuck her head in. 'Call for you,' she said.

'Who is it?' asked Daniella, distracted. She was squinting at the X-ray pictures, deciding what line to take with her incision before putting the local anaesthetic in. The needle had been in there for a few days, having broken off when the patient – a keen quilter – had stepped on it. In the thick foot skin, no evidence could be seen on the surface. The woman had finally come in when it had worked its way down to the bone and she was having difficulty walking. Daniella didn't want to miss it by making an incision in the wrong place.

'Said his name is Dr Bell too,' said the nurse. 'Relative of yours? He said it was important.'

This grabbed Daniella's attention. Her mobile was turned off for the shift, so her father calling the hospital meant two things: he knew she was there, and whatever he needed to talk to her about couldn't wait.

'Okay. Tell him I'll be just a minute.' She turned to the patient. 'I'm sorry, Joyce, I'm going to step out. I'll be right back, though, and we'll get this underway.'

'You're right, love. I'm not in a hurry. It's been in there three days already.'

Daniella de-gloved and washed her hands. The butterflies were flying manoeuvres in her stomach. What could be so important that her father had interrupted her at work? Her first thought had been Aiden.

She pushed the curtain aside and trotted towards the triage desk, smoothing back her hair and pulling at the stethoscope slung around her neck. Her heart racing, she picked up the phone. 'Dad? Is everything okay?' she asked. 'Is Aiden all right?'

'Yes, yes,' he said, then, 'what's this about a complaint?'

Daniella gasped in shock. 'What? How did you find out about that?'

'Someone rang my office and left a message with my secretary. They didn't leave a name. I thought maybe you wanted me to call.'

Someone had rung his office? Was it Dr Harris? No, he wouldn't do that, she was sure of it. She tried to focus. 'It's a bogus complaint, Dad. Just a misunderstanding. I don't know why anyone would call you.'

'Daniella, they're almost always bogus complaints. But consider how this might affect your career and your entry into training programs.'

'It's not going to come to that—'

Her father spoke over her. 'The experience up there isn't worth it. I want you to come home. I've organised for Dr Harvey to take you in the surgical unit at the Mater. Fantastic breast and endocrine unit there, a real leg-up.'

Daniella took a deep breath. She'd just been thinking about Brisbane again, but not like this. A year ago, she would have leapt at this opportunity but she wasn't the same as she'd been then. 'Dad, I'm not coming back right now.'

He grunted impatiently. 'I don't see the sense in sticking it out only a few months—'

'I mean, I'm not coming back to Brisbane. I applied for the rural generalist program. I'm staying here.' All right, none of that was true. But there didn't seem another way to stand her ground.

'What? But what about surgery? That's what you said you always wanted to do. I don't understand what's changed.'

She took a breath. 'Dad, I had a bad experience before I came here . . .' But the words were too hard to say, and her voice faltered. The secret was embedded inside her, too deep to speak of. And her father was so far away.

Her moment of weakness seemed to reassure him. 'We can talk about it when you get home. Lay it all out and go through it. I'm sure it's nothing – you do the work and you know your stuff. You should take this chance and get serious about your future. I can organise everything down here. Just say the word.'

Daniella felt her insides collapse. If he wouldn't listen to her, how could he understand? 'Thank you for calling,' she said shortly. 'I have to get back to work.'

She put the phone down. Her hands were surprisingly steady, but she knew it wouldn't last. And she had to get back to Joyce and the needle. But later, she knew she'd want to be alone to think about what she would do now. She picked up the phone again and called Mark's mobile. She got his voicemail, and spoke quickly. 'Mark, sorry. I can't see you tonight. Don't come up, okay?'

Chapter 16

Even upstairs in her pod with the doors and windows closed, Daniella could hear the rodeo. The distant roar came through the earth and air, all those trampling hooves, shouts and cheers. As night fell, clouds came over, as if the stars needed a blanket to drown out the shenanigans. It was the first time since she'd left Brisbane that she had been unable to see any part of the night sky.

But maybe that was fitting. She just wanted to be alone tonight. Fortunately, the mysterious night-shift doctor or nurse had evidently already left.

She dumped her work bag in her room and took her bathroom bag to the shower. At least the water was piping hot. She washed her hair. Twice. And shaved everything she'd neglected over the last few days. When she reached out a hand to grab her hardly used loofah mitt, she knew she was just dithering.

She shut off the water and grabbed her towel, still bothered.

She'd said she wasn't going back to Brisbane, but did she mean it, really? She thought of Jackie, desperate to leave Ryders behind. Daniella already missed her terribly.

She paused, thinking she heard something out in the lounge. She waited, but there was silence, broken only by the dripping showerhead. No, she must have been mistaken.

Wrapping the towel around herself she opened the door. Then she heard steps on the stairs outside, the handrail rattling as it always did when someone went down. Maybe the other doctor had locked themselves out. Feeling a little self-conscious in her towel, she trotted to the door and opened it. A familiar figure was on the stairs.

'Mark!'

He was nearly at the bottom, his broad back turned, red checked shirt bright in the streetlight. He looked up and grinned. Daniella felt herself go weak. Maybe she didn't want to be alone after all. She shook her head ruefully. How did he do that with just one smile?

'I thought I saw a light on.' He bounded back up the stairs and took her in his arms.

Daniella clung to him, burying her face in his shoulder. 'I asked you not to come,' she murmured into his checked flannelette, feeling a tear roll down her cheek.

'There was no way I wasn't coming,' he said. 'Hey, it's okay.'

Eventually, she pulled away so she didn't feel like a total sap.

'Christ, you're gorgeous,' he whispered.

'I am not!' she protested. She thought she must look like a snivelling train wreck.

'Come on, I'm only a man and you're wearing a towel.' He tugged playfully at the towel's free end.

Suddenly self-conscious again, Daniella tightened it around her.

'You want to go out?'

'Not really,' she said, smiling despite herself.

'Good, because I'm going to cook for you.'

'You are?'

'Yeah. Well, unless any of those people next door look like joining in. Who are they?'

'In the next pod? Med students. Why, what are they doing?'

Mark scratched at the back of his head. 'I don't know. But they have a beer keg.'

'Better shut that door quick then. It's just me here.'

'Oh, good,' he said.

Once she was dressed, she sat on one of the dodgy kitchen stools while Mark sorted through the available utensils. He put a few blackened pots in the bin. 'I wish we were at the station,' he muttered at one point. 'Kath would never stand for this. Christ.' He peered at her through a pot whose base was completely burned through.

Daniella shrugged. 'Abuse of the commons.'

'Common is right. It's worse than your place in Ryders.'

Finally he found a usable pot and retrieved a grocery bag from the ute. He offered her a glass of wine but she had to refuse as she was on call, so he poured her some sparkling water instead. 'So,' he said, 'tell me what happened today.'

'Oh, you know, the usual,' she said, turning the glass around so the bubbles made patterns on the unwetted sides.

Mark looked up from cutting mushrooms, his eyes seeking hers. 'You know, you do that a lot.'

'Do what?'

'Gloss over things. Leave stuff out.'

'I don't gloss,' she lied.

He stopped cutting. 'You don't have to hide from me,' he said softly.

'I'm not hiding,' she said. *Not much.*

He didn't argue. A silence settled, and Daniella resisted filling it. But Mark proved himself just as stubborn, and finally she couldn't bear it. He'd been good to her, a complete gentleman. His face was tender, just like his touch.

'All right, all right. My father called today,' she said in a rush. 'Somehow he'd heard about why I was here – it gave me a shock.'

Mark leaned against the bench, giving her his full attention. 'What did he want?'

'For me to move back to Brisbane, now.'

Mark's face went very still. 'Ah, I see.'

'Anyway, I don't really want to talk about it.' Daniella took a slug of sparkling water.

Mark nodded slowly. 'He must miss you.'

Daniella felt a pang. She missed her father too, but not the domineering approach he'd taken on the phone. 'He's more concerned I don't go to waste in the bush,' she said wryly.

Mark raised his eyebrows. 'You want me to fight him for you? I'm good with a rope.'

Daniella laughed. 'Oh, are you?' The mood lightened. After a pause, she said, 'How're things at the station?'

'All right.'

'Mark, now you're doing it.'

'What?'

'Glossing over. What is it?'

He put both hands on the bench and looked down at them as though weighing up his words. 'You remember I said that the Morgans have a financial stake in Ryders? Dad and I have been working hard to get the property back on track, but of course it takes time. Now the Morgans have told us there's a foreign buyer interested, and they also keep talking about mining exploration. We don't want to sell or allow mining prospectors on the land, but we're running out of time before the Morgans start pressuring us to show a return on their investment. As I mentioned, I've been looking for other ways to make the station profitable, but Dad doesn't want to talk about those things either. He can be really stubborn.'

'Why doesn't he want to talk about it?'

Mark rubbed his hair. 'I think he's just holding on to the way things used to be. He's not being rational about it.'

'Do you think he'll come around?' she asked, remembering William Walker's curtness when she met him at Ryders station.

'Something will have to happen,' he said grimly. 'I'll just have to convince him.'

'Sounds like hard work,' Daniella said sympathetically. 'I don't think he liked me much either.'

Mark's face softened. 'It's not you specifically. Apparently he doesn't think I should be dating someone . . . not from the land.'

Daniella felt no surprise after what Valerie Turner had said, but it was still unsettling to be disapproved of. 'And what do you think?' she asked tentatively.

He gave her a cheeky smile. 'I don't like you being in Isa. When are you coming back?'

Daniella threw a dishcloth at him. 'You're as bad as Dad! Anyway, it's not my decision.'

'I know. But I hope it's soon. Want me to fight Dr Harris for you? I'm—'

'Good with a rope, I know! Is that why you're here tonight? You going to the rodeo to show off your skills?'

'No. I wanted to see you.'

Daniella looked down to hide her smile of pleasure at his simple statement.

The meal he cooked was excellent, pasta with chicken and mushrooms and fresh thyme. Daniella finished it all, in spite of the awful chipped plates. When the dishes had been washed and put away, she sat down next to him on the couch.

He pulled her in close. 'I think my Latin's got rusty again,' he murmured.

She couldn't resist him, and soon they were kissing again as they had that night at the station, pure fire and sparkle that made her breathless.

'Which is your room again?' he asked between kisses. She pointed, and he picked her up and carried her. He laid her on the bed and undressed her, caressing every curve with his large hands before pulling her into his body.

Then Daniella heard her phone ringing.

'Leave it,' Mark muttered.

'I can't, I'm on call,' she gasped, wriggling out from under him. She left him wearing just his jeans, his belt undone, looking like a Calvin Klein model against the sheets. Jesus, if this was a nothing call . . .

'Dr Bell?'

Something about the man's tone sobered her immediately. 'Yes?'

'Chris, on dispatch. We've got an MVA on the highway and we're down crew because of the rodeo. One crew is en route, but they need support. You're on call and I've got one officer in an ambulance leaving now. Can he pick you up outside your accommodation? Five minutes.'

Instantly, Daniella's head was in a different place. Her heart accelerated and adrenaline tingled her fingers. 'I'll be waiting,' she said.

Daniella rode in the passenger seat of the ambulance, the sirens setting her pulse rate. The ambo, Steve, got radio updates on the way there. Single vehicle, loss of control. Gone off-road across a ditch and rolled through a fence into a paddock. Four occupants. Two dead at the scene.

It was so close to town, they arrived in no time. She saw the spotlights as they came around the last bend. When they pulled up, her eyes settled on unimportant details: a disposable apron on one of the ambos, backlit under the lights. The expanse of skin between their blue gloves and rolled-up sleeves.

Two patients were lying on the ground, three people around each. Bags were open, equipment deployed; there was so much gear Daniella could barely see the person underneath. One ambo from the first crew was with each group, while the others were local police or fire service guys helping out. When the first crew saw Steve and Daniella, they quickly rearranged themselves so each team would be working on one patient.

'He's bagged already,' the female officer told her as she handed over. 'Heartbeat thready at one-sixty, BP holding at ninety on sixty. Fractured left femur, maybe the C-spine. Evac's coming in for our guy, headed for Townsville. Yours needs an OR. Need to get them both back to town as soon as we can.'

Daniella had never been this front-line close to an accident before, but she translated what she knew from resus in the A&E: get them stabilised, neck brace on. Stop obvious bleeding. Keep a check on the pulse rate. Pain relief. Fluids. She followed Steve's lead on the stretcher transfer. The patient was in and out of consciousness. He was young; they all were, probably teenagers. Daniella didn't have time to dwell on this, to think about their families, their futures. Then it seemed everyone was leaving.

As the rear ambulance doors closed behind her, Daniella saw the scene in a new way. Spotlit, the unrecognisable remains of the car balanced on its roof, discarded packets from gauze and tubes caught in the scrubby grass; and, overhead, the big cloudy sky thinning to let the moon see two covered bodies set side by side.

~

The first ambo crew had already headed back to the scene by the time Daniella handed over at the A&E. Her patient was with a visiting trauma surgeon in the operating room; he would have to sort out the broken femur before the patient could be transferred east. The boy the other crew had brought in had just left in the chopper for Townsville. His head injuries were very serious; it was touch and go.

Daniella helped the nurses pull the files from ID found in the injured boys' pockets; then, briefly at a loss, she walked around the A&E once without taking much in. She felt as though she'd been hit by a cyclone: one moment she was with Mark, and everything was calm and lovely, then boom! Her night was tossed into chaos. Now the eye of the storm was passing over her, but she was still wired, waiting for the turmoil to resume.

The A&E was bustling. A few people in the waiting room sported chaps over their jeans and competitor numbers on their backs. So the rodeo had claimed its first victims. She moved towards the triage computer.

'Hey, what do you think you're doing?' Her supervisor cut her off. 'You've done more than enough tonight – and if I need you on call again later I don't want you burned out.'

Daniella almost laughed; no one at the hospital in Brisbane would ever have said that to her.

'Go and get a coffee or something,' he went on. 'I'll see if one of the nurses is leaving and can drop you home.'

Daniella knew better than to touch the health-service coffee. But otherwise, her thoughts felt loose and broken, like the needle she'd pulled out of Joyce's foot earlier. She really needed to go home. And Mark, she should call Mark. 'It's all right, I've got a ride,' she told him.

She stepped outside the front of the hospital and pulled out her phone. She waited while another chap-clad teenager limped in the doors, supported by an older man. In the distance, she saw the ambulance returning up the road. The sirens were silent, unneeded. It would pull in around the back of the hospital with its grim cargo. Daniella watched it go past, her heart breaking for the parents who were about to be given the worst possible news.

Turning, she was surprised to see Mark's ute pulling into the car park.

'How did you know?' she asked, as he got out and jogged over. Then she saw that his face was white as the moon itself. 'Oh God, what is it?'

'I just got a call. One of the boys in the car was from the station. He was driving in with his mates for the rodeo. His uncle just heard from the hospital and knew I was here.'

Daniella felt hollow under her breastbone. She swallowed. Which of the four boys was it? 'Did he, was he—'

'They said he's in theatre,' said Mark.

Instantly Daniella remembered the file she'd helped find. It was her patient. 'Andrew Simmons?'

'Yeah, Simmo,' said Mark. 'Do you know how's he's doing? I need to find him, then ring his uncle back. He's the vet in the district. He's still trying to reach Simmo's parents – they're up near Darwin.'

Daniella told him the limited information she knew. He put his arms around her, cradling her against his chest. She was aware of how worried he must be, but her thoughts were all half formed; she couldn't think of anything to say that would help ease the shock, and then she realised that no words were needed. He simply needed her to be there. They held each other for a long time.

Finally, Daniella said, 'Let's go see if there's any news.' He nodded. 'Is it all right if I come with you?'

'Yes. Please,' he said softly.

~

To Mark, the hallway was an endless white tunnel. The air-conditioning cooled the sweat on the back of his neck.

The hospital smelled like the one where his mother had died. Sitting in a chair, waiting for a nurse, Mark looked down at his hands. The skin was red-toned, like the station's earth. He had a rare sense of panic: he didn't belong in here among all this white. He felt as though he would drown in it. Then Daniella took his hand. He turned her smooth fingers in his palm. Amid all this coldness she was warm; a bridge of colour into the white. The panic passed and he was himself again.

A nurse came in and told them all she knew, not much more than Daniella had already disclosed: Simmo was in theatre, where they were stabilising a fracture before the Flying Doctors would take him to Townsville. She said he was looking better than he had half an hour ago, but the injuries were still serious. Mark allowed himself a moment of relief, but he also felt strangely, irrationally responsible. Simmo was barely out of childhood. On the station, Mark took special care to watch out for him; it was hard to accept that he couldn't protect him everywhere.

Daniella walked with him back down the hall. He glanced sideways and saw the tiny frown between her eyebrows. He recognised that look of concern, and knew that it was as much for him as for Simmo. He sighed, feeling lifted.

'You going to be okay?' she asked, looking up.

Mark ran his hand through his hair, then pulled her to him and hugged her tight. 'I've got to make this call.'

His mobile battery was low, so she showed him the alcove where the phones were; she'd wait for him in the main seating area. Mark picked up the receiver and watched her walk away. For the first time he understood the true demands of her job. She was so strong inside herself; she must see these things every day – maybe that was why she wouldn't tell him everything.

When she had disappeared round the corner, he took a levelling breath, and dialled.

~

Daniella sat in the A&E while Mark made his call. She remembered the last time she'd sat in a waiting room, at the clinic, right after her father had called the first time, just after she'd come north. She remembered being upset then. But that was personal; nothing like the professional ache she had now.

She'd always associated the hospital with anxiety and grief: a dozen individual black clouds, all corralled behind curtains and doors. This allowed, just a few blocks away, the rodeo to be jubilant, and oblivious. And it allowed her also to leave the losses behind. All except one.

She watched the few children in the A&E, in various stages of exasperating their parents. None of them looked ill. But then, that was the problem, wasn't it?

When Mark finally came out, they drove back to her accommodation in silence. As they climbed the stairs, he took her hand. Inside, he led her to her bedroom. He made love to her gently, powerfully, both of them releasing the worry and frustration of the last couple of hours. They lay together for a long time afterwards, not speaking but feeling the closeness of their bond.

Gradually, long after midnight, the last clouds burned away and the stars came out. And into this silence, Mark began to talk about the future he envisaged, for the station and more. Daniella listened, noting he used 'we' instead of 'I', and in the comfort of lying beside him, allowed herself to imagine all this was possible.

Chapter 17

Daniella woke feeling clear and light. Mark was kissing her awake with a tenderness that reflected how the night had forged them closer. She stretched, enjoying the feel of his lips on her face, and the smell of him on her pillow.

'I just called Simmo's uncle,' he said quietly. 'He's in Townsville – he did really well overnight. They think he'll come good. His parents are on their way to him now.'

'That's wonderful,' she said, feeling relief spread like the sun's glow.

'Do you have a shift today?' he asked, his stubble tickling her as he kissed her neck. Her attempts to wriggle away were ineffectual.

'No!' She tried to escape by tumbling out of bed, but he caught her foot and hauled her back.

'This,' he said sweetly, gathering up the captured leg with her two hands, 'is a roping move.'

'What's that?' she asked, lying still, trying to make him think she'd given up.

'Rodeo event,' he said.

'Ah, the rodeo.' She made a dive for it, but he was too fast. A moment later, she was back on the bed, pinned under him, laughing. 'I'll start playing dirty!' she threatened.

He affected a hurt expression. 'Hmm . . . what makes you think I wouldn't go for that?'

'Because you're too well mannered,' she said, finally escaping by digging an elbow into his ribs.

'They're the ones you have to watch,' he said, grinning. He lay back on the bed, the sheet only just covering his hips, trying to entice her by flexing. She allowed herself to admire the bed-tousled sandy hair, the flat muscles of his chest.

'That's not fair,' she complained.

'Just using the tools available. Come closer.'

'I'm not falling for that!'

He laughed. 'Come with me to the rodeo today?'

She chucked a pillow at him. 'You pull a rodeo move on me, and then you expect me to go with you? Won't it give you ideas?'

'Come on, it'll be fun. I'll wear my hat,' he grinned at her, 'which I know you like. You can wear that ratty thing you're so fond of. And you can meet my brother.'

Daniella relented. She was curious about this elder brother who'd braved his father's displeasure and left the station for life in the mines. But she didn't want Mark to think he could win so easily. 'Are you sure you want to do that? Is he good-looking too, your brother?'

Mark didn't bite. He winked at her. 'It's okay, I can take him.'

'I heard the tickets were sold out.'

'That's why I bought a couple, weeks ago. Aren't you glad Dave didn't want the other one?'

~

The rodeo grounds were in a big park on the outskirts of town, but close enough that they could walk there. The streets were bursting with traffic, and the announcing mike was audible everywhere, though hollow and unintelligible. Daniella could smell the cattle yards long before they got there.

'Ah, that's the smell I remember from when the rodeo came to Brisbane,' she said.

Mark soon had them installed in prime seats near the middle of the main grandstand where they could see the ring and the giant screen. The stands were packed, the crowd expectant. As they sat down, Daniella caught a blur from the corner of her eye as a calf streaked out from one end of the ring, chased by a rider swinging a rope loop overhead. The rider released the rope, catching the calf around the neck. The horse slid to a stop and the rope came away from the saddle, tipped with a bright pink ribbon; it dragged across the ring after the calf, who disappeared into a chute at the opposite end. The whole thing happened in only a few seconds.

'Wow, what was that?' exclaimed Daniella, now realising that the roper was a woman.

'Breakaway roping,' said Mark. 'It's a women's event. You have to rope the calf, then stop and let the rope pull away. The clock stops when the judges see the ribbon come off the saddle.'

'That was fast, wasn't it?' said Daniella.

'Yeah, about six seconds. It looks really easy, but the horse has to hold the line on the calf, otherwise the rider can't hope to throw, and they have to stop on a dime.'

Daniella nodded. 'Things that look easy are often deceptive,' she said.

Mark smiled at her. 'Yeah, I know. I thought that the first time I saw you work. You made it look effortless, but that's only because you've been dedicated and practised.'

Daniella shifted, uncomfortable with the praise.

'It's true,' he insisted. 'Don't you know how amazing you are? I mean, last night, dropping everything to go help those boys?'

'It's my job,' she said.

Mark made a face. 'Things like that are never just a job.'

The next competitor came in, but missed the calf altogether. The rider left the ring shaking her head. Daniella felt for her, knowing it might have been months of practice all scrubbed out in an instant. The events were ruthless like that. Two more ropers made their catches, but neither were as quick as the first one Daniella had seen. She found herself rooting for the first roper and hoping she would win.

'I'm surprised your father isn't here,' she said. 'Wouldn't he love this?'

'He does,' said Mark. 'He'd usually come up, but he's already travelled a lot in the last two weeks and he wanted to push through with some things on the station.'

Daniella looked down at her hands. 'Will you be going back today? I can't imagine you can stay away for long either.'

Mark kissed her. 'Tomorrow morning at the earliest.'

Daniella relaxed, but only fractionally. This happiness should have felt wonderful, but it made her nervous. She glanced sideways at Mark and wondered what she'd done to deserve him.

She let the event recapture her attention. Six more competitors came and went, and still no one could beat the earlier time. It ended with the first rider as the winner and Daniella felt gratified. She decided she was going to try to pick the winner in everything.

'What's next?' she asked, excited.

Steer wrestling followed, and Daniella gripped Mark's thigh as each rider and hazer chased a steer down the ring, the rider throwing himself onto the horns and wrestling the steer to the ground. Mark explained that the clock only stopped when the steer was on its side, all four legs pointing the same way.

These guys were faster even than the breakaway ropers; the winner took the steer down in five seconds.

'Is this something you do?' she asked Mark, excited at the idea of seeing his physical prowess on display.

He laughed. 'Not in a ring, but I can do it well enough if I have to. A few years back, I was in the rope and tie. That's when you rope a calf from the saddle, then dismount and take the calf down and tie three of its legs together.'

Daniella feigned outrage. 'I see! So that's what you were doing this morning.'

'Well, yeah, but without the horse.' He winked at her.

'Why did you stop competing?'

'It takes a lot of skill and practice to follow all the rules to protect animal safety. You can't take the calf down in certain ways, and your horse can't drag the calf once it's roped, or you get fined. When I got more involved in running the station, I let the practice slip. Unless you want to help me train again?'

Daniella punched him in the arm.

'Ouch. Fine. I get it, no tying you up.'

'I didn't say that,' she said with a sly glance. 'Just no treating me like a cow.'

'Deal.' He laughed and squeezed her hand.

Daniella marvelled at his easy physicality. He came from a different world, and seemed quite unaware of the fact. 'Does anyone else from the station compete?' she asked, treading carefully after last night's awful accident.

'If my sister was here, she'd be entering the barrel racing – that's another women's event. Some of the stockmen will be competing at the campdraft later in the year.'

After the steer wrestling ended, there was a break for lunch and Mark stepped out to make a call. A moment later, he came back. 'Will can meet us down by the food vans,' he said. 'That okay with you?'

Outside the main grandstand was an area that reminded Daniella of the Brisbane Ekka, where sideshow-style food vans were selling everything from hamburgers to Dagwood dogs. Oh yes, and Chiko Rolls, doughnuts and fairy floss. Exactly like the Ekka, she thought. She felt like a kid again. She hadn't been to the Brisbane show in years, but today was bringing back all those happy memories.

'Mark!' A man approached them dressed in jeans, a pink shirt and cowboy boots and Daniella immediately saw the family resemblance; they had the same open Walker face, but Will was slighter than Mark, his hair darker. Daniella liked him immediately.

'You must be Daniella,' he said warmly. 'Really like that hat – you look quite the part! And Mark, how the hell are ya?' They slapped each other on the back. 'Dad here?' Will asked quickly with that same wrinkle between the brows that Mark had.

'Just me,' said Mark.

'Right then. Well, you hungry?'

'Starved,' admitted Daniella.

'Oh no. Mark, what are you doing not feeding this woman? Disgraceful.'

'Didn't think all this carnival rubbish was good enough,' Mark shot back good-humouredly.

'It's fine with me!' said Daniella. 'I told you about the Ekka, remember?'

Will winked at her. 'Well, I have the answer. Care to join me for a catered lunch?'

'Catered where?' asked Mark suspiciously. Will pointed up into the grandstand. 'Corporate box?' Mark said incredulously.

'Yep. The mine booked it, then all the white-collar boys got called back to a meeting. Should have heard the whingeing. All ours if you want.'

Both brothers looked at Daniella. 'Sounds good to me,' she said.

From the box they had a fantastic view over the ground, and the seats were much more comfortable than in the grandstand.

'I reckon I could sit here a full hour without my arse going numb,' Daniella said, which made Will and Mark burst out laughing.

The tables were covered with massive platters of sandwiches and small pastries; the three of them barely made a dent, so Will sent the rest down to the yards for the stockmen. They were waiting for the grand entry parade to begin when Mark went outside, saying he was going to phone Simmo's folks and see how he was doing.

Will turned to Daniella. 'So, how are you enjoying Ryders Ridge?'

Daniella hesitated, wondering how best to phrase her reply.

'Ah,' said Will. 'Enough said.'

'No, no,' she hurried to explain. 'It's great, really. Dr Harris is fantastic to work for, and I've really enjoyed getting to know the patients and working at the hospital . . .'

'I sense a "but" coming.'

'Well, it was all going well until last week.'

Will raised an eyebrow. 'Want to talk about it?'

Daniella paused. He was easy to talk to – must be a family trait – but she shook her head. 'No, not really.' Not wanting to appear rude, she changed the subject. 'Is it hard for you, being so far away from the family?'

Will glanced down. 'Ah, in a way. But I like it. Mining is a different game altogether. I'd rather be down in the earth than driving cattle across the top of it. And I like my father better when I'm here and he's there. I miss Mark, of course – and Catrina. We were always really close. Us all being apart is hardest on her, I think, because she's the youngest. And Mum dying was a terrible shock for her.'

Down in the ring, Daniella saw a line of banners approaching; the parade was starting.

'Mark said Catrina was in Brisbane?'

'Yeah. I sometimes fly down for the weekend and take her out to shows or whatever she wants to do.'

'Wow, you're a good brother!' she exclaimed.

He shrugged. 'I make good money. I like to spend it on her. Mum probably would have been horrified about spoiling her. You got brothers and sisters?'

The riders were now halfway around the ring. Daniella could read a few of the banners, for sponsors and other associations involved with the rodeo. 'One elder brother. He's in the army, so he moves around a lot. He's in Victoria right now, but he might be going back to Afghanistan soon. I don't get to see him much.'

'That's hard.'

'Yeah.' Daniella didn't really want to talk about her brother. Thinking of him going back overseas was terrifying. 'So, Mark tells me you're a ute man?' she asked, changing the subject.

Will gave her a sidelong glance, again reminding her of Mark. 'He hasn't been driving my girl, has he?'

'Oops, did I just get him in trouble?'

'Get me in trouble for what?' asked Mark, reappearing in the doorway of the box.

'You. Driving my girl.'

Mark sat down on Daniella's other side and shrugged. 'I had no choice. Had to go to town. Dad took the Rover and the stockmen had the utes. I was gentle.'

Will put his head in his hands in mock despair. 'Oh Christ, the cattle grids!'

Mark looked thoughtful. 'Well, you know, Dave's a pretty decent panelbeater. I'm sure he can—'

'Stop, stop. I don't want to know.' Will grinned at Daniella. 'What are you driving?'

'Nothing. I flew into Isa and got a lift down to Ryders with Dr Harris. Everything there is pretty close together so I haven't needed a car.'

'Oh, that's no good,' said Will. 'You gotta have a vehicle out here. We should fix you up.'

Mark's phone rang. 'Sorry, last one,' he said, stepping out again.

Daniella and Will sat for a time in companionable silence.

'You know, he's really into you,' said Will, cocking his head in the direction of the door. 'I mean seriously into you. Talks about you all the time on the phone. I think it's great. I've never seen him like this before.'

'Oh well, we haven't really known each other all that long,' she demurred, hoping she wasn't blushing.

Will looked at her. 'But do you like him? I mean, seriously?' he asked, his face grave.

She was definitely going red now but was pleased to hear Mark was so keen. 'Yes, I like him.'

'Good. I can see exactly why he likes you. Lucky bastard. He's a better man than me.' Then Will rubbed his hair, just like Mark. 'You know, he looks at you like Dad used to look at Mum. Hey, don't look so worried. Mark tell you about Mum?'

'A little . . . not much.'

'Yeah, well. Things aren't the same without her. I'm seriously glad he found you. I like you.'

Daniella smiled at Will's enthusiasm but filed this information with all the other things that were making her uneasy. After last night and meeting Will the relationship with Mark was gaining momentum. This wasn't why she'd come north at all; it was both exciting and frightening at once.

They watched the parade, now nearly filling the arena. Mark came back a moment later, obviously tense. 'I just got a text. Dad's here,' he said.

Will raised his eyebrows and glanced around.

'Can you look after Daniella for a bit?' asked Mark. 'I need to go and sort out what's happening on the station.'

Will relaxed. 'Sure.'

Mark kissed Daniella before he left. 'Sorry, babe. I'll be back soon.' Then he was gone.

'Babe, is it?' grinned Will.

Daniella felt her cheeks flare again, and made a show of checking her mobile. 'They must be handling things okay at the hospital. No calls.'

They watched the end of the parade, then waited for the grader to make its way around the arena, smoothing the surface. Then a trailer came in loaded with forty-four-gallon drums.

'Barrel racing next,' said Will, rubbing his hands together.

'Mark said this was a women's event?'

'Yes indeed.' Will explained the rules. Three barrels were laid out, one at the head of the ring, the other two near the sides, like three points of a cross. 'It's a clover-leaf pattern. The rider races from the gates at the other end, around the right-hand barrel, then across to the left one, then around the head barrel, then fangs it back down to the start.'

The ring was now set up and Daniella could see the first competitor, a teenager waiting in the gate. She was off. Daniella watched as she galloped down the ring with abandon, then swung into the first barrel.

'Too wide, oh dear,' murmured Will.

The girl was soon around the barrel and beating towards the second. She pulled this turn tighter, but came out of it slowly. At the top, she brushed the barrel and it swayed. Then she galloped back down the ring, arms and legs flying, the crowd cheering her on, for a time of 17.73 seconds.

'Was that any good?' asked Daniella.

'Well, she was pretty slow and wide on the barrels, plus if you knock one over, you get a time penalty. You'll see.'

The first rider was followed by a cowgirl on a dappled grey who attacked the course. She leaned right out on the turns, her fingers touching the tops of the barrels as her horse pivoted. After the first two turns, the crowd were on their feet, going berserk as she rounded the top and pounded for home. After clearing the finish, she skidded to a stop, then rode out, happily waving to the crowd as her time of 17.25 seconds was announced.

'Now, that's how it's done,' said Will. 'See, you have to let go. You train and practise so your reactions are automatic, so you're not thinking about it. You just let the course have it, and your horse trusts that you know what you're doing. Let him have his head and go for it. That's going to be a hard time to beat.'

The cowgirl was followed by several more competitors. One knocked over a barrel, and none of them came close to the time set by the second rider.

The next competitor was announced. 'Now, riding from Ryders Ridge, Stephanie Morgan!'

'Christ,' muttered Will.

Steph looked amazing on her horse, a real country belle in her white jeans and tasselled chaps, blue tucked shirt and broad hat. She rode towards the first barrel at a good speed, but had to rein in hard to make the turn. The second barrel was the same. Then the third. By the time she was pounding down towards the finish, losing her hat, it was obvious her horse was the fastest sprinter, but the turns had slowed her down. Her time was 18.03 seconds, not enough to put her in the top five after the first round.

Will stroked his chin meditatively. 'That's what I was talking about. When you're too in control you can't trust yourself, or your horse. So, it doesn't matter how fast her horse is, she's always jabbing him in the mouth to make sure the turn feels safe to her.' He sighed. 'Typical Morgan.'

'Typical?' asked Daniella, intrigued.

'You haven't noticed? Look, the Morgans are fine when you're on their good side. But if they don't like you, or they think you're threatening their position, watch out. It's not personal; they're businesspeople at their core. I used to call them the Gorgons. Dad would threaten to strap me for it; then Mum would talk him down. Maria made Mum's life pretty hard for a while, talking behind her back about her travelling, that she wasn't a proper wife or mother, crap like that. I don't think Mark would remember; he was too young. Thank God Maria moved to Townsville. I still can't believe Dad took their money. Then again, I guess he didn't have much choice at the time. The banks wouldn't help. I wouldn't trust them, but hell, I've been gone a long time. Maybe things have changed. Still, I'm betting Steph drove Dad up with the float, and now Mark's flying around trying to find out who's covering the station.'

Right then, Mark was in fact waiting in the marshalling area for Stephanie to come out of the ring. When he'd called his father's mobile it had rung out, and he was trying to keep a lid on his anxiety. Not that things could go horribly wrong in a day or two, but Kath would be at the station practically on her own now that the muster was over. The horses still needed taking care of, there was a feed delivery due, and other issues were always cropping up.

'Steph,' he called, as she slid down from her horse.

She turned, eyebrows raised in surprise, cheeks flushed pink from the race. 'Mark! I didn't expect to see you.' She pulled him into a quick hug. 'Did you see the round?'

Mark stepped back, annoyed. 'No, I didn't,' he said tersely. 'Do you know where Dad is?'

Her smile slipped a little. 'I think he was going to the stands, but I'm really not sure. I left him with the horse float because I was running late.'

'Do you know who's on the station? Did he arrange anything?'

Stephanie's hand floated across her mouth. 'Oh, I didn't even think. He brought the float and picked me up in town. I'd been entered for ages and I didn't think I was coming, then I decided I would. He offered to drive. I didn't even know you'd be here.'

Mark found this incredible. Stephanie knew what things were like on the station, and he was sure William would have mentioned Mark's being here on the drive up. He didn't know how she'd managed to convince William to come, but he had a bad feeling about it. 'When's he planning to go back?'

'Not sure,' Stephanie said breezily, pausing to receive her lost hat back from a steward. 'But look, I'm sure it'll be fine. Why don't you give Dave a call, get him to check on things, and then we can grab a beer – maybe dinner later?' She smiled, her hand drifting up to Mark's side.

As her fingers settled just above his belt, Mark felt a surge of discomfort. He took another step back, out of her reach, trying to decide how to handle this. 'Look, Steph,' he said eventually, as gently as he could. 'I like you, and I appreciate what you and your mum have done for the station. But I'm with Daniella. I want to work with you on the business side of things, and I want everything to work well. All right?'

Stephanie's face tightened. 'Of course,' she said. She gave him a quick smile with no warmth. 'I heard she was here too. Hope you have a good time.' Then she turned on her spurred heel and led her horse away.

Mark stood in a swirl of arena dust and lingering unease. But thoughts of the station quickly drowned out any other concerns. He pulled his phone from his jeans pocket and called Dave.

'I guess you saw,' said Mark as he came back into the box.

'Yeah,' said Will. 'She come up with Dad?'

'Seems so. I can't get through to him, though. He'll be here somewhere. But Dave's in Ryders so I've asked him to go out and check on things. He can handle himself, of course, but it's not his job. I'm going to have to go back.'

Will got up tactfully. 'Excuse me a minute.'

When he'd gone, Mark put his arms around Daniella. 'I'm sorry.'

'It's all right, you have to go,' she said. Inside, though, she was angry and hurt. Stephanie had managed to take Mark away; her perfectly made-up face and woman-on-a-horse image just made it worse. Daniella couldn't compete with that, and she didn't want to feel like she had to. But she'd be damned if she'd show that to Mark.

'I'll call you as soon as I get in,' he said. 'When are you coming back to Ryders?'

'I'm not sure. I'm here at least until Friday, but—'

Will stuck his head back in. 'Mark, I just rang Dave. He says he's fine till tomorrow and everything's under control. So there's plenty of time to find Dad and see when he's planning to go back. Don't go rushing home. Take Daniella out tonight and head back tomorrow.'

Daniella saw the conflict on Mark's face. He was worried about the station, but he wanted to be with her too. Knowing how much the station meant to him, it was scary to be the reason for his staying. It would be like her turning down an emergency call from the hospital to be with him. Would she do that? No, it wasn't right.

'He still on the line?' asked Mark. Will waved the phone at him. Mark took it.

'He shouldn't go,' Will whispered to Daniella. 'This smells all wrong. If Steph brought Dad up here with some ulterior motive, I'll quite enjoy thwarting her. I'm going to take you both out somewhere tonight.'

Mark came back. 'All right, I'll head back tomorrow.' He was more relaxed now.

'I've just told Daniella we're all going out.'

Mark grinned. 'Okay, but not to the Irish. You promised last time.'

'I remember. I know another place. It'll be great.'

~

In the end, they had a good night. They walked all around the town, taking in the sights, while Will told them stories about things he'd got up to in each pub. By the end, Daniella was laughing so hard her face and ribs ached. It was in the midst of this that they'd passed an electronics store, and a display gave Daniella an idea. She'd had to shush both men – who complained good-naturedly about how hungry they were – while she scrutinised the sleek white boxes in the window, containing computers and tablets, trying to read the fine print. Finally, she'd allowed them to lead her away.

Will took them to a Chinese place for dinner, but didn't linger after they'd eaten. He kissed Daniella goodbye and she was sorry to see him go.

As they arrived back at the pod, Daniella's phone rang. It was Dr Harris. 'Daniella, how are you doing? Apologies for calling so late.'

They exchanged status reports. Then he said, 'I heard about last night. Awful thing to happen. I've known Andrew since he was a young lad.'

'I know,' sighed Daniella. 'But it seems he's going to be all right.'

'Yes, that's a miracle really. Not so sure about the other lad in Townsville. And as for the other two boys, it's such a waste. But Andrew's still going to have a long recovery. Actually, that's why I'm calling you. I'd like you back in the clinic. My registrar is still here until Wednesday, but I want to fly out to Townsville and see Andrew's parents. They're good friends and I haven't seen them in a long time, and I can also touch base with the treating doctors on his recovery. I'd like you back on Tuesday so you can cover the half-day when the reg goes.'

'What about the complaint?' Daniella asked.

'We'll talk about that when you get back.'

'I'm coming back early in the week,' she told Mark when they'd rung off.

He grinned and hugged her. 'That's my girl. Then you'll come with me to the movie fundraiser next Saturday? *Jurassic Park*, remember?'

Daniella groaned. 'That's this week?'

He nodded.

'All right then. But I'm scared of those damn raptors.'

'Good. Then you'll just have to stick close to me.'

Chapter 18

'I'm so glad you're back,' said Jackie, linking her arm through Daniella's.

'I was only gone a week!'

'I know, but Dr Rimar isn't half as much fun as you.'

They were just leaving Jackie's house for the oval. It was Saturday night, clinic was over for the week, and Dr Harris had taken the on-call duties. Jamie was with Jackie's mother, *Jurassic Park* being deemed far too scary for him.

'So, did you see Mark last night?' asked Jackie.

'No, I've been on call. I haven't seen him since Sunday. They were tagging and branding this week, and I think a shipment was going too so he's been busy. And he went to Townsville with Dr Harris on Wednesday.'

'At least Simmo's getting better. But it's horrible, isn't it? Those two boys who died . . . I think their parents lived in the Territory; who knows when they were last home, and then that happens. If anything ever happened to Jamie like that . . . Well, it's awful, that's all.'

They reached the end of Jackie's street and turned onto the main road. A few other people were walking down too, all carrying picnic baskets, and they waved to them. They passed by Margaret's bench, where Daniella had taken to stopping every night on her way home from the clinic. She did her thinking there, enjoying the solitude, and in the last few nights, she'd even found herself wondering about where else she might go. Such thoughts, however, sat uncomfortably with the roots she was forming in Ryders, and she'd pushed them aside.

As they reached the oval, the approaching crowds thickened. The sun was just going down and everyone was busily setting up. Vehicles were allowed behind a tape, and all the best spots had been taken by caravanning travellers; meanwhile the ground in between them and the huge screen – erected on the western goalposts – was filling with picnickers with blankets. Around the edge, stalls were taking orders: coffee, tea and beer from one, hot chips and pies at another. A merchandise store was capitalising on the film choice, selling everything from dinosaur T-shirts to fossil-hunting kits. The crowds were particularly thick around that one.

'Thank God Jamie isn't here,' said Jackie. 'He'd be begging for everything from that store.'

'Where will we sit?' asked Daniella, scanning around for a good spot.

'Anywhere you like. Listen, I forgot to say, I promised I'd help out at the drinks stand for a while. Here, take the basket.'

'What? When did that happen? I thought you said—'

'I was weak.' Jackie bowed her head as if in shame. 'Roselyn was going to do it and then couldn't make it. I'll try to be quick. Do my best to be back before the T-rex turns up. But look, you'll be all right – there's Mark. See ya!' And she was off towards the tent.

Daniella shook her head. She was wondering if she should go and offer to help too when Mark reached her.

'There you are,' he declared, sweeping her off the ground and spinning her in a circle.

'Mark!' Daniella was aware of curious glances. 'What will people think?' she whispered.

Mark put her down, but said in her ear, 'I don't care.' He kissed her. 'I haven't seen you for a week.'

Absurdly pleased, Daniella slipped her arm around him. 'How'd the cattle processing go?'

'Good. Shipment's gone. The rest of that herd's on its way back out into the fallow paddock, which looks untouched. They'll have plenty of fresh grazing.'

She lowered her voice. 'How was Townsville?'

Mark rubbed his hair. 'Sad, and positive at the same time. His parents took it pretty hard when they realised how bad the crash was. But Simmo's doing better – and his brothers came down to see him, too. They were on properties in the Territory and hadn't seen each other for ages. It's going to be a while before he comes back here, though – if he decides that's what he wants.'

'How about you?' she asked. Everyone was closer to each other out here, bound together by their remoteness. And all that time in a hospital must have brought back memories of his mother's illness.

He kissed her again. 'Much better for seeing you.'

Together they made their way into the picnic area in front of the big screen. They settled on a spot just off-centre, about halfway back. Daniella spread out the blanket and they sat down, chatting while they waited for the entertainment to get started. Mark hugged her close. Night steadily crept in; soon, only a pink blush could be seen in the west behind the screen.

'There's Dave,' said Daniella, waving as she spotted him securing something behind the goal-mounted screen. He finished tying off and strode over to them.

'Hey,' she said. 'Looks like a big turnout.'

Dave rolled his eyes. 'Yep. And Murphy's Law says that means mechanical problems. Plus the equipment's not the newest.' He tapped the spanner slung through his belt. 'Hey, how's Simmo doing?' he asked Mark.

'Much better. He's starting on the rehab.'

'Good, good.'

'Would you like to join us?' asked Daniella. 'We've got sausage rolls and chips and every form of sugar the supermarket sells.'

Dave shifted on his feet. 'Sounds tempting, but I'm on projector duty. They're running the whole lot off gennies down the back. Don't like the look of one, personally. I'll come back after I check it.'

'How'd you get landed with that?' asked Mark. 'The committee paid for a full crew.'

'Steph said some of them didn't turn up,' said Dave, before pacing towards the back of the oval. Daniella twisted around to look. In the back of a truck, a short scaffold was set up with a chunky, industrial-looking projector on it; cables ran off to an area behind the stalls, and the distant hum of generators could be heard under the babble of voices. Two guys in black were now moving around the pole-mounted speakers, checking their orientation and talking into walkie-talkies.

'Did I see Jackie heading to the stalls?' said Mark. 'She's been gone a while.'

'She's helping out,' said Daniella. 'She promised to be back before the T-rex shows up.'

Mark frowned.

'What?' said Daniella.

'Oh, nothing. Just got a funny feeling.'

'It's raptors,' she said. 'They spook everyone.'

He laughed. They went through the picnic basket and laid out a few things, but both of them felt bad eating without

Jackie, who'd gone to all the trouble of packing the basket in the first place. The movie began and Daniella leaned back against Mark. After a few problems with the sound, everything settled down. People mostly ate happily and watched, but some drifted off to the side to visit the food tents or chase after small children.

The on-screen party was just being shown into the electric land rovers when Mark squeezed Daniella's shoulder. 'Dave should've been back by now. I'm going to see if he needs a hand.'

'You're leaving me just before the T-rex starts eating people?' Daniella affected outrage.

'I think you're tough enough to handle it if I don't get back in time,' he said. 'That's why I love you.'

Daniella tried to conceal her surprise. Love? Had he just said that? So smoothly, openly. In a daze, she said, 'Will you check if Jackie's okay too?'

On the screen, the land rovers set out into the park, heading towards mayhem and destruction. Daniella watched without registering what she saw. Her heart was beating fast; had he meant to say it, or was it just a turn of phrase?

She probably would have continued mulling it over for some time, except that she caught the name 'Jackie' in a nearby conversation. Daniella looked over. It was two teenage girls; she thought they worked at the same supermarket as Becky. Eavesdropping was difficult with the blaring soundtrack, but when she also caught 'Jamie' and 'Dave', a nasty feeling began to rise up in her stomach.

Mark returned a few minutes later, his hand on her shoulder startling her. The speakers were playing the braying goat. He tugged her hand. 'Come over here for a sec,' he said.

He led her towards the edge of the oval, behind the speakers where it was quieter. As they walked, the heavy footsteps of the T-rex sounded, and the water cup rippled ominously on screen. Daniella rubbed her arms, suddenly chilled.

When he stopped and turned to her, Mark's face showed a mix of concern and surprise. 'Do you know anything about Dave being Jamie's father?'

Daniella hedged; Jackie had sworn her to secrecy. 'Why?'

'Because I just had three different people ask me that on the way back here. Is it true?'

Daniella shook her head. 'Not for me to say. Give me a minute.'

She left Mark and skirted around the blankets to the drinks stand. The queue was short now that the action was heating up on screen. The T-rex roared. There were three women serving, one of them was Stephanie Morgan.

'Hi, Dani, can I get you something?' she asked brightly.

'I'm looking for Jackie.'

'Oh. She left. Are you sure I can't get you tea? Or lemonade? You look tired.'

Daniella tried to remain polite. 'No, thanks. Where did she go?'

'She wasn't feeling well and decided to go home.'

Daniella looked into Stephanie's immaculately made-up face with its carefully set expression of friendly interest and didn't believe a word. The other two women were talking to each other behind their hands. Daniella could guess exactly what had happened to Jackie and she suspected Stephanie knew too.

'When did she leave?' she asked.

'Oh, not that long ago. But look, if you're not going to buy something, could you step aside for the customers? Unless you want to make a donation?'

Daniella turned and walked away from the stand, afraid that if she stood there any longer she might punch Steph's obnoxious face. On the screen, the T-rex was free, crushing cars, running after the jeep. Things would never be the same in Jurassic Park again.

Or in Ryders Ridge . . . Mark had heard the rumour from at least three people. Out there, on the blankets, were dozens of people who would probably hear it before the end of the night.

Jackie's secret was out.

Daniella had never quite appreciated until now why it was such a big deal. In the city, privacy was easy, unless you were a celebrity. Only now, looking at all those faces, the conspiratorial gossiping of the ladies behind the drinks stand, could she begin to understand the level of scrutiny in a small town where everyone knew you.

She pulled out her phone.

~

Giving up on waiting for Daniella, Mark headed away from the screen, towards the projection truck and all its cables. Now that the movie was playing without a hitch, there wasn't a lot of activity there, just the two crew in their black jeans and T-shirts, leaning against the truck, smoking.

'Hey, you seen Dave Cooper?' he asked.

'Who?'

'Guy who helped you with the screen and the gennies. Jeans, white shirt?'

'Oh yeah. Nah, man. Not for a while.'

Mark cursed under his breath. Rumours took off quickly in a small town. If anything sordid was discovered, the proverbial fan spread it fast and thick. But Dave being the father of Jackie's kid? It didn't make sense. Sure, Dave had been keen on her a few years back, but as far as Mark knew she'd never returned the feeling. And Jackie had been living down in Brisbane when she'd got pregnant. No, he didn't believe it; after all, Dave was a decent guy. If he was the father, he'd have stood by her.

Mark slipped behind the tourist vans, then down the bank where the generators had been set up. Bingo. There was Dave, fiddling with the third generator, an open jerry can sitting beside him.

He looked up and waved over the din. Mark jabbed a finger around the bank, away from the generators. Dave followed. 'What's up?' he asked.

'Okay, be straight with me. Are you Jamie's father?' Mark only had to see Dave's expression to know the answer. 'Fuck, it's true, isn't it? What the hell?'

Dave rubbed his face, looking off to the side. 'Did she tell you?'

'Never mind about that for a minute – is it true?'

'Yeah, it's true.'

Stunned, Mark struggled to form a coherent question. 'Why didn't you . . . I mean, why isn't Jackie—'

'Because I was stupid, all right? I really liked her and we were having a good time – then I knocked her up, and she hated me for it.'

'Why the secret, though? Make it all official!'

Dave shook his head. 'Mark, she wanted to study down in Brisbane and make something of herself, and I ruined that for her. And she thought I was playing around on her too – I wasn't, but she didn't believe me. Things got all screwed up between us. We couldn't talk without fighting. She doesn't want anything to do with me, doesn't want people to know.'

Mark shook his head in disbelief. 'Holy shit. How did you bear it, Dave? He's your son.'

At this, Dave looked physically wounded. He sat down against the bank. 'With fucking difficulty,' he said fiercely. 'Look, back then, I tried to convince her we'd work it out. But she was so mad, and I made it worse because I wouldn't listen to her. She was proud of the dream she had, and I wanted to drag her around with me instead. I said some stupid stuff, trying to convince her it was what she wanted, and she didn't forgive me. It's all my fault. I tried to send her money and she wouldn't take it – she just sent it back so I gave up. But if she won't have me then at least I can do what she asks. Some day, who knows? If she can get back to Brisbane, do those things she missed out on, maybe she'll have me then. I hope so.'

'Christ,' said Mark, sitting down beside him. 'Why didn't you tell me any of this?'

'She asked me to keep quiet. It was hard as anything. I thought it'd get easier, but it didn't. If anyone asks, she tells them it was some guy from Brisbane. Man, that hurts.' Dave stabbed his finger at the ground. 'Jamie . . . I've never even properly met him. Never held him when he was born . . .' His voice cracked. 'I can't believe she told you.'

Mark began to comprehend how bad this might get. The moral police would soon have their talons out. Even if Jackie left now, years of apparent non-involvement made Dave look heartless. The town might become a very cold place for him.

'Dave, about that. Jackie didn't tell me. I heard it from three different people tonight. Why do you think I'm here? The whole town's going to know by tomorrow morning.'

'Oh . . . shit. She's going to think it was me.'

'Does anyone else know?'

'I haven't told anyone. Maybe Jackie did?'

'Okay, well. If you need to come stay at the station, you do that. And for Christ's sake, bring her with you. This could get bad. And you know it's going to be worse for her.'

Dave nodded, absent with shock. Then he grabbed Mark's arm. 'Look, if this really is out in the open, I'll need to talk to Jackie, but I might need you to help me out. Or Daniella. Jackie's going to be pretty mad.'

'Let me know if you need anything,' said Mark.

He strode back to the oval and eventually found Daniella pacing behind the big screen, from where the rumble of the movie's soundtrack was muffled. The hastily gathered picnic gear was thrown over her arm.

'Jackie left and she's not answering her phone,' she said. 'I'm sorry, but I have to go and make sure she's okay.'

Mark didn't need more direction. 'I'll drive you,' he said, putting an arm around her.

But five minutes later, they found Jackie's house in darkness, her ute nowhere to be seen.

'You don't think she'd do something stupid, do you?' asked Daniella.

Mark hated seeing Daniella so worried. An urge to drive her out to the station – where he could comfort and protect her – surged within him. But that wasn't possible. Instead, he drove the Ryders streets while Daniella checked the tav and every other place Jackie might have gone. Finally, she had to admit they weren't getting anywhere.

'Maybe she just wants some time alone,' she said reluctantly.

Daniella was probably right about that. But later, as Mark drove back to Ryders by himself, being alone had never seemed so unappealing.

~

At lunchtime the next day, Daniella finally managed to get Jackie on the phone.

'Where were you last night? I was worried!'

'I drove around all night,' said Jackie flatly. 'Didn't even care about the roos.'

'Are you okay?' Daniella asked.

'Oh, just peachy,' said Jackie, with slathered irony. 'Everyone knows, Daniella. Everyone.'

'They can't hurt you,' said Daniella, trying to find a way to console her.

'That's not the point,' argued Jackie. 'I don't want them talking about Jamie and moralising on what I should do. It's none of their business.' A tense silence stretched between them. Then she said, 'Who did you tell?'

Daniella was taken aback. 'I didn't tell anyone. Maybe Dave—'

'Dave's kept quiet for three years. You're the only one I've told, Daniella. Then, two weeks later, everyone knows? I *trusted* you.'

Daniella couldn't breathe. Jackie's voice was quiet, almost reasonable, but the words stung like hot barbs, and tears burned the back of her eyes. 'I swear, Jackie, I didn't tell anyone. Look, I want to talk to you about what we can do.'

'Why, you got a time machine there?'

'I'm serious.'

'How about you seriously leave me alone,' Jackie said, and hung up.

Chapter 19

Later that day, Daniella walked grimly to Margaret's bench, desperately needing distance from all the turmoil that surrounded her. The sky was again covered with clouds. Daniella sniffed back tears. She hadn't told anyone her friend's secret, she knew that, but Jackie wouldn't believe her. Losing the friendship hurt most of all. How were they going to work together now? Then there was the lingering complaint made by Becky's parents. And, of course, the halfway place between desire and fear where her feelings for Mark had parked themselves. Things with him had suddenly turned serious, and faster than she was comfortable with. Christ, what a mess. The need to escape was stirring within her.

As she approached the bench, she was surprised to find it occupied. Mark was there, his broad back towards her, looking out towards the station. The light had faded to a late afternoon glow, the scrub on the plain blue and sleepy, ready to become the slumbering shadows that were all she could see out there at night.

'Hey,' Mark said as she sat down. He seemed preoccupied and looked down at his hands. 'Daniella, I know now might not be the best time, but this whole thing with Jackie and Dave has got me thinking about it. Well, thinking about it more.'

'What's that?' asked Daniella, not sure what he was talking about.

He turned towards her, taking her hands. 'I think you're incredible, the most wonderful woman I've ever met. I want more for us. You know, more than just meeting up in town once or twice a week.'

Daniella shrank back. She had come here seeking a calm space where she could think about what had happened with Jackie, and instead she felt as though she was about to get tackled from behind.

'Mark—' she began.

'Move to the station with me,' he said quickly. 'I know you don't really like your place here in town. And I'd love you to live there.'

Daniella felt the momentary heat kindled by his words, but it chilled swiftly. She couldn't believe he was asking her to move in with him. 'Mark, I couldn't . . . I mean, when I'm on call, I have to be able to get to the hospital in a hurry. If I was at the station I'd be forty minutes out, at least.'

This sounded very reasonable. But inside, Daniella felt trapped. Those small thoughts about where her training might take her next pushed forward in her mind. She'd only just begun to think about the possibilities. Mount Isa hadn't been as bad as she'd thought. She knew she had to talk about that with him, but now he'd jumped ahead of her, and too many steps.

Mark sighed. 'I know. I'll just have to keep dreaming about that one. But what about the nights you're not on call? Dr Harris usually takes the weekend, doesn't he? Could you come out and stay with me then?'

Daniella swallowed. Panic boiled on her tongue. She needed him to be what he'd been until now: steady and sure and gentle. If she was going to sort out her working life, decide what she was going to do, that couldn't change. She needed his patience and understanding. 'Um, I-I'm not sure,' she stammered. 'If an important case comes in, I wouldn't be here to see it.'

Mark nodded, his lips moving against her hair, but he was quiet for a while. Daniella felt his disappointment.

'Besides,' she continued, 'what about your father? He's not exactly going to like that.'

She felt Mark stiffen. 'I don't care what he thinks, and neither should you. He doesn't get a say in who I date, who I sleep with, who I marry. It's not an issue.'

Daniella flinched at the *marry*. Her rising panic began transmuting into anger. She was now way beyond being tackled from behind: she was down in the dirt, off-balance, struggling to get up again. Mark was coming too close, now. Asking too much of her. She couldn't get her thoughts straight enough to even consider what he was asking, and now he'd gone a step too far.

However, she didn't want a fight. She couldn't handle it after her conversation with Jackie. 'Mark, I know all that,' she whispered. 'But we haven't been together all that long. And people are going to talk. That makes it hard for me in the clinic. I mean, there's already been one complaint about me.'

She was pedalling hard now, trying to put some distance between them. Hanging on to the hope that he'd leave it alone and and they could continue as they'd been up until now: she'd be able to work through her turmoil and they could talk about this later. But she also knew how determined Mark could be; he wasn't going to drop it. Daniella felt the same spinning sensation in her chest as she'd had when she was desperate to escape from Brisbane.

'What if I came to town, then? Stayed with you?' he suggested.

'What about the station?' she replied quickly. 'Wouldn't it be better if we just kept things as they are?'

He made an unhappy sound. 'Dad's on the station.'

'Yes, but don't you have to . . .'

'I know,' he said.

He let it go after that, and Daniella was relieved. But Mark was quiet as he drove her back to the house. Unease settled around them like a dust cloud.

'Wow, this really hasn't changed,' Mark said as he came inside, taking in the plain lino and laminex kitchen, all in unpleasant shades of off-white and grey, and the couch, which looked as though it might collapse on itself at any moment. To distract them both, Daniella offered to give him the grand tour, which only involved showing him the bedroom that he'd never seen. Her case still lay open on the floor under the window – nothing had made it to the wardrobe – and though she'd started sleeping on the bed, it wasn't properly made up with sheets; she'd just laid out the blanket and pillow on top of the mattress.

'Looks like you're sleeping rough in here,' he joked. But she saw the quick frown, heard the forced humour. Daniella felt bad about what had happened on the bench; it hurt her that he was upset. She wanted to make it up to him, but here in the stark reality of her home she felt exposed. She realised what it looked like: that she might be ready to go at any moment.

She headed back out through the front door and looked up at the sky. Mark followed. A dreadful sense of foreboding crept between them. Daniella could find no words. Instead, she put her arms around him.

He returned the pressure, but stiffly. 'Were you ever planning to stay?' he asked her softly. 'On the station that night, you said you'd moved here, you were going to stay here for the long haul. But you haven't even unpacked.'

'When I first came here I wanted to stay . . .' she hedged.

He called her on it. 'I'm not sure I believe you.'

Daniella pulled away. 'All right. I came here because I wanted to get away from Brisbane. And then I liked it, and I thought that yes, maybe I could stay for good. But when I went to Isa and saw a different place, it ended up being a good experience. Professionally, I need to be able to manage different situations. Besides, certain things have got out of hand here.'

He winced. 'That's what this is about? That you need to be in control?'

'Well, yes, actually. It's important for my job. I have to be able to respond and keep on top of things. If I'm not in control—'

'I'm not talking about your job,' he said. 'I'm talking about everything else. Is that why you don't want us to be together?'

'I didn't say I don't want to be together—'

'But you've been thinking about leaving, and you didn't say anything? What else is going on that you haven't told me? Because I can tell you're keeping something quiet.'

He had her there. 'I can't,' she said, her voice faint.

'Christ,' he muttered, pacing. 'And you really don't want to be with me, even if it's here in town?'

Tears gathered in her eyes, but her anger returned too. She *did* want to be with him, but it was too fast and she couldn't deal with it now. Other things had to be straightened out first. She looked at him and saw he couldn't let it go; he wouldn't leave it alone until she told him what was bothering her. And that was absolutely out of the question.

'I'm not ready for that,' she said, with force, with heartbreak.

He stopped pacing and caught her hand, so gentle, and took a breath. 'I love you, Daniella. I won't apologise for that. I'll do whatever it takes to make this work, but I need to know I'm not the only one trying.'

She couldn't say it back to him. She needed to escape. 'Mark, I think we should stop seeing each other.' The pain was a shock. Her whole being protested that this wasn't what she wanted. She shut it down, crammed the feeling back in the place where she hid all the out-of-control stuff. A rip started, somewhere in her gut, threatening to spread and tear her in half. But she kept herself immobile, expressionless.

'I don't,' he said. He still had her hand. 'I think you're running. You ran away from Brisbane and you're doing the same now.'

He was too close to the truth. 'You don't get to decide that!' she shot back at him.

'I get to decide what's worth fighting for, and this is it,' he said. His eyes were shining with tears, his voice thick. 'I don't want to lose you over this. Won't you tell me what's going on?'

Daniella sat down on the long top step. Her hands were shaking, so she jammed them between her legs. She wouldn't last much longer before she broke down; she had to get out of this. She couldn't admit he was right; she couldn't save herself.

So she drowned. 'Please leave,' she said. She kept her eyes fixed on the ground, where she could see only his boots.

'Daniella, please—'

'Don't call.' She screwed her eyes tight. She heard his ragged breaths. For such a long time. Waiting for her to give him something. But she simply couldn't; not in this emotional inferno where her throat and heart were raw and broken, her thoughts all tangled. She just needed him to leave.

Finally, his boots strode across the dirt. The Rover door opened and closed. The engine roared to life, and he was gone.

Silence returned. She opened her eyes. The sky seemed huge overhead, the space around and within so empty.

Daniella felt herself crack, as though someone had rammed a sixteen gauge between her ribs and was sucking out all the air. 'He left,' she gasped to the sky. God, this was real.

The house was too stark, all its fluorescent lights exposing every ugly detail of her pain.

She ran. She kept going until she was near the end of the main street, that slight rise that let the town slip away and the clouds take over. She reached the bench once more. God, she couldn't breathe. The pain that had started as a needle prick grew as if she were bleeding out, the thick fluid filling her windpipe. When it reached her larynx, she began to gasp, but it kept rising. It touched the back of her throat, burning hot, then her nose. Then it was in her brain and her eyes.

Her vision blurred. And then, finally, the tears came. Daniella cried in great racking sobs, heartbreak and guilt crashing together. She cried and confessed until the clouds had heard all her secrets. Then, when she was spent, the moon burned through and the starry sky came out.

She didn't want this thing inside her anymore; she needed to tell someone. Someone she trusted. She wanted Mark badly in that moment. She needed to explain why she'd done what she'd done. Why she'd come here, why she'd felt she had no choice but to push him away. But could she do it? Clarity came on the slow walk back to the house. Tomorrow, she told herself, she would call. Apologise, at least, as he'd done the first time he'd called her. They had a lot to talk about.

~

Mark drove back to the station in a blur of disbelief. Perhaps he'd been stupid to ask her so soon, but he couldn't help it. He loved her. He wanted her to know that, didn't want her to be in any doubt. And given how hopelessly he'd fallen for her, it was probably a good thing he knew now that she didn't feel the same.

Ah, fuck. It hurt. He clenched the wheel. He could feel the blood thrumming around his body, remembering every moment they had spent together, every time she'd smiled at him. The Rover ate up the dusty road, but the thought of home gave him no comfort now. Without the hope of seeing her again, the station seemed a desolate place. His love for the station had become entangled with his feelings for her. Everything he saw hurt now. He had a gnawing need for space.

He pulled the Rover into the carport and went inside; for the first time, he left his boots on. He had to remove himself from the situation or he was going to crumble. But where could he go? He paced, avoiding the lounge room with its happy family photographs.

Suddenly, an idea struck. He went straight down the hall to the phone and punched in a number.

'Will?'

'Hey, Mark. Good to hear fr—'

Mark spoke over the top of him. 'Will, is that shut work still on? You mentioned it a few weeks ago.'

'Yeah, sure. Dave interested?'

'No, not Dave. Me.'

A short pause. 'Something happen with Dad?'

'No. Is it on or not?'

'Yeah, it's on. Something happen with Daniella?'

Mark heard the plastic handset groan as his fist clenched around it. He made himself breathe out.

'Mark?'

'Yeah, something like that. Can I come or not?'

'Sure, come up. When you leaving?'

'About ten minutes. I'm bringing your girl.'

'Wow. All right.'

Mark hung up, aware that he was being irrational but too upset to care. He threw three sets of work clothes and a toothbrush in a bag. He zipped it up and grabbed the Commodore's keys off the hall rack.

As he strode outside, Dave and another stationhand were pulling up. Dave took one look at the bag and said, 'You piking out?'

'Going to do the Isa shut.'

'What the hell happened?'

'Need you to fill in for a while, okay? Help Dad for a couple of weeks?' Mark knew he was being a coward, but he couldn't face telling his father he was leaving. He was really losing it now, he felt the tears on his cheeks.

'Jesus Christ,' said Dave.

'I'll check in tomorrow. Call me if there're any problems,' Mark called over his shoulder.

He couldn't believe it had come to this. He was driving away from the station. But he loved her, and it was all he could think to do.

Chapter 20

Jackie swapped the Monday shift with Roselyn so she didn't have to brave the clinic. It was strange and awful to think that just a week ago everything had been going so well. Her bank account wasn't quite there yet, but she had the application forms on top of the fridge, away from Jamie's inquisitive fingers. The only reason she hadn't filled them in was the superstition that this would be tempting fate; she needed the ute to hold together for a bit longer.

She stared meditatively at her cleaning cupboard. Mr Sheen was an excellent therapist, so she grabbed him first and started on the sticky TV cabinet with gusto.

She was angry as hell with Daniella. Jackie had kept the identity of Jamie's dad to herself for three long years – it stung that the first person she'd confided in had betrayed her. She still found it hard to believe, but it must have been Daniella. Dave had always kept the secret, and the timing put the issue beyond doubt.

What surprised Jackie was how much the loss of the friendship hurt. Daniella had been such a fresh breeze – she was fun, supportive, and the first person to really understand Jackie's dreams for a different life. And that made the betrayal all the worse.

Jackie moved on from the cabinet, working around the flaking edges of the chipboard cupboards in the kitchen. She cleaned until Jamie woke up, then played with him until his cheerful exuberance made her cry. Dave had been like that once, when they'd first liked each other. It seemed so long ago that she'd felt that young, when she'd loved him and had hopes for their future together. It made her heart ache that Jamie so powerfully reminded her of Dave. She'd wanted her feelings for Dave to move past longing and anger, yet she seemed powerless to achieve it.

At around two thirty she ran out of surfaces to clean, so she started looking in cupboards instead, daring the dust bunnies to show themselves and submit to her wrath. The idea made her smile. She spun about the kitchen, making light-sabre moves with the duster. *Zoom-zoom*. She stopped when she realised she was just putting dust back on the floor, but it had cheered her up a little. She would make dinner early, watch a feel-good movie tonight, one where the bad guys got what was coming and the good guys won. Probably, it should have Bruce Willis in it.

Investigating the pantry, she discovered a hitch with her plan. Dinner required food. She picked through the ancient tins of tomato soup, found a bottle of satay sauce and three half-open pasta packets. She looked towards Jamie's room. Could she face the store now, with everyone talking about them?

To hell with that, she decided. She couldn't hide forever. Best get on with it.

Jamie fell asleep in the stroller on the walk down. Jackie breezed around the aisles, selecting things without really looking. After all her bravado, there was no one else in the store, and she felt oddly disappointed. She wanted someone to give her a disapproving glance so she could shout at them, get some of this fire out of her system. *What are you looking at?*

When she realised the desired fight wasn't going to materialise, Jackie finally went to the checkout. She slapped her purchases down on the counter. Becky was at the register and gave her a wide-eyed look. This only made Jackie feel tired; she wouldn't get any satisfaction out of yelling at a teenager, especially not one who always looked as sullen as Becky.

'Hi, Jackie,' the girl said.

'Hi, Becky.'

'What a cutie,' Becky said, smiling at Jamie as she scanned the groceries.

'Yeah.'

She leaned over to look closer at the sleeping child. 'Got your curls. Maybe his nose looks a bit like Dave's . . .' she continued.

Jackie's hands tightened on the pram handles and she missed a few words.

'. . . I couldn't believe it when she first said it, but now I can maybe see it.'

Jackie frowned. 'I'm sorry, what?'

'I said, I didn't believe her when she first said it. Thought I'd heard wrong.'

Jackie's senses tweaked. 'Who's she?'

'Stephanie Morgan. When she came to talk to my parents. I mean, she comes round a lot because of the organising committees, but last week she was telling them about Dave being . . . well, you know, that he's Jamie's dad. She was saying she thought it was awful how he'd never supported you and—'

Jackie listened in disbelief. Steph Morgan? What did she know about it?

'That's not true,' she said quickly. 'He's a good man. I didn't want people to know and I didn't want someone else's money.'

Becky tilted her head to one side. 'Oh. Well, that's good then. I didn't want that to be true. Dave always tells the other girls to quit teasing me when he comes to fix the fridges. And—' she looked around and dropped her voice 'I don't really like Stephanie Morgan.'

Jackie felt more kindly disposed towards Becky in that moment. 'Oh?'

'Yeah, well, I didn't want anyone to know about the . . .' Becky went bright red and whispered, 'You know, that I'm on the pill now. But my mum found them and told Steph about it when they were meeting about the fundraiser. And then Steph told her she should complain about Dr Bell.'

'Really?'

'Yeah, I mean . . . I sometimes listen at the door because they always know what's happening in town. I know I'm not supposed to but . . . I mean, like this morning, before I came to work, Steph was there again. It's so sad about Mark, isn't it?'

Jackie had been staring out towards the street, her mind racing as she tried to figure out how Stephanie had unearthed her secret. She had been spending a lot of time in Townsville already when Jackie had moved back from Brisbane; there was the B&S, but Jackie knew neither she nor Dave had said anything then. Her attention snapped back to Becky. 'What about Mark?'

'Didn't you know? He's left town.'

'What?'

'Yeah, that's what I thought they said this morning, and one of the stationhands was in here maybe an hour ago. He said Dave's filling in because Mark's gone to work in Isa. He was really upset about something and took off for a while.'

'Holy shit,' said Jackie out loud.

She walked home in a daze. She'd never liked Steph Morgan, but she hadn't given her too much thought. Now, though, she saw a pattern. Disrupting the dinner party, encouraging a complaint . . . both things that got at Daniella. Daniella, who was new, and who wouldn't do as she was told. Daniella, who was with Mark. Jackie also remembered that on Saturday night – before she'd heard her secret on everyone's lips – Stephanie had been asking questions about Daniella; how long had she been back in town, was she going back to Isa? And despite her foggy recollections of parts of the B&S, she thought perhaps Steph had been asking then, too. Maybe Steph was spitefully targeting Jackie now because she was Daniella's friend. Jackie thought back on the years she'd known Steph. At school she'd been a gossip and an occasional bully; in recent years, Jackie had avoided her organising committees, and would never have confided in her. And she knew Dave had always disliked Stephanie, an animosity that went back years. Perhaps the man had some good sense after all. Jackie thought about how Daniella must be feeling right now, thinking Jackie hated her and with Mark gone too. Jackie felt awful.

She was home by half past three and grabbed the phone. Then she realised Daniella would probably be too busy to talk. She tapped her foot. She would have to wait.

The phone was still in her hand. She smoothed the keys under her thumb. Then, for the first time in three years, she called Dave.

~

Daniella had – somehow – managed to get through the day. She'd tried to call Mark but had only reached his voicemail. Nothing new there; coverage on the station was patchy.

She found the note when she got home. It was in the letterbox, which she rarely checked (no one sent her mail here), so she had no way of knowing how long it had been there. All she knew now was that he was gone.

There wasn't a trace of bitterness in his words, no regret. He explained simply that he loved her. He was sorry he'd come on too strong, but not for what he felt. He wouldn't stand in her way, or make it hard for her in town by hanging around as a reminder. So, he was gone. She was free to leave, to do whatever she wanted.

Now here she was, sitting on the bench at the crest of the main street, looking out on Ryders Station as though he might still be there.

Her phone rang and she saw Jackie's name on the caller ID. Daniella cut it off. She wasn't ready for another bollocking right now.

She was shocked, however, when she walked home in the dark, white-rat eyed and sniffly, to find Jackie sitting on her front steps.

Daniella approached warily. 'Hi.'

Jackie launched herself off the stoop. 'I'm sorry,' she said, grabbing Daniella in a bear hug. 'I know it wasn't you.'

Daniella rocked backwards under the impact. 'It wasn't, I swear!'

'It was Stephanie Morgan!'

The whole tale came tumbling out, starting with Becky's revelations at the supermarket, then looping back through snatches of time in Brisbane, the B&S and a lot of deviations along the way. Daniella listened as she unlocked the door and made them both tea. Finally, Jackie got back to Becky and the supermarket.

'So, yeah, basically, Steph is a Sith Lord!' declared Jackie.

Daniella grinned despite her dismay. 'And Becky seriously reckons Steph encouraged the complaint against me?'

'Yeah. Seems Becky's a pretty good eavesdropper.'

'It's so bizarre.' Daniella leaned back in her chair, stunned. 'How did Steph even find out about you and Dave? Do you think she overheard something or guessed? Did you say something to him at the ball?'

Jackie shook her head. 'I don't know. I never said anything, not even at the B&S – I was pissed, but it's not something I'd ever just blurt out. Anyway, despite my recollection being not that great, I'm pretty sure it was you she was talking about that night. Dave and I were never together here, and no one knew that we were together in Brisbane. Daniella, I'm so sorry about the things I said to you. Just everyone talking about it was such a shock. Maybe I shouldn't have kept it quiet in the first place. Another big mistake for me.'

Daniella leaned forward. 'Jackie,' she said gently, 'if any of it was a mistake, you and Dave both made it. And don't you think it was a mistake worth making? I can see how much you love Jamie.'

'Yeah.' Jackie blew her nose.

'So, what are you going to do? Still going to Brisbane?'

Jackie nodded, her expression determined. 'When the money's sorted.'

'What about Dave?'

Jackie sucked in a pained breath. 'Don't know. Might be too late to change all that's happened in the last few years. But I talked to him.'

'You did?'

'Yeah. I just realised how stupid it was to still be angry about it. People like Steph are the real problem.'

'So you're going to try?'

'Not sure,' said Jackie. 'Nothing too fast. If we promised not to kill each other, maybe we could meet up, somewhere private. And I won't tell Jamie about Dave being his dad, won't even think about it until I've seen how everything goes.'

Daniella nodded. 'Probably a good idea to take things slow.' But the thought only reminded her of Mark, and the tears welled up again. 'I'm sorry,' she sobbed a minute later. 'I screwed up. That's why he left.'

She showed Jackie the note. Jackie read it several times while Daniella pulled herself together.

'God, this is amazing,' said Jackie, putting down the letter. 'There's no spite or anger in it. He loves you enough to take himself out of the picture and let you decide what you want. What are you going to do?'

'Nothing. He was right. I love what I do, so that's what I'm going to do.' Though this decision still made Daniella feel hollow inside, she hoped in time, that feeling would go away.

Jackie pursed her lips. 'Look, Daniella. I know I'm the last person to be giving relationship advice, but take it from someone who screwed up her chance at love because of pride – don't do it. You and Mark don't have any secrets between you, so go for it.'

Daniella looked away. She told Jackie she'd think about it, but she knew exactly what would occupy her thoughts. She did have a secret, and Mark knew it. She kept it close to her chest, the reason she needed control.

Jackie left around nine. At the door, Daniella said, 'Hey, you want to know a good spot for a private outing? For you and Dave, I mean.'

'Yeah?'

'The dam!'

Jackie gave a dismissive wave. 'Lots of people go there, you saw that!'

Even though the memory cut painfully, Daniella explained about the path, and the hidden beach where she and Mark had spent their first evening together. Jackie looked thoughtful. 'Thanks for that,' she said.

Daniella closed the door behind her. Now, all she could think about was the dam, and therefore Mark. The memories threatened to overwhelm her again, and she prowled around the house looking for distraction. *Offspring* was on the television, but Daniella couldn't face watching a romance. Instead she braved the bedroom that contained her tiny desk. Yes, a good dose of *Gray's Anatomy* was what she needed – the original. She took the tome to the desk and sat down in the uncomfortable chair. She flicked through until she found a picture of the reverse side of the liver, with all its grooves and prominences labelled in Latin. She hated the back of the liver; she'd always found it hard to remember the names. It also reminded her of surgery, and therefore her father. But some hard kernel inside her wanted to be able to stare him in the eye, even if it was through the lens of anatomically correct viscera.

She studied until eye strain made the text blur, and then shut the book with a thump. The gust of air scattered her notes.

With a groan, she grovelled under the bed to retrieve one of the sheets of paper, and instead came up with the shopping bag she'd brought from Mount Isa. It was from the same electronics shop she had looked in when out with Mark and Will – she'd gone back there before returning to Ryders. She took out a slim box and turned it over in her hands, pondering. When she'd bought it, she'd been full of enthusiasm. Then, later, she'd doubted it was a good idea – she'd put it under the bed and told herself she would give it to Aiden for Christmas instead. But in the vacuum of Mark leaving, she resolved to follow her original thought: this was for Valerie.

With renewed focus, she opened the box and got down to work, wrestling with the unfamiliar device until her eyes were gritty. But when she crawled into bed, satisfaction glowed inside her. It was even better than she'd anticipated. She only hoped for two things: first, that Valerie would accept it; and second, that in her exhaustion, she'd sleep without dreaming of Mark.

~

The next afternoon, Daniella called in to Valerie Turner's house without phoning ahead. She wasn't sure what reception she'd get, but all Valerie said once Daniella had knocked and entered was, 'Oh, it's you.'

'Hello, Mrs Turner. Sorry I didn't call first.'

'Didn't think I'd speak to you, did you? After you abandoned me?'

Daniella blew out a breath and sat down on the couch. She noticed the dressing on Valerie's leg was much smaller, and her face looked a little tanned, as if she'd been outside more. 'I had to go to Mount Isa for a week,' she said.

'I know. I made that nurse tell me all about it last week when she came with Dr Harris.'

'Jackie?'

'That's the one. Heard something interesting about her too. The cleaner wouldn't stop talking about it. Is it true about David Cooper?'

'Seems so,' said Daniella carefully.

'Bloody people,' said Valerie, shifting indignantly in her seat. 'Can't mind their own business. I can't imagine Jackie's thrilled everyone knows?'

'She's not,' said Daniella.

'And who was it that blabbed about it then?'

Daniella paused. 'I don't think I should talk about this, Mrs Turner.'

'Valerie,' the old woman said. 'I don't suppose it was you, or the nurse, or David for that matter.'

'No, it wasn't.'

'So, someone else has been doing some digging, then,' Valerie surmised with a shrewd expression. 'I wonder why.' Daniella could see her mind working, but she wasn't going to get drawn into talking about Steph Morgan, so she sat in a determined silence.

'Hmph,' said Valerie after a few minutes. 'And what have you got there?'

Relieved to change the subject, Daniella slid the box out of its bag, opened it, and passed the shiny screen to Valerie. She hoped the woman wouldn't cast it across the room.

'What's this?' Valerie looked at it suspiciously.

'It's an iPad. So you can write letters any time you want to,' Daniella explained. Before Valerie could come out with any objections, Daniella started showing her how to switch it on, and how to make the device read out what was on the screen. She desperately hoped Valerie would take this chance to reconnect with the world. She had already dialled up the size of the icons and text to maximum, and Valerie admitted, after several minutes of peering at it in ominous silence, that she could see them well enough. Daniella then produced a set of headphones and showed her how to use voice input to control the device and record text.

'Now, if you want I can help set you up with an internet connection,' Daniella went on. 'So that you can send the letters to Bruce as emails. If you do that, then the iPad can read out his replies. Or if you're feeling really brave, I can show you how to use Skype.'

Valerie said nothing for a long while, thumbing through the icons and menus and making the iPad tell her what different things were. 'This looks expensive,' she said. 'How much?'

Daniella evaded that one. 'Just think of it as a permanent loan. I want to see if it actually works for you.'

'Does this mean you're not coming round anymore?' Valerie demanded.

Daniella smiled. 'Not at all. I just don't want you to have to wait for me if you want to write a letter.'

Valerie turned back to the iPad. 'Thank you,' she said finally.

Daniella nodded, trying to hide how pleased she was by Valerie's acceptance. 'Well, try it out.'

'How's that man of yours?' asked Valerie suddenly.

Emptiness immediately opened in Daniella's chest and drained the strength from her arms. The plastic bag she'd been folding dropped to the floor.

'Ah,' said Valerie. 'And I suppose he's a bastard now?'

Daniella just held the tears in. 'No, it's not like that. We had a fight, and now he's left town.'

'Left town?'

'Gone to Isa,' said Daniella.

For the first time, Valerie actually looked shocked. 'This is Mark Walker, isn't it?'

Daniella got up hastily; there was no way she could deal with Valerie's pity right now. 'Sorry, Valerie, I'd really better go.'

'He'll be back,' Valerie called after her. 'Those Walkers always come back.'

But Daniella wasn't sure that was true.

Chapter 21

Mark clocked off after another twelve-hour shift and was out the mine gate five minutes later. He drove to Will's place in town, where he was staying.

There were things about Isa he didn't mind. The place was bigger than Ryders Ridge, and very few people knew him, so no one ever stopped him to ask how he was or how things were on the station. Plus he was making good money, which couldn't be a bad thing.

On the other hand, he had few outlets for his despair.

He'd never been a big drinker; on the station, there were always early starts and he hated feeling hung-over. So it scared him how quickly the pubs and drinking holes had begun to look attractive. That had happened after only a few days, so Mark had taken up exercise instead, something he'd never worried about on the station. The mine work was physical, but nothing like what he'd done each day at home. So now he ran through the streets each night, for at least an hour, hoping to wear himself out enough to sleep.

The problem was, it wasn't working. Nearly three weeks had passed since he'd left, and he felt no better. In fact, his longing for Daniella had only grown worse. He'd even removed her number from his phone so he couldn't call her at a weak moment.

Tonight, Friday night, was the worst. A free weekend stretched ahead; the shutdown ran 24/7, but due to safety guidelines, they wouldn't put him on any more shifts. He also had to face the fact that in another week, the rolling shut would be complete across the site and the work would be over. What he would do then, he hadn't yet thought through.

'Mark? You home?'

He heard the flat's front door open, followed by the clump of Will's boots on the entry tiles.

'In here,' Mark called.

'Coming out tonight?'

'Nah—'

'I should rephrase that. You're coming out tonight,' said Will. 'You're fucking suicide on a stick and you need to get over it.'

Over the past three weeks Will had tried on several occasions to find out what had happened, but Mark had shut down. Talking about it made it worse – or at least that was how it felt. Will had eventually given up, declaring Mark was impossible. It was a temporary reprieve only; he'd avoided taking any calls from his father, but Catrina would soon be home for the September break. When she discovered he wasn't at Ryders, Mark knew she wouldn't leave it alone until she'd uncovered the truth.

Cranky at the thought, he turned on the big-screen TV and flicked through Will's cable channels. Golf. Some horrible reality show featuring orange women with large hair. A romantic comedy, several inane sitcoms. If he stayed in, he was going to go mental.

'Where are you going?' he asked Will.

'No, just come. It doesn't matter where.'

'So, you're going to the 'Rish.'

'Just come out.'

To his surprise, Mark actually did feel a little better after he'd washed the mine off his body and got dressed in jeans and a white shirt. By the time they'd reached the Irish and were heading down the stairs to the club itself, he even felt a little pumped, keyed up. They sat at the bar and Will talked while Mark steadily shredded the label off his first beer, then started on the sweaty coaster. The bar girl made a face as she cleaned it up.

They ordered another round. Tuning out Will's voice, he started watching the other clubgoers. Many of the guys were from the mine, but there were other businesses in town too, and a number of out-of-towners stopping over during the long drive west. From time to time, he heard snatches of Jimmy Barnes being murdered, karaoke-style, from round the corner.

'. . . want to come?' Will asked.

Mark had been watching a group of guys in King Gees who'd approached two women, both drinking from cola-filled lowball glasses, and standing around one of the far tables. They were behind a pillar and he couldn't quite see what was happening. He realised Will had stopped talking and was looking at him expectantly.

'Ah, sorry, what did you say?'

Will rolled his eyes. 'I said, do you want to come shooting? Harry's going at the end of the swing. Got a spare space.'

'Not sure,' said Mark, still watching the table. He thought he recognised one of the guys, but he could only see his profile. The other men had begun to wander off, but Mark kept watching because of the way the women were playing with their straws, their shoulders hunched; neither of them looked comfortable. The guy probably couldn't take a hint. Mark turned his empty bottle meditatively.

'Come on, it'll be good. Besides, Harry's bringing his sister—'

'Why would I care about that?' snapped Mark without looking at Will.

'Because she's gorgeous and I know she'll like you.'

Mark stilled; he felt as though he'd just been kicked in the guts. He slowly placed his empty on the bar and put his hands together. 'Let it go, Will,' he said.

Will shrugged. 'Worth a try.'

Across the floor, the two women were making to leave. The guy was still standing there. Then he moved, blocking their exit.

Mark was on his feet and across the room before he could think. He brought his hand down on the guy's shoulder. 'Hey, buddy. Buy you a drink?' Under his hand, the shoulder was angular and ropey with muscle.

The guy shrugged him off, turning on him. 'Push off,' he growled. 'Talkin' to these ladies here.'

With a shock, Mark realised where he'd seen him before. The last time they'd met, Pete Stein had been eating dust out the front of the Ryders Ridge hospital. From the expression on the other man's face, Mark knew the recognition was mutual.

The women backed away, scenting trouble. Mark made his hand into a fist around Pete's shirt and leaned his weight in. 'Outside,' he hissed.

He manhandled Pete through the club and up the stairs towards the exit, caught in a sense of whirling déjà-vu; he felt the same rage that had filled him at the hospital when he'd seen this man threatening Daniella. He needed to be taught a lesson. Again. People stepped back to let them pass.

Soon they were outside in the car park, under a yellow spotlight. Mark gave Pete a shove and let him go. 'You need to learn some manners,' he said, as Pete recovered his balance. Mark put up his fists. 'Let's go.'

'Fuck you,' said Pete, twitching his shoulders as though he could still feel Mark's hands on him. 'No one asked you to stick your cock in. 'Snot the way it works around here.'

Mark realised too late that he and Pete weren't alone. Someone came at him from behind and landed a decent hit below his left ear. Mark twisted away, but he was knocked off-balance, his head spinning. Looking down, he counted several pairs of boots. Right, he thought, good idea to haul the guy out who's here with his mates. He couldn't see Will anywhere, and a shot of fear for his brother went through him.

The big guy who'd come up behind him took another swing. Mark ducked, coming back with a rough right that landed in the guy's generous beer belly. Shit, padding.

Mark tried to get his back against the gardens, but they cut him off. He sidestepped another guy who tried to tackle him, and got a body shot in. The guy went down onto the pavement, and provided an inconvenient lump that the others had to move round. So, he could take a breath, try to get out of this—

His head snapped to the side and he crumpled. There was no pain at first; he only registered he'd been hit. With something much harder than a fist. He put a hand forward to stop himself falling and found he was on his knees. There was blood raining down on the bitumen. His left eye started throbbing, a smash of pain with each heartbeat. Then a wind-sucking kick landed below his ribs and knocked him onto his back.

Blood ran hot down his face and into his ear. Dimly, through his stunned semi-consciousness, he heard furious voices. Then urgent footsteps. A hand shook his shoulder.

'Jesus, Mark!' It was Will. Dazed, Mark tried to get up. 'No, stay there.'

Women's heels clacked on the bitumen. Something soft was pressed against his face.

'Here, hold this on,' said Will, moving Mark's hand to cover it more firmly.

'Ow, fuck!' declared Mark.

'Yep, stitches for you,' said Will.

~

Afterwards, Mark wasn't entirely sure how they got to the hospital. He knew there wasn't an ambulance; he'd have remembered the flashing lights. Maybe they walked, maybe Will had bundled him into a taxi. In any case, he spent the journey torn between rage at Pete and his mates, and hoping against hope that Daniella would, by some miracle, be in the Isa hospital again.

She wasn't. Of course.

Will leaned against the bench in the minor procedures room, leafing through an ancient *Who Weekly*, while one of the doctors stitched up Mark's face.

'You're lucky,' the doctor told him. 'The split's right above your eyebrow, so it won't show too much once it's healed. It's pretty deep though. Bled nicely.'

Mark grunted. He was lying down so the doctor could patch him up, and his ribs ached. He wanted to curl up to take the pressure off them, but all he could do was pull up his knees.

'Still numb, or do you need a top-up?' asked the doc, waggling a syringe of local anaesthetic.

'I'm good,' said Mark. He didn't want to talk. Despite only drinking two beers – a couple of hours ago now – he felt empty and nauseous. And it was doubly awful here in the hospital, with its clean scent that only reminded him of Daniella.

The doctor didn't sense his reluctance, chatting on as he worked. 'Big cut – what'd you get hit with?'

'Beer bottle,' put in Will, from above the Kardashian sisters. 'One of them threw it at you.'

'Ha,' said the doc.

'Makes sense,' said Mark, wincing. 'Didn't think it was a fist.'

'Got a discerning face, have you?' chuckled the doc. Then he got serious. 'Look, there's nothing broken in your face, as far as I can tell on the X-ray. But those ribs could be cracked. At the least they're bruised pretty bad, and you're going to be sore. I'll write you a cert for work. You'll need a few days off.'

Mark almost laughed. He was about to tell the doctor not to bother; he was a grazier, after all, he didn't have an employer to report to. Then he remembered: he did.

The doctor excused himself to attend to other patients, telling Mark to stay put for a while. Mark closed his eyes and obeyed. Man, what a shitstorm. A few weeks ago, everything had been perfect.

Well, maybe not perfect. He hadn't known then what was going on beneath the surface, but it had *felt* lovely. He missed Daniella. The longing was so strong, he thought he might be sick.

A bedpan appeared under his chin. 'You gonna chuck?' asked Will. 'You look a bit off.'

'No,' Mark croaked. Though maybe he should. Something to do.

Will threw the mag back on the bench. 'Okay. You going to tell me why you picked a fight with that guy?'

'He was messing with those girls,' mumbled Mark.

'Aw, come on. You were spoiling for a fight. Don't think I didn't notice.'

Mark took a shallow breath and kept his voice low. That way his ribs hurt less. 'He's the same guy I turfed out of the Ryders hospital. Trying to steal drugs.'

'And threatening Daniella. You told me about it, remember?'

Mark closed his eyes, stung by the sound of her name. 'Yeah.'

'All right, that makes a bit of sense. But look, you're clearly not over this girl, Mark. Sooner you realise that the easier it'll be for you.'

Mark tried to sit up so he could tell Will again how much he didn't want to talk about it. The pain was excruciating, and Will had to help him, stuffing pillows behind his back for support. By the time that was done, the heat had gone out of his anger. 'I'll be fine,' he said. 'I just need more time. When she moves on, I'll be fine.'

'Listen to you,' said Will. 'You have no idea. It'll kill you if she moves on with someone else.'

'I meant when she leaves town. She's going to leave, Will. She told me she was planning to stay, but she never even unpacked. Sooner or later she'll be pushing off somewhere else.'

'Like me?' asked Will gently.

Mark was quiet for a while. 'That's different,' he said.

Will sat down carefully on the bed. 'It's not different. I know how much the station means to Dad, and to you, but it's not for me. It's not what I want for my life, and if I made myself stay there I'd be unbearable to be around. Sometimes, you can't stay somewhere just to be with the people you love; it's just not enough. Dad'll understand that eventually. At least, I hope he will. It doesn't mean I love the place any less, but I can't stay there. And maybe it's the same for Daniella.'

Mark was unmoved. 'She can do what she wants.'

'Going down swinging, huh? Look, Mark, she's in your blood, right? Hiding out here and hoping she'll leave town before you have to go back won't help you get over her.'

Mark knew Will was right, but that just made him angry. 'What the hell do you know about it?' he demanded.

Will refused to bite. 'Mark. The way you talk about her – that's exactly how Dad was about Mum. He loved her absolutely, but he could never accept that she had to travel to be herself. She was a teacher and she loved Ryders too. But she was more than that – she needed the world outside as much as she needed him. His problem was that he could never understand how she could love and need both things. I've always thought I ended up like her. But you, my brother, you're like Dad. You want things to be too simple – your way.'

Mark chewed on this, his anger slipping away again. 'I don't want to be like that,' he whispered.

Will shrugged. 'I'm not going to go all Dr Phil on you, but you're not completely like Dad. You've been travelling too. You've seen some of the world. Right?'

Mark nodded, but he realised that those days seemed a long time ago. It felt as though for years he'd thought of nothing but the station, and getting it right again.

'Right,' continued Will. 'And you went back to Ryders because after seeing what was out there you still knew you preferred home. Good for you. But Dad stayed put because he was jealous of what the bigger world meant to Mum. He didn't want to know about it, he didn't want to try and understand that. That's why they fought so badly. But you're not that lug-headed. So don't act like it.' Will paused, then put his hand briefly on Mark's shoulder. 'Okay, end of lecture. It's late and I don't know how long they're going to keep you. I'm getting a coffee.'

'Will, wait.'

Will stopped in the doorway, eyebrows raised. Mark remembered his mother standing like that sometimes, just waiting, happy to hear you even though she was bound for somewhere else. Waiting for as long as it took to say what you needed to.

'Don't drink the coffee here. Daniella said it's bad.'

'Right.'

Mark sat back against the pillows. He was still wearing his white shirt, but there was blood down the front and someone had undone the buttons to look at his ribs.

He threw his legs over the side of the bed, testing to see whether he could sit up. He had to know if he could drive.

He had to go home.

Chapter 22

Saturday morning found Daniella and Jackie in an unusually quiet clinic. Dr Harris was in with a patient, but two other appointments hadn't shown up, so re-stocking was on the agenda.

'How's it going with Dave?' asked Daniella, tearing open a box of syringes and stuffing a handful into the wall container. She knew Jackie had only seen him a few times in the last three weeks, introducing him slowly to Jamie.

Jackie had her head down, stocking up the vaccination fridge, and didn't answer.

Daniella tried again. 'Jackie? How'd it go last night?'

'Oh, um . . . okay, I guess.'

'Only okay?' Daniella stopped trolling for needle tips that had ended up in the wrong size bin.

'Yeah.' Jackie sighed and sat back on her heels. Then she closed the fridge and leaned against it. 'It's just . . . it's weird. It's not too bad when Jamie's there, because I can focus on him and talk about what he's doing. But Dave and me . . . it's awkward. There's all this stuff we don't discuss, especially about me going away. But we can't talk about it. And I don't think it'd help if we did.'

'I'm so sorry,' said Daniella. 'Maybe you just need more

time. Would you consider counselling? If you can't talk about it together, maybe you need someone else there?'

Jackie made a face. 'Ha! Can you imagine? No. Besides, we'd have to go to Isa or something to find a counsellor, and Dave's so involved at the station right now with Mark gone – shit, sorry.'

'It's all right,' Daniella said softly.

'Anyway,' said Jackie. 'I haven't told Jamie yet about Dave being his dad, but they're getting on well together. I don't want to wreck that for him. And I feel like if we tried counselling and it didn't work, we might blow everything. When we move away, I want Jamie to know he has a dad who loves him, and who might come to visit.'

'How're those plans going?' asked Daniella, starting to tidy up the desk. She really needed to stop avoiding talking to Dr Harris about her own plans for moving on and start organising. Valerie – having shrewdly deduced from the iPad gift and Mark's departure that *something* was going on – was now emailing her, asking for the details. Jackie could only laugh about Daniella unleashing a monster.

'I still haven't got round to filling in the application forms,' Jackie said ruefully. 'Can't seem to get five minutes together and I have to post them on Monday to make this year's deadline.'

'Can I help?'

'Maybe. Well, actually . . .'

Daniella looked up from rummaging through the second drawer. 'Yes?'

'I was going to do them tomorrow but Dave wanted me and Jamie to go out to the station. They're flying out to check fences in the morning and Jamie wants to see the chopper when they're back. I haven't given Dave an answer, but Jamie's been asking about it every five minutes. He's even stopped playing with his dinosaurs. Could you come with us? If you could keep an eye on Jamie around the chopper for an hour, I could do the forms then.'

Daniella took a breath. It would mean seeing the station again, which would bring up so many memories of Mark, and besides, William Walker might be there. She hesitated, anxious.

Jackie saw this and said, 'I don't like the chopper anyway—' she wrinkled her nose '—and it would be a big help. I'll be too stuffed by evening to concentrate.'

Daniella considered; Mark was away, and Jackie was a good friend. She relented. 'Okay,' she said.

Daniella turned up at Jackie's at nine the next morning, but by the time Jamie was organised, Daniella and Jackie were late heading out to the station. Jackie's ute bounced them over the cattle grids, and with each passing minute, Daniella's stomach tightened further.

Finally, they drove over the last rise and saw the homestead with its honey-coloured stones sheltering under the verandah in the morning sun. Daniella's mind flooded with mixed emotions: the peace she'd felt here with Mark beside her, and the ache of knowing that time was gone.

The ute ground to a stop beside the nearest shed, and Jamie tumbled out of the back. 'Little bugger's got good at undoing that,' hissed Jackie as she scrambled to catch him before he could get too far.

Daniella eased herself out, her eyes scanning nervously round. Actually, the place seemed deserted. Dave would still be out flying, and the cattle yards were empty except for a few horses. In fact, it was a lot like the first time Mark had brought her here.

The front door of the homestead opened and Kath appeared, swaddled in an enormous apron. 'Yoo hoo! Come in!' she called. Daniella had met her only briefly before and wondered how much she knew about what had happened with Mark. Would Kath blame her for his departure?

She needn't have worried. Kath greeted her warmly, ushered all three of them inside and installed them at the huge kitchen table, which was loaded with sacks of potatoes, boxes of onions, vacuum-packed meat.

'There you go,' she said, pouring a glass of lemonade for Jamie. 'They're still out, I'm afraid, but Dave told me you were coming, and to clear you some space, Jackie. Daniella, my dear, I might have to put you to work.' She nodded towards the table, which had been cleared at one end but was otherwise groaning under the produce.

'You're not cooking all that are you?' asked Jackie.

'Not all of it – some's going to the larder. But we've got a full house tonight so I wanted to get started early. The Morgans are coming in from town later. The men are all out on the long routes today, and it's hot and dusty, so when they come back they'll be starving.' She hefted a sack of potatoes into the sink, then put the others into a huge bin in the pantry.

Daniella soon found herself at the sink with a peeler in hand. 'What's happening today?' she asked.

Kath kept moving the supplies as she spoke. 'Well, they're doing the long fence run in the chopper this morning and then moving stock to the back paddock. This afternoon there're orders to sort and they're starting on a shed extension.'

Daniella only half listened as she swept the peeler across the first potato, laying bare its pale glistening flesh. Being inside the house, especially here in the kitchen, where she and Mark had made sandwiches, where he had kissed her – the memories were even stronger and more painful than they had been outside. Trying to distract herself, she asked, 'What's happening out on the long routes?'

'Gate repairs, and checking a bore for starters.' Kath smiled as she watched Jamie investigate the dark recesses of the pantry. 'No, you keep on with what you're doing. He's all right,' she said to Jackie, who had looked up from her paperwork to see what mischief Jamie was up to.

Kath turned back to Daniella and her smile broadened as she said knowingly, 'You must be looking forward to seeing them when they get back.'

Daniella looked at her in confusion. 'I'm sorry, why?'

'After Mark's been away in Mount Isa all these weeks.'

Daniella's heart stopped momentarily, then pounded noisily in her ears. 'I'm sorry,' she said again. 'You mean Mark's back?'

'Yes, love. You didn't know? He got back yesterday. Looked a little worse for wear.'

Oh God. Daniella felt ill. 'No, I didn't know,' she whispered.

'Oh well. Nice surprise then.' Kath went to the window and peered out down the station's front paddocks.

Daniella nodded weakly. Jackie caught her eye and raised an inquisitive eyebrow. Kath turned back from the window and looked at her watch. 'Those boys. Must've stopped somewhere. Said they'd be back by now.'

Daniella picked up another potato, then put it back on the pile. 'Excuse me for a minute,' she said.

She stepped out onto the verandah and walked away from the kitchen, trying to find air that wasn't cloying. She pulled the phone from her pocket and checked the reception. Two bars; not bad for out here. After the way they'd parted, she felt intrusive being here. She had to talk to him before he came back and found her.

Her hand shook as she dialled. There was a moment's silence, before an electronic voice responded. '*The mobile telephone you have dialled is switched off or not in a mobile area—*'

Feeling helpless, she hung up. Heading back towards the kitchen she found Kath standing in the doorway, her hand shielding her eyes, staring down the range.

'Really expected them back by now,' she said, frowning.

'What time did they say they'd be back?' Daniella asked.

Kath looked at her wrist. 'Twenty minutes ago.'

Jackie came up behind Kath, Jamie on her hip. He'd somehow managed to smear chocolate across his cheek. 'What are we looking at?' she asked.

'Seeing if we can spot the chopper coming back,' Kath answered.

At the mention of the chopper, Jamie wriggled to be let down. He pressed himself against the verandah post, eyes fixed on the horizon.

'Kath said they're late,' Daniella said to Jackie.

'I'm sure it's nothing,' said Kath reassuringly. 'They often make extra stops. But lunch always brings them back, even Mark.'

Daniella's pulse thundered in her throat. 'Mark? He's flying with Dave?'

Kath nodded. 'They sent the others to move the herd and took the chopper for the fence.'

Movement caught Daniella's eye. Jamie held his arm up, flapping his fingers as though trying to fly. But just one arm. He noticed her looking and beamed up at her. 'Look!' he said.

Daniella squinted. And there, on the horizon, floating and almost indistinct, was a puff of red dust.

~

Kath grabbed binoculars from inside, but even with the magnification, all she could report was rapidly dissipating dust. She looked over the top of the lenses. 'Could be the herd,' she said, passing the binoculars to Daniella. 'Except there's no herd up there in the long pocket.'

Kath's lips were pinched. Daniella knew she didn't really think it was the cows. And there was still no sign of the chopper. Kath tried to raise them on the radio, and got nothing. She came back out and gave Daniella a searching look. Understanding passed between them.

'Jackie, we need to borrow your ute,' said Kath decisively. 'Stay here with Jamie and call everyone else back in. Channel sixty, all right? They're all probably at least thirty minutes away, maybe more. And keep trying the chopper. Let us know if you get anything.' Kath pressed a hand-held radio into Daniella's hand. It felt like lead in her palm.

'What are we going to do?' asked Daniella.

'Take the ute to the long pocket and check it out.'

They were soon rattling off the graded road and into the front paddock. Kath didn't drive anything like Mark had when he'd taken Daniella down the ridge; she floored the ute, roaring down the fence line until Daniella could see a column of dust rising up behind them. Every time they hit a bend, Daniella felt the ute's rear tyres slide a little. She kept thinking about Mark and Dave, somewhere out there in the endless sky; she hoped at any moment they would see the chopper flying towards them and find the dust cloud was just a bunch of escaped cows or stationhands doing circle work.

But as the fifteen-minute mark ticked by, they lost the dust cloud. Daniella leaned forward, desperately scanning the ground and sky on each side of the fence. She tried not to despair, but the property was so large, and she couldn't see very far in each direction. How would they spot them?

'Hope they were still on the fence line,' muttered Kath, as if she had heard Daniella's thoughts. She came to a halt, letting the dust behind the ute settle. The homestead was just a light smudge on the horizon behind them. The source of the cloud had to be close by.

They pressed on, around four more bends, over some deep ruts, and then the road changed. The earth here was fine, sandy and pale beneath a thin red dust coat. Then, over the next rise, they saw it.

The chopper had come down in the soft earth, tearing out a gash of topsoil and grass as it tumbled over. Daniella couldn't tell for a minute exactly what she was looking at; pieces of wreckage seemed to be strewn everywhere. Then she saw that the tail had come off, and lay twisted, the rotors crumpled and broken. The cabin appeared intact and was leaning on its side, covered in fine dust and dug a foot in.

Daniella threw herself out the door before the ute was fully stopped. She heard her own footsteps, then the creaking of metal as fragments shifted in the breeze, then something splashing. Kath was behind her, calling frantically on the radio for help.

'Mark! Dave!' Daniella yelled as she ran towards the wreck.

She saw Dave first.

He was lying on the ground beside the dented cabin bubble, on his side. Daniella had visions of the car crash in Mount Isa – the bodies amid pieces of wreckage. Only now, there were no ambos to help. No equipment.

She checked him quickly. His face was bloodied and he was unconscious, but she found a pulse and felt some breaths. He looked as though he'd managed to climb out of the cabin before passing out.

She smelled a fresh, sharp scent. It reminded her of the airport. The sound of splashing acquired a new, sinister meaning. Fuel. Leaking fuel.

She stood up and looked towards the cabin.

Mark was still in his seat, slumped forward, his head resting on the central control panel. Seeing him move, Daniella ran to the leaning side of the wreck. The door next to Mark was bent inwards, the window cracked. Daniella's professional brain kicked in. She needed to get his head upright or he might suffocate. A few yanks on his door did nothing to budge it. She tried again, with all her strength, and the catch released, but the door only opened a short way before sticking; she had to wedge herself against the cabin and kick at the door to force it open.

'Mark!' she yelled. His face was slippery with blood; it took two attempts to tip up his chin. His eyelids flickered. Blood ran down his forehead, soaking a dressing she briefly noted above his eyebrow.

The smell of fuel was potent now, stinging her nose. She thought she smelled a trace of smoke, too. And with that came cold terror. She had no idea how long they had before the fuel caught fire. Nothing mattered at this point except getting away.

'Kath!' she yelled, seeing the older woman running towards Dave. 'Move him! Drag him back!' She turned away. 'Mark!' she shouted again. She fumbled, managed to release his seat-belt, but she could hardly shift him. He was too heavy, and she realised that one foot was caught on a pedal. Something black protruded from his pocket, catching the belt. His phone. Daniella shoved it into her own pocket.

He turned his head to look at her, eyes glassy and unfocused. Blood ran from his nose, making his teeth into little orange squares rimmed in red.

She tugged on his leg, heard the fabric of his trousers tear as it came free. She tried to get under his shoulder. It didn't quite work. He wasn't conscious enough to walk, or even stand. As soon as his feet hit the ground he crumpled, and Daniella went down with him.

With her nose in the dust, she couldn't get enough air. The fuel filled every breath. Her vision swam; she had to get up. She made it to her knees. Mark slumped against the red earth beneath her. The smell of smoke was stronger now.

A primal sense drove her to action. She got her feet underneath her and heaved up, then grabbed Mark's collar and pulled. He didn't move. She crouched and pulled again with all her strength, leaning over until he shifted a few feet. She stopped, lungs burning, legs screaming, then pulled again, not daring to stop until her energy gave out. Something was definitely on fire now; she could feel the heat on her back. When she turned, she saw Kath still struggling to drag Dave. With a last effort she stumbled back towards them; together, they pulled Dave away as flames spread around the chopper.

She managed to get both men laid out, then she collapsed alongside Mark, shaking, all the adrenaline spent. Kath knelt beside her, exhausted.

As soon as she'd caught her breath, Daniella checked vitals as best she could. There was blood coming from Mark's ear – not a good sign. His pulse was rapid, thready. A horrible chasm opened in her mind: a panicky sensation that cancelled out rational thought. She saw again the A&E in Brisbane. This was the way she had felt then, too – blank and empty, useless. And the patient had died.

She sensed Mark slipping. Her beautiful Mark, who'd loved her, wanted her. She hadn't had the chance to tell him she loved him too, which she knew now with hopeless certainty. Failed once; now failing again. She threw her arms across his chest and hugged him, keeping his heart beating in her ear.

The explosion came then. It wasn't Hollywood spectacular; there was no rain of burning fragments, but suddenly, the wreckage was engulfed. A heat wave licked them and a column of charcoal smoke funnelled into the sky. That big sky she loved so much . . . Mark had fallen from it, and she couldn't even think what to do.

Silent tears washed the dust from her face as she sat in the dirt, listening to Mark's pulse slipping, hoping help was coming soon.

It took nearly two hours for the four-wheel-drive ambulance to arrive, load Mark and Dave and make it back to the Ryders Ridge hospital. By that time, Daniella was frantic. Mark's breathing had grown very quiet. She could do nothing but watch, shaking and useless, as the volunteer ambos did their work.

The A&E doors seemed frighteningly unfamiliar, but everyone was prepped. Dr Harris and Roselyn worked with practised efficiency. The Flying Doctors were en route to the air strip but were still a long way off. Dimly, Daniella was aware of Dr Harris working to stabilise both men: equipment was rolled out, pulse oximeters were attached, lines put in, saline bags hung. His calm assurance brought more guilt, as did the fact that Jackie was capably working alongside them. Daniella herself was dizzy, shaking so much she hadn't even been able to put a drip in. Calmly, Dr Harris took it out of her hands and sent her to sit on a gurney.

Only then did she become aware of what was happening outside the door. William Walker paced in front of the plastic chairs in the hall, rubbing his face. She didn't know when he'd arrived.

She turned away. Dr Harris now had the ultrasound machine out and was pressing it up near Mark's rib cage. Roselyn was hanging two red bags. Blood. A moment later, the red streak ran from the bag down the IV line. Dr Harris had started a transfusion.

He stepped away and drew Daniella out into the hall where William stood.

'How's he doing?' asked William, his voice not quite steady.

Daniella hugged herself; from what she'd just seen she already knew what Dr Harris had likely found.

'William, I'm not going to beat around the bush,' said Dr Harris. 'He's bleeding internally, probably from the spleen. Blood pressure's low. Probable head injury too, like Dave. They both need to get out of here and to Townsville as fast as possible. I'm not a surgeon, and he needs one. RFDS say they're still at least half an hour away. We need to try to hold out for that long, and then for the journey. At this point we're preserving organ function.'

Daniella felt cold trickling dread. For the first time in her life, she was on the wrong side of this conversation, having to hear bad news about someone she loved. In that moment she regretted everything: lying to Mark, telling him to leave when she should have fought as hard as he had. The idea that he might die before she could tell him how she felt was infinitely worse than anything she'd experienced before.

'He's going to need a lot of fluids and blood,' Dr Harris went on. 'So we've called—'

'The community donors,' interrupted William. 'I saw them. They're waiting out front.'

Dr Harris nodded, satisfied. 'Yes, good. Daniella?'

She looked at him blankly, and he put his hands on her shoulders. 'You've done a lot today already, and I know you're in shock, but I need your help taking blood. Get a full bag from everyone you can.'

Roselyn appeared and passed her a box of blood donation bags. Daniella took it in a daze, still with the dreadful blankness inside. Then she thought of Mark and how important this was. She forced herself to focus. She remembered being in Isa, where she'd used the donation bag without trouble. Somewhere inside, she knew what she was doing. She followed William down the hall. In the waiting area were six people, who all looked as though they'd come straight from work. She recognised Donna from the tav, and Rich, the copper. These were the volunteers from the community who made up a living blood bank, O-negatives who came when they were needed, because Ryders hospital didn't store much blood.

And now, they had come for the man she loved.

She took a steadying breath, squared her shoulders. 'Mr Walker, could you get me that trolley, please? Now, I need each of you in a chair, with an empty chair beside you. You first,' she said, pointing at a young man in overalls with scruffy hair. From the look of his lean, muscular arms, he'd have the best veins.

She pulled a chair in close, and the trolley appeared beside her. Nothing looked familiar. She stared at the kidney-shaped dish, at the rolls of tape and the blood bags in their packets, the stack of cotton balls. Panic heated her blood and her face flushed. Time accelerated; she felt the blood donors' eyes on her. She reached for the dish and knocked a multicoloured elastic strap onto the floor. What was that even for . . . ?

Amid the panic, a cool thread of clarity. It was the tourniquet. She snatched it up and shakily wrapped it around the guy's bicep. She was rolling now, little rivulets of memory running together. She felt the veins at his elbow, remembering one step ahead, then two. But when the red stream finally flowed down the tube and into the bag, no satisfaction came with it, only relief.

Chapter 23

Mark seemed to hold on by sheer force of will, but Daniella was all too aware of how bad things were. His only chance was to reach a hospital with a good surgical unit and a good surgeon.

The RFDS plane touched down just as the ambulance pulled into the tiny terminal shed. Dr Harris and the volunteer ambos helped the transfer team to load Mark and Dave. With two patients, there was no room for passengers. Daniella had to let go of Mark's hand and watch as the plane closed its doors, roared down the short runway and vanished into the big blue sky.

On the journey back in the empty ambulance, she didn't know how she could just go home and wait for news. But mercifully, Dr Harris offered her his car. 'Go,' he said simply.

She raced home, threw a few things into a bag, then hit the highway, heading for the Townsville hospital, six hours' drive away. Jackie still had to go home and get Jamie, and said she would follow as soon as possible.

Daniella was only half an hour down the road when her mobile rang. She glanced down at the screen and saw it was Jackie. She almost picked it up while driving, but then pulled Dr Harris's station wagon to a stop on the shoulder of the road, leaving a cloud of dust floating across the highway.

'They're not going to Townsville,' said Jackie grimly, when Daniella answered the call. 'The evac coordinator called back, said ICU there is full; they just had a bad smash on the highway. And the boys might need a neurosurgeon, too, so they've diverted the flight.'

'Where to?'

'Straight to the Princess Mary trauma unit in Brisbane.'

Silence.

Faintly, Daniella heard Jackie's voice, far away, saying, 'I'm putting Jamie in the car and driving to Isa with William Walker in an hour.'

But all she registered was: *Brisbane*. The place where bad things had happened.

Daniella pushed the car door open and put her feet on the road. The bitumen arrowed off in both directions, dividing the still, golden grass, and shedding ripples where it met the sky. The sun spilled across her forehead in a hot rush. No wind, no breath.

Alone.

The sky waited.

She ran her fingers across the keys of her mobile. Jackie was gone; hung up or dropped out, Daniella had no idea. The reception bars were down to one; soon, when she drove on, there would be none. She bit her lip, tasting salt on her dry, cracked skin. She was too aware, in that moment, of her vulnerabilities, all of them. The churning shame she'd carried since Brisbane; the ache where Mark had touched and changed her heart; her body alone under the sun. Mark was vulnerable too; he would arrive in Brisbane long before she did. She couldn't stand the thought of him being alone like this.

She keyed the number. The one bar of reception held.

'Peter Bell.'

'Dad.' Crackles on the line.

'Daniella?' Concern in his voice. 'Something wrong?'

She tried to sound matter-of-fact. 'I'm on my way to find a flight to Brisbane.'

'Well, that's great—'

'Please, Dad, just listen.' She breathed out to quell the shaking in her voice. 'There are two patients being medevaced to the PM right now. One of them is Mark Walker. Out of Ryders Ridge for internal bleeding. He was in a chopper crash.'

Daniella could hear scratching sounds around the crackling. Her father was making notes with a pencil.

She went on, 'He's my . . .' She wanted to say *boyfriend*, but that wasn't true, and *patient* was too cold. 'He's important. I want to be there but it'll take me a few hours to get to Isa and I don't know the flight times. Can you meet him when he comes in? If you're off that's okay—'

'I'm on shift soon,' he said quickly. 'It's not a problem. What's kidney function like?'

'Dad, I don't know. I wasn't the treating doc,' she said, frustrated and afraid.

More scribbling. 'I'll go and find out who's managing this end, but I'll probably be the one in theatre.' Her father's voice was flat, professional. He was in his zone.

Daniella felt relief lighten her. In her father, she had the highest confidence. 'Dad, I have to go. I need to keep driving.'

'All right. How long until you reach Isa?'

Daniella glanced at her watch. 'Two and a half hours, I think. Maybe three.'

'I'll have my secretary organise the earliest flight. Call her when you get to the airport. I'll have information for you when you get here.'

Daniella hung up and stared at the phone. In the distance, a crow settled on the road, then took off again. She had never before felt grateful that her father was a perfectionist who demanded the same of everyone else . . . but now she did.

Climbing back into the station wagon, she joined the highway again and headed for the Isa turn-off.

~

At nine thirty that evening, Daniella stepped out of a taxi at the Princess Mary Hospital, grateful that the trip had been short and she hadn't had to field the driver's attempts to chat for too long. The sluggish weekend traffic lit Sandgate Road in white and red; above, the hospital complex – a hodge-podge of converted heritage buildings steadily being muscled out by pre-cast concrete and glass at jaunty architectural angles – glowed white, and familiar.

As the big glass doors opened to admit her, Daniella's fears intensified. This was the site of her greatest failure, and she had left because of it. The distance had deadened the guilt; now, she had nothing to shield her.

Two escalators led off the grand foyer up to the mezzanine. She avoided them and headed for the stairs, finding her way to the surgical ward on autopilot. The nurse at the desk told her Mark was in surgery, and directed her to the waiting area.

She paced. A few other people dotted the space, as animated as the fake potted plants. A Coke machine hummed and gurgled, and Daniella rubbed at her arms, frustrated and helpless. Here it didn't matter that she was a doctor; she was just someone waiting for news. So she kept moving. After what seemed like an hour, she glanced at the clock. How long had it been? Ten minutes. Shit.

Time that had raced in the Ryders hopsital waiting room now ground to a halt. Her back ached. She sat in one of the hard plastic chairs, tipped her head back against the wall and closed her eyes. Mark was before her instantly. He was laughing, his green eyes sparkling under his hat, his hand reaching for her. Daniella jerked her own eyes open, tears already forming. She didn't want those memories now. She couldn't bear it. Not if . . .

Not if she lost him.

She shied away from the thought. But instead, all she could think about was the waiting room back in Ryders, not being able to remember how to take the donors' blood. Then other images flashed into her mind. A small limb, a purple rash. People watching her flounder. Her brow was sticky, her hand shaking. *She couldn't get the line in.* Daniella felt the fingers of dread push deeper inside her, right through her heart and into her lungs.

She heard her own sob as she wrenched herself out of the memory. She was still in the plastic chair near the Coke machine. An elderly lady across the waiting area stared at her. Daniella's heart beat in her ears and her fingers were white against the chair's arms. She pushed herself up and went into the ladies'. Three stalls, a plain sink dotted with pink soap from a leaky dispenser. She chose the last stall; closing the door, she crouched down beside the bowl, recognising a panic attack kicking in. She knew she had to break the cycle of the attack, but more than anything she wanted to feel sick, to purge herself from all these thoughts. She stared at the bowl, breathing slowly and waiting for catharsis, but nothing would come except gradual, undramatic calm. She was exhausted; tired of this internal battle. She finally got up and went out to the basin, where she splashed cold water onto her face.

She looked up into the mirror. Bloodshot eyes, a small graze on her left cheekbone. Otherwise, she looked normal. Nothing to show the hollowness inside.

Emerging from the ladies', Daniella eyed the Coke machine. She shoved her hands into her pockets, checking for coins.

Instead, she drew out two phones, and looked at them in confusion before she remembered. The second phone was Mark's. She'd taken it at the chopper.

She turned it over. It actually looked undamaged, although there was a line of dirt in every seam. She pushed the power button experimentally. The screen glowed, and a moment later, it was on. She put a hand over her mouth. The background image was a picture he'd taken of the two of them, in Mount Isa.

The phone rang in her hand; she fumbled and nearly dropped it. The desk nurse gave her a dirty look and pointed at the no-mobiles sign. Daniella managed to answer the call as she scuttled out into the hall.

'Who's that?' asked Will. 'Daniella?'

'Yes,' she croaked.

'Hey, nice to hear your voice. Mark there?'

Daniella inhaled sharply. 'How much do you know?'

'Know about what?'

She had to tell him the whole story, about the crash, the injuries, the evac, feeling desperate that he didn't know already. Will listened in disbelief, only stopping her occasionally to clarify details or ask her to slow down. For Daniella, it meant living the hell all over again; when she was done she felt drained.

'So that explains why no one was answering. I had two missed calls from the station during my shift, but no one's picking up there now. I assumed it was Mark. Hang on a tick,' said Will a moment later. 'There's something about it on the news. Jesus.'

'What?' asked Daniella.

His voice was rough. 'They're showing the wreckage.'

Daniella moved to the doorway so she could look at a monitor hanging in the waiting area. It was on a bad angle; all she could see was a black lump, then the shot panned back and she saw the black mark against the pale earth. She recognised it, but it still felt like another world, not somewhere she'd been just this morning.

'Fuck, how did the journos get in there?' Will was saying, but his voice was desperate with concern. He asked her again how Mark was now.

Daniella could only repeat what she had already said. Will fell silent; down the line, Daniella could hear rustling, a zip opening, drawers being opened and closed. She assumed he was packing a bag.

Finally, Will asked, 'How are you doing?'

Daniella leaned against the wall and sank down slowly. 'I feel like shit,' she said. She dropped her voice to a whisper. 'I'm scared.'

Will sighed. The background noises ceased. 'Oh, honey. Me too. But they're good down there, aren't they?'

Yes, they were, thought Daniella. Her father especially.

'Look, I'm nearly packed. I'm going to call Cat and make sure she knows. She plays sport on Sundays, and I don't want her hearing about it on the news. Then I'll get on the first flight there myself. Can you text me when Dad arrives?'

Daniella said she would, then ended the call and returned to the waiting area. She wondered how this would end. In a week's time, would there be grateful relief, or would her heart be aching forever?

~

An hour later, when Daniella was regretting a second cup of awful coffee, she felt a hand on her arm.

'Daniella?' Jackie stood over her, red-eyed, Jamie on her hip.

Daniella had never been so glad to see another person in her life. 'You're here.' She stood up, trying to hold back a fresh wave of tears. 'When did you get in?'

'Fifteen minutes ago. Dave's just out of surgery. They put a pin in his leg. And they're checking the scans for a skull fracture too. What about Mark?'

Over Jackie's shoulder, Daniella could see William Walker at the enquiries desk.

'Still in surgery. Don't know yet.'

Jackie grabbed her in a rough one-armed hug. 'It'll be fine,' she said, squeezing hard. But Daniella knew these were only words.

William Walker strode over, as imposing as ever but wearing a haggard expression. 'The nurse thinks he might be out soon, maybe half an hour,' he said. 'How are you, Dr Bell?'

Daniella realised he was extending an olive branch. Gingerly, she took it. 'Tired,' she admitted, sitting in one of the chairs. 'Worried.'

William grunted and sat beside her as Jackie took Jamie for a short walk. He cast an appraising glance around. 'Hate hospitals,' he said after a minute. 'They're always so cold. A person comes in here and you feel like they're not a person anymore. Sometimes I think it's better to be an animal; at least people always look at you the same way.' He spread his weathered fingers on his thigh, looking down at them as though they were the source of this wisdom. Daniella detected vulnerability in that small movement. She wondered if he was thinking about his wife as well as Mark.

'I know what you mean,' she said softly. 'Before this, I'd never had to see someone I cared about in here. I never realised how awful it is to wait.'

She was going to say more – that she was so sorry about his wife, about his son . . . something, anything. But then Daniella's own father appeared in the hall, and came towards them. She watched him, tall and familiar, comforting in his mere presence in a way he'd never been on the phone. She felt her heart tug; she wanted to run to him.

'Daniella,' he said, and she was on her feet in an instant.

'Dad, this is Mark's father, William Walker, and Jackie, one of the nurses from Ryders Ridge. Jackie and Mr Walker, this is my father, Peter Bell.'

Her father quickly shook hands. 'Right, folks, let's go over here where we can talk.' He ushered them into a little alcove with comfortable-looking chairs, but no one sat down.

Her father got straight to the point. 'We're in a tight situation. Mark's blood pressure was low on the way down here, but fortunately it stabilised before he went into surgery. I was able to stop all the bleeding, and I'm satisfied we've dealt with that, at least for now. We can never be completely sure in the first few hours, but I'm feeling confident.'

Here comes the 'but', thought Daniella.

'But his blood pressure was low for a long time. When that happens, some important organs don't get enough oxygen and they can start to shut down. His kidneys are the biggest worry right now. He's starting to show signs of acute renal failure. Now, that's recoverable. We need to support him through it. But there might be other damage. He's in the ICU, and they're going to monitor everything like hawks – he might need some dialysis.' He paused and smiled at them encouragingly. 'It's early days. I think we've reached the best situation we're going to get to right now. But we're not out of the woods yet.'

Daniella absorbed this. Her throat was already so raw, she felt beyond tears. Jackie had her hand across her mouth. Daniella's father put a hand on William's shoulder, a solid reassuring contact, honed from many moments like this.

Daniella found her voice. 'Can we see him?'

He nodded. 'Briefly, yes of course. Mr Walker, Mark has a number of machines keeping everything square at the moment. It can be confronting to see. I just want you to be prepared.'

William said stiffly, 'It's all right, doc. Went through that with my wife.'

Seeing Mark was what made the awfulness real. Daniella had been in the intensive care unit many times, but she'd never known the patients when they'd been fit and well. She felt cold terror gnaw her insides; Mark didn't look like the Mark she knew. He looked like a patient, with the endotracheal tube, the central line in the base of his neck, the hanging bags of fluid with their dosing pumps, and all the ECG dots on his chest with their leads snaking to the monitor. His face was swollen, his skin waxy, his eyes taped closed. He had bruises on his chest, scrapes on his cheeks. The dressing she'd seen over this eye at the crash site was gone, revealing stitches. On a drafting board at the foot of the bed was the big A2 monitoring chart.

Her father went with them into ICU and stood next to her the whole time, then walked them back out to the waiting area. In the middle of the room, he pulled her into his arms. 'I've missed you,' he said into her hair.

Daniella returned the hug, burying her face in his solid shoulder. The tension of their phone calls over the last few months was forgotten.

'Get some rest,' he said gently, when he released her. 'You'll need it.'

Daniella shook her head. She glanced up at the clock. It was late but she couldn't contemplate going anywhere. 'I'm staying.'

'You look exhausted,' Jackie told her. 'You need to rest.'

'So do you,' countered Daniella.

Jackie pulled a face. 'I know I should go and get some sleep. It's funny; as a nurse, I'm always encouraging patients' families to do that. Now I'm on this side, I understand why they don't want to leave, you know?'

Daniella nodded. 'Yeah, you don't trust them to call you if there's a problem.'

'Or if they do, you won't get here in time.' Jackie shrugged helplessly. 'I'd have to look for a hotel anyway.'

William Walker stepped in. 'Nonsense. My sister lives ten minutes away. It's not a problem.'

'Really?'

William Walker allowed himself a smile. Too like Mark's.

'You go,' Daniella said. 'I'm going to stay. These chairs look comfortable enough, I'll wait here.'

They couldn't persuade her otherwise. When Jackie, Jamie and William left, Daniella let herself breathe out. Her father sat down beside her.

'If you're going to try to convince me to go too, you can save yourself the effort,' she said, ready for a fight.

But he just sighed. 'I wasn't going to do that.'

'Oh.' She stole a glance at him. He was the same father she remembered, meticulous and formidable. But this time he wasn't looking at her as a colleague or a student, but with gentleness, as his daughter. He glanced down at his hands; his instruments. He'd worked on Mark with those hands. Daniella had to look away.

'Daniella . . . you said Mark's important to you. You seeing him?'

Daniella rubbed at the frown between her eyebrows, wishing her answer could be straightforward. 'I was. But we had a fight and he left. I just found out he was back.'

'What did you fight about?' he asked.

'I'm sorry?'

'You and Mark. You said you'd had a fight. What was it about?'

'Oh, Dad. I'm . . . not sure I want to get into it.' Not least because, at its heart, it was the same issue she'd argued with her father about.

'Try me. We're going to be here for a while.' He stretched out in the chair, his scrub shirt lifting to show the beeper clipped at his waist.

'You're on call?' she asked.

'No, darling. But I'm going to wait with you.'

Daniella didn't know quite what to say. 'All right.'

'So, what did you fight about?'

Daniella gave in. 'At first, because I wasn't going to stay in Ryders. I . . . might have given him the impression I was there permanently. The town's really small, and most doctors don't stay, as you know. Yeah, well, anyway. He thought I was staying and then I realised I wasn't.'

'I see. And after that?'

Daniella paused. The crux of this disagreement had been that she wouldn't let Mark in, wouldn't tell him what was going on inside her. She still wasn't sure she could do that with anyone. And now she felt as though she was under examination. Her father had been trained the same as she had; he knew how to do a mental health interview. She didn't want to feel evaluated. Her skin itched and she stood up.

'Dad, would you mind if I took a walk . . . by myself? I'll be back soon.'

'Sure. You want another coffee?'

'Ugh, no.'

She slipped into the fire stairs. Her hand on the stainless-steel handrail, she went down five floors until she reached the bottom, a grey pit with a single door. She pushed out into the corridor, and found herself behind the A&E. The familiar smell hit her; pine cleaner and plastic packaging.

She walked along the white corridor on autopilot. When she had been on shifts here she had often come in this way. It was the way she'd come in that night. Daniella looked down at herself; she was still wearing her jeans and T-shirt from that morning; it felt like such a long time ago. The shirt was streaked with dirt and had been soaked with sweat more than once. She could probably snap the thing in half.

She pushed through the staff-only double doors, and went past the back entrance to the treatment rooms. She came to the scrubs trolley. Alongside were the staff bathrooms. Daniella licked her dry lips, nervous about what she was doing. Yes, she worked for the health service, but not here. If she was caught, would there be trouble?

She stiffened her resolve, grabbed some scrubs and changed in the bathroom, leaving her clothes on top of the lockers. There, professional armour. She was ready for this.

She crept back down the hall and turned left into the treatment area. The corridor of curtained bays was nearly empty; only two curtains were drawn to signal that there were patients inside. It looked just the same as it had that night. The bay she'd been in then was the furthest one, right down the back. She absorbed the space; paced around it. It seemed so innocuous now. Hospital rooms didn't hold secrets. They never spoke of the lives that had departed in them. The staff carried that instead.

Daniella turned her gaze back towards the entrance. She could just see the edge of the triage desk, a resident slow-walking with his nose in a chart. Business as usual down here. As if what had happened had never been. Daniella's insides rolled over. She remembered, even if no one else did. Even if no one else cared.

Well, not quite. Mark had cared. And somewhere above her head, he was fighting for his life. Even if he made it, could she ever tell him? Could she ever tell anyone about what had happened?

She cast another look around, trying to find something that indicated what had taken place here. On roadsides, families left crosses and flowers. But here, there was nothing.

She left, silent and unseen, scoured herself clean in the staff shower, then put her jeans back on with the scrub top. The T-shirt went in the bin. At least she smelled better now, even if nothing else had changed.

She put the scrub pants into the laundry hamper and made her way back upstairs. Her outside was so easily cleaned. Inside, she felt as though she was balanced on a precipice, waiting for the perturbation that would push her off. As for what had happened here five months ago – it had disappeared without a trace. No reminders remained. Anyone who hadn't witnessed it could come and go and never know.

It was the same act Daniella had been following. Outside – nothing to see here. Inside though, she needed cleaning, fixing . . . absolving. The whole reason she had gone to Ryders Ridge. And now look where it had led her.

Back to the place she'd tried to escape, and waiting for heartbreak.

Chapter 24

The night passed with no new developments. After the shift change, her father spoke to the night super and Daniella was permitted to sleep in one of the staff bunks, waking what seemed like every hour. Her first thoughts then were about the reticular system, that deep part of the brain stem so intimately connected to consciousness. In her mind she saw pictures of it in her old anatomy sketch pad, recalled a snatch of a pharmacology lecture where the professor had been talking about anaesthetics. All the important stuff that kept you alive – breathing, circulation and sleeping – was deep down in the brain, low-level, unconscious. The higher brain centres could overpower those primitive drives, but only to a point. If you let go of consciousness, the ability to think and reason, then you returned to the most basic state. Heartbeat. Breathing. Sleep.

Each time she woke, she went to sit by Mark's bed, feeling as if that was all she was: a breathing heartbeat in need of sleep. Before her, Mark had all three, but she craved what he lacked: his consciousness, his eyes opening, recognising her, knowing he would pull through. She touched his sun-browned forearm with its golden hairs, sometimes resting her head against his bicep, wondering if somehow he knew she was there. But she remained silent. The ICU staff were never far away, making routine observations every fifteen minutes, and Daniella didn't want them to hear her private thoughts.

So she spoke to him with her fingers. She touched him gently, tenderly; it was the same way she had touched him when they'd been together and yet it had always seemed so natural then, so easy. Now she was aware how precarious those moments had been. How easily she had undone all their promise.

Inside, she felt herself teetering.

She noticed the tiny details. His hair was brushing his ears, which she knew he didn't like. He'd let it get away from him in the last few weeks. And he had those stitches above his eyebrow. Someone had cleaned and re-dressed the wound, but Daniella knew it hadn't happened in the crash – she'd seen the dressing when she dragged him from the chopper. Evidence of how he'd lived in the weeks they'd been apart. But what did it mean?

She wanted to ask those things; she no longer cared if he was angry with her, as long as he woke. The scrapes on his face were healing, the surrounding flesh pink as his body recognised the hurt and rallied to it. In a week, the flesh would be new. In two, the scrapes barely visible. Gone in a year. But inside, his organs, his brain, would he heal there too?

Dawn came and went. Her father dropped in, and left again on his rounds. Then the ICU's own rounds began, and Daniella stepped out to allow the staff some space.

She slumped against the wall facing a window, the bright sunny day outside mocking her depleted hopes. She spent her professional life dealing with sickness and injuries, but she'd never before understood what a tyrant anxiety was, how it drained, distorted and forbade you to sleep. Below, the city moved sluggishly beneath a hot day's hazy blanket. It looked just the way she felt.

'Hi,' said a gravelly voice.

Daniella jumped. 'Dave!'

He was supporting himself on a pair of crutches and trailing an IV stand with several packets of saline hooked into a dosing pump. His face was a mess – his nose swollen, both eyes rimmed in bruises. His neck showed a mass of shallow, scabbed scrapes. A memory of dragging him across the red earth flashed into Daniella's mind.

He was also a sickly shade of green. 'For God's sake, sit down,' she said, helping him lower himself into one of the comfortable waiting chairs then propping his braced leg up on another. Above the brace, a mass of white bandage disappeared into the hem of his hospital gown.

'Thanks,' he rasped. 'Is anyone following me?'

Daniella straightened and glanced down the empty hall. 'No . . .'

'Good. Clean getaway. Wanted to come see Mark. How is he?'

Now he was sitting down, Dave's colour had improved to a pasty grey. Daniella sank down beside him. 'No change so far,' she whispered, then cleared her throat, hating to sound so weak. 'I mean, he's no worse, and that's something. They're watching all the vitals really closely. Just . . . waiting.'

Dave nodded. He didn't speak for a while, and it seemed his thoughts had drifted. Then he said, 'I hear ya. I'm not good with waiting. As you see.' He raised his eyes up to the pilfered IV trolley.

Daniella was amazed to see him up at all, barely twelve hours out of surgery. The relief was like a warm bath. 'I'm so glad you're all right,' she said. 'They're doing rounds in there now.'

He eased back in his seat. 'Actually, I wanted to see you too.'

She raised her eyebrows in surprise.

'I don't remember a lot about the crash. Something hit us, I think. We came down and I sort of remember thinking about climbing out. Next thing, I was outside, on the ground. Then I don't really have anything until I woke up here. Can you tell me what happened?'

Daniella tried to think of what she'd seen, but all that came was the smell of fuel and smoke. Finally, she said, 'You got out on your own. I don't know how. I found you on the ground already.'

'Okay,' he said, and waited for her to go on.

'Mark was still inside. I tried to pull him out. Kath was there with you. It took a while to get Mark out. Once he was on the ground, I dragged him away, past the ute.'

Dave's gaze was fixed now, as though he knew this already. 'Why did you do that?'

'Fuel,' she whispered. 'There was fuel everywhere. I could smell it, and something was burning, up high, near the blades.'

'What then?'

The words kept coming, as if of their own accord. 'Kath couldn't move you on her own. So I went back and helped. I grabbed your collar and dragged you.'

'That's what I thought. I've been dragged by a horse before, got scrapes just like these.'

Daniella broke into a smile. 'Did you ever think maybe you and animals aren't a good mix?'

Dave gave a brief chuckle, then he shook his head. 'Jesus.'

'What?'

'Daniella . . . I weigh ninety-five kilos. And Mark's heavier than me. I can't imagine how the hell you did that. And shit, coming back again, when it was already on fire? There was a lot of goddamn avgas in the tanks. I saw it on the news – once the thing was done burning there wasn't anything left of it.'

He shivered. 'Thank you,' he said finally. Daniella could say nothing; what she'd done didn't seem anything special.

They sat a few moments in silence before he said, 'I suppose I should go back to the ward.'

'How's the leg?'

'Throbbing like a bastard. Letting me know it's still there, I guess.'

'You want some help?'

'Nah.' He edged himself forward and got as far as shuffling his braced leg off the chair before he said, 'Actually, would you mind?'

Daniella got up. 'Stay there.' She ducked into the ICU's equipment room and grabbed a hospital wheelchair, complete with IV bag stand.

Dave looked impressed. 'Wish I'd thought of that.'

They'd nearly made it back to the medical ward when a nurse found them in the hallway.

'Aha! I knew you'd be trouble,' she said, good-naturedly shaking her finger at Dave. 'Hadn't got him out of the ambulance before he wanted to be off. You didn't damage yourself did you?'

Dave said that he was okay, and Daniella decided not to mention that he'd originally set off on crutches. But she did dob him in on the pain. 'His leg's hurting,' she told the nurse.

'Well, I'm not surprised since you missed the rounds.' She took over the wheelchair. 'Let's get you back and fixed up with the good stuff in your chart.' She turned to Daniella. 'You look familiar, love. Were you here last night?'

Daniella swallowed. The nurse looked familiar to her too. 'I used to work here,' she said quickly.

Fortunately, the nurse was more concerned with getting Dave back. Daniella trailed behind, noting the bed number so she could visit again later. The nurse drew the curtain around them and Daniella could hear her patter as she checked all the drips and organised the pain meds. Dave's was the only occupied bed in a group room of four. It had a big window facing over the grounds, and Daniella was drawn to it.

The sun was a little higher now, kissing the green trees of the golf course in the distance. Closer was the curving roof of the bus stop. When she'd worked here, she'd caught the bus almost every day. And walked past this view a hundred times without seeing it. She sank onto the low sill, just to rest a moment.

She heard footsteps in the hall, then the swish-swish of Dave's bed curtain being opened and closed again. Daniella assumed it was the nurse, until she heard a voice she knew well.

~

Jackie held Jamie's sleeping weight against her beating heart.

The night had been long and restless with thinking and worry. She'd been uncertain about many of the things she'd done in the past three years, but now she was sure about something. She hesitated only because Dave seemed to be asleep, and she wanted to look at him. Even with all the bruising, he was perfect. She'd been so angry with him for so long, but he was part of her, his face as familiar as her own. She had clung to her hurt pride, her dignity, and tried to deny how much he meant to her, but nearly losing him had made that seem senseless and petty. Even if she was too late for him to still feel the same way, she had to do this.

She sat down gently on the side of the bed. Dave smiled and opened an eye. Then the smile slipped a little as he saw who it was.

He turned his head towards her. 'Ow,' he whispered as a grazed ear brushed the pillow.

'Sorry I woke you,' she said, biting her lip.

'I wasn't asleep,' he said.

They looked at each other for a long time. Dave's dark eyes were steady, waiting for what she would say, but he waited with such patience, such hope, Jackie found she couldn't speak. Her throat was choked with memories. The way his hair had felt silken in her fingers. She also remembered all the times she'd wanted to say nice things to him and somehow they had ended up fighting instead. She couldn't do that again.

Rather than speaking, she cradled Jamie in her arms as if he were a newborn again and then passed him to Dave. Dave's arms came around Jamie protectively, and he gazed down at his son, his eyes drinking him in. After a few minutes, Jamie stretched out an arm and his eyes flickered open.

'Hey there,' Dave said softly. He tried to smile, but there was such sadness in his face. Jackie's heart broke for everything that had happened.

'Dave,' said Jamie.

Jackie reached out and touched Jamie's foot, warm in his socks and gave it a little squeeze so he'd know she was there. 'Jamie, Dave is your daddy.'

She watched as Jamie quietly accepted this. She had thought it would be harder, but somehow it was the simplest thing she'd ever done.

Dave looked up at her then, his eyes streaming. The tears ran down his cheeks and fell on the hospital gown, his chest rising with each big breath. Jackie put her other hand out towards him, wanting to touch him gently on his arm. To show him she was sorry that she had ruined things between them.

But he caught her hand and pulled her towards him so that he held both her and Jamie in his arms. He crushed her against his chest and she felt his breath against her skin as he kissed her hair. She was crying now too; she had come without much hope, and now it seemed possible they could forgive each other everything they had done.

'Daddy?' asked Jamie in a worried voice, clearly wondering what was going on.

That word broke the last dam. Dave's tears became sobs that he buried in her hair, and he hugged them tightly, his arms shaking.

~

Daniella left the ward, tears in her eyes. She hadn't meant to eavesdrop, but she hadn't wanted to interrupt. And the curtains were flimsy. She was so happy for Jackie and Dave, but it also set her isolation in stark relief. What if she never got the chance to tell Mark she'd been wrong? Would she have to carry the regret around with her forever?

These thoughts threatened to overwhelm her. Combined with an empty stomach and semi-sleepless night, they left her feeling weak and nauseous. Then she turned a corner into another white hallway, and stopped. She noticed a little dip in the wall as if the builders had got the alignment wrong. And alongside, a phone. The next moment, she had her hand on the receiver.

'Clinic.' A bored-sounding nurse.

'Hello. Does Dr Bell have any space this morning? It's his daughter.'

The sound of shuffling papers. 'Yeah. A double this morning. Someone just cancelled.'

'Can you tell him I'll come down?'

The nurse didn't seem to care. 'Sure. But don't keep him late. Backs up the clinic.'

~

So, just after eleven Daniella found herself in the familiar white-walled, blue-carpeted clinic area. She hovered by the desk, waiting for her father's patient to come out. He was even on time; Daniella didn't know if that boded well or not.

Her father beckoned her in and closed the door. 'Any change?' he asked as soon as she'd sat down.

'No, same as earlier,' she said. She paused, wondering if she was really going to do this.

'I'll come up to see him when clinic's done,' he said.

'Thanks. Look, there's something else I want to talk about.' Here goes, she thought.

Her father took off his glasses. 'Mmm?' He waited calmly to hear her.

She swallowed. 'Something happened at work, here in Brisbane, before I went up north,' she began. 'It was five months ago. That was the real reason I left.'

Her father didn't say anything, just watched her face, nodding slightly.

'I left because every time I came to work I remembered what happened,' Daniella continued. 'I thought if I went away for a while, it would get better. I could fix it somehow. And then I could come back.'

'Did that happen?'

It wasn't the question she'd been expecting. She'd been waiting for him to ask exactly what had happened, for the details, so he could analyse them. She'd been so preoccupied with thinking about what she might say, she had to stop to reroute her thoughts.

'No, not really. Sometimes I get panicky, and I worry that my mind will go blank and I'll forget what to do. That hasn't gone away.'

Her father rubbed his mouth. 'That must have been really hard for you.'

Again, she felt surprise. 'What do you mean?'

He gave a little smile. 'Because I think you expect yourself to be perfect. And when you're less than perfect, you think you've failed. You were always like that.'

She frowned. 'But you're perfect! You have to be perfect if you're going to be a good surgeon, a good anything!'

Now that she'd said the words, they hung ridiculous in the air. Her father looked around as if he could see them. He shook his head. 'What you're seeing as perfection is just years of practice and training, and sometimes getting it badly wrong,' he said. 'You know better than this, Daniella. I don't think you really expect other people to be perfect, and you can't demand it of yourself, especially in this profession.'

Daniella bowed her head. 'Do you mean you don't think I can forget about it?'

Her father leaned forward and put a finger gently under her chin. 'You're never going to forget about it. And you shouldn't. But you have to learn how to think about it so it doesn't sabotage you. I wish I could help you with that, but I'm not the best person. There's a blurry line here – you can see that.'

Daniella nodded, realising why he hadn't asked. They were related, and she was talking about a professional issue. It was ethically murky. 'See, I knew you were perfect,' she murmured.

He scoffed. 'I have my moments. Do you have your own doc? GP?'

She shook her head. 'But I think I can get one.'

'Do that. And make sure you go. I'm going to nag you about it . . . don't think I'll forget.'

She sat there, unable to move. She looked at the clock on the wall behind him and watched the second hand move around. She'd come hoping for professional absolution, she realised, but that wasn't going to happen. Something else was bubbling in the back of her throat.

'Dad, I'm scared.'

'Of what?'

'That he's going to die.'

'We're all going to die,' he said gently.

'I mean that he's going to die before I can tell him I'm sorry.'

'Ah.' A long pause. 'He's my patient, Daniella, remember that. We did our work well. Now it's up to him. He's young and strong. But he's been through a lot, so you're going to have to remind him why he wants to be here.'

'I can't,' she said desperately. 'There's always people around and I feel stupid.'

He squeezed her hand. 'Talk to him. Tell him everything you think you won't be able to say later. Believe me, the nurses have heard it all before.'

He stood and pulled her to her feet. 'I'll walk you back up there.'

Chapter 25

Late the next morning, Mark surfaced from a weird time-warped dream. He'd been formless, floating, hearing a voice from the whiteness, but now he felt his fingers against sheets, the breath in his chest, his eyelids still closed. He tried to open them but he couldn't. Strange. But it proved he had a body again.

He felt stiff; he tried to change position, but there was a tugging, and a dull ache in his gut.

'Mark?' An unfamiliar voice. 'Mark? Do you know where you are?'

Something peeled across his eyes and he saw flashes of light. He cracked an eyelid. For a moment, just lots of too-bright white.

Slowly, his vision focused. White beds, surrounded by machines, tubes and cables. He was in a hospital. A nurse was leaning over him.

'There you are,' she said. 'Do you know where you are?'

Mark frowned. Hers wasn't the voice he remembered, much less where he was. He began to notice all the things he was hooked up to. Two drips, one in each hand. Something up around his neck. And what was that? A warm line right across his thigh. He connected the dots on that one fast; for some reason it was the worst.

The nurse made some notes on a chart. 'How's your pain? Zero to ten, ten being the worst imaginable.'

Mark had to take a minute to process this, then he tested his voice. 'Four,' he croaked. His throat felt as if he'd gargled with a blow torch.

The nurse nodded and noted it down, then stepped away. 'Buzz if you need anything. Doctor will be in to see you soon. I'll leave you to it.'

Mark then realised someone else was beside the bed; trying not to intrude. He turned his head to see more clearly.

Daniella was standing beside an old hospital chair, her fingers laced together, lip tucked into her teeth. Her voice, he realised. That was what he remembered. He tried to reach for her, but only managed to move a few of his fingers.

Immediately, Daniella rushed closer, taking his hand in her own. Dropping to the chair beside the bed, she pressed her forehead against his skin. She felt cold; he didn't like that. With great effort, he moved his other arm, trailing tubes, and stroked her hair. The texture shocked his sleep-numbed senses; his memories of her were strong, and pulled him back to reality.

'I'm so sorry,' she whispered.

Mark was confused; he couldn't quite think what it was she might be sorry for. And how had he come to be here? Why couldn't he recall that? The last he remembered he'd been on the station, about to head out in the chopper with Dave.

Oh God.

'What happened?' he managed.

Daniella looked up and wiped her eyes. She would always be beautiful to him, but now she looked drawn and tired, fear and exhaustion written on her face. He sensed the depth of what he didn't recall.

'What do you remember?' she asked.

Through the long night, Daniella's fears for Mark had become a cold stone that lodged in her stomach and pressed on her heart. Past this mass she'd forced every word she'd spoken to him, until her body ached with the effort. Now, her relief was like a fever. He was awake, and all that had been cold was warm again: the tears in her eyes, his skin under her fingers. Her chest felt so light she thought her heart might fly away on its own.

To anchor herself, she steadily filled in the details for him, telling him about the accident, assuring him that Dave was okay. She explained that he was in Brisbane, that he had been unconsious for forty-eight hours. Then she watched as the exhaustion caught up with him and he slept again.

Daniella stayed where she was, resting her head against his shoulder where she could hear his breaths. Several hours passed before she felt him move again. Slowly, he reached for his own face, as if to make sure that everything was still there. Then he brushed the stitches above his eye and winced.

'How did you get that?' Daniella asked.

'Long story,' he said, his voice still hoarse. He touched his neck.

'It's all right,' she said. 'Your throat must feel awful from the tube. I won't stay if you want to rest.'

'Stay,' he said.

She took his hand gently, avoiding the cannulas and tape. Now the immediate danger was over and he was more alert, she was worried how the gesture would be received – was he still hurt, would he be angry with her? But he folded his fingers carefully around hers.

Now though, she had no idea what to say, and she saw his eyes were dull beneath the bruises. He needed to rest. 'I'll let you sleep,' she said. 'And come back later.'

'I don't want to sleep,' he said. 'Talk to me.'

'Okay, just until you feel tired.' She chewed her lip. 'What happened to your face?'

He winced again. 'Honestly? I got the shit beaten out of me.'

'By who?'

'Like I said, long story.'

For just a moment, they both smiled. A thread of connection sparked between them, and Daniella saw Mark as he had been when they'd been together. Then the moment vanished. Mark closed his eyes with a silent sigh. 'Maybe I'll sleep a little.'

~

Mark's condition continued to improve steadily and he was transferred to the ward the next day. Around lunchtime the day after, a doctor came to remove his central line. Cat had been allowed in, clearly relieved to see him in one piece. She looked older than he remembered, but still had her enthusiasm; she was excited to meet Daniella and the two of them got along well. Now Daniella had gone away to make some calls, organising leave, clothes and food, all of which he knew she'd been neglecting while she waited at his bedside. He'd also had a long talk with Dave – who'd appeared on a pair of crutches – about the trials of recovery and then the accident itself. Dave was clearly anxious about what had happened, and about Mark's injuries. Mark reassured him: he was recovering, and they'd both have to wait for the investigation report. Will had made it too, just missing their father, who had had to head back to Ryders: there was only so long things could be left to run themselves.

Now, restless and bored, he flicked through the TV channels. He could hear the squeak of shoes on the linoleum in the hallway outside the room, the dripping of the fluid bag into the IV, the creaking of the mattresses across the room when someone shifted position. Whenever footsteps approached he felt absurdly hopeful, and then swiftly deflated; he'd know Daniella from twenty metres away.

Late in the afternoon new footsteps entered the ward. A young woman in a polo shirt drew aside the curtains and introduced herself as Liz, the physio. Liz joked that she was there to make Mark's life miserable. The upside was that she would get him back to condition as fast as possible.

She turned out to be kind, patient and good at her job. Mark was grateful; it took him ten minutes to move to the side of the bed and swing his legs to the floor. Liz didn't hurry him; she let him wait for the dizzy spells to pass before resuming. Thank God the bloody catheter would be gone soon. He appreciated now the awfulness of being a patient, of depending on other people. For the first time, he began to understand his father's reluctance to accept care, and what his mother must have gone through with the chemo and surgery.

Somehow, it was easier that it was a stranger seeing him like this. Liz was a professional, here to do a job. It was okay for him to struggle in her presence, but not to quit. A clean, simple relationship. But it was his thoughts of Daniella that motivated him. He wanted to be strong again for her.

Suddenly, he was on his feet and walking. He couldn't stand fully upright because his middle was still tender, but he was walking, no longer confined to a bed. It was amazing how much this meant to him.

They went down the hallway and back twice, Liz holding his arm, the drip on a mobile trolley beside him.

'Again?' Liz asked him after his second trip.

Mark clenched his teeth, hating that he had to walk past the nurses' station and be on display in this weakened state. He felt more determined than ever to recover quickly so that Daniella would never see him like this. 'Yes.'

They went again, after which Liz clucked her tongue approvingly and angled him back towards the bed. 'All right, that's probably enough—'

'Once more,' he said. He wanted to make sure the first three hadn't been flukes. Then, halfway through the circuit, he realised Liz wasn't steadying him anymore, that he was completely on his own. For a moment, he had an irrational thought of making a run for it, just to see what would happen. Dave had told him that was possible; they'd actually laughed about it. Well, Dave had laughed and Mark had guarded his sore belly.

Finally, Liz told him that was enough for now, occupying herself with moving the drip as he slowly pulled his legs back onto the bed.

She then nodded with satisfaction. 'Look, I can see you're going to do this for yourself later, so just keep it slow and steady. Your blood pressure's good now, but your baroreflex might be a bit sluggish – that's what stops you from passing out when you stand up – so watch the sudden movements. I think you're going to do just fine. Buzz if you want a hand again – I'm on for the rest of the day and the nurses can page me. I'll be back tomorrow anyway.'

After she'd left, Mark enjoyed the glow of achievement. It was the first step on the road to going back to Ryders, going back to work, back to Daniella . . . He paused, remembering. No matter how many steps he took, what difference would it make if she was adamant she wanted to leave?

~

When Daniella eventually made it back to the ward – showered and changed after a long call to Dr Harris, and even a meal in the cafeteria – she found Mark in much better spirits; there was colour in his face again and he wore a determined expression.

'Uh-oh,' she said. 'That's exactly how Dave looked when I found him on the run the other day. You're not thinking of checking out?'

He actually smiled. 'I thought about it.'

'But?'

'Well, turns out I might not be able to get further than the end of the ward.'

Daniella cocked her head at him. 'Physio been?'

Mark gave her a silly grin. 'How did you guess?'

She returned the smile tentatively. 'Patients always smile when the physio leaves.'

He laughed a little – shallowly, she noticed, because it probably still hurt. But Daniella hadn't heard it in such a long time. She loved to hear him laugh.

His face became serious again. 'Look, Daniella. I'm really sorry about what I said. Weeks ago, I mean, before I went to Isa. It was unfair. I shouldn't have pushed things so fast.'

Daniella bit her lip. 'No, you were right,' she said. 'I wanted to be with you but it meant dealing with what was going on inside me.' She felt the tears on her face. 'It was easier to let you go. I soon realised how stupid I'd been. But then this happened and I thought I'd never get the chance to tell you . . .' She sat down in the chair beside the bed, her fingers reaching for his. 'I love you,' she whispered. 'I don't know what's going to happen between us, but I do.'

She looked up and found him grinning at her. 'Say that again.'

'I love you,' she said, smiling through her tears.

Mark looked at her with pure abandon. 'Come up here,' he said, and made some room for her to curl in beside him. 'I missed you,' he said. 'I went a little crazy trying to deny it, but it's true. There's the evidence.' He pointed at his stitched eyebrow.

'Are you going to tell me the story now?' she asked.

'I ran into your friend Pete in Isa. I was looking for a fight and he was pretty happy to give me one . . . but I didn't count on all his mates.'

'Oh no,' said Daniella, putting her hand over her mouth.

'It was a stupid thing to do,' he admitted. 'I'm not proud of it. Luckily Will was there to fish me out.'

'Let me have a look,' said Daniella, twisting around, determined to see what sort of job they'd made of it. 'Hmm. Not too bad. But make sure you get those stitches out in a day or two or they might scar.'

He gave her an incredulous look. 'You're worried about that?' He gestured to his torso. 'I'm pretty sure your dad put some bigger ones down here.'

Daniella compressed her lips. 'I like your face just the way it is,' she argued. 'What other damage did you get?'

'A few bruises, but you can't tell them apart from the rest now,' he said. 'Oh, and these.' He patted his side.

'Ribs?'

'Yeah, cracked a few.'

'Show me,' she demanded.

Obediently, he pushed down the sheet and pulled up the gown. Daniella could see the yellow halo around his lower ribs, discolouring the lovely ripples of his muscles. She avoided the surgical dressings, and ran her fingers over the bruises.

Mark winced. 'Yeah, that's it.'

Daniella put her hand flat against him, very gently. 'Sorry,' she whispered. 'I didn't mean to hurt you. I really didn't.'

Mark pulled the sheet back up, taking her hand. 'It's not so bad.'

Daniella finally saw some hope. They could mend this. When he was out of hospital, when they were both back to where they'd been before. She didn't want to say what she had to next.

'I'm going to have to go back,' she said. 'Dr Harris is on his own again and everything's overbooked.'

Mark looked resigned, but he didn't pull away. 'When?'

'Tomorrow, probably, depending on flights. I'm not happy about it,' she added, desperate that he would think she was running off again. 'I want to be here with you more than anything. It rips my heart out that I have to go. But I don't have any more leave and there's something else I have to deal with, too.'

He tipped her face up to look into her eyes. 'Want to talk about it?'

She shook her head. 'I'm not quite ready for that. But when I am, I promise I will tell you. I want to work this out.'

'Really?' He looked at her with such an expression of hope that she nearly started crying again. She knew she needed to get herself sorted out if they were to have any chance together. If she didn't do something about the things in her head, they'd be back to where it all went wrong.

Chapter 26

Daniella, in fact, had already worked out exactly who she wanted to talk to. The problem was, she hadn't quite mustered the guts to do it. And it wasn't something to do by phone.

She slept most of the flight and coach trip back to Ryders Ridge, then went back to her house and slept some more in the ancient bed. She woke early the next day with a sense of purpose, but it never seemed to be the right time.

It was strange to be returning to work as if everything was exactly the same as before the crash. She was so busy that she didn't have time to dwell on it, and two weeks passed in a blur of work and daily calls to Mark. Valerie Turner was back on her house-call list, and quizzed her endlessly about everything that had happened. The woman seemed to have more energy than ever. Mark himself was doing better and better, and would be home in a few days.

His impending return was the final prompt. She took the long walk home from the clinic and stopped to look at the bench on the hill at the end of the main street.

Since her return she'd avoided coming here; too many memories. But now the sight of its plain wooden slats and the little brass plaque, was a powerful reminder of her life here before the crash. It spoke to her of a routine she was fast slipping back into. The one where nothing changed. She could not put this off any longer.

The next morning, just after eleven when Daniella knew Dr Harris had a double appointment free, she put aside her stethoscope and ushered herself into his office, a new file tucked under her arm.

'How's young Mark?' he asked as she sat down.

'Doing well.'

'Good to hear. Dave's been in already. Leg incision's healed well and he's getting around.'

Daniella was nodding along. She stopped herself. 'Dr Harris, that's great. But I'm actually here to talk about something else.' She handed across the file and watched as he read the cover: it was her own name.

'Of course,' he said, betraying no surprise. 'Go ahead.'

She balled her fists in her lap and forced herself to start. 'Something happened at work, in Brisbane, before I came here. About six months ago now,' she trailed off. Dr Harris waited patiently.

She tried again. 'Anyway, I was on an emergency rotation and there was a case where . . .' She stopped, taking a breath. Maybe she couldn't do this.

'Take your time,' Dr Harris said gently.

'I killed a patient,' she blurted. Oh God, she'd said it now. It was out, this terrible secret. 'A child. A little girl. She . . . ah, her parents brought her in. Irritable, not eating. They'd been to see their GP that day and were sent home, but it was Friday night and they were still worried. She was very young, only two. She had a fever. There was a lot of that going around.'

She put a hand up to her face; her cheek was burning hot against her palm, as though she was feverish herself.

'Okay,' said Dr Harris. 'What then?'

'We were busy. It was a bad night, two MVAs, so they had to wait a while. She was on the list for the senior reg, but he'd just got started with them when he was called away. Triage gave her to me instead. When I saw her, I checked for meningitis. I thought she had neck stiffness . . . but, to be honest, I'd never seen it before in a child. She wasn't vaccinated.

'I wanted to give her antibiotics straight away, before we tried for a lumbar puncture. I couldn't get the needle in on my first try and I went looking for the registrar to help. But I couldn't find him, so I tried again. By then, the rash was coming in. As I tried to get that line in I watched the thing spread.'

Daniella stopped. She saw that rash again, those awful spreading purple spots on such tiny limbs. Remembered calling over her shoulder for someone to help. Dr Harris waited.

'I panicked. I was so focused on that line. I should have put an interosseous needle in so the line couldn't collapse, but I'd never done one. By the time I thought of it, I'd finally got the line in. But it took a long time – too long.'

'What happened then?' Dr Harris asked.

Daniella made herself unclench her hands and wiped her palms on her trousers. 'I'd called a nurse to get the antibiotics but she hadn't come back. So I went out to get them myself. When I came back, the child had a febrile seizure and the line tissued out – I don't know if the cannula moved or the vein collapsed, but I couldn't get anything through it. I couldn't believe how fast it happened. I . . . ah, I couldn't remember what to do. So when she finally came back, I sent the nurse to find the senior reg, or the consultant or someone and I kept trying to put in a new line.

'She crashed not long after. That got the resus team in – eventually. It was out of my hands then. They did the interosseous and gave her antibiotics, but they never got her back.

Pathology on the lumbar puncture diagnosed meningococcus. I think she hung on for a few days in ICU before they turned off the life support.

'Nothing happened afterwards,' she continued, rushing now she was close to the end. 'It wasn't an unexpected death because the infection was so obvious, so there was no inquest. And the reg was the supervisor, so he did all the paperwork. It felt . . . wrong somehow. I was the one in there. I kept expecting more to happen, but it didn't.

'The reg said it was awful and unfortunate, but things like this happen. But it kept coming back to me. I'd find myself panicking in some situations, and I started to worry that something like that would happen again. I came here because I thought in a smaller place, I wouldn't get lost in the chaos. I thought I could find my confidence again and then go home. If I was somewhere small, I couldn't get lost. But it hasn't gone away. And then, after the chopper crash, I felt it happening again. I couldn't get my head together and I couldn't help. Sometimes I've wondered if I shouldn't be doing this at all.' She waved her hand around, indicating the clinic, medicine in general. 'Other times I can't think of doing anything else, but not with all this inside me.'

She took a breath, thinking there was more to say, but then realised there wasn't. She was done. She stared past Dr Harris's shoulder, feeling wretched and worthless. Getting it all out hadn't made her feel better; in fact, she felt more vulnerable.

Dr Harris rubbed his chin. 'Let me ask you a couple of things. What antibiotics did you get?'

'Vancomycin and ceftriaxone,' she whispered.

'What else was going on?' he asked gently.

'What do you mean?'

'How long had you been on?'

Daniella thought back. 'I'm not sure. Probably since early that morning. I think I was covering someone's shift.'

Dr Harris was quiet for a while. 'How do you think it could have gone differently?' he asked her finally.

Daniella wasn't expecting that. She'd been nursing the sense that she'd simply been wrong for so long, she hadn't thought about alternatives. 'Well, if those antibiotics had gone in earlier, maybe . . .'

'How much earlier would you have been able to get them in?'

'Um . . . maybe fifteen, twenty minutes?'

'Do you think that would have made a difference?'

She thought about it. 'I don't know,' she admitted.

'That's right.' Dr Harris sighed. 'Daniella, I want you to listen to me very carefully, because you're a good doctor and that was an awful thing to experience. Very confronting. I had something similar happen to me early in my career; I might tell you about it sometime. I think the only reason I'm still here is because someone told me what I am about to tell you.

'You didn't kill that child. You took on someone else's patient and you made the right call. The system around you didn't help. None of us work in isolation, all right? Not even me, in this place. When you're in the A&E, you're the last line of defence, not the first, do you understand? That child could have been vaccinated, but she wasn't. The registrar could have been there to help you. The GP could have recognised it earlier in the day. I'm never going to be able to fully remove the burden you're carrying around inside you, because you wouldn't be a good doctor if you didn't feel a sense of responsibility. The experience is going to stay with you. But you must stop telling yourself that you were careless, that you alone could have changed all the things that went wrong for that poor child. That but for you, everything would have been fine. The thing is, you can't control everything that happens.

You can only do your best. And sometimes, your best isn't enough.' Dr Harris took off his glasses and rubbed his eyes. He looked tired.

'I've loved having your support here,' he went on. 'It would be a great shame to lose you because of something like this. You must have felt very alone with these feelings.'

Daniella could only nod.

'It has to happen to everyone I think. And as for after the crash . . .' He gave her a sympathetic but exasperated smile. 'Can I remind you that you'd just been at the scene and pulled two men away from a burning wreck? Can you give yourself a break about that?'

Daniella frowned, then suddenly perspective came. Put that way, it did sound utterly ridiculous. 'Maybe,' she said.

'There you go,' he said. 'Now, I don't think for any money that this chat has resolved these things. We should talk about it more and do some structured therapy. But I'm glad you told me.'

'Me too,' she said honestly.

'All right. Well, let's leave it there for now and make another time. Maybe take a day off tomorrow.'

'I don't do too well with days off,' she said. 'I get bored of reading and television.'

'What about cooking?' he asked with a smile.

'What about it?' she replied suspiciously.

'I'm thinking about hosting another dinner, this weekend or next. Maybe you could plan the menu, if you feel up to it?'

Daniella made a face, but she considered it. She'd been thinking about the community blood donors, and Mark, not to mention Dr Harris himself. She owed people a lot: it would be a small way to say thank you.

'Can I do the invites too?' she asked.

Chapter 27

For Mark, the last weeks had been – to use a phrase he'd picked up from Jackie – a special kind of hell. Spending days bored in a hospital bed, interspersed with painful physio, had been bad enough even when Daniella was there, but after she'd returned to work it was infinitely worse. He was restless to see her, and for normal life to resume. As the days passed, however, he'd recovered quickly, and now he was finally allowed to go home.

He flew in to Isa, where Catrina and their father met him and drove him back to Ryders. It was good timing with Catrina nearing the end of the semester. He let Daniella know he was back, but she'd been busy with the clinic and being on call. Exhausted, he'd slept through the afternoon and the evening.

But the next morning, with the familiar sounds of home filtering in through his curtains, he woke feeling truly rested. His body felt like it belonged to him again, and he was keen to get back to work.

He found Catrina in the kitchen; she'd clearly slotted into the routine as though she'd never been away. 'Hey, you're up. Want some?' she asked, pointing to a stack of toast.

Mark ate slowly, testing the return of his appetite, while they chatted easily about the events of the last week, her plans for the day and for the rest of the semester in Brisbane. Then Mark steered the conversation back to things they'd discussed on the phone long before the crash: whether Ryders could improve its operations using new technologies.

Cat laughed. 'Typical! Always thinking about the station, even when you've been back for just a day.' But there was enthusiasm in her voice as she went on. 'My professor's still interested. He said he'd know more about it after the break. What are you up to today? Ready to be roundly thrashed at Monopoly?' The game had become a tradition between them – they always played at least once when Cat came home for holidays.

But Mark couldn't bear to be inside for another minute. Promising he'd play Monopoly later, and that he'd take things easy, he slipped away.

As he strolled down the hill towards the sheds, his thoughts kept returning to Daniella. She would be at work, so he wouldn't call her, but he was impatient to see her. To distract himself, he took a quad bike and went up the main fence line to the crash site. The Civil Aviation Safety Authority agents had gone all over it, but they hadn't taken anything away. Mark spent an hour slowly walking round the blackened hull. Dave had told him what had happened, but he had no memories of the accident himself and it remained unreal. He paced from the chopper's remains to where he guessed Daniella and Kath had waited with Dave and himself. Something brown had clumped in the dirt there, maybe blood, and he could still see the drag marks. The investigators had even pegged it out.

When his pacing took him over a low rise, he spotted something caught against a grass stump, limply shifting in the occasional breeze. Recognising it, he plucked the battered hat from its snare and beat the dust off it across his knee. Daniella's dirty old hat. His desire to call her surged in his chest.

He returned to the homestead and busied himself in the office. Much later, when he considered himself up to date, he took a quad bike down the ridge, loving being home again, until the sun was sinking, the light slipping into blues and purples. He drove the quad bike back into the main shed just on dark, then found Catrina in the small stock yard, feeding Buttons, her favourite horse. Her blonde ponytail was a mess, her T-shirt covered in dirt, but she looked happy.

'There you are,' she said accusingly. 'Dr Harris called to check on you. He said you have an appointment tomorrow. I was just about to send out a search party.'

'You were not. You'd let me rot out there with the roos.'

'Well, maybe. You okay?' When he nodded, she added, 'Steph Morgan is here, too.' She pointed a carrot in the direction of the stables.

Mark took a slow breath. For the last few weeks he hadn't had to think too much about the Morgans and their demands; it was one thing he hadn't missed.

'Thanks.' He took a little longer than necessary to walk towards the stables. He hadn't seen Steph since just before he'd left for Isa, and his father hadn't told him how any discussions had gone in his absence. The Morgans had sent flowers to him in hospital, but now it would be back to business. He hoped he had the strength. Mark was especially uneasy about what the financial ramifications of the crash might be. The chopper had been on lease; it was insured. But he didn't yet know what costs they might have to cover.

He found Stephanie grooming one of the stock horses. She looked up and smiled. 'Hi, Mark. How are you? Not working too hard?'

She seemed at ease, betraying no sign of remembering their uncomfortable exchange at the rodeo, so Mark relaxed a little. 'I'm fine,' he said. 'Didn't know you were in town.'

'We're organising the campdraft, so I thought I'd drop out to confirm some details. Is it still all right to use the cottage for a night?'

'Of course.' Keen to keep busy, he stepped into the feed shed and bent down to pick up a bucket, gratified that he no longer felt unstable on his feet. As he slowly put together the stock horses' mix, he checked the feed stock levels. The chaff bin was low. He ran his finger along the stock list, neatly pinned on the wall, and pencilled it in for the next order.

Stephanie appeared at the feed-shed door. 'Are you coming up to the house for dinner?'

'Not sure yet.' Though he didn't like to admit it, the day had tired him and he didn't know whether he'd have the stamina to sit at the table and make conversation. He took down a bridle that was hanging crooked, straightened it and put it back.

'Well, I'd like to talk to you.'

'About what?' Mark poked around in the electrolyte bins, assessing the levels. Still a few months' supply left. He felt his energy fading fast now. Maybe he had overdone it today.

'The campdraft. I know it's a few weeks away but . . . well, we can talk over dinner.'

'Ask me now.'

She shifted on her feet. 'Well, we need some cattle for the events and—'

Mark looked up. 'We're already providing them. Dad signed the contract months ago.'

'Right.' A moment's silence. 'You know, Mark. Since the accident . . . I wondered if you'd had a chance to think about your options here. The buyers are extremely keen. They keep asking us.'

Mark straightened. 'We're not for sale, Steph. And Dad should be here for this conversation.'

'Of course,' she said evenly. 'But they won't wait forever. And you know the finances aren't great. We're still looking at the impact of the crash.'

Mark's mood descended. Carefully he grabbed a saddle from the cleaning rack and moved it back onto the permanent peg. All was in order now. He moved towards the door, keen to be alone.

'Wasn't it a shame about Dave?' Stephanie commented from behind him.

'Shame?' he asked, stopping reluctantly in the doorway.

'You know, about Jamie. Dave being the father all along and never saying anything. He hasn't behaved very honourably, has he?'

Mark turned around and looked at her steadily. She was picking at the wooden door frame with her fingernails. An odd feeling stirred in his gut. 'I don't see it that way,' he said.

She folded her arms. 'It's not exactly decent.'

'Steph, it's not the fifties,' he said, trying to contain his irritation. 'Jackie wanted it kept quiet – it's not for us to judge.'

Silence. The gut feeling became stronger. Something about her posture and the look on her face, told him there was more to this.

'It was you, wasn't it?' Mark demanded. 'You were the one who started everyone talking about Dave and Jackie!'

She didn't try to deny it, her expression unapologetic.

'Jesus, that's low.' He pointed his finger at her. 'You should know better. Like I said, it's no one else's business. If Jackie didn't want anyone to know, you should have kept your trap shut. How the hell did you know, anyway?'

'Oh, come on, Mark! It wasn't like it could be kept secret forever—'

'That wasn't for you to decide.' Mark was surprised by how angry he felt in that moment. He hadn't thought Stephanie capable of such malice. Rumours were rife in small towns, but to spread them deliberately, and about people who had been your friends . . .

He turned away and left her in the stables. As he walked towards the house, Cat was coming up from the yards with Buttons' halter dangling from her hand.

'Everything okay?' she asked, her eyes scanning his face.

Mark sighed. 'Fine.' But his mind was working hard. The arrangement with the Morgans, which had never been a comfortable one, now had a sour taste. He wondered, too, why Steph hadn't bothered denying her role. It was as if she wanted him to know she'd done it. And that made him very uneasy.

Cat fell in beside him and they walked up to the house together. In his tiredness, Mark resisted the urge to lean on her. As they went through the back door, his phone rang. One look at the caller ID and Mark told her to go ahead without him, all thoughts of Stephanie forgotten.

When he entered the kitchen a few minutes later, nothing could dent his elation. Daniella's work day was over and she wanted to see him. As soon as he'd had a shower, he would be on his way to town.

Cat glanced around the pantry door at him. 'You going to see her?'

Mark grinned; his tiredness had evaporated.

'Good,' she said.

Chapter 28

Mark pulled up just after seven thirty, when Daniella's hair was still wet from the shower. She was unsure about how this would go, she didn't want to have expectations . . . but that didn't stop her watching him from the window. He looked like the old Mark: confident and sure, only a little thinner than she remembered. Daniella felt a surge of excitement. She opened the door before he could knock.

'Hi,' she said.

'Hi.' He stopped uncertainly. They were both aware they hadn't seen each other for a while.

She stood aside and he walked into the living room. Daniella perched on the arm of the couch and he sat in the hard chair across from her. Despite their last meeting in the hospital, the memory of the last time they'd both been together in this house intruded; echoes of that painful conversation seemed to hang in the air.

Daniella's face flushed as they searched each other's eyes, both looking for how to begin, how to make what they'd had before real again. Something was there. Daniella felt as though she only had to touch him, and the gap would close. But before that could happen, they would both need to be sure it was what they wanted.

Then Mark shifted on the seat. Daniella saw the hesitation in his movement: he was still being careful with himself. And suddenly, she remembered how it had felt when she'd thought she might lose him forever; as though her chest was paper thin, not strong enough to contain her pounding heart. She couldn't lose him now.

Before she lost her nerve she got up and grabbed his hand. 'I need to show you something,' she said. She steered him towards her bedroom, pulled him in the door and turned on the light. 'See,' she whispered.

The change in the room was still so new, Daniella saw the place as though it was someone else's. The bed was made up properly, with crisp new sheets, and the case had been unpacked and put away. She slid open the wardrobe so he could see her clothes hanging up inside.

'Does this mean what I think it does?' he murmured. He edged towards her, rubbing his fingers across his mouth, trying to hide his smile. With his other hand, he reached out. Daniella stepped into the embrace. He pressed his lips into her hair and she turned her cheek into the muscle of his shoulder. She knew he understood: she was staying. That was the decision. She'd unpacked, made a home here. She'd chosen him.

'I've missed this,' he said. 'I've missed you so much.'

'No more packed bags,' she said. She hugged him tighter, tears gathering in her eyes. 'I want things to be the way they were.' Then she let go in alarm. 'I'm sorry, that was too hard.'

'It was not,' he said. 'Do it again.'

She laughed, enjoying the sensation of his muscles bunching against her when he tightened his arms. He drew her towards the bed and pulled her down beside him. She felt the luxury of having the whole evening ahead of them as he began to kiss her, gently at first and then hungrily. 'I've missed this too,' he said roughly, slipping his hands under her T-shirt to stroke her skin.

'Are you sure you're up to it?' she teased. But her fingers traced down his cheek to where the scar from the central line nestled in the base of his neck. The crash could so easily have changed everything. 'Show me?' she whispered, moving her fingers across the fabric of his shirt.

He pulled it free from his jeans and lay back on the covers. Then he put her hand against his skin. His stomach was warm. Daniella pushed his shirt higher. She tried to see him through detatched, professional eyes, but she knew the landscape of his body too well for that. The arc of his scar showed plainly beneath his ribs. Her father had done good work; that scar was his mark, the line between Mark's living and dying.

When he'd let her examine him to her satisfaction, Mark slowly undressed her. Then, warm skin on skin, he showed her just how well he'd recovered.

Afterwards, they held each other, all the remaining tensions between them gone. Daniella was too comfortable to think about getting up.

'Are you hungry?' Mark asked eventually, planting a few kisses down her cheek and searching for her mouth.

'No,' she lied, snuggling into him so she could kiss him back. Her stomach gave an audible, traitorous rumble.

'Ah ha!' he said, pushing himself up. 'I knew it. Get ready. I'm going hunting for the biggest feed I can muster.' He groped for his jeans on the floor. It felt just like old times.

'All right, I suppose, as long as it doesn't bite you!' And then she had to tell him the story of Joe and the pig. Finally, to buy more time in bed, she said, 'Speaking of food, Dr Harris wants me to give another dinner soon. But this time I actually want to do it. I'm inviting all the blood donors, and I want you there too.'

'No problem. And Catrina would probably love to help out, if that's okay?'

Daniella smiled, remembering Mark's sister, who she'd met briefly in the hospital in Brisbane. 'I'd like that.'

Mark raised his eyebrows. 'Well, I'm sure people have said that before and regretted it. Cooking's not her strong suit. But, you can only learn. And I wouldn't mind getting her off my back – she keeps telling me to rest.'

Daniella made a noise in her throat. 'Well, resting's bad for recovery. I can show you the research.'

'Good. I want to see it.' Then the frown crept back between his brows. 'Are you really sure about staying?'

Daniella pulled him closer and smiled reassuringly. The qualm she felt at the idea would pass. 'I'm sure about you,' she said.

~

At around five thirty on Sunday night, Daniella finally took a breath. The dinner had many more invitees than the last one, and Dr Harris had brought home chairs from the clinic to cram around the table. Daniella had found her forte in making dessert, and in happily directing proceedings for the main from a high stool at the breakfast bar where she could see everything that went on. Catrina was great fun and spent a while quizzing Daniella about her own uni days, and then about Mark, conversations that had never been possible in Brisbane. Daniella laughed as she avoided the more personal queries about Mark. Catrina took this with good humour and applied herself to stirring pots or prodding the meat, all under Dr Harris's careful supervision.

Cat also spent a while scrutinising the guest list for people she knew. 'Who's Samuel Parsons?' she asked.

'One of the community blood donors,' said Daniella. She eased off her stool and inspected her caramel sauce, which was bubbling on low heat. Time to get on with the pudding.

'Why don't I know him?' Cat demanded of Dr Harris.

'Just moved here this year,' said Dr Harris, buffing a wine glass. 'He's the electrician's apprentice. In his final year, I think he said.'

'Why's Steph Morgan on this list?' Cat asked, looking up.

Daniella shrugged. Mark had told her, and later Cat, about his discovery that Stephanie had spread the news about Dave and Jackie. When Daniella saw how angry he was, she decided not to tell him about Steph's involvement in the complaint, too.

'Figured she couldn't surprise me that way,' she said, going down the hall to wash her hands in the bathroom. When she emerged, the photo in the hall caught her eye again, and she stood inspecting it until Cat called that she'd better come look at her sauce.

At around six o'clock, the house began to fill up. Jackie and Dave arrived first, installing Jamie in the lounge, now a toy heaven. Then they came into the kitchen. Dave was still wearing a brace on his leg, but his bruises had long since faded.

Daniella hugged them both. 'How's it going?' she asked Jackie.

Jackie smiled carefully. 'Better,' she said.

Samuel arrived next, scrubbed, scruffy hair tamed and in a clean pair of jeans and a white shirt. Daniella caught the moment when Catrina looked up from the pot she was stirring, took him in, then realised she was staring and quickly looked away. Daniella smiled to herself. Samuel was followed by Donna from the tav and Rich, the constable, who'd both given blood after the crash.

Daniella put her mind to opening a wine bottle. Dave wasn't up to drinking, but everyone else accepted a glass.

Soon, conversation was rising around the table on the deck while the delicious smell of roasting pork wafted out from the kitchen. Daniella stayed in the kitchen, enjoying a moment to herself. Her senses were tingling with anticipation; Mark would be here soon.

A minute later, Dr Harris came in to scrutinise the meat through the oven door. His reflection reminded Daniella of the photo in the hall. 'Did I tell you the secret to perfect roast pork?' he asked, for perhaps the third time that day.

'Freshest meat you can get, well-salted rind, and add some milk to the roasting tray,' she rattled off.

He brandished a carving fork in her direction. 'Exactly.'

'Dr Harris, can I ask you about the photo in the hall?' she asked. He turned slowly, with a look of surprise. 'I'm sorry, it's none of my business,' she said. 'But it's such a lovely picture and I wondered who it was.'

Dr Harris looked thoughtful. 'Well, it's me,' he said. 'And my wife. In Sydney, at Circular Quay.'

'Ah, that must be the Harbour Bridge in the background? It's a little hard to tell . . . You could probably have it restored, you know.'

Dr Harris smiled slightly. 'No, no. I let it fade on purpose, Daniella. Theresa died soon after we moved here. We knew she was sick, and there wasn't much we could do. She wanted to make sure I was settled somewhere before she died, and it's been the right place for me – lots of work to do, not much time to think about her being gone, even with all her things still here. Not long after she died I put that photo on the table where the sun comes in the window in the morning; I told myself that when we were both faded away in that picture, it would be time to move on.' He gave her a quick smile as if this was not the deeply emotional thing it clearly was. 'It looks like I might be here a few more years yet,' he acknowledged.

He marched back outside to talk to his guests. Daniella turned his words over in her mind. People could be so complex; even the ones you thought you'd worked out could surprise you. She was still thinking this when the doorbell rang again. She slipped off her stool and padded down the hall. Mark and his father were standing on the porch.

'Hi, Mark. Hello, Mr Walker. Come in.'

She went to step aside for them, but Mark gathered her up in a hug, planting a kiss on her lips. Daniella suspected that William Walker's own lips would be a thin line of disapproval. Well, she was staying; he would just have to get used to it.

'How are you, Daniella?' he asked, when Mark had let her go.

'I'm well, thank you.'

'That's good,' he said gruffly, and Daniella noted that he seemed more uncomfortable than anything. She relaxed a little and led them through to join the others. William Walker went out to the deck while Mark stayed in the kitchen with her.

'Hi,' he said mischievously, once they were alone, taking her face in his hands to kiss her again.

She happily kissed him back, enjoying the softness of his lips. She broke away when one of the kitchen buzzers shrilled. Dr Harris and Catrina both headed inside.

'It's mine!' declared Catrina, racing for the stove.

Dr Harris grumbled about being usurped in his own kitchen, but he was clearly enjoying her high spirits. 'Mark, you're looking even better than when I saw you a few days ago,' he commented.

'The meat's ready,' called Cat.

'Everything's done then,' said Daniella. 'We're just short the Morgans.'

'I forgot – they've got some business to attend to and sent their apologies,' said Mark.

'Oh well, then I can put away the folding chairs,' said Dr Harris.

'Everything all right?' Daniella asked Mark quietly.

He made a dismissive noise. 'Don't worry about it. Let's eat.'

The food was wonderful. Dr Harris and Daniella both tried to deflect the credit onto each other and Cat. Dr Harris could hardly deny responsibility for the roast pork, for which he was justifiably famous. But everyone agreed Daniella's sticky date pudding was the best they'd ever tasted.

'Kath'll be down here looking for the recipe,' said William Walker with an uncharacteristic smile.

Catrina had managed to manoeuvre Samuel into a corner, where he was making a decent effort at keeping pace with her conversation, while Dr Harris chatted to Donna and Rich. Jackie and Dave didn't say much to each other, but there was clearly an easy gentleness between them.

Mark sat beside Daniella, refilling her glass and drawing her into his conversation with his father.

'So, Mark tells me you're planning to stay in town,' William said to her at one point.

Daniella paused with food halfway to her mouth. She put her fork down carefully. 'Yes.' Only a little flutter of doubt now. The feeling would go away, she was sure. She was just adjusting to the idea.

William nodded, his expression hard to read. 'Are you planning to see the campdraft? Folk from all over the district will be coming in for it.'

Daniella confessed her ignorance. 'What's a campdraft? Is that like a rodeo?'

Mark went to explain but William cut him off. 'It's an event that tests the skills of a rider working with cattle. There're six of them in a ring – that's the camp – and the rider cuts a steer from the pack. They prove to the judges they've got the animal controlled, then they have to work the steer around a figure eight. That's the draft. It's a great event.'

'Great for business too,' said Jackie from across the table. 'Even more casualties than the rugby last year.'

Daniella looked at Dr Harris. 'Well, if I'm not on call, I'd love to see it.'

'Done any riding?' asked William.

'A lot when I was younger. Not for a while though.'

'Mark's going to ride this year,' put in Dave.

'Really?' questioned Daniella, turning towards him, wondering if he was up to it.

Mark looked determined. 'Yeah, got the all-clear to ride again from Dr Harris, and it's still a few weeks out so I have time.'

'So, am I finally going to see you work?' she murmured.

'I'll show you work. Later,' he breathed in her ear as he rose to help Dr Harris with the coffee. Daniella flushed pink as she saw William looking right at her.

After dinner, Mark and his father both insisted the cooks shouldn't do any clearing up, and retreated to the kitchen. Daniella sat back in her chair and looked out at the trees. Inevitably, her eyes were drawn up. Dark sky, sparkling stars. Even without the Morgans accepting the dinner invitation – or perhaps thanks to their absence – she counted the night a success. She felt contented and safe, with the beautiful skyscape above, the murmur of happy conversation all around. Daniella sipped her water. She could make a home here. She pushed down her last hesitation.

Yes, this was definitely home.

Inside at the sink, Mark washed while his father dried. The pile of pots and pans was impressive, though not as daunting as when Kath cooked for all the stationhands during the muster.

Suddenly his father said, 'I went out to the crash site, you know.'

Mark was thrown, 'Really?'

'I wanted to make sure those TV bastards didn't nick anything.'

Mark smiled. 'I think Kath frisked them on the way out.'

William grunted. He was silent for a few moments. 'I didn't realise how badly it burned up.'

'Yeah.'

'That must have been frightening.'

'I don't remember it.' Mark stopped washing the plates and put his hands on the sink, thinking about his own trip out to the wreck. 'What do you want to know, Dad?'

'Kath told me that Daniella got you out herself, then helped pull Dave away – that she came back when it was burning.'

Mark pushed himself up off the sink. 'Yeah. I'm told that's what happened.'

William said nothing more, just hung up a wet tea towel and grabbed a dry one. Mark watched his father's thick, work-roughened hands as they reached for the next plate.

'Pots aren't going to wash themselves,' William said finally.

Chapter 29

The campdraft smelled of dust, cows and excitement. Jackie and Daniella drove to the ground together, windows down, Jamie happily playing with his dinosaurs in the back. Dave and Mark were already out there. It was the first truly summery day of the year, and the road was shedding heat in waves.

Once Daniella was sure he was physically okay to ride, she had become excited about Mark competing in the event; something about the idea of him on a horse, controlling cows, was frighteningly sexy. She confessed this to Jackie.

'Yeah, it's a recognised mental illness with city girls,' Jackie said, fanning herself as she drove. 'You dig horses, we get mango madness.'

'What's mango madness?'

Jackie rolled her eyes. 'Seasonal affective disorder. It'll start in the next few weeks. People start to anticipate summer coming and they go a bit crazy; some get depressed, some start acting weird. Like in Sweden when winter's coming and they know it's going to be dark for weeks on end. Or so I've read.'

'Is that real or are you making it up?'

'Just wait and see. You haven't experienced the proper summer here yet. This is nothing.'

Daniella tugged down the cap she'd bought to protect her from the fierce sun; she hadn't been able to find the old felt hat in weeks, and she felt strangely bereft without it. Of course, neither the cap nor the hat could do anything about the warm dusty air she sucked in with each breath. Once the heat really hit she knew she'd be thankful for the clinic's air-conditioning.

'Still, don't get too excited about seeing Mark compete today,' Jackie went on. 'Odds are we ride back to the clinic in the ambulance before he gets a turn.'

A few minutes later they pulled up alongside a line of other parked utes. The campdraft was held in one of the cattle-holding yards outside town, the huge main ring fenced with wooden posts and separated by a gate from a smaller yard. A mob of cattle was held in the smaller yard, and there were more waiting out in another ring connected to it by a chute. Horse floats overlooked the line of cars; behind the fences, spectators flanked the ground. A few marquees were set up, and PA speakers on poles.

'There's Dave,' said Jackie, waving with Jamie.

Daniella saw Dave on horseback in the opening between the spectators and the parked cars. Next to him was Mark. She caught her breath. Yes, she definitely had the city-girl horse sickness. He looked magnificent: faded blue jeans, white shirt, western hat, easy smile. Mark and Dave came towards them and they met halfway to the main ring. Even in the heat, he was barely breaking a sweat, quite back to his old self. His horse had a kind, intelligent face and she flicked her ears towards Daniella. Jamie instantly insisted on being lifted up, and Dave dropped his reins to oblige.

'Hey, you made it.' Mark got down and hugged her. 'How are you, babe?'

'Wonderful,' she said honestly. He grinned at her.

'Ahem,' said Jackie, looking pointedly at Dave.

'Not fair,' he complained, trying to contain a wriggling Jamie while staying on his horse.

Mark shrugged. 'Sorry, mate. You'll have to make it up to her later.'

Daniella stroked his horse's nose. The mare's muzzle was velvety smooth, and she closed her eyes and stretched her neck like a cat, blowing hot air into Daniella's hand.

'This is Rocket,' said Mark. 'Aren't you, girl?'

'Is she good?' asked Daniella. 'Jackie said the horse matters a lot in these events.'

'Yeah – you'll see why,' said Mark. 'And she's not bad. No Acres of Diamonds, but still.'

'Who's that?'

'Really good mare on the circuit. Amazing to watch.'

'She here today?'

'Not sure, but there'll be plenty of other good ones. It's starting pretty soon. You should go find a seat. Cat's waiting for you.'

Catrina had saved seats for them in a portable grandstand by the main marquee where there was some shade. The announcer was also in the marquee, so they could hear perfectly even though they were behind the main speakers. Jamie continued to play with his dinosaurs, making them slide down the grandstand's railing. To Daniella's surprise, William Walker joined them just before the first rider came into the small side ring. He sat down in the spare seat beside Daniella and proceeded to give her a running commentary on the action.

The first rider was a novice who struggled even to cut a cow out of the pack. Finally, the gate to the main ring was opened and the cow took off merrily, the rider chasing after, skittishly trying to turn the animal around the first of two pegs that marked out the course. They managed it eventually, but messily, the cow running circles around the ring.

'See, no trust between them.' William gave a bark of laughter. 'And that horse is scared of cows, too.'

A much slicker performance followed: the horse and rider guided a steer neatly around the figure of eight, the animals' hooves kicking up puffs of dust.

'Better,' said William, clapping as the rider finished the course to cheering.

This was followed by three more riders; one managed the course successfully, but the other two fell off. The first one flew off his horse while attempting too tight a turn when the cow was getting away; the second horse stumbled over backwards, depositing the rider in the starting ring. Fortunately both men got up unscathed, dusting themselves off to catcalls. 'Got it on camera! Smile, Kevvie!'

Jackie gave Daniella a meaningful look. 'I see what you mean,' said Daniella, hoping selfishly that if anyone was going to injure themselves it would be after Mark so she could see him in action.

'Are those Ryders cows, Mr Walker?' she asked a moment later.

'Call me William,' he said, rubbing at his chest. 'And yes, only the finest,' he added.

Daniella took a breath, full of earthy scents: cows and dust and sweat. William looked as though he was struggling with the heat and wiped his brow. 'It's a good name, Ryders,' she said.

He raised his eyebrows, giving her his full attention despite the cow currently careening around the main ring.

'For a station, I mean,' she went on. 'Seems a natural pairing. Jackie told me they named the town after the station, so I figured it must have been named a long time ago – is that right?'

William nodded. 'In the 1850s. John Walker, who was first here, named it for his lost love in England or so one story goes.' He proceeded to tell her the rest of the story she'd heard from Mark. Then, he said, 'It was my father who really re-established the place. He started a new bloodline and worked hard to build the town too. That was back in the days when they did everything on horses. All his stories were about riding out over the country, moving stock or mustering, or checking the pastures, and they'd always start and end at the house, on the ridge. Regardless of where the name came from originally, that's how I like to think of it.'

'That's so fitting,' said Daniella, touched by the pride in his voice.

'He was a master of cattle breeding,' William continued. 'Over the years we've diversified, of course, even gone into all the artificial techniques. You just can't compete in this business anymore without that . . . But the first bull he brought was the original. Perfect bull, excellent temperament, made quality beef.'

'And all your cows are descended from that bull?'

'Undoubtedly.' William looked away, took out a handkerchief and mopped his face. Clearly, this was the end of the conversation.

Daniella sat back. There was still some awkwardness between them, but she was satisfied with the progress they were making, and encouraged by his openness.

The action paused as a new batch of cows was brought into the small ring. William stood and straightened his lapels, then sat again as Mark rode into the ring.

Daniella instantly focused; she loved the way he moved. He kept his hands low, Rocket seeming to read invisible commands as they expertly cut a heifer out from the pack, then weaved back and forth to show they had the animal covered. Mark hardly moved in the saddle, his hat just tilting to and fro.

Then the gate was opened and the heifer took off. Rocket rose off her hindquarters and caught up quickly, keeping behind and to the outside to bend the cow back towards the pegs. William got up and leaned against the railing, watching the round. Daniella held her breath, waiting to see what would happen.

They were around the first peg now, Mark shifting his weight as Rocket changed sides on the heifer, guiding her around the second peg to complete the course. The spectators erupted into cheers and hollers. Daniella clapped madly as Mark made a lap around the ring, tipping his hat once. A good fast round.

Daniella turned to William to say so, and her smile fell.

'Dad?' cried Catrina, getting up.

William was curled over on himself, a fist pressed into his chest, his face twisted in a mask of agony.

Daniella felt her head shift gears. Heart, she thought. Myocardium. Ischaemia. Heart attack. She scrambled up and steered him into a seat. 'William, talk to me. What's happening?' she asked, leaning forward and reaching for his wrist to check his pulse.

'Pain. Bad,' he gasped. He was sweating heavily now, the beads coalescing.

'Do you have a spray?' she asked, hoping he had his angina meds on him.

'He's got one somewhere,' said Catrina, looking panicked and helpless. But William shook his head.

People were gathering round now, murmuring, unsure what to do. 'Let's make some room,' Daniella said, then turned to Jackie. 'Go get the ambos. Run. Cat, go and find Mark. Right now.'

~

On the way to the hospital, Daniella gave William the under-tongue nitrate spray from the ambulance stock, plus morphine and aspirin, and stuck him on the high-flow oxygen mask. Dr Harris met them at A&E, the ECG machine primed and waiting.

Together, they monitored his pulse and blood pressure, took blood and repeated the ECGs.

Before long, two more patients came in, both from the campdraft. One guy had fallen with his horse and been rolled on; the other had also come off, badly breaking his lower leg. Daniella got Jackie to do the X-rays while she slapped a neck brace on the first guy.

Twenty minutes passed before she could return to Dr Harris and William.

'How is he?' she asked, once they'd stepped into the hall.

'No pain now. Blood pressure's come down, pulse is a little high. But no way he's staying here – I want him in a cath lab. Might even need a bypass.'

Daniella glanced at William through the door, lying back against the white sheets, his face pale beneath the oxygen mask. 'Do Mark and Cat know?'

'I was just about to tell them. What have you got down the hall?'

'Concussion with a query on the C-spine, and what looks like a closed displaced tibiofibular fracture. Jackie's doing the films now. Might need surgery.'

Dr Harris nodded. 'I'll ask Roselyn to see if we can get a dual evac, then. I'll go look at the neck films. You want to be the one to speak to Mark?'

Daniella found him and Cat in the waiting area. Cat was shaky and red-eyed, Mark looked wretched with worry.

'What's happening?' asked Cat. Mark stood beside her, clearly steeling himself. Daniella could see that they both expected the worst.

She sat them down. 'He's fine for now,' she said. 'The ECG result shows us he's had a heart attack, but we got onto it very early and gave him meds to try to avoid as much damage as possible. We're keeping a close eye on him, though. Sometimes problems can creep up afterwards.'

Mark blew out his breath. Cat hugged herself in relief.

Daniella continued, 'He'll have to be transferred so a cardiologist can work out what to do. Probably he'll need some kind of procedure, but we won't know that for sure until they've looked at him.'

'How soon?' Mark asked.

'Roselyn's trying to organise an evac now. We've got another guy who needs to go too.'

Mark nodded, looking spaced out. 'Do me a favour?' he asked. 'Don't tell Dad about the other guy. If he finds out, he'll probably refuse to go, thinking the other guy should go first.'

'Can we see him?' asked Cat.

'Of course,' said Daniella. 'I'll give you a minute alone, but I'll be right down the hall if you need me.'

~

As he walked into the room where his father was lying on a bed, Mark couldn't help thinking of the last time he'd seen his mother in the hospital. To be back here again, within a year, now for his father, was rough. His whole world was shifting beneath him. For the first time since his father's initial bout of chest pain all those months ago, he had to accept how serious it could be. And that one day, he was going to have to run the station alone.

Cat began to calm down once William had spoken to her and allowed her to hug him. After that, she launched into remonstration.

'Where's your spray?' she demanded.

'Left it at the station,' he admitted from around the oxygen mask.

'Well . . . don't do it again!'

'All right, darling,' he placated her. He looked down the bed at Mark. 'Cat, can you give us a minute, please?'

'Why?'

'Please, darling.'

Cat looked pained, but gave in. 'Fine. But I'm coming back in ten minutes.'

When she had gone, William beckoned Mark closer. 'Dr Harris says I've got to go to Townsville.'

Mark pulled a chair towards the bed and sat down. 'Yeah, that's what Daniella said too. They're organising the flight now.'

'Another flight,' said William, shaking his head. 'But then, I've avoided doctors so long, maybe this is payback.'

'Dad, you really shouldn't be talking,' said Mark.

'The hell I won't,' came the reply.

Mark sighed. Even under an oxygen mask, this was the William Walker of old, refusing to go down without a fight. But he didn't speak again for a while.

Then, out of nowhere, he said, 'I want to apologise to you.'

Mark's head snapped up. 'Christ, Dad, you're not dying.'

Behind the mask, William laughed, which came out as a gurgle. 'That bad, am I? Think I'd only apologise if I thought I was gonna die?'

Mark thought about it. 'Pretty much, you hard-arsed old bugger.'

William actually looked pleased. 'Still,' he went on, 'I was wrong. I shouldn't have said those things to you about Daniella. Should've known better.'

Mark rubbed his hair. 'We can talk about this later.'

'No, we won't,' said William. His face grew serious and he pulled the mask aside.

'Put that back on,' said Mark.

'Just listen for a minute. This is important. Are you serious about Daniella?'

'Dad, this really isn't—'

'Are you? Because she's obviously serious about you. And now she's talking about staying here.'

Mark felt his heart flutter. 'Yeah, I'm serious.'

His father gave him a hard look. 'Then be very careful about what you're doing. You've been uneasy these last few days. I noticed. Don't string her along if you're not—'

'Christ, it's not that,' said Mark, horrified that his father thought he was looking for a way out. 'I love her. More than anything. But before I went to Isa, we fought because she said she was thinking about leaving town for work.'

'Go on,' said his father, as if he understood where this was going.

'Yeah, well. Thing is, I spoke to Dr Harris last week about how doctors do their training. She's not supposed to stay in one place. She's meant to move around to different hospitals so she can learn. And I think she's giving that up for me. She didn't tell me that, but it's bothering me.'

William said slowly, 'Because you're worried that, even though she thinks she's giving it up willingly now, in a few years she'll resent you for it. And you'll feel awful for taking her freedom from her. And once that happens, things will never be the same again.'

Mark stared at his father dumbly. Yes, that was his fear.

William replaced the oxygen mask for a few breaths, then moved it aside again. 'It was exactly the same with your mother and me. She was a traveller. She loved the station, she loved us all, but she couldn't be tied to one place. I tried to move around with her for a while, but I couldn't do it. I resented her because I thought it meant she loved the outside world more than us. I couldn't understand it.

'It wasn't until she was dying that I finally got it. And then I wished I'd tried harder while she was well. Daniella has that same look your mother had when she tried to settle here with me. Somewhere inside she knows what she's giving up. In a while, she'll realise it. Your mother did.'

William stopped for a few more breaths. 'I've wished every day I could have made her life a little easier, and not blamed her for just being herself. She'd drive into town and sit on that bench by the main street, just looking out on us. That was as close as she could bear to be to me, sometimes. That's not what I want for you.'

Mark couldn't speak. He sat back in his chair, completely gutted. He'd never realised that was why his mother had spent so much time on that bench. He felt as if he'd gone down in the ring earlier and Rocket had rolled over him. A few times, actually. He felt as though he was going to lose Daniella all over again. Sooner or later, it would happen. And he couldn't bear that. Maybe he was the one who needed to change . . . Could he leave the station, as Will had done? He'd done it before, but he'd always returned.

'There's one more thing,' said William.

Mark raised his eyebrows, dreading what his father might say next. Hadn't he said enough?

'Your ideas about the station. The new technologies, or looking at crops if they free up the river water or whatever you were trying to tell me about. We should do it.'

'What?' Mark couldn't believe what he was hearing.

'I've been talking to Cat,' William continued. 'She told me about your discussions. About the CSIRO research programs that some of the universities are involved in. They might be interested in working with us. Is that about right?'

Mark nodded, dazed. 'Yeah, that's right. They reckon they can use satellite pictures to track the herds, even work out if they're sick, or where the best grazing is. Make operations more efficient, save on fuel and guesswork. And there's a research grant in it maybe. But you're kidding, right?' he added. 'I thought you didn't want any of that going on at Ryders.'

William touched a hand to his chest. 'Deep in this buggered old ticker, no, I really don't. But the world's changing. I don't want the station to go under.'

Mark was still processing all this when Cat came back.

And still, an hour later when the ambos packed his father into the ambulance to go to the air strip. They had space on the flight for one family member, so Cat went with him. Mark had work to do at the station, so he'd drive up on Tuesday.

As the plane took off into the late afternoon, great waves of heat rolled off the tarmac, catching him in the chest. Daniella was watching the fading speck, her hand up to her eyes, with that determined expression he'd first seen when she was working on Dave after the rugby. He felt intensely possessive as she turned towards him. He wanted to bundle her into his arms, take her back to her house and spend a few hours forgetting everything his father had just said to him.

But that wouldn't be fair.

'Hey, you doing all right?' she asked, coming over and putting her arms around him.

Mark made himself smile. 'Yeah. He's a tough nut. And he was talking like he was dying, so that means he'll pull through.'

She laughed. 'True. I'm not going to tell you it's not serious, but he's in good hands.'

Impulsively, Mark kissed her. 'You know I love you, right?' he asked.

She looked up at him, suddenly serious, catching his tone. 'Yes. Why?'

'I've got to go back out to the campdraft, take the cattle back to the station. Dave's there by himself.'

'Okay.'

He kissed her again. Oh, man. How was he going to resolve this problem – how could they be together without ruining each other? And he felt awful for not sharing any of the thoughts that were tumbling round his head.

Chapter 30

Daniella was just stepping out of her after-clinic shower the following evening when she heard loud knocking on the door. 'Coming,' she called, pulling on a pair of trackies and a T-shirt.

She found Jackie on the doorstep, practically hyperventilating.

'What's going on?' Daniella asked, concerned.

'Oh my God, am I crazy? I'm crazy, right?'

'Why? What's happened?'

Daniella stood back and Jackie came inside, hands flapping as fast as her mouth. 'Can this even work? I mean, can it really? I must be nuts!'

'Jack, what the hell are you talking about?'

Jackie collapsed onto the couch. 'Dave. He's gone insane.'

'Why? For Pete's sake, start at the beginning.'

'Okay, right.' Jackie paused as if to put her thoughts in some order. 'Well, he tried to talk to me yesterday, but it was kinda crazy with all the drama. So, he came round this morning. He said . . .' she took a big breath, 'he's applied to work in Brisbane. He wants us to live there together while I do radiography. I'm even thinking of applying for med next year, which I never dared think about before.'

Daniella was thrilled. 'Oh, but that's fantastic. I mean, is that what you want? To be together?'

Jackie began to cry. 'I thought I didn't. I thought he'd stay here and I'd be moving away and that would be that. I never imagined he'd want to come with me.'

'Of course he would,' said Daniella. 'I've seen the way he looks at you – at both of you. He's always going to want to be with you.'

Jackie laughed through her tears. 'Maybe I should send bloody Steph Morgan a thank-you card. If she hadn't blabbed, I'd probably still be trying to work out how to get away on my own. I mean, I still don't know quite how it's going to work. We'll have to find somewhere to live and child care for Jamie soon. God knows how I'm going to study.'

'I think you'll work it out somehow.'

Jackie took a wrinkled tissue from her pocket and blew her nose. 'I think so too. Can you believe it? I didn't think this would ever happen.'

Daniella was so pleased for her; it was wonderful. But the news settled heavily in her. 'I'm going to miss you,' she admitted, hugging Jackie close.

'Will you come and visit?'

Daniella smiled. 'Definitely.'

'What about you and Mark?' asked Jackie, holding her at arm's length. 'Are you moving out to the station?'

'I can't,' said Daniella. 'It's too far from the hospital when I'm on call.'

'Uh-huh. So he comes here for sleepovers, then?'

'Yeah, for now.' That little flutter was still there.

'He coming tonight?'

'Don't think so. He had things to do.'

'You want to come watch *Battlestar*, then?'

Daniella took a breath. 'Actually, can we do it tomorrow? I wouldn't mind a quiet one.'

'Sure – I was really only coming to tell you the news.'

Jackie took herself to the door. She turned as she went down the steps. 'Look, Daniella, Mark's a really good guy, I know that. But is this really where you want to be forever?'

Daniella put her hands on her hips. 'You giving me relationship advice now?'

'I know, I know. I can talk. But just think about it.'

Daniella knew she wouldn't be able to avoid that. 'I will. Hey, Jackie, can I borrow your ute? I need to go for a drive. Only be an hour or so.'

'Sure.' Jackie tossed her the keys. 'I can walk from here. Just drop it back when you're done.'

Half an hour later, Daniella sat on the hood of Jackie's ute and watched the sun go down. She'd driven round to the secluded spot Mark had shown her all those weeks ago; as usual, no one else was there.

In spite of the beautiful setting she was uneasy, though not about the usual things. That morning she'd met with Dr Harris again to work through more of the issues around the incident in Brisbane. She was getting better at thinking about it without the crippling guilt. It might take a while, but she was beginning to think she would get there. What Jackie had said was bothering her, though. She loved everything about Mark, but she'd been trying to avoid thinking too long term. She would stay in town, she'd committed to that; but it meant they could never properly move in together. And what if things went further, like she caught herself imagining? What if they got married, wanted to start a family? Would she give up her job?

Daniella sighed and leaned back on the hood. The metal was still warm from the engine, but the heat of the day itself was fading now. She had come to Ryders to escape her guilt about the incident. She'd begun to heal that hurt, but in making her new life here, would she just create others?

She pulled her mobile out of her pocket and looked at the screen. Amazingly, there was actually a bar of reception here today. Practically civilised. For what seemed like the tenth time that day, she thought about starting surgical training. But that was out of the question for now. Which was fine. She had Mark. And he was enough. Of course he was.

A few stars were beginning to show. Daniella counted them, trying to spot new ones just as they became visible. She heard a vehicle coming down the dam road, its headlights briefly illuminating the trees across the lake before it went around the corner. Someone else must be coming to the dam to watch the stars. That was fine. The sky was big enough to share.

She was surprised a minute later when the engine sound grew closer. The vehicle was coming down the path to the secret spot. Then she saw the Rover.

Mark pulled up alongside and got out looking unsurprised to see her. 'Hey.'

'Hey, yourself. I was just thinking about you.'

'Were you?' he responded, striding over. 'I was hoping you'd be here.'

'You came by the house?'

He shook his head then leaned on the hood next to her. 'No, actually, I came here first. I just had a feeling you might be here.'

They looked at each other steadily. Daniella knew he could see through her, that he knew she was uneasy. She took a deep breath, trying not to cry. 'We need to talk, don't we?'

He nodded, and pushed himself up onto the hood. He put his arm around her.

Daniella said, 'I meant it when I said I was staying.'

Mark looked out at the dam. 'I know you did. But I think you should go.'

Daniella sniffed. 'You're breaking up with me?'

'Christ, no! Where did you get that idea?'

She shrugged.

'Daniella, I told you. I love you.' He smoothed her hair, smiling at her stricken face. 'But I don't want to ruin this by being too selfish. I know with your job you're not meant to stay in one place. I don't want you giving up everything for me. You might think you want to do that now, but I've seen you work. You love it. So I know you're going to have to go away. For a while I thought about coming with you. I thought I could . . .'

'But you love the station too much, I know,' she said brokenly. She had known that for a long time.

'That's true.' He spoke warmly, urgently. 'But what I want to know is, will you be with me anyway? Even when you go, will you be mine? I'll come and visit you as much as I can wherever you go, and there'll always be a home here for you. I don't want to let you go, but even more than that I don't want you to stay here and always be wondering what else you might have done.'

Daniella searched his face. Now it was his turn to look anxious. He thought she was going to refuse him, tell him his idea wouldn't work. She took a breath. 'Mark, I need to tell you something. It's something I haven't told anyone except Dr Harris.'

She laid it out for him, describing what had happened in Brisbane. How she'd felt afterwards. He listened intently, just nodding and asking for a detail here and there.

'You were right when you said I tried to control everything,' she acknowledged finally. 'That was exactly what I was doing. I came to Ryders because it was small. I thought it would be easier to get a grip here, and to avoid my father, and the training programs. I've been hiding out.'

'I can understand,' he said. 'Sometimes we lose calves on the station. I'm not saying it's anywhere near what you went through, but I always feel ratshit about it. I can't imagine what that would have been like for you. And when I went to Isa, that's what I was doing too – hoping that running away would solve my problems. Guess there's only one difference.'

'What's that?'

'Well, I'm glad you came to Ryders. I'm not happy I went to Isa.'

She laughed. 'Yeah, that's the crucial difference!'

'It is for me.' He kissed her slowly, between his sentences. 'I don't know if this will work. But I want it to.'

'Me too. And there's something else.'

'Mmm?'

'I want to spend weekends on the station. I'll be here for another four months at least before I could even think about getting a program place. I want to spend time with you.'

Without a word, Mark got off the bonnet, walked to the Rover and retrieved something from the back seat. When Daniella saw what it was, she gasped. 'Where did you find that?'

Mark plonked the battered felt hat on her head and tipped up her chin for another kiss. 'I found it trying to escape near the crash site,' he whispered. 'So look after it. I like how it looks on you.'

'Did I mention I love you?' she asked, kissing him with her whole heart.

Chapter 31

The next Saturday afternoon, Mark was sitting on the main yard fence, watching Daniella riding Rocket.

'You really did used to do this, didn't you?' he called. He loved that she was keen to learn about the station, and now everything was out in the open he was confident they could make it work. The details would come later; he'd promised they'd ride up the main paddock tomorrow morning to give them time together to plan.

He glanced around to see his father coming down from the house.

William had spent a week in Townsville before returning to the station. Since then, he'd actually heeded advice to take it easy, but he'd also been distracted.

'Need a few minutes with you in the office,' William said.

'Will you be all right for a bit?' Mark called to Daniella, who brought Rocket round again and reined her in at the fence. Under her hat, she was pink-cheeked, a big smile on her dusty face.

'Of course,' she said.

Mark followed his father towards the station office, which was attached to the stables and faced down the plain. Inside, the walls were covered with feed charts, stock charts and meteorological data. There was paper everywhere, organised into folders and bundles and filing cabinets.

'I've been busy,' was his father's opening line.

Mark raised his eyebrows. 'Well, you did just have a heart attack. Somehow, though, I don't think that's what you mean.'

'It isn't. The Civil Aviation Safety Authority investigator called earlier. They're releasing the report on the crash in a few days and wanted to let us know in advance what they found.'

Mark's stomach flipped over. 'What did he say?'

'Bird strike,' said William. 'Pretty definitive, really. They reckon Dave did a good job of putting it down the way he did.'

Mark raked a hand through his hair. He still didn't remember the crash at all, but he carried the consequences in his body. In the days since, he'd felt for the first time that his own life was as precarious as their grip on the property. And it only made him more determined to see the place right.

'There's more,' said his father, moving to the window. 'I happened to get a very interesting call from Valerie Turner's son the day after I got to Townsville. I don't know if you remember him.'

Mark frowned, searching his memory. 'Bruce, right? He works in Townsville, doesn't he? Valerie's still here though – Daniella's talked about her. She won't admit it but I think they're friends.'

'That's the one. Bruce used to come out here often when he was a teenager. You might not remember so well; you were only small then. He became a lawyer. Works for the Morgans' firm now, as it turns out.'

'Really?'

'Yes. At least he did until last week, when he resigned.'

Mark wondered where this was going. 'What did he say?'

'Apparently the Morgans have told us a bunch of crap. They weren't approached about mineral exploration or a sale.

They've been actively looking for a buyer and preparing a case to have the government approve the sale to a foreign company.'

'What?' Betrayal sliced Mark through the chest.

'Not only that, but they've been scouring the contract, looking for a way to force us out.'

Mark slowly absorbed this information, anger replacing helplessness. He remembered the way Stephanie had pretended to be on board with his determination to keep the station running, always insisting she just wanted them to know the options. Perhaps he could have understood if they'd wanted to get their money out and into something more lucrative, but the way they'd gone about it was so underhanded.

At the same time, he felt out of his depth. He understood the land, how it responded to him, how to get the best out of it with what they had. But contracts and lawyers were so far removed from that, and he felt a jolt of panic. 'How do we stop them?'

'I did a lot of thinking about that in the hospital,' William said. 'I didn't tell you because I wasn't sure I could do it, and I didn't want an argument.'

Mark froze. His father had his hands in his pockets now, as he looked through the window and over the land that he had always loved. Mark had an awful feeling. 'What did you do?'

William dipped his head. 'I'm selling the Roma station, and some shares. And a few other things.'

'You're what?'

'Once the sale goes through, there'll be just enough to buy out the Morgans' share. Won't get us out of the existing loans, but we won't have anyone else to answer to. We're going to direct this place again, outright.'

Mark tried to take this in. He couldn't believe it. The Roma property wasn't large, but it was steady. Too good to sell, but easiest to liquidate.

'What did Maria say?' he asked.

His father laughed grimly. 'We didn't actually speak. That's the only thing I like about lawyers. And I've asked Bruce Turner to take over the rest of the process. He couldn't be happier, but I can't imagine the Morgans will be pleased, what with losing the possibility of all that lucrative cash they'd get for a foreign sale or exploration rights. I suspect that's really what they were after all along.'

'I'll be amazed if Maria accepts it,' said Mark.

'She doesn't have to,' said his father, his voice revealing just how proud he was of himself. 'I would never have taken their money in the first place if it meant surrendering control. I made sure there was a clause in the contract that if we could front the cash, we always had the option. But before it just always felt like it was too hard to do.'

Mark felt lighter. 'Dad, that's . . . fantastic. How the hell did you have time to do all that while you were in hospital in Townsville?'

'Bruce Turner's a good friend to us, it seems. Organised all manner of lawyers and paperwork. And since those stents, I've never felt better. I had to do something. Besides, I have it on good authority that bed rest is bad for recovery.'

Mark swore. 'You and Daniella are going to team up against me, aren't you? I can just smell it.' But he hadn't felt this happy in years. All the pieces seemed to be coming together. He had Daniella back; his father was on the mend. And the station had a future.

'There's one more thing,' said William. 'Bruce heard about that business with Jackie and Dave and Jamie from his mother – apparently she's emailing him with all kinds of news. After she mentioned it, he remembered something he'd seen in the office. He went back through some papers and found a request for Jamie's birth certificate.'

'What was that doing in the Morgans' office?'

'He wondered the same thing. The transmittal came through their office. He thought it was odd because they don't deal in family law. After he'd seen the Morgans going over the contracts on this place, he had some suspicions about their methods. So he called Jackie to check whether she'd authorised it, because the request had her signature. She didn't know anything about it. Turns out it was forged, and he's pretty sure who by. He decided he couldn't work for them anymore. Resigned on the spot.'

'Jesus.'

'I asked Steph to come down for a meeting this morning, but I've been putting her off. She's at the cottage waiting. I haven't told her anything yet. I'm going to leave that to you.' William clapped Mark on the shoulder. 'Then let's talk about what we do next.'

A long minute later, when his father had gone, Mark realised what had just happened. William had actually made it possible for Mark to try out his plans for the station. He'd made the last big effort; now he knew it was safely in family hands, the rest was up to Mark. He had control. He was trusted to fight the battles on his own.

All this had passed tacitly in a moment of contact from father to son; a small cloud of the land's dust raised by a weathered hand, and it was done.

Mark rode the quad bike down the spur to the cottage. Steph answered promptly when he knocked on the door. 'Mark,' she said, as if surprised to see him. She looked as immaculate as ever, but her expression was pinched. 'Would you like to come in?'

Mark jacked his boots and stepped into the short hallway. The kitchen table was deep in papers: posters for the next fundraiser, planning sheets and rosters. Steph did do a lot of good for the community, he reminded himself, suddenly uneasy. They'd known each other since they were both small children and her family's money had helped the station out of a tight spot; he didn't want to believe she was capable of the things he'd just heard. He was determined not to make this unpleasant.

'How's your dad?' she asked, sitting back down in the seat where she'd been working. 'Is he ready for that meeting now?'

Mark stayed in the kitchen doorway. 'He's doing really well. But the meeting's just with me.'

'Oh?'

Straight to it, then. 'Dad's going to buy out the Morgan share of the station.'

Stephanie surprised him by laughing, leaning back in her chair. 'I didn't need you to come and tell me that. I already know. Of course we know. As soon as he started the paperwork, the lawyers called from Townsville. I was just speaking with them before, in fact.'

Mark straightened, feeling uncomfortable at her unfriendly tone. 'All right.'

She gestured around the cottage. 'That it then? Want me to leave?'

'There's no need for that. You and your mother have had a stake here for a long time. No need to go rushing off.'

Her eyes flared. 'Going to be the good guy, huh?'

'I hope so.' He did. He no longer harboured any illusions about the Morgans, but this didn't have to be hostile.

She tapped her fingers on the table, looking longingly out the window. 'I don't suppose you'd reconsider?' she asked. 'There'd be a lot of money in a sale. Enough to discharge all the debts. You could easily start again somewhere else with none of that hanging over you.'

The thought of losing Ryders was behind him now, and Mark was annoyed by her persistence. 'Not on your life,' he said stiffly.

Her voice dropped. 'Hmm. And what if that wasn't the only thing at stake?'

He leaned against the door frame, arms crossed. 'What do you mean?'

The chair scraped across the floor as Steph stood up again. 'Well, let's see. Ryders Station isn't the only thing you care about, is it?' She prowled around the table towards him. 'There's your lovely doctor girlfriend. And there's Will.' She was right before him now, only a foot away. Her pearl earrings were perfect orbs, as white as her teeth.

Mark narrowed his eyes. 'What are you talking about?'

Stephanie leaned in, pressing the full length of her body against him as she whispered in his ear, 'I've found out some things about Daniella Bell that I'm sure she doesn't want anyone to know. But her patients would be interested. There're other things I know, too, things I'm sure your family wouldn't want out. But I won't say a word about any of those things, if you'll just be reasonable and look at the terms of this sale.'

Mark instantly saw how wrong he'd been about Steph. The shock of her words, of seeing her true nature, was a landed blow, one he wanted to fight off. Trapped between her and the wall, he instinctively raised his hands to push her away.

'Don't even think about touching me,' she hissed. 'It's just the two of us here. Who knows what I could say?'

His heart hammering, Mark slid sideways, forcing her to step back to keep her balance. He edged away, his thoughts a momentary tumble. Would she really make up some story about him? He could guess what secret of Daniella's she was referring to, but was she bluffing about the rest? He moved towards the door while she watched him with cold anger in her eyes.

'You know, right up till a minute ago I felt a little sorry for you,' he said.

She served him a withering look. 'Whatever, Mark. This is business. And you need to be reasonable.'

Mark shook his head as she came towards him again. 'This is hardly reasonable.'

'I just want you to think about what I'm saying to you. It's a good deal.'

Mark stopped moving. 'You know, this is why things never worked between us. You don't get it. You could never understand what this place means to me.'

'You were always too sentimental about everything,' she shot back.

Mark pressed his fist into his chest, where he carried both his loves, for the station and for Daniella. Daniella understood that about him, and she carried within her the same twin love: for him and her work. Steph had nothing like that. It wasn't a weakness, this feeling. It was the way out.

'Take your things and go,' he said. 'This is over.' He turned for the door.

'It's not over!' she yelled, losing her calm. 'You have no idea who you're dealing with. We're not finished with the contract yet. You should start packing.'

Mark rounded on her, finally letting his anger crack like a whip. 'Let me make myself perfectly clear. You haven't got anything I want. Our association is over. You don't threaten me, my family, my friends or Daniella ever again. And you don't contact us either.'

Steph laughed. 'Or what?'

Mark smiled cooly. 'I'm pretty sure it's illegal to forge someone's signature. I think that's called fraud. And I know you did that to find out about Dave. We have the proof, so don't push me to take it further. Could be very bad for business.'

Steph said nothing, and Mark strode to the front door. When he turned back, she was framed in the doorway to the kitchen, her hand on the jamb. She stared at him as if he were a stranger, eyes wide, mouth frozen open in surprise. Caught. Then she glanced away. Mark saw her searching for some way to come back at him, but clearly nothing came. Her hand fell.

'I'm glad we understand each other,' Mark said as he left.

Six months later

It had been a long week. Daniella counted down the minutes to the end of her shift while she shuffled the paperwork for her last patient into a fat hospital file. He was a twelve-year-old boy with Type I diabetes, diagnosed at age three. This week his blood sugar had been all over the place and he'd ended up with a bad hypo. The blood work showed the sugar control had been off for a long time. They were trying to sort it out, but this happened a lot. It wasn't right that someone so young should have a file so thick already, but she'd seen all too often how unfair life could be. It made her all the more grateful for her work.

She often caught herself thinking she was back at Ryders Ridge or Mount Isa, but that was easy to do within the generic walls of a hospital. Inside, Nambour looked indistinguishable from the other hospitals she'd worked in: the white walls, the odd collection of prints, the scuff marks on the hall corners where the gurneys and linen trolleys took the paint off.

She replaced the file in bed five's pigeonhole and grabbed the computer in the registrars' room before anyone could waylay her with something else. There were two emails from Jackie, keeping her up to date with what was going on in Brisbane. The university semester was just winding up for her and Dave was flying again. Things were crazy, but happy crazy.

There were photos attached, which Daniella would have to download another time. Another email was from Valerie, who was still riding high on Bruce's defection from the Morgans and setting up his own practice. She smiled, looking forward to reading it later.

She heard footsteps in the hall, so she logged out of her email and trotted back to the nurses' station.

Blake, the night reg, was yawning as he stuffed his bag in a locker.

'Hey, Blake,' she said.

'Hi, Daniella. Man, I'm not used to these night starts yet.'

'You'll never get used to them. They're one of the cruel and unusual punishments of this job.'

'Thanks very much,' he complained.

'Hey, you said that to me last week.'

'Indeed I did. Damn your good memory. And I suppose you want to go home now. All right, what've we got?'

Daniella went through the handover notes for each of the kids on the ward. Blake nodded along. 'No red flags so far,' she finished. 'Just watch Trent in five. He's not keen on the hospital food and we need to watch that postprandial sugar if he hides any of it.'

'Gotcha.'

Daniella stepped out into the balmy Sunshine Coast late summer evening, her eyes shaded as usual by the old felt hat. She'd tried to clean it, but it remained intractably grubby looking, an object with a history. It went most places with her now, reminding her of all she'd learned in Ryders Ridge, and particularly of the weekends on the station that she'd missed these last few months. She couldn't wait to get back there for a visit. She pulled out her phone.

Mark picked up on the second ring. 'Hi, babe, you just get off?'

She grinned into the phone. 'You know, it always sounds rude when you say that!' He laughed at her. 'How many sleeps now?' she asked plaintively.

'One more and I'll be there. You better still have that leave booked, and not be lying to me about that bikini.'

'It's all set, as long as you bring your hat like you promised.'

'Done.'

Daniella turned right out of the hospital's main entrance and headed down the road towards her shared house. 'One other thing,' she said. 'I've got a surprise for you.'

'Yeah?'

'After this placement, I've managed to get the next stint in Townsville. And then probably a year in Isa. I'll be able to see you more easily.'

'You know what I like to hear. That's amazing. Is that really what you want to do, though?'

'Definitely.'

'You didn't do this because Cat came up to visit you on the weekend and talked you into coming back north?'

'No,' Daniella said. 'It was fun. We went shopping and she told me about the research project. Ryders is going to be a national study, huh? Satellite tracking for your herd?'

She heard him groan. 'I told her to keep that a secret. I was going to tell you all about it. We just got sign-off from the research board this week.'

Daniella reached the peak of the hill and stopped to look down. The rolling suburbia of Nambour, which seemed vast to her after Ryders, ended at the horizon, but just over it were Maroochydore and the ocean. And tomorrow, she and Mark would be sitting on one of the perfect Alex Heads beaches. After that, it would be two months before she'd see him again, flying to the station for four days. That was how they were staying sane: booking ahead, so they always knew when they would see each other next.

'As it happens, I've got something for you too,' he said.

'Oh? What is it?' she asked as she started down the hill.

'Can't tell you, you'll have to wait.'

'That's not fair! Is it a cow?'

He sounded deflated. 'How did you guess?'

'Really, you got me a cow? What kind?'

He laughed again. 'No, not really. But I had you going, didn't I?'

She laughed too. 'I love you.'

'Say that again.'

'I love you, Mark.'

'Ahh . . . do you really want a cow? I can get you one. I think we have some around here somewhere . . .'

'Yeah, I'd like a cow.'

They walked together for a little way; she could hear his footsteps through the phone, and she knew he could hear hers. They did this most nights as she walked, either to work or home, a ritual.

'Babe, it's not a cow,' he said finally.

'But I'll have to wait, right?'

'Well, maybe not as long as you think.'

Daniella stopped. 'What do you mean?'

'Just keep walking.'

She turned the corner, feeling tingly. And there he was. Mark, leaning against an ancient, beaten ute, in blue jeans and a white T-shirt. Mark, with a big grin on his handsome face.

'Surprise,' he whispered, pulling her into his arms.

Daniella kissed him, incredulous. 'What are you doing here?'

'Being early. You wanna go for a drive?'

He opened the passenger door and ushered her into the cab, which Daniella noted had been worked over by a very meticulous cleaner. Mark climbed in the driver's side and threw the ute into first gear with purpose.

'What's going on?' she asked suspiciously.

He gave her a sidelong grin. 'We're going for a drive.'

It didn't take long to reach the edge of Nambour. Daniella twisted around to look at the receding town, then stared at Mark with her eyebrows raised.

He refused to be drawn. 'Just wait.'

Still, it wasn't until they'd crested the seaside hill and were looking down on Alex Heads that Daniella twigged. 'We're not supposed to be here until tomorrow! And I'm still in my work clothes.'

'Your bag's in the back. Your housemate was very helpful.'

He drove down to the esplanade, where the blue waves were spreading lazily over the golden sand of the pine-spiked shore. Where the sea road rose up over the cliffs at the headland itself, Mark pulled the ute into a car park and got out. For once, Daniella didn't try to rile him by stepping out before he could open the door. Holding it for her, he took her hand. 'Come on.'

They walked right to the edge of the grass to stand at the top of the cliff above the waves and rocks; below them the sea stretched into the day's last light. The sky was streaked with pink, and as yet starless. They stood together, Daniella enjoying Mark's warmth by her side. This was about as far from the station as Daniella could imagine, but these days place didn't seem so important. It was all the same sky; and Mark was here.

'Daniella, there's something I have to say.'

She leaned her head against his shoulder. 'Is it something about the view?'

'No. Why don't you see what you can find in my pocket?'

Daniella hid her smile, and slipped her hand into his jeans. Her fingers closed on a small velvet bag. Without opening it, she could feel the fine arc of metal within.

'Oh, Mark . . .'

He took both her hands and sank down on one knee. A few other people at the lookout turned and smiled. Daniella could see nothing but Mark.

'I know we're not usual in the scheme of things, but I love you more than anything,' he said. 'I want you for good, wherever you are. Will you say the same?'

Daniella thought of all the travelling they'd been doing back and forth, all the lonely nights without him, the study and the work. And then she thought of how she felt right now, when she was with him.

She smiled. 'I will.'

Acknowledgements

Ryders Ridge began in a conversation at our writing group retreat, and I thank all my Sisters of the Pen – Bek, Fi, Kim, Meg, Sal and Nic – for your support throughout. Special thanks to Rebekah Turner, who read the manuscript several times and talked through many points with me. You are the bestest writing bud ever. Kim Wilkins, thank you for getting me started in this writing business, and for your ongoing friendship and wisdom. To my husband Kevin, thank you for your love, support, humour, patience and suggestions. I also am indebted to many friends: Barnaby, for the conversations about satellite technologies in agriculture (and the ISS); Nic and Ben, for your hospitality and guidance on choppers and cows; and Craig, for the laughs, and the advice on utes and all things army. Finally, I would like to thank the fabulous publishing team at Hachette Australia, including Bernadette Foley and Kate Ballard. Working with you has been an absolute delight.

INTRODUCING

IRON JUNCTION

ALSO BY CHARLOTTE NASH

Chapter 1

Brisbane, November

'Beth Harding, what the hell is going on?'

In the midst of her youngest sister's birthday party, Beth Harding pressed her phone to her ear and crept inside, her pulse racing. She steadied her camera against her chest.

'Hi, Tom.' She heard waves in the background. She imagined her former fellow resident, Tom Black, the headland of Manly beach rising up behind him. They'd known each other since medical school, and for the past week she'd been sleeping on his couch.

'How's the beach?' she asked.

'Nice try,' he said, clearly ropable. 'I called the hospital to swap a shift and instead I find out you resigned yesterday. I thought you were just flying home to Brisbane for Vicky's party. So, what the hell?'

Beth glanced around. Thirty guests crowded her mother's covered patio. Her uncle Jim was mustering the meat, brandishing the long tongs and a tasteless apron covered in a French-maid print, the air thick with barbecue smoke. Across the tiles Victoria, the birthday girl, radiated charm. Her white sundress, Christmas-bell earrings and blonde chignon were flight-attendant perfect, despite her coming off-shift early that morning. Vicky was in a huddle with Anne, her middle sister, and their mother, while Vicky's boyfriend, Ryan, hovered at the edge of the conversation. But no one was looking her way.

Tom went on, 'I know you've been frustrated with work, and getting over Richard is going to take a while . . .'

A strangled sound escaped Beth's throat.

'Beth? Beth?' He tried his best reasonable tone. 'Look, I'm worried. Why don't we have a coffee when you're back tomorrow and talk about it?'

'I can't, Tom.' Beth couldn't help glancing at her case resting in the hallway, its belly stuffed full of Murtagh's *General Practice*, *The Oxford Handbook of Clinical Medicine*, her album and enough clothes for a long trip. She pushed a wayward length of hair behind her ear and cupped her hand around the phone. 'I'm going away for a while.'

A pause. 'Where?'

Beth took a breath. 'I'm taking a locum post. I'm just waiting for the call to confirm.'

Tom suddenly laughed. 'Thank god. Finally!'

'What do you mean, finally?'

Tom only laughed harder. 'Beth, you've been miserably stale for three years. I'd given up thinking you were going to climb out of the rut.'

'I wasn't in a rut,' hissed Beth indignantly. But he had a point. She was five years out of med school and still without any direction. No specialty had called her, and the world had contracted around the monotony of her inner-city hospital.

'Are you really sure, though?' Tom continued. 'You're a beach girl. What if you end up in the desert?'

'It's only a few months,' she said.

Tom sighed. 'I wish you'd told me,' he said. 'But I'll hold your boxes. I want to hear all about it.'

Beth ended the call and eased back around the doors, her fingers stroking the camera around her neck, a bead of sweat on her lip. The barbecue sizzled unattended, the crowd clustered at the patio's far edge; from the shouts, one of her younger cousins was doing tricks on the backyard trampoline. Beth hovered by the patio doors, smoothing her blue sun dress, an anxious impatience turning in her gut.

The next moment, her uncle Jim appeared, tongs in hand, his apron stretched across his belly, a net of broken capillaries over his nose.

'Beth!' he exclaimed. 'Good to see you, love. Everything all right? Your mum said she was a bit worried about you. Where's that fine fiancé?'

Beth evaded neatly. 'I'm fine, Uncle Jim. And he's working.' Just a little white lie.

'Good, good. Well, listen, now the old cooker's under control, can you take a look at something for me?' He cast a glance over his shoulder.

Beth steered him inside. 'What have you got?'

Jim pulled up his shirt, displaying angry red skin across his stomach. 'Came up all by itself and itches like crazy,' he said.

Beth peered at the rash. 'Could be an allergy. Have you changed washing powder, or something like that?'

Jim scratched at his stomach. 'No, but I was in Thailand last week. Got some new shirts.'

Beth raised her eyebrows. 'You should see your GP,' she said firmly. 'Promise me you will, Uncle Jim?'

'Okay, okay. But there's also this other thing, too,' began Jim, turning and gripping the seat of his pants.

'For goodness sake, Jim, leave Beth alone,' scolded a familiar voice. 'No one wants to look at your behind, least of all your niece.'

Gratefully, Beth found her aunt Judy striding in from the patio. Judy had the same curly, pale ginger hair as Margaret Harding, Beth's mother, but that was where the similarity ended. Her mouth was bracketed with deep smile lines, and energy and wit sparkled in her eyes. Beth had always thought Judy and her mother could make a good pair of drama masks, one sweet, one sour. Jim retreated, red-faced, to the barbecue.

'That man has no sense of shame,' said Judy. 'How are you, dear? Getting on well in Sydney, still?'

'Fine,' said Beth brightly.

Judy's eyes fell on Beth's camera. 'Oh, you've still got that old thing!' She ran a finger across the lens cap. 'I remember when your father bought it. Are you staying long?'

Beth shook her head. 'I just came for the party. I promised Victoria I would.'

'You're a good sister,' said Judy. 'But you'll be glad to get home. I know it's tricky for you here.'

Beth swallowed a curdling mix of guilt and secrets. *Where was home now?*

Soon, the meat was served and a long line formed around the salad table, hands batting away the flies. Beth waited until the queue was shorter. With spare seats in short supply, she pulled a dining table chair up to the French doors and tucked her camera underneath. She'd just sat with the flimsy paper plate on her knees when a shadow fell across her chair.

'Beth, here.' Beth stood reflexively, nearly losing her food plate as her mother handed her a tray of spent glasses. 'These are for the dishwasher. It should have finished the last load. Oh, and Ryan needs a fresh beer. They're in the sink.'

~

Beth carried the tray into the kitchen with its familiar worn wooden cupboards and seventies brown tiles. She stacked and reloaded the dishwasher, and then as she made a move back to her dinner plate her mother reappeared, cross lines circling her mouth. Her sun dress was a jovial yellow, a light colour for her slender frame. But her eyes were pinched and tired.

'I nearly tripped over this,' Margaret said, thrusting Beth's camera case into her hands. 'And Ryan's been looking for that beer.' With a tut, she extracted a bottle from the ice and left.

Beth scanned the camera for damage, all its old-fashioned dials and hand-painted numbers. When she'd tucked it away, Margaret reappeared with Beth's dinner plate. 'Someone might have sat on it,' she said, moving to tip the lot into the bin.

Beth leapt for it. 'I haven't eaten any yet!'

'It's cold.'

'I'll still eat it,' said Beth, rescuing the plate.

'You're lucky to have such an appetite,' her mother went on. 'I've barely been able to eat anything. Had horrible stomach pains all week, and my back before that. Must be the stress of the party. I had to go to the doctor yesterday.'

Beth glanced up. Her mother leaned against the sink, her ginger curls limp. Beth's heart tightened. 'What did he say?'

'Kept me waiting too long, so I left. But all doctors are quacks anyway. I'm going to see Anne's acupuncturist on Thursday. He'll sort it out.'

Beth stared at the puddle of tomato sauce, bleeding into her paper plate. Her free hand had bunched. Slowly, she relaxed. 'I just . . . want to know it's not serious.'

Margaret's hand flew to her chest. 'Do you have to say that? I was stressed enough already. Christmas is only six weeks away. Everyone's here. I've been packing boxes for the business orders all week and I had to make all the desserts myself. Vicky's only twenty-one once. You should have come up earlier to help.'

Beth reached her hand to her mother's arm, desperate to make amends. 'I didn't mean it like that.' But her mother moved to adjust her bracelet, out of reach. Beth retracted her fingers.

'I didn't expect you to come without Richard,' her mother went on. 'You might have told me for the numbers.'

Beth knew the adult thing to do was to tell the truth, but all bravery left her. 'Sorry. I didn't think.'

Her mother brightened. 'Have you looked at your guest list yet?'

Beth swallowed. 'No. Sorry.'

'You're not wearing your ring either. Richard's a good man, Beth.' Her mother's gaze flickered, her mouth setting like toffee. Beth detected the familiar topic. 'Not like your father. No-good deserting bastard.'

'*Mum*,' Beth said. Even though her father had been gone nearly fifteen years, the idea of him cut like shards of glass.

'Well, he was,' Margaret insisted but Beth heard her voice waver. 'Left us for that mine job, but I stayed. I did the hard work bringing you all up. I worked hard so you could have things I didn't.' Tears gathered in her eyes, and the facade cracked. Margaret fanned a hand over her chest. 'I'm sorry,' she mumbled. 'I don't know why you put up with me.'

Beth reached out a hand and her mother pulled her into a hug wrapped in familiar floral perfume. Beth had always been tall for her age, and now her mother seemed fragile, her shoulders all bones under Beth's hand. 'It's okay, Mum,' she said soothingly. 'I know it still hurts. I'm sorry, too.'

Her mother pulled away, dabbing under her eyes. 'There, I'm fine,' she said. 'Now, just . . . I'll just be outside.'

Beth leaned against the bench, trying to assemble the pieces of the conversation into some kind of meaningful order, but all that came was shame. How on earth could she go across the country?

Then like a beacon, her phone rang.

'Doctor Harding? This is Greg at the MedFirst agency.'

Beth hung on the words. 'Yes?'

'I've confirmed an immediate start position in Iron Junction. It's a Pilbara mining-town med centre and one of their FIFO doctors is sick.'

'FIFO?'

'Fly-in, fly-out. You'd do ten days on and four off back in Perth, which they call a swing. Does that sound okay? I know you were keen and we can have you travelling today. It's two flights and a drive, I'm afraid.'

A muddy emotion surged through Beth's soul. Joy and uncertainty, hope and doubt. She turned the name of the town over in her mind. *Iron Junction*. A mining town. It sounded remote. She'd been hoping so much for this call, and now she wasn't sure why. What did she hope to achieve? *See the world*, reminded a tiny voice. Beth bit her lip. The crowd was forming a knot on the patio, now. Maybe it was time for cake. They hushed, and she dropped her own voice. 'Yes, but I'm in Brisbane,' she said.

'That's all right. I'll see what we can book and call you back.'

Beth ended the call with a smile on her face and the first sensation of lightness in the long, difficult week. She stepped into the hall with its soft pink walls and ornate plaster cornices. Such a familiar place. Even Victoria's and Anne's rooms were exactly as they'd been while they were at school. Beth's had become the office after she'd been the first to leave home for Sydney and the room now smelled of Australian pepper and smoky salt that were her mother's best culinary mail-order sellers. But heading off to remote Western Australia was something else. Maybe she should phone Greg back and call this off.

She slipped out the patio doors, where Victoria's birthday speeches were underway. She might be at a crossroad, but this was a happy day for her family. Ryan was speaking now, telling everyone how amazing Victoria was, and wishing her a happy birthday. Claps and cheers.

Then Ryan hushed the crowd. 'That's also why,' he continued, 'I have something else for Victoria.'

Beth took in Ryan's satisfied smile, Victoria's perplexed expression, the murmur of expectation. Ryan was down on his knee now, offering up a ring box. Victoria's eyes were wide and spilling tears.

Beth's elation evaporated, and her stomach turned in a protective, leaden ball. Just a few short months ago, that had been Richard on his knee, and her happiness. Things she no longer had.

Stiffly, she found the bathroom and splashed water on her face, then stared at herself in the mirror. Her long dark hair was caught behind her ears, but her eyes now had that same pinched look her mother always carried.

'Go,' she told herself sternly.

Beth in the mirror refused to budge. Her thoughts turned back to Sydney and how she'd left. She closed her eyes. 'Please, go,' she whispered.

A droplet of water tracked down her face, a tiny sensation that cut a clean path in her thoughts. She must leave now or she would never have the chance. It was time to cast off the old Beth like a cloak, and go looking for the self she'd left somewhere behind. So, silently, she picked up her heart and her case, and left the party behind.

Chapter 2

'I don't suppose you have a small car?'

Two flights, a late night, and a 3-am wake-up later, Beth stood in the gravelled parking lot of Paraburdoo airport, staring at a four-wheel-drive monster. The woman beside her cackled. She had a tight red perm and a flush of sunburn across her nose and cheeks, her shirt damp around the armpits even at six in the morning. 'First time up here, huh? This is the smallest we got.'

Beth swallowed. In Sydney she'd had a tiny hatch, parking like she owned the place, never worrying about blind spots. This car had running boards as high as her knee, a bullbar that could hold up a small house, and a strobe on the roof like a dull orange eye. But when she lifted her gaze to the lightening sky, breathing in the bright air of this new, red-dusted world, she had to admit the car was probably made for this place. Out the plane's window she'd seen the land stretching to the horizon, a russet smudge wrinkled with hills, and streaked with shadows and scrappy trees. From the air, the terminal had resembled a lonely truck-stop petrol station. A great primal landscape, across which she faced a three-hour drive to her new job.

The woman pushed the Prado's key into Beth's hand. 'Where you headed?'

'Iron Junction,' said Beth.

'Ah, nice. Follow the signs. But watch the mine roads – do you know about that?'

'No?'

She pointed to the roof. 'If you're on a mine road, turn your strobe on. Switch's under the dash, but remember to turn it off when you stop. And if you see a haul truck, you're in the wrong place.' She wrinkled her eyes as the sun burst through the building's edge. 'You could be fined if you get caught without it on, so don't forget.'

'Right,' said Beth. Nerves tickled her belly. The new land had strange rules.

The woman gave a cheerful wave and turned back to the demountable shack, emblazoned with the company logo. Beth licked her lips. In the slanting rays of early sun, sweat was already soaking the dark hair against her neck. She wished she'd worn a singlet, not the stiff cotton work shirt tucked into woollen suit pants, which were now sticking to her legs. Silence stole upon her. The flight had been full of hi-vis-clad workers, but they'd vanished in a convoy of dust-stained utes and four-wheel drives.

'This is an adventure,' she muttered as she shoved her case into the back seat and hauled herself up. The vast interior swallowed her, roll-bars arching over her head. The engine rumbled to life and soon, Beth eased onto the asphalt strip, a lone car on the lonely road. The steering was surprisingly light, her position high over the road. Beth sat straighter, a smile on her lips. In the rear view the abandoned airport receded, its windsock lifting a limp end. Just like a scene from the zombie apocalypse. Abruptly, a fist gripped her stomach. Maybe she should have stayed in Sydney. Maybe she should have worked things out . . .

Stop it.

She set her face, drawing power from the engine's deep grumble. Iron Junction was just the first step, a safe haven. All she had to do was get there.

Three hours later, Beth rounded a bend between the scrub and spied a neat township nestled between two rises. All the mental games she'd been playing – of wild, frontier towns – turned out to be quite wrong. Iron Junction's streets were a neat grid hanging from the connecting highway and rimmed in a twin row of train tracks. A large billboard announced the town: *Iron Junction, The Pilbara's Finest Community*, and the company logo in red and green. And when she found the medical centre, a new, white, modular building with a cheerful patch of wilting perennials rimming its base, the company logo was there too.

Outside the centre, a man in a suit waited alongside a woman with cropped grey hair, a clinical coat and a coffee mug. Beth's cheeks burned as they watched her two attempts to park, and her careful descent from the cab.

The man strode forward, his broad smile surrounded by a trimmed beard, his hand extended. Beth noticed the perfect windsor knot in his tie as he squared his shoulders. 'Doctor Harding, I presume? Dale King, the mine manager. Welcome to the Junction.'

Beth had her hand warmly shaken. Dale turned. 'And this is—'

'Maxine de Wet,' said the woman briskly in a thick South African accent. She tipped her mug out on the perennials. 'How was the drive?'

'Fine, once I manhandled the beast,' Beth said, holding out her hand towards, she presumed, her new colleague.

Maxine shook it briefly. 'Right. Inside out of this heat,' she declared.

Dale gestured ahead into the clinic. Beth followed Maxine through a large door and into a white-and-blue waiting area, pristine with white chairs, water cooler and kids' play area. The seats were even padded, and a receptionist clicked away at a sleek monitor behind the desk. The whole set-up looked like an inner-city private clinic.

'Jennifer, this is Doctor Harding, the locum,' said Doctor de Wet to the receptionist, not stopping as she marched towards the hall.

Dale King came to a stop by the desk. 'Well, Doctor Harding. Elizabeth?'

'Beth's fine,' she said.

'Beth. Well, I'm very glad you could come. Three years at Royal Sydney, second in your class at med school. Your CV is very impressive.'

A pink glow spread across Beth's cheeks.

'I just wanted to meet you and give you a quick run-down. I'm sure you won't have any trouble with our procedures. Did the agency give you our information packet?'

'Yes, I read through it,' said Beth carefully, aware Dale was watching her reaction. The agency had stressed the mine's importance. She remembered sheaves of glossy photographs and bold headlines on sustainability and community engagement, which hadn't meant much to her. She smiled anyway.

Dale nodded and warmly returned the smile. 'Excellent. So, you understand the medical centre is a partnership? I personally make sure everything is top notch. Any issues at all, you just let me know. I'd like us to be on good terms. Now, we've got contractors in town for the expansion, so Doctor Gregg's illness has left us short. He handled all the company cases and paperwork. A really good educator, too. He does a lot for the mine, and I'm sure I can count on you.'

Dale grabbed two forms off Jennifer's desk, one pink, one blue. 'Fill these out for any worker. Then, into this internal envelope to come back to me. Clear as mud?'

Beth peered at the forms. 'Okay . . .'

Dale patted her shoulder. 'Anything you don't understand on here, just call me directly. Here's my card,' he finished, pressing the white oblong into Beth's hand. 'And make sure you come to the company Christmas party this Saturday, down at the creek. Everyone will be there.' He stuck his hand out a second time. 'Maxine will show you around. I'm sure we'll speak again soon.' He winked.

Beth stared after his departing back. She'd never had such a personal welcome anywhere. She raised her eyebrows at Jennifer, who was still smiling after him. Then Beth noticed Maxine waiting in the hallway and hurried to catch up.

'Minor procedures in there, eye room there,' Maxine said, striding on. 'Vaccination fridge. Supply room . . .' Beth tried to keep up as they made a complete loop around the U-shaped hallway, Maxine outlining in detail the contents of every cupboard. 'The tea room's back on the other side,' she went on as they circled back. Finally, she stopped outside a door.

'And this here is Doctor Gregg's room. You heard what happened?'

'He's sick?'

'Pancreatitis,' said Maxine, ushering Beth into Doctor Gregg's desk chair. 'He's in the Royal Perth. We had to evac him down there last week.'

'Pretty serious, then.' Beth glanced around. Standard exam table behind a curtain, bookshelf over the desk, slimline computer monitor, pot of tongue depressors, a smaller one of jelly beans. She could survive the length of a pancreatitis bout in this place. What would it be, six weeks? Eight?

Maxine shrugged. 'I'm sure he'll recover. I just want to know if you can stay until he's back.' Beth assured her she would, but Maxine lingered, giving Beth the once-over. 'You don't look like the sort we usually get in here.'

'What sort's that?'

Maxine folded her arms. 'In it for the money. Broken by what they've been doing before and looking for a holiday. People like that.'

'Oh?' asked Beth, her stomach squirming. She might be a little bit broken. But she wasn't looking for a holiday, just a good night's sleep before she started tomorrow.

'Don't worry, the roster soon sorts them out,' went on Maxine. 'We run on the mine time, twelve-hour shifts, except Friday, which is a half-day. Your first appointment's in an hour. You can get your key from Jennifer when you finish tonight. The apartment's across the road.'

Beth's jaw was still open as Maxine disappeared.